LEAVING BEFORE
IT'S OVER

Also by Jean Reynolds Page

THE LAST SUMMER OF HER OTHER LIFE
THE SPACE BETWEEN BEFORE AND AFTER
A BLESSED EVENT
ACCIDENTAL HAPPINESS

LEAVING BEFORE
IT'S OVER

JEAN REYNOLDS PAGE

AVON

An Imprint of HarperCollins*Publishers*

LEAVING BEFORE IT'S OVER. Copyright © 2010 by Jean Reynolds Page. All rights reserved. Printed in the United States of America. No part of this book may be used or reproduced in any manner whatsoever without written permission except in the case of brief quotations embodied in critical articles and reviews. For information address HarperCollins Publishers, 10 East 53rd Street, New York, NY 10022.

HarperCollins books may be purchased for educational, business, or sales promotional use. For information please write: Special Markets Department, HarperCollins Publishers, 10 East 53rd Street, New York, NY 10022.

FIRST AVON PAPERBACK EDITION PUBLISHED 2010.

Designed by Diahann Sturge

Library of Congress Cataloging-in-Publication Data
Page, Jean Reynolds.
    Leaving before it's over / Jean Reynolds Page.
       p.   cm.
    ISBN 978-0-06-187692-9 (pbk.)
    1. Married people—Fiction.   2. Birthfathers—Fiction.   3. Families—Fiction.
    4. Domestic fiction.   I. Title.
PS3616.A33755L43   2010
813'.6—dc22   2009045502

10 11 12 13 14   OV/RRD   10 9 8 7 6 5 4 3 2 1

Dedicated to the memory of the amazing Blue girls:
Grace (Blue) Reynolds Massengill
Lois (Blue) McQueen
Edna Lee (Blue) Smiley
Frances (Blue) Thompson

And, as always,
To Rick

Acknowledgments

The seeds of this book began years ago in a writing workshop at Southern Methodist University. More than a decade later, Lola (who was thirteen in the original book and named Leola) is no longer carrying the narrative with her voice alone. Layers of family conflict have been added. But I want to thank the champions of that early incarnation: Al Silverman, Juris Jurjevics, and Barbara Wedgwood. Their encouragement gave me the hope I needed to go to the computer every day.

I continue to need a steady voice of encouragement these days. Most often, I turn to my agent and friend, Susan Ginsburg. Not only does she handle the business side of my writing life, but she puts on an editorial hat for early drafts, and switches to the role of psychotherapist when the need arises. There is no end to my gratitude. Thanks also to Bethany Strout and all the wonderful folks at Writers House, my literary home.

My wonderful editor at HarperCollins, Lyssa Keusch, made the book better at every stage with an excellent eye and gentle prodding. Wendy Lee kept everything on schedule with extraordinary patience and grace. Many thanks.

And as usual, I rely on early readers to keep me from certain disaster. Ian Pierce, Mary Turner, and Jeanne Skartsiaris of my writers group in Texas read and offered valuable insights at various stages of the manuscript. Rick Lange took time out of his chaotic physician's existence to read and correct. Others in my

Texas group, Kathy Yank, Lou Tasciotti, and Chris Smith kept me going with laughter and moral support.

With medical questions about Rosalind's blood disorder, ITP, my thanks go to Dr. Janis L. Abkowitz at the University of Washington. She answered thoroughly (and in terms I could understand!). She then answered more questions and a few more after that, always with good cheer. I don't pretend to have gotten everything right with regard to this illness, but every accurate detail came from Jan's input. (Any mistakes are, unfortunately, my own.)

When considering my journey from writer to published writer, I again (and always) must thank Colleen Murphy who led me to the amazing Victoria Skurnick. I still can't thank you both enough for believing in me.

There are many others—past and present—who have offered support and encouragement. Among them, I must mention a few. Joyce Ross and Lynn Saunders are always just a phone call away. Ralph Reynolds remains a calm voice of sanity. Andy Ziskind keeps me from aging a day (at least in my author photo). Diane Hammond talks me off ledge after ledge. Hilda Lee (with a nod and a red pencil) got it all started. Bob Reynolds helps me remember who I am.

And finally, gratitude to my most important allies—my family. Franklin, Gillian, and Edward, who keep the world real to me. And my dearest Rick who manages to be everything— husband, best friend, first reader, and constant partner in the adventure. All my love.

LEAVING BEFORE
IT'S OVER

One

Lola heard from other kids that if you stand in front of a mirror in a nearly dark room, close your eyes, and turn around three times, all ghosts who have cause to be near you will appear. She pulled together her courage, got out of bed, and went into the bathroom. Charlotte said she tried it at her grandmother's house once and saw her uncle, her daddy's older brother, who'd died when he was only twenty-two. Charlotte said he looked as real as somebody in the grocery store.

Lola had never put it to the test because, if there were ghosts anywhere close by, she certainly did not want to know about it. Not before, anyway. But for the first time, she had a reason to try it out.

She stood in the dark bathroom, trying to get up her nerve. In the mirror, she could see herself—just barely—by the glow of the nightlight in the hall. Her sleeveless nightgown pulled tight against the fullness that had come to her body. All that filling out had happened sometime during the year before, but she hadn't really noticed until the summer came and she put on her old bathing suit. Most of her friends had already gotten more shape to them and she'd wished her time would come. But the embarrassment of flesh spilling out of the too-small suit made her feel strange inside.

As she looked into the mirror, her curves, so fascinating on a normal day, barely registered as she stared at the shadows behind her. A disturbing turn of events had forced her to consider the unthinkable. Her fun-loving, sweet daddy had left that morning and hadn't come home. He skipped work and took off somewhere and she had no idea where or why. Mama had closed herself up in her room and wouldn't come out. If Lola's daddy was dead in a ditch, she wanted to know it.

Lola closed her eyes. She touched her fingers lightly on the sink to keep herself oriented. Slowly she turned, keeping her eyes shut, touching the sink each time she came around. Once. Twice. Three times. Her heart raced as she stood with her eyes tight together. She shook and found that she needed to seriously steady herself against the cold porcelain in front of her. As she opened her eyes, the shadows of the empty room behind her in the mirror made her weak.

If it was true, the whole ghost thing, then that meant her daddy was still alive somewhere. Both relief and hurt flooded through her. If Roy Vines was still in this world and breathing, where the hell was he? What could make him leave and why hadn't he come home?

Lola felt foolish. At sixteen, she ought to know better than to believe in ghost tricks. She went back to bed, thinking that when the morning came, she would make Mama come out of her room. She'd find out the truth about what happened while she was at school. One way or another, she'd find out where her daddy had gone.

* * *

In her bed once more, but unable to sleep, Lola went over in her head all the things she did know. She'd gotten home from the bus to find Mama shut up in her room tight as preserves and not saying a word. The truck still sat in the driveway, so wherever Daddy was, he was walking. That was all she could figure out right off the bat.

When she thought back, there had been an eagerness at work in him for days. It was something she only realized after the fact. It was an anticipation of one kind or another. He must have had an awfully good reason to leave in the middle of a workweek. Lola knew for a fact that he loved them. What she didn't know was what could have been so important that he'd leave Mama sad in her room and Lola wondering where he could be.

Everything had gone wrong from the start of the day. Mama forgot to give her lunch money, so Lola had to eat a jelly biscuit and milk, which is what they give you at the high school if you're not paid up. The lunch lady, trying to be nice, told her she could sign up for the free lunch program if there was ever a need. She didn't plan to tell Mama about that one. Charity was a hateful word to Rosalind Vines.

Lola got home late because the bus broke down halfway through the run. For over an hour, Charlotte had played solitaire on the empty seat beside her while Lola sat across the aisle and watched.

"You want to play a game or something?" Charlotte asked her after about five failed hands.

"No," Lola said. "I'm having fun watching you lose to yourself."

Charlotte shot her the bird and went back to another round.

When the bus driver finally let them off at their road, Lola was starving and half sick from the smoky smell of whatever had gone wrong with the engine. Charlotte wanted her to come over, but Lola wasn't in the mood for Charlotte's sour-tempered mother or their loud little dog, so she said good-bye and went to her own house.

Right away, she knew something was wrong. She shut off Janie Ray's television program because it was a show Mama didn't let her watch. Mama didn't meet her in the kitchen and tell her she was going to fix a little snack.

"Where is she?" Lola asked Janie Ray.

"In her room," her little sister told her. "Been there near 'bout all day."

Lola went to her mother's door. "Mama?" she said, knocking lightly on the thin wood.

"I'm not well, Lola," her mother answered, in a voice so choked and full of hurt that Lola barely understood it to be her mama's. Her first thought was that somebody must have died, Grandma Simsy or Aunt Louise.

"They were fussing before he left." Janie Ray came up beside Lola.

"Before who left?"

"Daddy," Janie Ray said. She said it like it was no big deal, but Lola could see how scared she felt by the look in her eyes.

"Daddy's at work, sweet pea." She tried to reassure the child.

"No he's not," Janie Ray told her. "I heard him call on the telephone and tell Jerry he wouldn't be at work for a while. That's when him and Mama got to fussing."

"What about?"

"I don't know," her little sister answered. "Something about money, and about how Daddy had to go off somewhere. After they yelled a little bit, they both got to being mad without talking. Mama sent me off to my room when it all started, but I stood in the hall and listened. After the fussing stopped, Mama went in her room and shut the door. Daddy hugged me and told me to behave and to look after Mama—and then he left. That's all I saw."

Lola knew about the money problems—not just for them, but for nearly everyone in town. The Bicentennial should have been a big year for tourists to come through. 1976. The whole country was gearing up to celebrate all summer. But with the new interstate open, tourists were flying by Linton Springs with no more than a glance, and Daddy said business at the garage had slowed week by week. On Main Street, all the pottery stores, restaurants, and gas stations that relied on that traffic sat empty—and the people who owned or worked in those places decided to put off paying for repairs on their cars until things picked up again.

Lola's daddy said, "That little two-lane highway used to get people to the mountains like a paper boat moving down a creek, but the interstate gets them there like a bullet at a target range. It's a lot harder to stop a bullet."

Did that have something to do with Daddy going away? Lola's head hurt trying to figure it out. She decided to think about something else. She'd never get calm enough to sleep if she let images of her daddy keep running through her mind. She pushed her thoughts to something happy—the meeting she'd had with Mrs. Jessup, the counselor, at the beginning of the week.

"Lola," Mrs. Jessup told her, "your exceptional abilities have brought you to the attention of the Graham School. It's a private academy in Charlotte for gifted students."

The academy wanted to take her for her last two years of high school.

"But I don't live in Charlotte," Lola said.

"It would be a drive," Mrs. Jessup told her. "I can't deny that. Forty-five minutes each way, I'm guessing. But it would be worth it, Lola. I know you've been bored with what's offered here, hon.

I've heard it from all your teachers. I know we've talked about the option of having you graduate early, but you shouldn't cheat yourself out of your high school years."

Mrs. Jessup had been 1956 Homecoming Queen at Linton Springs High. Two decades later, she still talked about the thrill of that honor. Clearly, the woman's own high school experiences left her with a warped vision of what Lola's days were like.

"Your teachers try to challenge you, but they have whole classrooms full of kids to think about. The Graham School would introduce you to a lot of influential people. You'd have so many new opportunities."

Lola was too proud to say her family didn't own but one truck. They couldn't afford to get a car for her. Hell, they couldn't afford the gas for her to drive to Charlotte and back every day. Mrs. Jessup took all that for granted. She'd moved on to explaining why the school was interested in the first place.

"President Ford has started a program. He's freed up funding for places like the Graham School to pay partial tuition for gifted students who aren't financially able to cover the entire cost. This means you'll have a better shot at some of the good colleges, Lola."

Partial tuition. This woman has no idea what my life is like. Lola almost wanted to laugh, but the disappointment coated any part of the conversation that might have seemed funny. The way things stood, partial tuition might as well be double tuition for all the good it would do her.

She'd wrestled with whether to even tell Mama and Daddy. In the end, she decided they'd be pleased she was asked, even if she couldn't go.

"I wish it could work out for you, darlin'," Mama told her. "You are something else, and you'll be something special with or without a private school diploma."

Daddy had been pleased for her, but seemed to blame himself for her inability to go.

"I should be able to give you the things you need," he told her.

"I don't *need* to spend an hour and a half every day in city traffic just to get a diploma, Daddy." She'd laughed it off as crazy, something she wouldn't have done even if she could. "I'm just glad they recognized me. That's all."

Thinking about that conversation brought her right back around to thinking about him and how he was missing. She gave up on sleep, stared at the ceiling and waited for morning to come.

Two

Rosalind Vines heard her daughter moving around in the hall. Lola had called to her several times in the afternoon. Each time, Rosalind had answered through the door.

"Bear with me, Lola," she'd said. "I'm not feeling well."

It was true. She wasn't well. Better to let Lola think she meant cramps from her period or a headache from thinking about Roy's leaving. But it was worse than that. It was the kind of sick that she could barely feel other than the fatigue. The kind of sick that was eating her from the inside. The tiredness came first, then the rash. That's when she went to the doctor. Mono, he told her, but brought on by something else causing the rash. She needed a doctor that knew about blood problems.

Rosalind pushed these thoughts from her mind. She tried to conjure images of Roy—where he was and how soon he would be done and come back to her. In her lowest moments, she feared that he'd give in to his family and leave her for good. She knew him better than that. But what if that was the only way they would give him what he wanted—what he needed? What if they said, "Stay away from her and we will make sure your precious Rosalind gets the kind of doctor she needs."

Except for her children, there would be no life worth living without Roy.

She couldn't get rid of her chill, which was crazy since it was almost June. But she was used to the heat of Roy's skin next to her when she lay in bed. She didn't know if she'd ever be able to sleep without him.

I'm sorry, Rosie . . . She could still hear his voice, full of regret, but not changing his mind.

She wondered if he'd made it to Virginia already. In the truck, he would have been there in a few hours, but he didn't want to leave her with nothing to drive because she had a follow-up with the doctor scheduled later in the week. With Roy hitching rides or even taking the bus, she had no idea how long it would take him.

Rosalind couldn't stand to think of him in the same town with that first wife of his. But he was, and she had to live with it. Besides, he'd chosen Rosalind. Chosen her over not just Sherry, but his entire family. She had to stop being petty.

She got up to put socks on. If she could get her feet warm, maybe she could go to sleep. The knock on the door came through so faint, she wondered if she'd imagined it.

"Mama?" Lola. At the door again.

Rosalind pulled on her cotton robe to cover the places on her arms.

"Mama?" Lola called a little louder than before.

"I'm coming, hon," she said.

The days were hot, and covering herself, uncomfortable. But

for the time being, she wanted to hide the prickly red spots on her skin. She didn't want to explain anything to her girls when she understood so little herself.

"Are you okay?" Lola asked when she finally opened the door.

In the dark room, Lola's voice seemed to float out of nowhere.

"Just fair." Rosalind put her arms around her daughter. "How about you?"

"I can't sleep," Lola said, her face pressed into Rosalind's neck.

"That's two of us, then, darlin'." She stroked Lola's head.

"Can I get in bed with you?" Lola asked. Full-grown and put together like a woman, Lola was still so much a little girl. Rosalind had to remember that. She had to remember not to ask too much of the child.

"Come on." Rosalind kept her arm around the girl, walked over to the bed. "Just don't ask me about your daddy. I won't talk about him right now. You promise?"

"Why not?" Lola asked.

"Promise, Lola," Rosalind said again. "I'm not up to it right now."

"Okay."

The deception, begun so long ago, rendered easy explanations about Roy's absence impossible. Saying something like *Your daddy's just gone to visit his folks* would be normal under most circumstances. But Rosalind and Roy had told the girls that his parents were dead. That seemed the kindest explanation for the fact that they had no grandparents on their daddy's side to count on for visits and birthday money.

"You sure you don't mind if I crawl in bed with you?" Lola asked, already settling into her daddy's side of the bed.

"I'm glad to have you," Rosalind told her truthfully. "I hate sleeping by myself."

The girl looked just like Rosalind, with that dark, wavy hair and fair skin. Her strong-willed ways she got from her mother, too. But thank God she was a little furnace like her daddy, generating blessed warmth that eased Rosalind's chill.

"Just tell me if he's coming back," Lola said, unable to keep her word as she lay with her back to her mother.

"He will," Rosalind said. "But I don't know when. Sweet Jesus, I hope it's soon." And then before Lola could ask anything else of her she said, "Go to sleep, Lola. We're done talking for the night."

"Yes, ma'am."

No more words passed between them, but Rosalind doubted that her daughter slept even one second of the hours before dawn. If that was the case, that meant there was no rest for either of them.

Three

Roy Vines looked at the farmhouse where his parents still lived. It sat at the top of a small rise with acres of Vines family property laid out in every direction. Roy's father, Taylor Vines, built the house in '35, a year after Roy and his twin brother, Montgomery, were born. The Vines called the place a farm, although, with the exception of a family garden out back, the only crop had been lumber for as long as Roy could remember. The real family business was hardware. Taylor Vines owned the largest retail store in three counties.

Mountains rose up on either side of Gray's Hollow, a valley in the Blue Ridge hills. Roy had spent most of the night in a truck stop south of Wilkesboro. From there, he'd gone forty miles with a guy hauling aluminum. His last ride picked him up just before the Virginia border. Nice fellow, the driver. Liked to hear himself talk. He worked as a medical supplies rep covering Virginia territory, and he went out of his way to bring Roy to the dirt drive that led directly to the old home place.

The morning light, coming over a distant ridge, gave the house an aura. The intense, low rays would be streaming through the kitchen where Lydia was, most likely, making eggs to fill Taylor's belly for the day's work in front of him at the store. Three generations of Vineses had been in the hardware business.

Vines Hardware. Started by his granddaddy in the twenties, it had weathered the Depression and two world wars. Roy figured it would outlast all of them because, no matter how rough things got, people always needed wrenches and potting soil, paint and nails. But it wouldn't be his business. Not ever. Not like he thought when he was young. He'd walked away from that as surely as he left his first wife, his brother, and his parents when he took Rosalind and put that part of his life behind him. Eighteen years had passed since then, fifteen since he'd set foot on the property.

The windows were open and he stood close enough to hear the clang of pans landing on the burners of his mother's stovetop. She'd have an apron to protect her clothes from the grease. Lydia Vines never left her bedroom in the morning without getting fully dressed. And unless things had changed considerably over the past two decades, she would be wearing a dress or a skirt. No pants. In all his years growing up, he'd never seen his mother in a pair of slacks.

The last time he'd even spoke with either of his parents, eleven years before, his father had called to say that Roy's mother was getting treatment for breast cancer.

"They say they caught it early," Taylor had told him.

"Should I come?" Roy asked.

"I expect that would make it hard on everybody," Taylor replied. "I'll have Montgomery call you if things take a turn for the worse."

Mont shared Roy's looks down to the freckle, but couldn't be more different in temperament. Roy's curiosity, his enthusiasm, irritated the serious Montgomery. Obligation ruled Mont's world and that alone endeared him to the elder Vines—especially Lydia.

Roy knew that his mother held the tightest hold on the long-standing grudge against him. His father, who didn't even know the full story, would have softened years before if not for her resolve. But Lydia Vines's ambition for her family rivaled her devotion to the Word of God, and in fact, she managed to intertwine the two more often than not. It was as if God Himself supported the sanctity of the Vines name. In Lydia's view, Roy had sinned against God *and* the family when he fell in love with Rosalind Clark. It didn't seem to matter that Mont had made his share of mistakes, too. Roy's fall from grace set it all in motion, and as far as Lydia Vines was concerned, there was no middle ground.

Roy stood fast in the yard. He never expected to find himself on that property again—at least not without an invitation extended to the family he'd built with the woman he loved. He certainly never intended to return asking anything of his parents. But he'd also never expected to be without money when he needed it so very much. He'd required little of it over the years. It had taken almost nothing to be happy and get along. But in a week's time, all that had changed.

Finally, he took in a deep breath of courage and walked up the slope of grass. He went around the side of the house toward the kitchen door. Through the window screens he could hear the radio playing a gospel song about walking in the garden with God. Roy hadn't heard that one in years.

"You want bacon, too?" Lydia asked her husband. Taylor Vines sat at the table hunched over the morning paper. "Sausage is done and the pan's still hot if you want me to fry some up before I cook the eggs."

"Sausage ought to do it," Taylor said to his wife.

Roy hated to break into the routine of their day. The minute they saw him at the door, the normal ebb and flow would be replaced with long-standing conflict. He thought of all the anger that had passed between him and his folks. It was almost enough to make him turn around and head back toward the road.

"Hey," his mother said over her shoulder when she glanced up and saw him standing outside the screened door. "You're early. Looks like you're dressed to go stomping around in the woods. Come on in and I'll make you something to eat before you and your daddy head out."

Her response paralyzed him for the moment. He found himself unable to speak. Obeying her words, he opened the door and came inside.

His father looked up and smiled a brief greeting, then glanced back down at his newspaper. "Have a seat," he said.

Again, Roy blindly obeyed, taking a chair at the table next to his father.

"Hate to read the news these days," Taylor said, shaking his head. "No matter what story I open to, I can figure out in a sentence or two how it's going to cost me more money."

"Isn't that the truth?" Lydia said. She looked again at Roy. "Scrambled okay, son?"

He nodded, still dumbstruck by their response to his arrival. Then it occurred to him. They thought he was Mont. With the passage of a decade and a half since he last saw his twin brother, was it possible that he and Mont still looked that much alike?

"I thought we'd start over at Southback," Taylor said to him. "The lumber guy will be here early afternoon. We should have time to walk that section and get a fair price in mind for the timber. You've got a better eye for that sort of thing than I do. Always have. They'll come in low, for sure, but we're not desperate to cut just now. If we aren't happy, we can hold out, get another bid or two."

Lydia turned to look at them. "Can Jacob handle the store by himself all morning while you two are traipsing around out there?"

"He'll be fine," Taylor told her.

Roy wondered who Jacob was. It struck Roy as strange that even if this Jacob had worked at the hardware store for a decade or more, Roy would not have met him. Could he have been away that long? Lola was sixteen, so it had been that long and more since he'd been in the place. She'd been one when he made his last, unsuccessful attempt to ease things with his folks. He thought they'd want to know about their granddaughter, but he'd been mistaken.

"I don't know," his mother said. "Sometimes I think that boy couldn't make change for a dollar if his life depended on it. Isn't that right, Mont?"

Roy hesitated. Part of him wanted to prolong the moments before his parents knew he was Roy and not his twin brother. All his life, Roy had wanted to be treated by his father with the same respect given to Mont. Respect for his ideas, his judgment. But it was always Mont his daddy turned to for advice. Roy could do little more than bring an easy smile to his father's face. That was, until the day he found himself unwelcome in his parents' home.

"It's Roy, Daddy." Roy's voice scraped through his dry throat. "I'm not Mont."

Lydia turned to look at him, stood staring as if she'd seen a ghost. The only sound in the room was the sizzle of sausage in the pan on the stove. Roy looked from one to the other. He didn't know where it would go from there, couldn't think beyond that very moment.

"Roy?" His mother looked at him as if he might be the one mistaken about his own identity.

"Yes, ma'am," he said.

Taylor stared at him, had yet to speak. Lydia turned off the flame underneath the burner.

"Have you left her?" she asked, finally.

"Her" would always mean Rosalind. In Lydia's mind, Roy's love for Rosalind precipitated all that came after. Mont, the ambitious, loyal son, was therefore absolved of his part in the family's undoing.

"Have you come to your senses after all this time and cut that woman loose?" Lydia pressed. Roy suspected his mother's feelings arose from fairly concrete underpinnings. Rosalind, a country girl, came from nowhere, offered nothing to elevate the Vines name. If Roy chose to be an adulterer, he could have at least aimed higher than his first wife rather than lower.

"Lydia," Taylor said, standing up from the table and walking over to his wife. "Don't jump into the fray so fast. Let Roy tell us why he's here."

Roy didn't know what he'd been expecting. All those hours between Linton Springs and Gray's Hollow. He should have been thinking about what he would say when he finally got to where he was headed. But he hadn't. Looking at his parents, he was no longer a forty-two-year-old man. He was a boy again, and a foolish boy, at that. No wonder his daddy had never taken him seriously.

"I need help," he said, the words turning bitter in his mouth. That was the plain truth, as good a place as any to start. "I never planned to come back and ask you for anything. But here I am."

He heard the sound of someone moving around upstairs. A toilet flushed and pipes creaked as whoever it was turned on a spigot. Lydia glanced at the ceiling above her, then looked over at Taylor.

"Who else is here?" Roy asked. The looks on their faces suggested they'd rather not say.

Finally his mother spoke up. "The boy," she said. "He's living with us. Been here for a while now."

Roy felt the blood leave his face. A weakness went through him. It had been a mistake to come back. Rosalind had been right all along. How could he have ever thought it was the best thing to do? Again he heard the movement on the floor above him. Panic rose in his gut and he breathed deeply to quell it.

"Where's his mama?" Roy managed.

Lydia looked away, as if she couldn't stand the sight of him.

But Taylor Vines stared hard at Roy. "She's been gone for about eight years now," his father told him, but didn't explain any further. "We took him in. It was the right thing to do."

"Gone? What do you mean, *gone*?"

"She passed," his father said.

"How?" Stunned, Roy tried to imagine Sherry lifeless and in the ground, but it didn't make sense.

"Now's not the time," Lydia said, cutting her eyes upstairs where he could still hear the boy moving around. "He needed someone to step in when she was gone."

She didn't say more, but the implication was clear. Until her last breath, she would hold Roy responsible. He'd made the mess and he wasn't around to clean it up. That's what she was saying. The successful, driven Mont may have stumbled and fallen into the trap, but he didn't set it. Maybe she was right. Some days Roy felt that way himself.

Roy felt lost. He had no real case to make, nothing they would attempt to understand. He thought again that he should never have come. But the road behind him offered no better options, and he was left to move ahead with his plans. Before he could think of how to respond to the news about the death of his ex-wife, he heard more sounds above him in an upstairs room, then footsteps descending the stairs. He didn't want to see the child again—Lucas was his name—and certainly not in his parents' home. This put him at an unfair disadvantage. But it seemed he had no choice.

He braced for a vision of a young boy to emerge in the doorway. Instead, a tall figure, more man than boy, came into the room. The last time Roy had seen Lucas he'd been little, maybe two. But Roy recognized him immediately. How could he not? The boy looked just like him. He would be seventeen, a year older than Lola.

"Morning, Nanny," Lucas said as he opened the refrigerator to take out the milk. "Smells good. Is there enough for me?"

Roy saw his mother look at Taylor. Her husband's expression shared her concern. "Plenty," she said.

Lucas didn't seem to notice the awkward silence. "Uncle Mont?" He looked at Roy, pouring milk into a glass as he spoke. "You think I could borrow your truck on Friday?" The request had a nervous quality about it, as if he expected to be reprimanded for asking. He kept his eyes on Roy. "I need to haul some prom decorations from this kid's garage to the school and Pap doesn't like for me to drive his truck."

"You can borrow my truck, Luke," Taylor jumped in before Roy was forced to respond to the request. He shot Roy a brief look of warning. The old man didn't intend to tell the boy who Roy was. "We'll lash everything down tight. It won't be a problem."

Lucas looked up in surprise. "Really?" Clearly he'd had an earlier conversation with his grandfather that contradicted the current one.

"Sure," Taylor told him. "It's not that far to the school, anyway. You're a good driver. I know you'll be careful."

Roy saw the pleasure of the compliment rush to the kid's face, and Roy couldn't have spoken if he'd wanted to.

"Come on outside with me, Mont," Roy's father said, looking him in the eye as he spoke. "We can go over how to play the lumber estimate we get from these fellows today."

Roy stood up and followed his father to the door. As he glanced back, he saw Lucas digging into the plate of eggs and sausage Lydia had put in front of him. It was like watching a home movie of himself at that age, sitting at that very same table before high school. The resemblance was uncanny. But then why wouldn't it be? He and Mont had always been interchangeable in looks. People could only tell them apart when they spoke. Why wouldn't Mont's son look just like him?

"If Luke's going to see you again, it can't be like this. It's too much of a shock for him to find you sitting in the kitchen one morning without any warning," Taylor said to Roy when they were well out in the yard. "Better to let him think you're Mont for the time being."

Luke now. Roy could only think of him as Lucas. Sherry had called him Lucas.

Lydia knew what had happened between Mont and Sherry. She'd known all along, always turning the blame back to Roy and his wandering eye. But Taylor still believed that Roy was actually the boy's father. *And Lucas believes it, too.*

"I don't plan to stay long," Roy said. "Might be best if he doesn't know who I am at all."

Taylor's mouth drew up in a tight line of disdain. "You ought to be ashamed of yourself, Calderoy Vines." He shook his head. "Letting your brother do what you should have been doing all along."

"What do you mean?" Roy asked.

"Mont's been like a father to that boy," the older man said.

Roy stared at his father, unable to muster a response. The irony of the elder Vines's words grew thick in the air between them. If Roy countered his father's admonition with the simple truth, he'd send the old man reeling. He didn't have the stomach to cause that. He never had. Rosalind was all he'd ever wanted before, and he had her. Better to leave them be.

But as he stood in the yard with Taylor, part of him thought he ought to just speak the truth. If they wouldn't help him, maybe he could enlist the old man that way. But what would that do to the kid? Besides, the habit of silence had grown all too familiar.

What was he doing in Virginia in the first place? Asking his parents for help suddenly seemed impossible. But he had to find a way. He couldn't leave Rosalind's condition up to the whims of the county health department. She had a follow-up appointment with the local doctor, but he'd told her at her first appointment that her problems looked to be over his head.

"We have a relationship with a public hospital in Gastonia. We could send you there for further testing," he told Rosalind. "But they're backed up most of the time and the wait can be pretty long." She'd likely have a better outcome with a specialist at one of the major centers, he explained, and he mentioned a hospital in Winston-Salem. "They have some of the best people for this sort of thing. It's expensive though."

Free or nearly free medical care was worse than none sometimes. They'd found that out when Lola was born. Roy had to get that specialist for his wife. And that would take money.

After a few moments of awkward silence, Lucas Vines came out the kitchen door.

"Off to school?" Taylor called out as if it might be any other day.

"Yes, sir." The teenager waved his good-byes to the two of them as he got into an older model Buick that sat in the driveway by the house.

The dust the car churned up from the gravel lingered, even after Lucas left the driveway, heading out toward the main road.

Four

Lola woke up confused, the sun high outside her parents' bedroom window. Then she remembered why she was there and settled back onto Daddy's pillow. The pillowcase smelled like Vitalis, the stuff he used on his hair. She breathed him in and felt some small comfort in spite of the fact that he was still off somewhere and she had no idea when he might return. Still, with daylight came a renewed hope that everything might go back to normal soon.

"Hey, sleepyhead." Mama came into the room carrying a basket of clean clothes. She still had on her bathrobe, which was strange. Usually she was up no more than five or ten minutes before she got washed and dressed.

"Are you sick?" Lola asked. She put her feet on the floor beside the bed. "Why haven't you changed?"

"I haven't gotten around to it yet," Rosalind answered, staying busy putting laundry in drawers. "You better get moving. You'll miss the bus."

"Any word from Daddy?" Lola ventured.

"I expect he'll call today," her mama said, by way of a nonanswer. She continued with the laundry as if Lola had asked what time it was.

Lola left her there and went to get ready for school.

The window in Lola and Janie Ray's room was open, with only the screen keeping the flies from coming in. Lola heard Charlotte's dog barking down at the Benson house. Pinball, the Pomeranian. Little, bitty dog that served no purpose, best Lola could tell. He stayed in the den every night, but during the day, Charlotte's mama got tired of listening to him in the house, so she put him in the yard.

In addition to the barking noises, the smell of smoke came through the screen. It would grow faint and then a small gust of wind would stir it up again. It was the wrong time of year for burning dry leaves, but that's what it smelled like—only different. Not leaves, but something sweeter. Lola couldn't put her finger on what it was exactly, but the odor struck her as exotic and earthy all at once.

She looked at the clock and forgot about dogs and smoke. She had to hurry if she didn't plan to miss school. Janie Ray came in and picked up a stuffed bear off the floor by her cot. They'd been promising her a bed like Lola's ever since she gave up her crib, but so far, the cot was the best they could manage. Looking at her made Lola miss Daddy all over again. Janie Ray looked just like him. That brownish-red hair that curled around her face. Those same hazel eyes.

"Come here," Lola said, sitting on the edge of her bed. Janie Ray came over, and Lola wet a Kleenex with water from a glass by the bed. She wiped a smear of jam off the girl's cheek. "There," she said. "Now you're perfect."

Janie Ray smiled at her, stretched up and kissed Lola's chin. Then she took her bear and went back into the kitchen.

Dressed and ready to go, Lola found her mother, still wearing her robe, in the bathroom hanging up her stockings. "Are you going to be okay with Janie Ray today? I can stay home if you need me."

"I'm fine," Mama told her. "You go on. I'm going to make Janie Ray some biscuits for breakfast in a second. Did you get breakfast?"

"I'll get something at school." Lola felt uneasy looking at the pale unkempt figure of Rosalind, who was trying to pretend it might be a normal day. She hoped Mama would eat a biscuit herself, because as far as Lola knew, the woman hadn't had a bite in twenty-four hours.

"Lord, I don't know what Mr. Thomas is burning down there," Mama said, "but that smell is giving me a headache."

"Yeah, I noticed it was weird." Lola turned to leave. "See you after school," she said, and went out. The slap of the screen door against the frame signaled a kind of freedom. Freedom from worrying about her little sister. Freedom from figuring out the next thing that might happen at home. It felt good to be out and away from that, and she wondered if that was why her daddy had gone out the door and kept right on going. Was he just tired of worrying about everything and everybody, too?

She cut through the yard to get to the road. Charlotte stood waiting for the bus. Beyond Charlotte's house, down behind a patch of evergreens, smoke rose from the Thomases' property.

"Can you believe this?" Charlotte said when Lola reached her. "Smells like old Mr. Thomas just fired up the world's biggest bong."

"Damn," Lola said, "you're right. That's what it is. I couldn't figure out the smell when I was up at the house."

"That's 'cause Miss Goody-Two-Shoes has never even tried the stuff."

"Shut up," Lola said. "I'm not Shirley Temple and you're not exactly a stoner." She tried to sound casual, but it was a sore point and Charlotte knew it. Sometimes Lola got so sick of herself. Always the good kid. But she couldn't bring herself to act out. Mama's anger and Daddy's pure grief didn't seem worth it.

"What's he doing down there?" Lola got back to the subject at hand.

"I don't know," Charlotte said, suddenly serious. "He can't know what that stuff is. They're both too old to have a clue." She stopped as if thinking. "But he and Mrs. Thomas are really nice old people. You know how some people, when they get old, just turn nasty? Makes you appreciate the good ones."

Lola wondered what her parents would be like when they were old. Her mama would be kind, but inclined to keep to herself. Her daddy would be fun. Sweet, same way he was now. But then, what did she know? She would never have predicted that her daddy would take off and not come home.

"What's wrong?" Charlotte asked.

"My daddy went off somewhere yesterday. He wasn't at work and he didn't come home last night," Lola told her. "I still don't know where he is. Mama's acting strange. She didn't come out of her room until this morning. And when I left she was in her housecoat. I don't know what the hell's going on."

"He just took off? Holy shit." Charlotte's eyes were wide. Lola had the most normal family of anyone they knew. "Where do you think he is?"

"I don't know," Lola told her. "I don't even know if he closed up the shop or if Jerry's running things. He's never let Jerry take over by himself before—not for more than a couple of hours anyway."

"When's he coming back?" Charlotte asked.

It was a simple question, but Lola had no simple answer. She wished she could say *Tomorrow*, or even *Next week sometime*. But she didn't know. She didn't know anything.

"Soon, I hope." *Soon*. The bus would come soon. The weekend would come soon. Her daddy? The idea that no answer came to mind made her feel small. As small as Janie Ray.

The bus turned onto her road and when it pulled up, she and Charlotte got on like it was the most normal of days.

Five

Luke stopped at the end of the road. He looked back to see if Pap Taylor was watching, but the old man and Mont had launched deep into some discussion and weren't paying attention to which way he went. So Luke turned right. He was headed toward trouble and he knew it but, damn, it was worth it. He rounded the turn, going straight toward Kendra's house, instead of school.

Man, the girl was on fire every time he was with her. They'd been at it for three months, and he couldn't stay away. Part of him felt bad. He and Deedee had been going out for a few weeks now. He was going to the prom with her on the weekend. Still, he couldn't seem to quit things with Kendra.

Kendra was two years older, and out of high school. After she graduated, she got a job cutting hair—which meant she could leave that sour old bitch of a mother and rent a place of her own.

She'd never given him the time of day when she was at the high school. But once she was out on her own, all that changed.

"Everybody's gone," she complained one day sitting naked on the bed after they'd finished. "Bunch of old men flirting with me in the shop while I cut their wives' hair. That's all the excitement I get these days."

Luke knew that was the only reason Kendra let him in the door every time he showed up. He didn't care. Hell, he was grateful that all the jocks who used to follow her around had either gone off to school or, at least, left for someplace bigger than Gray's Hollow. Luke, too, would leave at the end of the summer, and Kendra would be the last thing on his mind as he drove away. But for the time being, she could use him all she wanted.

Five minutes to Kendra's house, half an hour in bed with her, and he could get to school before third period.

He pulled into her driveway, already hard just thinking about her. She must have seen him drive up because he found the door open when he got on the porch. She stood just inside wearing nothing but a bathrobe that trailed completely open down the front. Damn! He wasn't even going to make it through getting her off if he didn't settle down a little. And he'd learned pretty fast he didn't get to have his fun until she had hers.

He tried to think about something else. Ms. Jacobson and her fat ass in homeroom, calling out his name for attendance at that very moment. It didn't work. All he could see was Kendra, the pale blue cloth of her robe framing her nipples as she stood in front of him just inside the door.

"Before I forget," she said, undoing his belt as she spoke. "I got a cash box from the shop I need for you to drop off at Larry's on your way back through town, okay?"

"Again? Does it have to be done on my way?" he said, his

voice straining to sound close to normal. "How about this afternoon?"

"He's got to deposit it this morning or checks'll bounce, he
says."

Luke hesitated. That would put him getting to school at the
middle of third period history. He had a final paper due in that
class by next week and they were supposed to go over the drafts.
But hell, he was graduating in less than two weeks. What could
they do to him at this point?

She pulled his jeans and boxers down in one easy motion,
then stood and moved his hand up to her breast. He could feel
the nipple harden as he put his fingers over it.

"Sure," he said, closing his eyes. "No problem. I'll drop the
box by to him."

He could miss history again. Shit, he was making his own
history and that was more important.

He bent to kiss her mouth. *Anything you say.* The thought
raced through his mind—and not for the first time. *Anything.*
She pulled away slightly, bent her head back, and let the robe
slide off her shoulders and onto the floor.

Luke moved her toward the couch. The bedroom seemed way
too far to go. As he reached down to touch her, a cool shadow
of worry passed through him. Something was off. But minutes
later, after she came and when there was nothing left between
him and a blessed relief from the storm raging inside his own
body, everything seemed right again.

"Here, baby." She handed him a condom.

He smiled and took it. *Anything you say,* he thought again.
God, life just couldn't get any better.

Six

How'd you get here?" Taylor Vines asked Roy. The old man looked around the driveway and then the yard, as if a vehicle might be hidden behind the bushes somewhere.

"I hitched a ride," Roy told him. "Several rides, actually. The last fellow brought me right to the house."

Taylor frowned. "You out of something to drive these days?" He pulled a pack of cigarettes out of his pocket and offered one to Roy. Lucky Strikes. Taylor's brand for at least thirty years. Roy cut back a few months before, but he hadn't managed to quit altogether. He preferred menthols, but took one of his father's cigarettes anyway. He'd finished the last of his pack that morning, and besides, he could use some calming down.

"I've got a pickup. But I left it with Rosalind. It's all we've got and she . . ." *She has to get herself to the doctor,* he thought. "She needs it to get the girls around," he told his father.

"The girls?" The elder Vines ran his tongue along his lip, spat out a piece of tobacco. He looked at Roy, his forehead in a wrinkle. "More than one?"

"We had Janie Ray four years ago," Roy said. The notion that it had been a terrible idea to come to Virginia flooded his thoughts again. "I should have let you know, I guess," he said. His parents hadn't seen so much as a picture of Lola since she was a year old. He didn't think they'd want to hear about another grandchild they didn't plan to see.

"I never thought things would be this way when you were growing up, son," Taylor said, looking off toward the acreage that lay beyond the yard. But then he added, "It's the way it is, I suppose." No concessions. Apparently, no regrets.

"Rosalind has health problems, Daddy." Roy came to ask for money, so he decided to get it over with. "The garage is hurting right now. The whole town is hurting. The interstate took away most of the traffic coming through and people are looking after their own cars instead of paying me to do it."

Taylor nodded, looked off toward the house, and took in a deep breath. Roy could hear the creek that ran by the side yard—cold water that came straight off the mountain. As a boy, he'd spent summer hours sitting in that creek to get cool. The friendly sound of water seemed at odds with the tension between him and his father.

"I let go of our health insurance about six months ago," Roy said. "I had to. It was either that or fire Jerry, my boy at the shop. His wife is expecting. They'd just found out and I couldn't tell him he was out of a job. I figured things would pick up and I'd reinstate the policy. Daddy, I've been through the county health system before. That's all we had when Lola came along. It . . ." He shook his head. "They do what they can to take care of people, but Rosalind needs a specialist. I wouldn't ask if it wasn't—"

"I don't have the money, Roy," Taylor interrupted his son. To his credit, it looked as if it pained him to say it.

It took Roy a minute to process the words. "Is business down for you, too?" he asked. He felt his heartbeat in his neck, along his shoulders. This had been the unthinkable last resort—to ask his parents for the money. He never imagined that he could fall lower than the decision to turn to his folks.

Taylor shook his head. "Business is fine," he said. "It's just that three years ago, I turned everything over to Mont. I set up a salary for myself and put everything in Mont's name. I set up a decent amount for your mother and me to have, but not enough to . . ."

Not enough to give Roy what he needed. He stared at his daddy. The words weren't there. What could he say? Had he expected that some inheritance would eventually come to him? It couldn't be a shock that his parents had written him off entirely, not given the decade of silence between them. But it *was* a shock. Again, he felt like a foolish boy who'd been given his comeuppance.

"Okay," Roy said. He looked wildly around the property. He wished there was someplace to go. He wanted to leave in the worst way. But he didn't even have his truck. "Okay," he said again.

"Mont's been big in local politics for a few years now," Taylor said. The words seemed to be a non sequitur, but Roy waited for more. "More than a few, I guess. Time gets away from you. He started thinking several years back that he'd like to try for a seat in the state house. He's been building a campaign since the end of last year, and he's on the ballot in the fall. I turned the business over to him, you see. He needed resources to put together his campaign and he's good with the business. He was doing more and more of it anyway."

Taylor's explanation had taken on a defensive tone, and rambling set in. But Roy barely listened anyway. His father would have gone along with it, but giving the business to Mont had been his mother's idea, and Roy knew it. She had two boys. Two chances. Roy may not have had the drive to achieve greatness, but Mont would exceed all expectations. A state congressman.

As if on cue, a large car—a new model Cadillac from the looks of it—turned off from the road and came into the driveway. When the driver's door opened, Roy had the odd sensation of seeing an image of himself emerge from the car. The brothers might not have seen each other in fifteen years, but they had aged in sync, still identical, in spite of their best efforts at severing all bonds of fraternity.

Mont stared at Roy, no doubt sharing the same eerie recognition of his own features. Even his clothes, jeans and a workshirt, seemed to mirror Roy's. After a moment, Roy saw his brother's face change from the perplexed expression of someone taken completely by surprise, to a kind of resigned acceptance of the situation at hand.

"Hey, Roy," he said, his mouth set in a scowl.

"Hey, Mont," Roy echoed.

And with that, the three of them stood in the yard, all seemingly unwilling to make a move toward what might come next.

Seven

It had been an hour since Luke left Kendra's house. A little less, actually. He should have been sitting in history by then, but instead, he was in a small room at the sheriff's office that smelled like cigarettes and sweat. A good portion of the sweat smell, he decided, was coming from him.

"Don't lie to me, son." Everett Maycomb looked at him. "How long have you been working for Larry and that bunch?"

He stared at the deputy's gun that sat in the holster on the officer's hip. Luke had a hunting rifle and Pap Taylor had shotguns and rifles at the house, but Luke had never held a pistol before. His fascination with the firearm momentarily distracted him from the fact that he was scared shitless.

"Are you listening to me, Luke?" Maycomb said.

"Yes, sir."

Maycomb looked bored, as if he dealt with drug-toting kids every day of his life and Luke was less remarkable than most.

"You think you could answer my question, then?" Maycomb ran a hand through his hair—the hair that was left, anyway. Symmetrical V-shaped recesses framed his forehead, and the gray-black hair that remained, he'd cut short. Military-style.

"I thought it was a cash box from the beauty shop," Luke told him. "I swear that's the truth, Mr. Maycomb."

"Officer Maycomb."

"Yes, sir, I'm sorry. Officer Maycomb." Luke knew Maycomb's daughter from school. She'd let him feel her up once at a party after she'd had something to drink. They made out for about half an hour in somebody's laundry room before she'd sobered up enough to put a stop to the whole thing. Luke suddenly had the irrational fear that the deputy could somehow read his thoughts. He tried to focus on images of other things—trucks and hamburgers, anything but Lucy Maycomb's breasts.

"This is serious, Luke." The deputy seemed to soften a little. For the first time, Luke had the barest hope that the guy might end up believing him.

"I know it is, Officer," Luke said.

"These people aren't your friends," Maycomb said. "If you try to protect them, you could end up in jail."

Holy shit. Luke's mind raced, trying to come up with something to trade for his freedom. That's the way they did it in cop shows. But he didn't know anything. He'd screwed around with Kendra Hinkle and taken a box of what he thought was money to Larry Ames. Uncle Mont, he was a big shot in county government. Maybe Mont could get him out of this mess.

"Could you call my uncle Mont?" Luke asked Officer Maycomb. Should he ask for a lawyer, too? That's another thing they always did on TV. But Mont was in charge of the board of commissioners, and that was kind of like being a lawyer.

"We've already put in a call to your granddaddy," Maycomb said.

Luke thought of Pap Taylor hearing that he'd been brought to the courthouse for carrying around a box full of pot. He could see the look on Nanny's face when Pap told her. He wanted to cry or throw up, but kept himself from doing either, thank God.

"Okay," he said. "I think I ought to wait till somebody from my family gets here to talk to you anymore."

The honest truth was, there wasn't much more to tell, but instead of easing his mind, that only made him feel more ridiculous somehow. At least Mont had been with Pap Taylor when he left the house. Pap would get pissed, but Mont would move on past that to figuring out how to get Luke out of the mess he'd stepped into. Uncle Mont was his only hope. He sat back and waited. Maycomb pulled out a cigarette, and after lighting up, again rubbed his hand through the newly mown hair down the middle of his head.

"You think I could have one of those?" Luke asked, nodding toward the pack of Marlboros that rested on the table in front of Officer Maycomb. What the hell, he figured. He was already being questioned for selling drugs. A cigarette habit was suddenly small potatoes.

To his surprise, Maycomb shook a cigarette halfway out of the pack and inclined it toward Luke for the boy to take. The officer gave him a light, and the two of them settled back to wait for Luke's family to arrive.

Eight

Rosalind stood by the wall phone in the kitchen. She'd put her finger up to dial twice and pulled away both times.

Janie Ray lay curled up on the couch in the den with the television at a low mumble. If Rosalind was going to make the call, her best opportunity had arrived—while her youngest was asleep and Lola was still at school. But Roy would be upset. He'd take it personally as a failure on his part. Roy had always been so proud that he made enough to let Rosalind stay home with their girls. But he wasn't making enough anymore, especially if they had large medical bills added into the mix. They couldn't pretend that he was.

Maybe this trip to visit his folks would solve their problems, but she doubted that would happen. She told him flat-out not to go. And while he was off doing his best to help their situation, she couldn't bide her time and do nothing. Besides, sitting around and thinking about how the blood running through her veins had turned toxic on her seemed a harder job than getting busy and forgetting about it for a few hours a day while she made some money. If she got too weak, she'd have to reconsider, but that time hadn't come yet.

She put her finger to the dial again, and this time followed through.

"Linton Grill," a woman answered.

"Mae Rose?" Rosalind asked, but it didn't sound like her.

"No, this is Cherry," the woman said. "She's ringing somebody up right now. I'll get her in a second if you can wait."

"That's fine," Rosalind told Cherry. She knew the girl. Cherry had married one of Mae Rose's sons a few years back and helped out now and then at the grill.

Rosalind again almost lost her nerve while she waited. She felt dampness on her skin, down her neck and under her arms. It could be nerves, or it could be that she had on sleeves when the air had turned ripe for bare arms. Either way, she kept her ear to the phone, determined to go through with the call.

"Hello."

Rosalind recognized Mae Rose's voice, deep for a woman. "Hey there," Rosalind said, "this is Rosalind Vines."

"Rosalind," she said. "What can I do for you, darlin'?"

"You still need help at the grill?" Rosalind asked. No need to prolong the small talk. "I remember you mentioned a while back that you were short on hands during lunch. I could use a few extra dollars if you still need somebody."

Mae Rose was quiet for a few seconds, and Rosalind wondered if she'd lost her connection. "Mae?"

"Is everything okay, hon?" the woman asked.

"What do you mean?" The obvious answer was no, but Rosalind didn't want to broadcast her problems to the world.

"I heard from Casey Wells who works at the bank that the boy Jerry was running the garage by himself yesterday. He seemed to think Roy had taken off somewhere in a hurry. Are you in trouble, darlin'?"

Rosalind should have expected people to talk.

"He's gone out of town on some family business," Rosalind told her. "We're fine, just strapped for money like everybody else lately. You're lucky that your business is holding steady."

"Don't I know it," Mae Rose said, sounding relieved to have inquired and gotten a reasonable response. "Cherry's done her best to chip in since Elaine quit, but she's due to have this baby any day now, so your timing couldn't be better. When could you start?"

"Tomorrow, I guess," Rosalind said. Would that give her enough time to get the girls prepared for the news? Would Roy be back by then and put an end to the whole thing? "I could at least come in and get acquainted with everything."

"Sounds good to me. Come on in about ten o'clock. You'll normally be working from about eleven to four-thirty, covering the lunch and after-school crowd. But if you come in at ten tomorrow, I can get you oriented."

"I'll be there," Rosalind told her.

After she hung up the phone, she felt exactly like she'd gone out and cheated on Roy. That sort of betrayal was an entirely new feeling for Rosalind and she purely hated it, but she'd have to swallow whatever taste it left in her mouth and get herself to the grill the next day. She would not leave Roy to manage this crisis by himself. That had never been her way, and she wouldn't begin at a time when their problems peaked at their worst.

Rosalind set about figuring out what the girls could eat when Lola came home from school. She'd also have to remember and call the health department and see if the doctor could see her a little earlier for her appointment the next morning so that she could get to the grill by ten.

She'd give the kitchen a good once-over. That would make

her feel better. Lola had done her best to stay on top of everything while Rosalind was holed up in her room, but the girl didn't have the thoroughness needed to keep things up to Rosalind's standards.

If Rosalind kept her hands moving, she could keep her mind off telling Roy she'd taken a job. She would work that out when the time came. And the time *would* come soon. She had to believe that.

Nine

I'll drop my stuff off at home and then come up to your house," Charlotte told Lola when they got off the bus.

Lola looked back, saw her best friend stopping halfway to her house to check out something down on the ground. Lola smiled. Charlotte had been the same since before first grade. Distracted by bugs and squirrels, boys and rainbows, Charlotte only saw what was right in front of her, and for that reason, school came harder than it should have.

Charlotte's house looked like a magazine picture. White with green shutters, it seemed like a permanent sort of place that you'd come back to when you were older and say, "This is where I grew up." Not like Lola's house—half of a half-empty duplex.

Most of the houses on Lola's road looked more like Charlotte's, but somebody with rental property in mind had built Lola's house on the cheap. Pretty soon, the owners figured out there wasn't a market for renters in Linton Springs, so they agreed to sell half of it to Lola's daddy just to get something out of the investment. Daddy always had in mind to buy the other half from the original owner, but never had the money. Except for the occasional relative of the owner who needed a place to stay for a while, the other side had been empty for Lola's whole life.

"I'm home," Lola called out when she got inside.

She found Mama in the kitchen where the smell of Ajax came on strong. On the table, biscuits sat on a plate, with butter and jam off to the side. A thin steam rising told Lola the biscuits had just been baked.

"Hey, sugar," Mama said. "How was school?"

"Okay," Lola said. "Did you hear from Daddy yet?"

"Not yet," Mama said. Lola could tell she was forcing a cheerful tone.

Lola watched her move a rag across the counter, inch by inch, erasing the last of the stains and dried spills that Lola had missed in her efforts at cleaning up. Lola stared, mesmerized by the rhythmic sweep of her mother's arm, a white dishcloth on the darker surface. The counter was gold linoleum, a color ugly as sin, with aluminum piping around the edges. Lola wondered, not for the first time, who might have picked it out. With so many colors in the spectrum, why that one? Did the man who built the place have a color-blind wife?

"Lola?" Her mother had asked her something.

"I'm sorry, Mama," she said. "I didn't hear you."

Her mama's forehead wrinkled up. "What's wrong with you?"

"Nothing," Lola told her. "What did you ask me?"

"I asked if you saw Janie Ray when you got here. She was asleep on the couch a few minutes ago."

"I heard her going into the bathroom when I came in," Lola said.

"Go tell her there are biscuits on the table," Mama said. "You eat a little something, then get started on your homework."

Mama acted like Daddy was at work. Like everything was back to normal. But it wasn't. Lola couldn't decide how she ought to feel. She went down the hall looking for her little sister. The phone rang in the other room, but her mama picked it up.

"Janie Ray?"

"Shhh," her sister whispered from down the hall in Mama's room.

Lola went in and saw the child on the floor, bent over a spill with a towel in her hand. The smell of Mama's perfume overwhelmed her as she got close to Janie Ray.

"Don't tell Mama." Janie Ray's eyes were wet with tears.

"I won't have to, baby girl." Lola squatted down next to the tearful child. "She'll be smelling this for weeks. You want me to tell her I knocked it off by accident?" It broke Lola's heart to see her little sister so distraught.

Janie Ray shook her head no. Her lips stayed pursed forward in an effort to stop crying. "I did it," the girl said. "I'll tell her."

"Okay." Lola took the towel from Janie Ray. "Come on. I'll go with you." On the way back to the kitchen, she dropped it into the bathroom sink and put her arm around her sister for comfort.

"I was wondering if I could make the appointment earlier on Monday," Mama said into the phone. "I've taken a job and I need to be in town by mid-morning. If I come in at eight-thirty or so, I could make it to the grill on time."

Work? Since when did Mama work? Lola stood in the doorway to the kitchen. Mama's forehead was damp with sweat. Strands of dark hair lay wet against the side of her face. But still she had on a long-sleeved blouse. So much was wrong with everything at home. Ever since her daddy left, nothing made sense.

Mama finished talking and turned around, looking startled that her girls had come in.

"Where're you going to work?" Lola asked.

Mama walked over and turned the window air-conditioning unit on, running it at the lowest setting. "Mae Rose needs some help at the Linton Grill," she said, her face flushing pink from either heat or embarrassment. "I'll just be working a few hours a day." Her mama explained about how the schedule would work with Lola and Janie Ray after school, and how she needed Lola's cooperation. But all Lola could really think about was what her daddy was going to say when he found out.

"Can you work with me on this, Lola?" Mama was saying.

Lola nodded, her mama's news still settling inside her thoughts. Janie Ray was still too ashamed of her mishap to take in the announcement. Just as well; the little girl wouldn't like sharing Mama with a job.

"What's that smell?" Mama asked. "Is that my good perfume?"

In spite of her best efforts, Janie Ray burst into tears, and all talk of the new job was momentarily put aside.

Ten

Luke saw Pap Taylor first. Then his vision seemed to go double. He saw two of Mont. But they were both clear as the edge of a blade, just wearing different shirts. It had to be Mont's brother, Roy. Luke's *daddy*. Holy shit. Roy was like a myth to Luke—someone he'd heard of, but with no hard evidence of his existence to anchor the stories. Only he was suddenly there—like the Loch Ness Monster come full out of the lake.

The brothers hung back near the door. Must be weird, Luke thought, to have someone walking around that looked that much like you. That was the first notion that came into his head. The second more pressing thought soon followed. *Why is my daddy here?*

He didn't know whether to be pissed at the bastard, the way he'd been his whole life, or embarrassed that the man's first sight of him since he was a baby occurred at the sheriff's office.

The man finally shows up and Luke is sitting there accused of carrying around enough pot to get the whole senior class high—with some left over. But he had no idea what was in the box. Would anyone believe that?

Pap Taylor broke away from his sons and came over to Luke. "What's this you've gone and done, boy?" Pap looked about as pissed off as Luke had ever seen him.

"It's a mix-up," Luke said, unable to keep from staring at the two Uncle Monts across the room. "I stopped off to say hi to Kendra on the way to school, and the next thing I know, I'm sitting in this room with Officer Maycomb. I thought I was taking a money box and dropping it by Larry's for her. Honestly."

"That's what you were doing from what I hear," Pap said. "Only it wasn't full of money. And since when do you take a detour by a girl's house on your way to school? What were you doing there?"

"Kendra's a friend," he said, realizing that he hadn't exactly answered Pap's question. "Is that Roy? When did *he* show up?" he asked, unable to hold off any longer.

"That was him this morning," Pap said, lowering his voice, "before you left."

"Talking to you in the kitchen?"

"Yeah, I didn't want to spring it on you when you were on the way out the door," Pap said.

Great, Luke thought. *It's so much better for me to find out here.* "Okay," he said instead. "What's he doing here?"

"I didn't get the full story," Pap said, raising one eyebrow at Luke. "We were interrupted by a phone call from the sheriff's office before we got around to finishing our conversation."

"Sorry," Luke said, his indignation giving way to guilt again.

"They're going to let you go with us for now," Pap said. "They're not sure what the charges are going to be. We may need to get you a lawyer."

"That's it?" Luke said. "I just leave with you?"

"For the time being, yeah." Pap's face was set into the worst kind of frown. "Lucky for you I've got a good name in this town and your uncle Mont has a few connections, too. It's all pretty quiet for the moment. No one knows that you've been hauled in here except for Maycomb—who's been keeping an eye on that Larry fellow for a while—and the sheriff, who's a friend of the family. I don't want you yapping to any of your friends about what's happened. We're going to work this out with as little fuss as possible. You hear?"

"Yes, sir," Luke said. "Pap?"

"Yeah?"

"Does Nanny know?"

"Not yet," he said.

For some reason, that made Luke feel more hopeful, although he had no cause for optimism. He stood up and braced himself to, for the first time in his own memory at least, walk over and meet his daddy.

Eleven

Roy stood by Mont and looked at the boy. Luke had just finished getting the third degree from his grandfather. He'd started to cross the room toward Roy when the sheriff called him and Taylor over to talk. Roy, feeling out of place, put his hands in his pockets and shuffled his feet.

Roy had lived for more than a decade without thinking about Mont, for the most part. The dismissal of his twin's existence kept the anger at bay. Standing next to him, there was no way around it. He didn't hate his sibling, but he no longer felt any love, either, and that made him sad. They'd been close as young boys, but had drifted in different directions by their teenage years. Brothers ought to be friends, especially when they are carbon copies of each other.

"You never did fully explain why you're here," Mont spoke up, keeping his eyes on Luke and Taylor.

"We'll talk later," Roy said. "It's too complicated to explain standing here." He hadn't had a chance to say anything to Luke yet, and he began to wonder what he *could* say. He wasn't even sure what the boy had been told about him, and now that Mont held the purse strings to all the Vines family money, he'd have to put up with whatever version of things they'd been giving Luke. For the time being, at least.

"It's been a long time, Roy." Mont looked over at him for a moment, gave him the once-over as if the answers to Roy's arrival might be found on his person. Then he looked away again as Taylor and the boy began to walk toward them.

"Luke," the older man said when they had crossed the room. "This is . . . Roy. Roy, meet Luke."

Roy put out his hand and Luke reluctantly shook it. A ridiculous gesture, Roy thought, but what was he supposed to do? Luke narrowed his eyes, his expression full of contempt toward Roy. *Why wouldn't the kid hate me? I'm sure he thinks I abandoned him and his mama.* What was he supposed to say? *No, I'm not your daddy, son. That honor would go to my son-of-a-bitch brother here.* Sure, there was the money to think about, but he also realized that he couldn't do that to the boy, not without putting a lot of thought into it. So they were left with an awkward handshake and then an even more awkward silence.

"Listen, Lucas—" Roy began.

"Luke." The kid cut him off.

"Oh." Roy was taken aback at the venom in the teenage boy's tone. "Sorry."

"Only people I think of as family call me Lucas sometimes." He stared at Roy, defying him to argue the point.

"Fair enough," Roy said.

"Let's get out of here before the whole town is talking about our business," Mont said.

They walked out in a cluster, for all the world, Roy thought, like a huddle of birds on a lake, nervous and aware of the dangers that waited around them.

Twelve

Charlotte walked into the Vines house without knocking and headed straight for the kitchen, where Lola sat working on homework.

Lola always rang the doorbell when she went to Charlotte's, but then Charlotte's mama was just as apt to be in her underwear as her clothes, so it was always a good idea. There were no such concerns at Lola's house.

"Your mama home?" Charlotte asked.

"She's in her room, I think," Lola said.

"Any news about your daddy?"

Lola shook her head, and felt grateful when Charlotte let it drop. Mama had cleaned up the perfume, but the overpowering odor lingered in the house and Charlotte made a face.

"Janie Ray spilled Mama's L'Air du Temps," Lola said. "Mama's not even mad. I think the whole world has flipped upside down."

"That's good stuff," Charlotte said, then scrunched up her face again. "But a little goes a long way." She sat down beside Lola at the table. "At least it's better than smelling that giant joint old Mr. Thomas lit up this morning. My house still smells like the stoners threw a party in our den. Mama was complaining this morning, but after inhaling it all day, I swear she was high by the time I got home. I've never seen her so mellow."

Lola laughed. "Is it still burning?" she asked, putting jam on a biscuit.

"I think so," Charlotte said, eyeing the plate, but not taking any food. "Stinks like it, anyway. Mama said she hoped those damn peacocks wandered into the fire and died."

Mr. and Mrs. Thomas kept a handful of the birds on their property. The mournful calling of the peacocks could be heard day and night. In the right mood—right around her time of the month especially—their sounds made Lola cry.

Outside in the backyard, Janie Ray rolled down a small hill of grass.

"Good Lord," Mama said, coming back into the kitchen. "That child is going to be covered in chigger bites from head to toe. Did you get a biscuit, Charlotte?"

"No, ma'am," she said. "Mama says I'm starting to look like the broad side of a barn and Shelby told me they'll kick me off the cheerleading squad if I get any fatter." Charlotte's older sister, Shelby, was a senior, and on her way to surpassing Mrs. Benson as the biggest bitch in town. "Mama's got me on carrot sticks and Tab in the afternoons, even though I'm hungry enough to eat the dog by the time I get home from school."

Lola felt sorry for Charlotte, stuck in that house with her mama and sister. Mr. Benson, who was just as nice as Lola's daddy, kept busy at the car dealership as long as he could justify staying away from his own property.

"Lord, child," Mama told Charlotte, "you're not heavy. You're a perfect size. Girls are supposed to have proportions, for heaven's sake. Go on and eat something. We just won't mention it to your mama."

Charlotte looked grateful and reached for the plate. She took the smallest biscuit.

"You girls keep working on your lessons," Mama said. "I'm going outside to brush the grass off Janie Ray before she tracks it all in the house."

Charlotte spread out her books and papers on the table. Lola opened her social studies book. It came easily to her, all of it— math, language, geography. Her only problems came when she got bored and distracted.

"You got any idea how I'm supposed to figure out this problem?" Charlotte bit at the side of her bottom lip. Charlotte hated all subjects that had definite answers. She'd be happy to let the whole world stay one big question mark.

"All you do is multiply this and then divide this into it," Lola explained. She couldn't believe how far back Charlotte's class was. She'd done problems like that in seventh grade.

They worked through the afternoon and finished as dark threatened to take over the day. Then Lola walked part of the way home with Charlotte. She tried not to think about how her daddy ought to be coming home. He'd always come in from work at the garage and head straight to the bathroom to wash up before saying hello. He washed his face, his arms all the way to the elbow. He even had a special brush to get the grease from under his fingernails. When he was done, he'd come into the kitchen smelling strong of Irish Spring soap.

"Listen, I'll be on the bus like normal in the mornings, but I won't be riding in the afternoons anymore." Lola decided to get the words out. Charlotte would get an earful about Mama's new job anyway, as soon as her own mother found out about it.

"How come?" Charlotte asked.

"Mama got a job at the Linton Grill for a few hours during the day. I'm supposed to meet her there after school and pick up Janie Ray."

"The Linton Grill?" The expression on Charlotte's face gave away her opinions before she caught herself. She was too good a friend to say more, but Lola knew she was thinking what everybody else would be saying. Anybody's mom going to work as a waitress was cause for a certain amount of pity. Lola didn't want to look at her friend.

"Okay," Charlotte said. "Then you'll come home after you get Janie Ray?"

"Yeah," she said. "Mama's going to drive us here and then go back for the rest of her shift, I guess."

Charlotte nodded. There wasn't much else to say. "See you tomorrow, then." She turned to walk in the direction of her house. She didn't look back at Lola, and Lola didn't blame her.

Lola stood by the side of the road, not moving. She wanted everything to go back the way it had been the week before— and the week before that. Peacocks called out and she felt tears threaten for no good reason. She must be getting her period. *Damn it. What is wrong with everybody?* The distinct smell of marijuana drifted over, giving the moment an added element of the surreal. And when Lola looked up she saw a deer, full-grown and standing motionless in the middle of the road.

Charlotte's head was down, brown hair falling over her shoulders, and Lola wanted to call out to her, but she didn't want to scare the doe away. It was beautiful. Majestic. It could charge her if it took a notion to do so, but she wasn't afraid. The animal seemed like something out of a fairy tale.

After a moment, it turned, and with no urgency in its gait, left the road and disappeared into the wood beyond. Again, the peacocks' call pierced the air already thick with heat and smoke. And this time Lola did cry as she turned to walk back toward her house.

The deer filled her mind with memories of Daddy. How one day a week or so before, he'd come in early in the afternoon wearing his regular work clothes from the garage, except they were all spattered with blood. He smelled of sweat and some other odor that Lola couldn't place. His expression wasn't anything out of the ordinary and Lola could only stare at him, afraid to ask what had happened.

"What on earth did you get into?" Mama said when she came into the den from the kitchen. Lola remembered that, as an odd coincidence, Mama had a white dishtowel slung over her shoulder, the cloth soiled red with either Kool-Aid or Jell-O. The bright stain of it contrasted with her daddy's darker, more threatening hues. Lola felt uneasy looking at the two of them.

"I got in a tussle with a deer carcass," Daddy said, and winked at Janie Ray. "Deer looks a damn sight worse than me though."

"Oh, hush," Mama told him. "You haven't been hunting deer in the middle of May. You'd get yourself arrested."

Daddy just grinned and walked toward the hall bathroom. They all followed—Mama, Lola, and Janie Ray.

"Not hunting," he said, still holding with his sly smile, but relenting to tell them the story. "I drove over to Hal's this afternoon. He couldn't get his car running and I told him I'd come out and take a look." He washed his hands while he talked, blood making the suds look like pink frosting. "Anyway, this fellow, black fellow from out in the county, came by and said somebody just hit a deer up on the interstate. Said the animal was stunned, probably with a back leg broken. He was wondering if Hal could bring his rifle and finish the poor creature off real quick. He said he knew a couple of families down in The

Shallows could sure use the meat if we could put the doe down and then help get it into his truck bed."

Lola's school bus passed The Shallows every day. It was a neighborhood near the north end of the lake, away from all the fancy houses, where the water was low and tree stumps broke the surface. Fishing was good around the dead branches, so on any given afternoon you could see groups of black men, mostly old guys, fishing, knee-deep in the brown water. The few shacks nearby stood on raised concrete or stilts in case of flooding. Deer meat would be a luxury for the people there, although Lola couldn't help but think that her own family could use a little meat in the freezer, too.

"Did you get the poor thing?" Mama asked, helping Daddy out of his shirt so she could get the blood out before it set in.

"One shot." Daddy grinned. "Hal gave me first crack at it once we tracked it a short ways into the woods. Not much sport in it. The thing's leg was a mess. It wouldn't have lived through the night." He looked younger than forty-two, standing there in work pants without a shirt, just a little gray in his reddish-brown hair.

Lola saw her mama looking at him; the expression on her face seemed to say that everything about him shined silver and bright.

He was happy at home. Not just that day, but almost every day. He wouldn't have left without a good reason, and he wouldn't stay gone. Mama had said as much. But what the hell was going on?

Lola went back toward her own house. She wasn't small anymore like Janie Ray. She ought to know if there was a problem in her own family. She'd ask, and this time Mama would tell her what was going on. That's all there was to it.

Thirteen

Rosalind watched Lola shove potatoes and green beans around on the plate. She'd made short work of the small slice of salty ham that Rosalind served up with it. Not much of a meal, but then they didn't have much to go on in the way of a grocery budget. That was another nice thing about going to work for Mae Rose. She'd get to bring home food. The temptation to feel sorry for herself lingered, but she refused.

"You want some of my ham?" Rosalind asked. "I don't have much of an appetite."

"That's okay," Lola said. "I'm full, too."

Janie Ray had finished every scrap and was already off building a fort in the den, so Rosalind got up to clear their plates and Lola joined in.

Rosalind felt pretty good, in spite of the doctor's concerns about her easy bruising and the places on her arms. The initial test had shown that something was wrong with her blood count.

She had a follow-up appointment the next morning when they would tell her a little more, but if it turned out to be what they expected, she would need to see doctors out of town. That's why Roy had taken off. When she thought of him in Virginia, she felt grateful and angry at the same time.

But she wouldn't dwell on her health. She had two wonderful children, a roof over her head, and a man willing to put aside every shred of pride and ask his folks for money to help her. There were people in the world who deserved pity, but she wasn't one of them.

Janie Ray came in and grabbed the last biscuit left over from the afternoon. The tiny child could eat three times her weight, it seemed. As Rosalind had predicted, red bug bites dotted the girl's arms and she scratched at them, turning the skin angry in spots.

"Can I watch TV from my fort?" the smaller girl asked, her mouth full.

"Finish chewing what's in your mouth," Rosalind told her, "and then, yes, you may turn it on."

The child made a show of swallowing, then took the empty biscuit plate to the sink. She had to stand on her toes to put it down, before heading back to the other room. Rosalind turned her attention to Lola.

"I know this is hard on you," Rosalind said. "Everything's going to be okay."

"I want to know where Daddy is," Lola said, not looking up from her plate.

The day had cooled enough to turn off the air conditioner in the kitchen, but the air that replaced the window unit's cool stream was humid. Rosalind felt the sleeves of her blouse damp at her wrists. Lola deserved more of an explanation than she'd gotten. Rosalind had hoped to wait for Roy, so that they could explain it together, but she'd had no word from him since he left, and truth be told, she needed an ally, someone in whom to confide.

"I guess the first thing to tell you is that you have grandparents," Rosalind said.

"Grandma Simsy?" Lola looked confused. She'd always been close to Simsy Clark, Rosalind's mother—and Grandpa Clark, too, before he died.

"No, I don't mean my family," Rosalind continued. She thought of her mama and daddy. Vernon Clark had a fatal car crash when Lola was twelve, just after Janie Ray was born. Her mama still lived in the mountains, not far from the Virginia town where Roy was at that moment with his own folks.

Rosalind's parents had doted on their granddaughters. Her mother still did. How to explain those other two? Taylor and Lydia Vines? How do you tell a child that her own blood kin never took an interest in knowing her?

"I'm talking about your daddy's parents," she said.

Lola's forehead furrowed, but she didn't ask the question. She waited for Rosalind to continue.

"I know we told you they passed already," she said. "We didn't want to be dishonest, Lola, but the truth is they might as well have died. They broke with your father years ago when he married me. For reasons I don't want to go into, they didn't take to his relationship with me and he had to choose. He chose me. He chose this family."

"Does that have something to do with where he is now?" Lola asked.

Rosalind couldn't tell how Lola felt about the news. It was as if Lola intended to process it all before registering any emotion.

"He's gone to ask them for money," Rosalind said. "It's killing him, I know, but he's doing it for me."

Lola waited. Rosalind had to tell her. The secrets were becoming more troubling to the girl than the truth. She rolled up one sleeve of her blouse. The patches of red on her arm were the color of Janie Ray's chigger bites, only the skin over them was as smooth as plastic.

"What's that?" Lola asked, for the first time looking genuinely frightened.

"I noticed these marks a little while back." Rosalind kept her voice calm. "They weren't this bad when they first showed up. They were on my legs first and then my arms, too. I went over to the health department, and the doctor told me there might be something wrong with my blood. He said I'll probably need to see a specialist. Daddy wants to get me the best. I may need some kind of treatment and Daddy's set on finding a doctor that works especially with this kind of problem. But that will cost money, so he's gone off to ask his folks for help."

"Could this problem make you real sick?" Lola asked.

Rosalind knew the real question that Lola couldn't bring herself to say out loud. *Could it kill you?* That's what she wanted to know, and Rosalind didn't have the answer yet. The county doctor told her that he was no expert, but he said that if he was right about his diagnosis, he understood the problem to be *manageable*—with the right treatment.

"They need to do more tests," she said, avoiding any concrete detail. "I don't know all the ins and outs of it yet. But even the tests themselves will run into money. That's why your daddy—against my wishes—took off like that. Part of me would almost rather get sick than make him go to those people for help." She saw a flash of panic cross Lola's face. "I don't mean that, Lola. I'm sorry. Of course I'll do what's necessary to stay healthy. I promise."

In her mind's eye, she pictured another figure standing with Roy's parents. That woman. She pushed thoughts of Roy's first wife out of her mind. She would not talk about Sherry. She wouldn't even think about her, or about how desperate the woman was to hang on to Roy.

"Everything's going to be all right," she said. "I don't want you to worry."

"Do they know about me and Janie Ray?" Lola asked. "These other grandparents, I mean."

"They know we had you," Rosalind said. "I don't think they know about Janie Ray. They're hard people, Lola. I can't imagine how your sweet daddy came from such stock. It kills me that he's asking them for help, but I can't stop him."

"Is that why you're getting a job?" Lola asked. "Should you be working with this . . . condition you have? Maybe I could work at the grill after school instead of you going in. I could get there by—"

"Hush." Rosalind got up and put her arms around Lola. She kissed the top of her dark head and took in the shampoo smell of the girl's shiny, thick hair. Such young skin Lola had. "You need to help me with Janie Ray. That's all. I'll be fine, and working some will keep me busy. I'm better off busy."

The phone rang. *Please let it be Roy.* She pulled away from Lola and walked over to pick it up.

"Hey, darlin'." The sound of her husband's voice gave her a rush of pure joy. He was okay.

"I got sick with worry when I didn't hear from you, Roy," she said, then regretted her words when she remembered that Lola was still in the room.

"I've had a hectic time of it. I didn't even get here until early this morning and this is the first chance I've had to get to a phone. I'm sorry. I knew you'd be fretting."

"It's okay," she said. "I'm just sorry you left with me in such a state. I'm not mad at you. I wasn't being fair."

"We were both upset. This isn't what either of us wanted, Rosie. But I had to do something."

She didn't tell him that she had to do something, too. She didn't tell him she'd called Mae Rose. There would be time for that conversation later. "Did your parents agree to help you?"

He hesitated, and her spirits sank.

"It's more complicated than I thought," Roy said. "I'll explain things later, but this is costing money on their long-distance bill. I think we'll be able to work something out. Don't worry."

"When are you coming home?"

"In a day or so," he said. "I mean it. Don't worry. I've got to go, okay?"

"Is *she* there?" Rosalind dropped her voice low.

He didn't answer right away, and she wondered for an instant if Roy's ex-wife was standing right beside him.

"She's not here," he said, finally. "I'm not sure what the whole story is, but they've told me she's dead. I don't know what happened to her."

Rosalind felt the power of his words. Dead. And Rosalind—even with all her problems—was alive. There was a certain sense of triumph in that. Relief that went through her followed by shame at the heartlessness of her reaction. In truth, Roy's first wife had more reason to hate Rosalind than the other way around.

"I have to go," Roy said again. "I love you."

"I love you, too."

Rosalind turned around to see Lola staring at her.

"He's fine," she told her daughter. "Everything's going to be fine."

Fourteen

The house smelled of roast pork and Pine-Sol. Roy sat in the back bedroom, his old room, having just gotten off the phone with Rosalind. His mother was making dinner, treating things for all the world like just any other night. Lydia had always been a master of keeping up appearances, but everyone there understood that the thinnest of veneers covered a family in crisis.

Luke shut himself up in his room the minute they got in from the courthouse. Mont drove home to fill Della in on the afternoon's events. Roy could only imagine his sister-in-law's response to Mont's news of the boy's behavior. He could see Della's cheerless eyes and the mute acceptance of yet another disappointing turn of events. It had been fifteen years since he'd seen Mont's wife, but he couldn't imagine that she'd changed much. She didn't so much react to news as she *absorbed* it. Made it part of the collective sadness that was her life.

Mont had a daughter, too. Nell. Roy wondered if she took after Della. Plump and sad without any personality to speak of. Or was she like Mont? Hell of a choice. Either way, the kid couldn't catch a break.

"Dinner'll be ready in twenty minutes," his mother called from the kitchen.

Roy felt hungry in spite of himself, but he didn't know if he could swallow food when the time came. He'd made his way to Virginia to talk to his folks. That had been hard enough. But this business with the boy . . . The look in Luke's eyes when he realized Roy's identity answered everything Roy needed to know about what they'd told the kid. They let Sherry's son believe Roy was a son-of-a-bitch who abandoned him and his mother for another family. Shit. What was he supposed to do with that? Pretend to be the kind of asshole who would run out on a baby? He realized that's exactly what he would have to do if he was going to do Rosalind any good.

He heard a car turn in from the road. He looked out the bedroom window and saw Mont's Cadillac stirring up dirt from the driveway as it arrived at the house. Roy could see Della looking out the window of the passenger side. Her eyes scanned to his window, and when she saw him, she quickly looked away.

There was a slight rustling in the hall, and Roy turned to see Taylor standing there. "Can I talk to you for a minute?"

Taylor Vines's figure filled the door frame. "Sure, come on in," Roy said. "It's your house." Roy didn't know why he added that last part. He had no cause to make things worse.

"If you're bitter about things, son, put it down right now." Taylor spoke in resolute tones. "We've got too much going on to add all the old hurts to the mix."

Taylor was right, he knew, but with no present to draw on, past hurts made up the bulk of Roy's feelings about his extended family. He couldn't make something out of nothing. "I'll do my best," Roy said, thinking of Vines Hardware. The family business, now firmly in Mont's possession with the papers legally drawn up in Mont's name. "What's going to happen with the boy?" He changed the subject.

Taylor took in a full breath of air and came into the room. He sat down at a desk chair across the room from where Roy sat on the bed. Roy wished Rosalind was with him. He'd always felt it took the two of them to stand up to either one of his parents. But her voice, still close in his ear from their conversation, would have to suffice.

"It's a bad time for all this to happen," Taylor said.

"Can you think of a good time?"

Taylor ignored his comment. "Mont's put everything into this election. The store's holding up pretty good, but people can turn fast if rumors about the boy start to spread."

Again, Roy thought of Rosalind. How she would have been worried about the boy and not about the rumors. How she cared about her family and to hell with everything else. At the courthouse, Roy began to feel an urgency to talk to his wife. He knew she'd be worried about him, but it was more than that. He needed her voice to ground him in some sort of reality. Nothing since he arrived at his old home place that morning had seemed consistent with the life he'd known since leaving Gray's Hollow. He called up the sound of her again in his mind. *I'm not mad at you.* She said that. And she said she loved him. That's all he needed.

". . . for a while, at least." Taylor was saying something. "We can revisit the whole thing in a month or two. The boy has college in the fall and—"

"I'm sorry," Roy interrupted him. "What did you say?"

Taylor looked pained. Whatever he said, he clearly did not want to repeat. He braced himself with his hands on his knees. "The boy needs to go back to North Carolina with you for the summer. His school finishes soon anyway. He's already taken his exams. I'm sure they'll let him finish up any remaining work he has on his own so he can get his diploma."

Roy didn't respond. He found himself unable to think, much less speak. Was Taylor really suggesting that Luke go with him? Live in his house?

"Mont can't have any questions being asked right now," Taylor went on. "If Luke just goes away, Al Handler, the sheriff, and Maycomb, that officer who brought Luke in, will be able to pass it off as something simple. Say he got smart-mouthed on a traffic stop or something. Gossip runs out of steam when there's nobody to point to."

Roy felt blood rise to his face. He heard the whoosh of his own heartbeat inside his ears. "Daddy, that can't happen," he managed. "I can't take a full-grown boy I don't even know back to my family. I can't believe you're even asking me to do that."

"He's your son, Roy," Taylor said, the words landing firm in the air of Roy's room. "It's time you took responsibility for that."

Surely his mother would speak up. Even if Mont planned to let him take the kid, she would have to tell Taylor the truth, wouldn't she? Immediately he knew the answer to his question. Lydia would protect Mont. She always had. He was the bright hope of the family, and in her eyes, a victim of Roy's poor judgment.

For the second or third time that day, Roy swallowed back the truth. Blurting it out to his father would sound absurd. Made up. But what could he do? There was no way he could take Luke Vines back and make Rosalind put up with him in her own home. Even under normal circumstances, it would be impossible. But Rosalind now had other struggles to overcome. Enemies inside her own body, inside her blood. Roy would not put this on her, too.

"I can't, Daddy," he said, keeping his voice low and strong in spite of his shaky nerves. "How can you ask me to do that right now? Rosalind is sick. I've got to look after her. I can't take on the boy."

Roy heard footsteps.

"The money's there, Roy." Mont came in and sat down beside Roy on the twin bed Roy had slept in as a boy. "The money you need to look after Rosalind. I can make that happen for you. But you have to do this one thing for us."

Roy looked at his brother. Mont was bargaining with Roy. Help for Rosalind in exchange for Roy's taking the boy and keeping his mouth shut.

"Think about it, Roy. Everybody gets what they need." Then Mont added, "It's the only way, brother."

Anger rose up inside Roy's chest. Anger both old and new, mixing into an all too familiar rage. But he thought of Rosalind. He thought of the pinpoints of blood that from a distance looked like a rash on her arms and legs. He thought of her and he could already see Mont's bastard son living under his very own roof. He immediately regretted his own meanness. It wasn't the boy's fault. Roy had to remember that much, at least.

"Have you told him about this plan yet?" Roy asked.

"Who?" Mont asked.

Was he serious? Who? "Luke," Roy answered, wondering how he and this man who looked just like him could be so different. "Have you talked to Luke about this?"

Taylor shook his head no.

"You don't think he'll object?" Roy was grasping at straws and he knew it.

"He doesn't have a choice, Roy," Mont said. Implied was that Roy had no more choice than Luke.

Roy looked from his father to his brother, both of them carrying the same blood that ran through his own body. But they were strangers to him. Rosalind and the girls were the only family he had. He felt a stab of pity for Luke. With Sherry gone, who did he have?

"Dinner's ready!" Lydia called from the kitchen, and since their conversation had come to an obvious close, all three men rose to answer her call.

Roy felt exhausted. Lack of hunger told him that he'd eaten, but he could barely remember what he put in his mouth. The small amount of conversation at supper, accompanied by the sound of forks moving around on china plates, made the meal one of the most awkward Roy had ever endured.

He figured that after dinner, they would all go to bed, especially after the day they'd had. But instead, Roy's brother and parents insisted that they sit there in the living room and work through the problems at hand.

Roy looked across the room to where Taylor Vines sat on the couch beside Mont and Della. For the first time in Roy's life, his father looked old to him. How many years would go by before Lola and Janie Ray looked at him like that? What the hell would happen between his present life and old age? Would Rosalind be there with him when that time came?

That's where he stopped. He would not consider life without his wife. Even with his children, life would be nothing but shadows without Rosalind.

"You brought this on all of us today, Luke," Mont was saying to the boy.

"I know you'd take it back if you could," Lydia said. She sat in an armchair identical to the one Roy occupied. "You've been trying to explain everything, but that's not the point anymore. We've got to decide how best to handle things as they are, and the fact of the matter is, you've put your uncle Mont in a terrible situation here. He's been like a father to you and his political opponents will use that against him if they get wind of it."

Luke sat in a straight-backed chair by the fireplace, looking miserable. The family meeting was taking on the tone of an inquisition.

It dragged on and on because Luke refused outright the notion that he should go live with Roy's family—and Mont, Taylor, and Lydia would not accept any other option. Not only would they not hear of anything else, but best Roy could tell, they wanted some kind of agreement from Luke that they were in the right. It wasn't enough to just punish him. They seemed to want to bring him as low as possible before that happened. The only thing Roy knew for sure was that the family tribunal would not end well for the kid—or for him.

"This is my last summer with my friends." Luke's voice had grown high-pitched and desperate. He'd said the same thing a dozen times, each time the plea falling on deaf ears. The repetition was becoming pathetic.

Roy wished he could help, but he was as stuck as anybody. He needed money for Rosalind. Mont held the purse strings, and Taylor and Lydia both—with very different reasons—would back up his brother without question. That left Luke with no foothold on his own life. Sure, the boy had screwed up, but he hadn't killed anybody. Hell, Roy pretty much believed that the kid didn't even know what was in the damn box.

But none of that mattered. Roy knew it. Everyone else in the room knew it, with the exception of Luke, who still seemed to believe that reason would prevail.

"I'm going to college in September," he said. "I'll be gone in a few months anyway. You're wanting to take away the last summer I have with everybody I've grown up with here? I've known these people since kindergarten. I've got prom this weekend. What's

Deedee supposed to do? She can't get another date this late. Hell, you're telling me I can't even *graduate* with them."

Taylor let out a long sigh. "Luke, you should have thought about your prom date when you were doing God knows what with that Kendra girl this morning. I'm sorry you've ruined things for yourself, but we're just cleaning up a mess you made. I'm not going to talk about this anymore."

"You can't do this," Luke said, the futile nature of his situation finally seeming to set in. "You've got to let me stay here."

"I'm sorry, son," Mont said. Della sat beside him, and something just shy of a smile played at her features.

She's happy about this. The certainty of this realization hit Roy, and he suddenly ached for the boy in a new way. Was it possible that Della knew the truth, too? Did she know that Mont was really the boy's father? Or maybe she disliked Luke for other reasons. Either way, Roy decided that he had to help the boy to the extent that he could. The entire extended Vines family had turned into a pack of jackals.

Luke shook his head, looked close to tears. He'd lost and he finally knew it. One mistake, and everything in his young life had changed.

Roy wanted to tell him that high school memories would become small one day. That contrary to what he believed at that moment, this disappointment would not dictate the colors of his life. But there's no way to convince a seventeen-year-old that his thirty-year-old self would outgrow what he felt with such fierce intensity.

What might matter to that future self of Luke's? Roy fought to think of what he could do.

"I'll take him under one condition," Roy said, keeping his voice steady as if he had some say in the matter.

Everyone else in the room looked up, surprised either at his tone or that he'd spoken at all.

"What's that?" Mont asked.

"He comes back to graduate with his friends." It was small, but Roy thought he could push that much through.

"That's too public." Taylor spoke up. "Just the thing we need to avoid."

"It'll be more conspicuous if he's absent," Roy pressed forward. "He's away with me for the next week and a half. Any rumors that bubble up will die down fast. We'll call his leaving with me family business. But then the boy comes back and walks with his class. He ought to have that, and you shouldn't take it from him. I'll drive him back here myself."

Luke's look of devastation eased ever so slightly. His eyes went from Mont to Taylor and back again.

"All right," Taylor said, and it wasn't so much a statement as a decree.

"Daddy, I don't think—" Mont began, but Taylor Vines put his hand out and stopped the argument in its tracks.

"He walks with his class," Taylor said. "Then he goes back to Roy's until he starts college in the fall."

Still slumped in so much defeat, Luke managed to give Roy a look. For the first time in their brief interactions, Luke's expression was unclouded by years of resentment against Roy. The boy offered a small nod of appreciation, acknowledging that Roy had spoken up for him.

Given that neither of them had a choice, Roy decided that was as good a place as any to begin.

Fifteen

The lights woke Lola before the noises. Red and white flashing swords cut through the steady dark of the room she shared with Janie Ray. By the time her brain registered the sirens—high-pitched wails alternating with low blasts—she was already standing. The lights seemed solid and full of danger. She looked at the clock by her bed. Not even midnight yet, but she'd been in the dead of sleep.

"Janie Ray, get up!" Lola said. She looked out the window to see if something close by was burning, but only smoke drifted by. No flames.

"Lola!" Mama called from the hall.

"Where's the fire?" Lola shouted back.

"Down at the Thomas house." Mama was in the room. "You and Janie Ray put your housecoats on and get outside. I don't want to take any chances, just in case it spreads this way."

Lola had the panicked thought that Charlotte's house was

closer to the problem than her own. She wanted to get down the road and check on her friend, but instead pulled a sleepy Janie Ray upright and guided her small arms through her housecoat. She felt around on the floor for flip-flops for the younger girl. Once Janie Ray was reasonably dressed, Lola found her own robe and sandals and they headed down the hall toward the front door. Mama stood in the kitchen talking on the phone.

"They're here already," she said, obviously talking to a neighbor who couldn't get through to anybody else. "The trucks just got to the fire. Don't worry. I'm sure they'll have it under control soon. Just get outside until it's over."

"Who was that?" Lola asked.

"Liddy Wren," Mama said.

"What's she worried about? She lives half a mile in the other direction," Lola said, as they all went onto the front porch.

"I know it," Mama said, and shook her head. "Old people get a little crazy when there's a fire."

Old people. Lola thought of Mr. and Mrs. Thomas. She looked in the direction of their house and saw orange and searing white flames. A hot breeze came from that direction.

"You think the Thomases are okay?" Janie Ray spoke for the first time, echoing Lola's thoughts.

"I sure hope so," Mama said. "Vicky Benson called a few minutes ago, said it looks like their whole house is going up."

"Is Charlotte all right?" Lola asked.

"Yeah," Mama said. "Vicky said everybody there is fine."

"How about Pinball?" Janie Ray asked in a strained, baby-sleep voice.

Janie Ray loved animals, and Pinball was the closest thing she had to a live pet of her own.

"Pinball's fine, I'm sure, honey," Mama said. "They wouldn't leave her in the house."

"He's a boy, not a 'her,'" Janie Ray said, obviously worried that if her mama had gotten that much wrong, the dog could be in serious danger.

"Whatever, darlin'," Mama said, only half paying attention. "The dog's all right."

Lola looked again at the wild glow of the flames in the distance. Arms of fire waving back and forth like one of those stoned-out hippies filmed dancing at Woodstock. If she didn't think about the danger of it all, the fire looked pretty, moving in the dark night. Even though the weatherman predicted rain, the night had come on clear. The moon, half full, had a fine edge. In the light of it, the gathering smoke gave the impression a storm brewed directly over the Thomas property. There and nowhere else.

"I see Vicky and her girls in the front yard down there," Mama said. "Let's walk on down and see if they've heard anything."

Not much short of a fire would get Mama in the same yard with Mrs. Benson, and Lola knew the feeling was mutual. That made it hard on Lola and Charlotte's daddies because they liked to watch ball games together—to fish and hunt on weekends.

"I want Bubbles," Janie Ray began to whine. Bubbles, her stuffed bear, provided comfort everywhere except the bathtub.

"I'll go get him," Mama said.

She went back in the house. The lights came on room to room, marking her path down the hall. Lola thought about their duplex. One side empty and lifeless, the other crowded and loud with a family barely able to fit inside four rooms. What if their house burned down? Where would they live? Grandma Simsy couldn't take them in; she lived in a home now. Then Lola remembered her mother's news about grandparents, her dad's mom and dad. Maybe they'd go live with them.

Lola tried to imagine what her newly discovered relatives

might look like. But all she came up with was images of people she knew from the movies, and she doubted that the real deal was anywhere near that glamorous.

Mama came out carrying Bubbles. She handed the bear to Janie Ray. "Come on," she said, already heading down the road.

Charlotte's mama didn't know anything more than Lola's. A third fire truck turned in at the main road screaming its warning, just like the others. Linton Springs had only two fire trucks and they were already hard at work. When the new truck went by, Lola saw that it came from the Creston Fire Department.

"I told you this would happen," Vicky Benson said to no one in particular. "All that burning he was doing this morning. There was too much smoke for it to be under control. I called this one right off the bat."

Even though that was true, Lola wished Charlotte's mama would get quiet. Mrs. Benson's lime green housedress stuck out from underneath her Sunday raincoat. With a net over her hair, she looked more like a lunchroom lady than treasurer of the town's snooty Kitchen Club.

Charlotte stood a short distance away wearing her daddy's canvas hunting jacket over her nightgown. The jacket was open in the front and Lola could see her friend's whole shape, even the shadow of her nipples, through the thin cotton. Sometimes Charlotte forgot that she wasn't little anymore.

"Look at it!" Charlotte was out of breath just standing there. "Can you believe there's a fire like that right here on our street? They've got at least twenty firemen down there. One of them told Daddy it's the biggest fire in the county in twenty years. That's since before I was born!"

Pinball caught her excitement and stood on his hind legs, turning in circles like a carnival dog.

Charlotte's daddy walked up the road from the direction of the fire.

"They know anything about the Thomases?" Mama asked when he got close enough.

"Alva's outside, but they haven't found Minnie yet," he said. "The old man is hoping she went out the back way. He thinks that maybe she's somewhere in all that mess of firemen. He said she should have been in bed with him, but she must have gotten up for something. He doesn't know where she was in the house when it started."

"Well, it's his own fault," Mrs. Benson said. "He's down there all afternoon acting like the neighborhood's made of Teflon."

"Shut the hell up, Vicky," Mr. Benson said, his voice tired and full of defeat. This got everybody's attention. Charlotte's daddy never talked like that to anybody, especially not his wife. Lola had the sudden impulse to give the man a hug.

Mrs. Benson looked like she might either hit him or start crying, but she didn't do either.

"We're all worn out," Mama said.

Lola looked again at the flames. They'd lost any bit of beauty they'd had just moments before. She thought of Mr. Thomas outside, scared and looking for his wife. She thought of her own daddy, also missing, but apparently okay. When people were absent from where they ought to be, the whole world got strange. Lola took hold of Janie Ray and hugged her even though the little girl tried to squirm away. But after a second, the child stopped struggling and turned to Lola.

"Pick me up," she said, her voice suddenly small and unsure.

Lola lifted her, and Janie Ray wrapped her legs tight around her big sister's waist.

"I miss Daddy," Janie Ray said, again following Lola's thoughts with eerie symmetry.

"Me too, baby girl," Lola said. "Me too."

* * *

Charlotte motioned for Lola to come over to the side of the porch.

"What is it?" Lola still carried Janie Ray. The child had dozed off in her arms, and even though she was getting heavy, Lola held tight and tried to keep her as still as she could while she walked over to Charlotte.

Charlotte motioned toward a figure sitting in the porch swing. Shelby, Charlotte's older sister, sat slumped against the chain that suspended the seat.

"She was out drinking with Bobby Langely," Charlotte whispered. "I think she's doing it with Bobby, but I don't know for sure. She's so *plowed* she came in my window instead of hers. She got in just before the sirens came by and Mama started yelling for us to get out. I don't think she can stand up without hurling."

"What are you girls up to over there?" Mrs. Benson called out to Charlotte.

"Nothing, Mama." Charlotte laughed.

Shelby dragged a droopy-eyed gaze over in their direction and worked on looking mean, but she couldn't quite pull it off. Lola laughed in spite of herself. She wondered if Shelby really was doing it with Bobby. She tried to imagine what it would feel like to be naked with a boy.

"It's not the time for jokes, girls." Mama looked over, and Lola felt embarrassment rise up through her cheeks. Mama couldn't read her thoughts, but she felt awful anyway. She adjusted Janie Ray's position in her arms and sat on the porch steps of Charlotte's house.

She thought about Minnie Thomas, wondered if she did get out like Mr. Thomas hoped, or if she was inside that furnace that just an hour before had been a perfectly good house.

Mrs. Thomas made tea cakes for weddings and other occasions around town. Lola would buy eggs from her sometimes, because they kept chickens in a coop at the back of their yard. Most days when Lola arrived at the kitchen door, Mrs. Thomas would be standing over the long linoleum table with metal legs that ran the length of the kitchen down the middle. She'd have pans and pans of sheet cake lined up on the table, ready for decoration.

Once, when Lola was about eight or nine, she stayed there for a whole afternoon, watching the older woman cut iced cakes into squares and then put a little flower on each one. She squeezed green leaves out of one tube and pink flowers out of another. Lola sat on a piano stool that Mr. Thomas twirled high enough so that she could see, and every so often Mrs. Thomas would look over at her, smile, and hand Lola a cake square to eat. When Lola left, she felt like she'd been to a party.

"Let's go over to Baker's Rock and sit," Charlotte said to Lola.

"That's a good idea," Vicky Benson chimed in. "Get away from this smoke a little bit."

Mama came over and took the sleeping Janie Ray from her, and Lola got up to go with Charlotte. Baker's Rock was a flat slab of stone embedded in the ground at the top of the rise behind Charlotte's house. The two of them used to make mud pies up there, dirt tamped firm into pie tins their mamas would let them take outside. They would line the tins up on the rock and say it was the oven. Lola's daddy was the first one to call it Baker's Rock when he saw their creations lined up there and cooking in the hot sun.

Lola and Charlotte huddled together on the rock with their knees drawn up to their chests.

"It's kind of pretty over there," Charlotte said.

"Their house is almost gone." Lola saw more fire than wood. "God only knows what's happened to Mrs. Thomas."

"It just doesn't seem real," Charlotte said.

Inside her truest thoughts, Lola had to admit that it was pretty. The house, still hot yellow on one side and starting to glow orange around the burned-out parts, looked beautiful really. Lights from the trucks washed over the glowing wood. Sometimes something awful could break your heart with beauty.

Firemen ran every which way dragging hoses and directing blasts of water that took in large swaths of wall. The lights and activity reminded Lola of the midway at the state fair.

"Look," Charlotte said, whispered really. "They've got somebody on a stretcher."

Sure enough, two firemen carried a stretcher away from the kitchen side of the house. Paramedics that Lola hadn't noticed before ran to help load whoever it was into an ambulance. Mr. Thomas looked like he was trying to get in, too, but they wouldn't let him. When he started to get agitated, one of the firemen came up and took him by the arm. The fireman led him off to the side, and Mr. Thomas dropped to his knees. He was either passing out or praying. Lola couldn't tell which.

Lola and Charlotte got up without saying anything, then walked back down the hill. The wind shifted and black smoke obscured their view of Mr. Thomas. Under the bright half moon, it looked like a curtain of privacy had been drawn to shield him as he bent over on his knees.

"You girls get back!" Mr. Benson shouted from behind them.

Lola turned and saw him dragging a fireman into a clearing and laying him on his back.

"Get his jacket open," another fireman called out as he came over to the hurt man.

Lola stepped closer so she could see.

"He went in after her," Mr. Benson said as he pulled the jacket away from the fireman's chest and got his helmet off. He bent over to check the man's breathing. "He pulled her out of that mess."

The injured man began coughing and rose up on his elbows.

"That's it, buddy," the other fireman said. "Cough it out."

With his helmet off, the hurt fireman looked young, not more than twenty, maybe younger even. Blond hair, damp with sweat, came down just past his neck.

Forgetting for a moment the horror of the fire, Lola stared at him. He was gorgeous. She wondered what his name was, then immediately she felt ashamed of herself. *A woman I care about is probably dead and I'm building a crush on some fireman.*

"How's my grandma?" Those were the first words he spoke when he stopped coughing.

"You did all you could," Mr. Benson said. "It's up to the good Lord now."

Grandma? The fireman was the Thomases' grandson? Lola had heard Mrs. Thomas talk about a grown daughter who lived in Creston. Said she hardly ever came home. This must be the woman's son. Lola remembered seeing a boy down there sometimes when she was little. This boy was all grown up.

"I've got to go check on her," the fireman said. He tried to stand with Mr. Benson holding his arm, but his head dropped down and he had to sit again.

"They won't let you in with her, Duncan." Mr. Benson seemed to know him. "They won't even let your granddaddy in there."

"She was in the root cellar with an old fan lying beside her," Duncan said. "I guess she went down to get it. She'd passed out by the time I got to her. Nothing had burned down there, but the smoke was bad. She was at the bottom of the stairs."

Mr. Benson shook his head.

"I should at least go check on my granddaddy," Duncan said.

The bustle seemed to be over inside the ambulance. Lola didn't think that was a good sign at all. One of the paramedics came out and headed for Mr. Thomas. Duncan had been walking toward the old man, but when he saw the other man heading toward his granddaddy, he stopped and watched from up on the rise.

"I'm Charlotte, their neighbor," Charlotte walked over to him and spoke up. "I hope everything's okay."

"I hope so, too," Duncan said softly, his eyes moving from Charlotte back to his grandfather.

In spite of herself, Lola felt a kind of anger rise against her best friend. Only it wasn't anger exactly. She was jealous. And for the third time that night, she felt ashamed of herself. But she couldn't help it. Charlotte standing there in her thin nightgown. But he barely noticed either one of them.

"This is my friend, Lola," Charlotte said. "She lives on the street here, too. We both know your grandparents. They're awfully sweet people." Charlotte had genuine concern and no motives in talking to Duncan. Lola could learn something from that.

"Hi," Lola managed, and hoped she sounded sympathetic. His face glistened with sweat and tears, and a scar, white where the rest of his face was tan, traveled from his jaw up over the edge of his ear and disappeared under that ragged blond hair.

"Duncan!" one of other firemen called from across the yard. "You're going to want to come down here."

Duncan moved all at once, stepped solid through the high grass until he reached his granddaddy. The old man looked up at his grandson, and Lola could have sworn she saw anger in his expression. Why would the old man be mad? He pushed away from Duncan, but the younger man followed him and took hold of him anyway. He took his granddad full in his arms and Mr. Thomas gave in, buried his head in Duncan's smoky jacket.

Minutes went by, but they kept hold of each other. They were still standing like that when Lola decided it was time to turn around and head back home.

Sixteen

Rosalind saw Lola walking back toward the house. Janie Ray woke up and scrambled off behind her sister. Minnie Thomas was gone, and there didn't seem to be much else for Rosalind to do except go home with her girls. Hal Benson said he'd gotten Mr. Thomas to agree to go to the hospital, and from what she gathered, the young fireman, his grandson, would be looking out for him. The boy could go call the rest of the family. It was almost too sad for words. Alva and Minnie Thomas had an old, strong love. It shouldn't have come to an end like that, without any good-byes.

Lola had been standing and talking to the grandson. Rosalind saw her. He was a boy, really, once he got the fireman's hat off, and the look on Lola's face reminded Rosalind of how she felt the first time she saw Roy.

Roy wore a crisp, white shirt that night, open at the collar. Flickers of light from a black and white television set lit up his face. He was in the reception hall at his church watching *The Wizard of Oz*. Roy's church hosted a movie night for anyone who wanted to come.

Even though Rosalind lived thirty miles away, she'd been invited to come with a friend from that church who went to Randolph-Macon Women's College. Rosalind had gone to the school for two years, then dropped out. That night, she and her friend came in late, after the movie had already started, and they settled into a couple of fold-out chairs at the side of the room.

"Who's that?" Rosalind asked her friend when Roy turned to look at her and held his gaze longer than he should have.

"Roy Vines," the friend told her. "Cute, isn't he?"

"The cutest," Rosalind said, staring at his profile after he'd turned back to watch the movie.

"He's got a twin brother who looks just like him. The only way I know that's Roy is because he's sitting with his wife, Sherry."

Wife. Rosalind looked away. Her disappointment felt solid and she didn't know why. She never even knew he existed before she walked into that room.

"How about the twin?" Rosalind asked, but knowing it wasn't exactly about his looks anyway. It was something in his expression as he glanced over at her.

"The twin brother's married, too," the friend said. "Their daddy owns Vines Hardware, so they had a business already set up and waiting for them after college."

"Too bad I didn't come around before those weddings," Rosalind told her, trying to make it all into a joke. But she couldn't shake the feeling of something special about this Roy.

After the movie ended, the wife, a pretty girl with light brown hair, helped clean up in the kitchen of the reception hall. Roy caught Rosalind's eye again and she looked away and walked out into the hall.

"Who are you?" he asked, following her out.

"Somebody who doesn't talk to married men," she answered. Her heartbeats came fast and hard inside her chest. She felt herself flushing hot.

"I just . . ." he started, but then lost whatever it was he'd wanted to say. "I'm sorry." He shook his head, as if to shake off whatever had come over him.

"Me too," she said, unable to keep herself from saying it. Her eyes were locked on his. She wanted to kiss him so much it felt like a physical hurt that she couldn't. "Lana's waiting on me in there," she said. "She's going to drive me back home."

"Where's home?"

"Murphy." She didn't regret telling him. She should have. She wasn't raised that way. She should have felt a crippling shame at giving that much information about herself to a married man. Murphy was about the size of a baseball field. She wouldn't be hard to find.

"You seem to know a few things about me. What's your name?" he asked, so softly she almost couldn't make out the words.

"Rosalind."

"Rosalind," he repeated.

Her own name had never sounded that way before coming out of anybody else's mouth. That was still true.

He did come to Murphy after that. He came with the excuse of a family friend nearby who needed his car worked on, and Roy knew everything there was to know about cars. He did work on the engine. Afterward, he cleaned up at the friend's house and came by her daddy's property.

"I'm Roy Vines from over at Gray's Hollow," he said to her daddy. "I heard you've got a rifle you're looking to sell." The rifle thing was true, but she didn't know who told him.

"Your daddy Taylor Vines from over at the hardware store?" Vernon Clark asked.

"Yes, sir," Roy said.

It went from there. He came in the house for a glass of tea, ended up buying the rifle and snagging an invite to hunt with Rosalind's daddy. She loved him and she knew it. She didn't know why because she'd barely even been alone with him. But it didn't matter, anyway. Nothing would happen between them no matter how much time he spent at her house. He wouldn't act on his feelings and she would never declare hers. The visits were just added torture that neither of them could seem to put to an end.

After they met, Roy stopped sleeping with his wife. Rosalind didn't know this at the time. He told Sherry that it was his problem. Suggested that it was a medical problem that some men went through. But there was nothing wrong with his desire. He just had it for the wrong woman.

One day, four months or so after he met Rosalind, the wife was crying when he got home from work. She insisted that he act like a husband and make love to her. He felt terrible, but he just couldn't bring himself to touch his wife when he loved someone else with all his heart. He didn't know what to do about it, but he knew pretending in bed wasn't the answer. When he made excuses, Sherry became angry, then frantic.

She was pregnant, she finally admitted.

"Who's the daddy?" he asked. What really got to him, he later told Rosalind, was that he was more curious than angry.

It was all Roy's fault, Sherry tried to say, and he couldn't deny it. She'd gone to another man for comfort when Roy pulled away from her. She'd gone to the person who seemed most natural to lean on, she said. The person who looked exactly like the husband who wouldn't give her the time of day.

Rosalind never knew exactly what passed between them, Roy and Mont. Roy's freedom for his silence, that much she understood. Mont kept his marriage to a boring woman whose daddy was an influential judge, and Sherry kept her reputation. Roy was vilified, but he said it didn't matter. The lie, and his subsequent marriage to Rosalind, cost him his extended family, but he said that didn't matter, either. He would have agreed to anything just to be with her, and he'd never given her cause to think he regretted it. Until her illness threatened everything, Roy had been paid for all his trouble with a happy life. Rosalind wondered what would come of his visit home.

"Mama?" Lola sat in the swing on the front porch that belonged to their half of the duplex.

"Hey there, my girl," Rosalind said. "Did your sister go inside?"

"Yes, ma'am," Lola said. "She was half asleep walking back to her bed."

"I know how she feels," Rosalind said. All that time so close to the fire had left her face raw, like a sunburn. The cool night air felt good on her cheeks.

"Seems like everything's changing," Lola said.

Rosalind sat beside her on the swing.

"What do you mean, darlin'?"

"Daddy going off like he did, you needing a special doctor, then deciding you're going to work—" She stopped, and when she looked up again she had tears in her eyes. "Mrs. Thomas."

"It's confusing," Rosalind told her daughter. "Why things happen. I don't understand it myself." She thought of the red places that lay under the sleeves of her robe. "We'll tackle everything as it comes. That's what all of us have to do. Although I think poor old Alva Thomas will have as hard a go as I can imagine. I expect the grandson will be a big help to him, as protective as the boy seemed of the old man tonight."

Lola nodded, but offered up no thoughts on the young fireman. The girl's silence didn't fool Rosalind.

"I wonder if Daddy will be different when he comes back," Lola said. The thought came out of the blue and it scared Rosalind to even consider it.

"Your daddy's been steady since the day I met him."

"I just feel like something's going to change," Lola pressed on. "I don't know what. And I don't know why I feel that way."

"It's been a strange night," Rosalind said. "You can't help but feel lost after seeing what we've seen. But who knows," she added, "maybe some things will change for the better."

Given the present hand of cards they'd been dealt, it took everything she had to even let herself hope.

Later in bed, Rosalind stretched out. She took up her side of the bed and Roy's, too, just because she could. Awake, she heard Janie Ray's sleep sounds coming from down the hall. She heard the hum of the refrigerator cycling through one cooling cycle and moving to another. And finally, with sleep no closer than when she lay down, she heard—no, she *felt*—the last of the fire trucks go by as it left the Thomas property. It shook the paneling of the duplex as it growled and rumbled toward the interstate, leaving them to live with everything the fire left behind.

Seventeen

Luke stared out the window of the car. They'd crossed the Virginia/North Carolina border about ten miles back. The countryside didn't look much different from one side or the other, but the state line sent a clear signal to Luke that his exodus was real. He really, truly had been thrown out of his grandparents' house. Bullshit. That's what it was. The whole business was messed up from start to finish.

"You hungry?" Roy asked.

"I could eat something if you want to stop," he said. He tried to sound like he didn't give a damn one way or the other about anything, but in reality, he was starving.

Nanny had put eggs and toast in front of him before they left, but he refused to eat it out of spite. He was so pissed off at the whole lot of them. Even this asshole in the car with him. His *daddy*. What kind of man shows up for the first time when you're seventeen? It'd been decent of him to insist that Luke get to graduate with his class, but that didn't make up for the rest of it. Not by a long shot.

"I've got to call home anyway," Roy said. "I should give Rosalind a heads-up that I'm not by myself. Start looking for a place that looks good to you."

Luke shifted in his seat. The vinyl on the upholstery had cracked in two places, and when Luke moved his butt to one side or the other, the hard edges of the torn spots scraped against his jeans. Pap Taylor wouldn't even let him take the Buick he'd been driving for two years. Instead, Mont gave Roy—who, best Luke could tell, had arrived on foot—the oldest chunk of metal any of them owned. A '68 Chevy Nova. Hell, Luke didn't even think the thing would run anymore. But after four hours of work, Roy finally got it going. For as long as Luke could remember, the Nova had sat unused in the back driveway at Mont and Della's house. He figured Roy must be some kind of genius with cars.

"How does that place look up there?" Roy asked.

Up the road, he saw a sign for Cagle's Family Restaurant. He would have liked to find a Hardee's or something, but they were on some godforsaken stretch of road, and he decided he'd better settle for what was there.

"Looks okay," he said.

Roy nodded, pulled the car into the gravel lot in front of the place. At least the man wasn't pushing conversation on him. Luke wondered how the hell he was going to live with these people. How had everything happened so fast? He'd only smoked pot, like, four times in his life and suddenly he's hauled into the police station for *dealing*?

And none of it would have happened if he wasn't such a horny bastard. He had Deedee lined up to go with him to the prom and that at least meant some fooling around. He should have held out and stayed away from Kendra. But it was too late.

He'd screwed up and now he was on the way to someplace even smaller than the pin dot on the map where he'd grown up.

"You go on in and get a seat," Roy said. "I'm going to that pay phone across the street and call home."

"Is your wife going to be mad?" Luke asked as they both got out of the car.

Roy swatted a fly away from his face, and his forehead settled into a wrinkle of thought. "She's sure not going to be happy," he said.

Luke didn't know what to say back to that. Part of him wanted to say Roy could just put him out when they got to something that looked like a real town, but he wasn't equipped to fend for himself and he knew it.

Halfway across the street, Roy turned around. "Order me a coffee and a barbeque sandwich," he said. "And get yourself whatever you want. I'll be there in a few minutes."

Luke said he would, then walked into the place. Reasonably cool air and the smell of fried food gave him some comfort.

"Anywhere you like," the lone waitress said to him as he stood near the cash register and waited. The woman, who was probably in her thirties but could have passed for fifty, disappeared into the kitchen.

He found a booth near a window and slid in. Across the street, he saw his daddy standing by the pay phone, pulling the cellophane off a pack of cigarettes he'd bought earlier when they stopped for gas. He took a cigarette out and lit it. Roy hadn't smoked during the whole ride down from Virginia. Must be a stress smoker, Luke guessed.

He watched as Roy put his free hand on the receiver and then took it off again. The older man took a deep breath and rubbed his forehead, then reached again for the phone. Luke didn't care for Roy all that much based on their history—or, more accurately, their lack of history—but at that moment, Luke couldn't help but feel sorry for him. The situation had come out of nowhere for Roy, too, and Luke didn't know why Roy had agreed to take him in. It wasn't because he wanted to, that was for sure.

It was so damn confusing. Roy looked just like Mont, and Luke had lived around his uncle since before he could remember. But with the exception of his looks, Roy was nothing like Mont. Mont saw opportunities, worked things to his advantage every chance he got. He had a talent for it. Luke hoped he'd be able to do that someday. He hoped he'd be successful like Mont.

Roy didn't seem to know how to work the angles like his brother. Truth was, in a lot of ways, Roy seemed more straight-up than Mont. But Roy had been the one to cut out on him while his uncle stuck around to help raise him. Luke had to remember that whenever he felt tempted to go soft on the jerk.

"Know what you want?" The waitress came up beside him.

"Coffee and a vanilla milk shake," he said, then glanced at the menu. "Two barbeque sandwiches and an order of fries."

"Hungry one, aren't you?" She smiled, but her eyes still looked tired.

"I'm waiting for my—" he stopped. *Daddy.* The word was there, but it didn't make any sense. "That guy on the phone across the street is with me," he said, finally.

She walked away and he turned to watch Roy. The receiver was at the older man's ear and he looked miserable. The cigarette still hung from the fingers of his free hand, and he took another drag before launching into more talk.

For as long as Luke could remember, he'd wanted his absent daddy to get what he deserved for leaving his mother with a kid to raise on her own. But he couldn't find much satisfaction in Roy's obvious distress. For the first time, he considered that there was probably another side to the story somewhere. Although he still wasn't sure he cared what it was. The bottom line was, he just wanted his own life back. He wanted his friends and the regular summer he'd planned on before starting college.

Luke's milk shake and Roy's coffee came, and he saw Roy crossing the street. *I hate this*, he thought. *I hate this but it's going to happen anyway.* He took a sip of milk shake and waited for Roy to come in the door.

Eighteen

Roy stepped into the restaurant. He saw Luke watching for him, waiting on him to come in. He wondered what the kid was thinking. What *did* Luke think of him? Nothing good. He'd figured out that much.

How was it that he never asked himself that question before? In all the years since he'd left Gray's Hollow, he'd never given the boy more than a passing thought. In truth, he'd been more relieved than angry at Mont and Sherry. Their betrayal left him free to live his life with Rosalind.

But Luke had been there all those years, too, and Roy never took a minute to imagine him turning four, eight, or twelve years old. How could Roy have lived for so many years without considering that fact?

"He's over there." The waitress nodded toward the booth where Luke sat as she passed out an armload of plates to a table of construction workers.

He walked over to join the boy. Coffee was already there, but steam rose from the cup. Good. Still hot.

"Sorry that took longer than I planned," Roy said, noting that Luke was already done with the milk shake in front of him.

"What'd she say?" Luke asked.

"She's pretty upset." *Upset* didn't begin to cover Rosalind's reaction. "She didn't say she was leaving me. I took that as a good sign." He meant it as a joke, but the words fell flat. Nothing he could come up with would make the situation any prettier than it was. "It's going to be an adjustment for everybody."

"Why did you bring me with you?" Luke asked.

The question had a loaded quality, and no right answer existed. The right answer would have been *Because I wanted to*, but both of them knew that wasn't the case. "Well," Roy said, "you may recall an incident of sexual relations with a young woman followed by possession of a box with dubious contents."

"That's why they sent me with you." Luke was having none of it. "Why did you agree?"

He would find out anyway. Might as well tell him, Roy decided. "Rosalind's got some kind of thing going on with her blood count. They've got a pretty good idea of what's wrong, and if they're right, she's going to need a doctor who knows how to manage her particular problem. I want the best for her, and I can't afford to get her the kind of care she needs."

Luke looked confused for a moment, then the logic of it settled in. "Mont and Pap Taylor have the money," Luke said. "And you have an empty bed. So you made a fair exchange?"

"Except for the bed part," Roy answered. "We're a little shy on space." He hadn't even thought of where the kid would sleep. Hell, they barely had enough room for three full-sized people and little Janie Ray. "Things are going to be tight. We'll figure it out though."

"You and your wife don't even have an extra room?"

"We do," he said, "but it's filled with my two daughters." Roy wondered if Luke even knew about Lola and Janie Ray.

"Daughters?"

There was his answer. Luke didn't know anything about Roy except the lie that Roy had abandoned all of them.

"Fuck," the boy muttered under his breath. "It just keeps getting better."

"You'll need to clean up your mouth some before we get to the house," Roy said. "My youngest doesn't need to pick up that kind of language." He tried to keep the suggestion to a matter-of-fact tone, without the kind of reproach the kid would have gotten from Taylor or Lydia. Roy figured if he treated him like an adult, Luke might begin to act like one. It was worth a shot anyway.

"How old are they? The daughters."

"Lola's sixteen," he said. "Janie Ray is four."

Roy saw the wheels turning in the kid's head. Sixteen. Lola was just a year younger. Luke hadn't just been abandoned. He'd been replaced. Roy knew that's what he would be thinking. Nothing Roy could say would take the sting out of that. Roy's anger toward his brother—anger toward Mont *and* toward his parents—bubbled up to the surface again. He could almost feel it agitating the nerves on his skin.

"I didn't cause this," Roy said, sounding more defensive than sure.

"Most everybody disagrees with you on that one," Luke said. He rolled his eyes and looked away from Roy. Across the room, the waitress looked at a newspaper some customer had left behind on the counter.

Roy was getting tired of the attitude. God knows what they would have done with him if Roy hadn't been handy. What would happen if he just told the kid everything? Mont would hold out the rest of the money he promised to send. And Luke would hear things about his mother that would devastate his memory of Sherry. Better to remain the bad guy—at least for the time being.

"You screwed up." Roy kept a hard edge in his voice. "You jumped in bed with some girl when you should have been in class, and you were thinking with your dick instead of your brains when you took that box from her. I don't like this any more than you do. It screws with my life as much as it does with yours. But we are where we are, Luke. Stop acting like a spoiled kid and help me figure out how to get through the next few months."

Luke drained the dregs of his milk shake and the waitress brought over two plates with identical sandwiches. "Another milk shake?" she asked.

"Water's okay," he said, still not looking at Roy.

Roy felt guilty for going off on the kid. But hell, he could only take so much. He was getting it on one side from Rosalind and the other from Luke. And he hadn't done a damn thing wrong. Rosalind would come around. She always did. She flared up bright and then settled down fast. But Roy didn't know the first thing about Luke. He guessed he'd learn. That was about the only given in the situation as it stood.

"I'm sorry about your mom," Roy said, trying a different tack. "I didn't know until yesterday."

The details had been sketchy. Sherry had been off for an afternoon of shopping with Lydia in Roanoke when she had some kind of fainting spell. Those spells happened once or twice during the time Roy was with her. The doctors called her "a sinker." Nothing dangerous, they said. She just needed to learn to identify when one was coming on so that she could sit down and put her head between her knees.

She'd been in the bathroom of a department store when she went down. She hit her head on the corner of the countertop, the blood building up against the side of her brain. They found her after about half an hour. She was dead two days later.

"Who are you closest to back there?" Roy asked.

"What do you mean?"

"Your mom's been gone a while," Roy said. "Who in the family have you gotten the closest to since she's been gone?"

Luke shrugged, took a bite of sandwich. Roy waited for him to come up with an answer, then realized the kid didn't intend to respond.

Roy tried to remember growing up in that house. Who had he been closest to during those years? Lydia had tended to him. Made him food. Washed his clothes. Taylor had been a companion for hunting and working on cars. Everyone assumed twins stayed close, but he and Mont had completely separate lives after the age of eleven or twelve. Parallel lives. They'd always wanted different things.

Roy wanted fun and sports. Grades came easily and he took them for granted. Same with girls. His guy friends were always there to make him laugh. Girlfriends listened if he needed to talk about things that bothered or confused him. He hadn't really thought about what his family should have given him. He got what he needed other places.

Even after high school when he and Mont both lived at home and drove back and forth to Roanoke College so that they could still work at the hardware store, he'd kept his life separate from his twin brother.

But what had Mont wanted? Control. Money. That's all Roy could come up with when he thought of Mont in those days. He'd been student body president. Head of a few clubs. All the stuff Roy didn't care about.

In addition to the hardware store, Mont kept other part-time jobs year-round, even during his college years when he carried a heavy load at school. Taylor would always go to Mont for serious talks about the business. It never seemed to occur to the old man to ask Roy's opinion about anything.

The last year or two of college, it started to bother Roy. He wanted Taylor to take him seriously. He wanted to feel his daddy's respect. And he started to want other things too. He matured enough to want just the barest amounts of understanding and love. Who had he gone to for support when that happened? Where did he find his comfort? He'd tried with Sherry. Succeeded with Rosalind. No wonder Luke turned toward the girl's house instead of school that morning.

"We'll work this out, son," he said. "You got dealt a bad hand. I know that. It'll all be okay in the end."

"I appreciate you standing up for me about going to graduation." Luke offered his first concession. "That was decent of you."

"It's a big day," Roy said. "You ought to have it."

They finished their sandwiches with that much of a truce between them, then got back on the road toward Linton Springs.

Nineteen

Rosalind scrambled to get out the door. She hadn't told Roy he was making her late. Even though what he said was hard to take, she wanted to hear his voice for as long as possible. Anything else could wait. Her doctor's appointment. Her new job. Roy didn't know about the last part and it was better left that way until she could tell him in person.

He'd blindsided her with news that Sherry's boy was with him. She should have known that awful family of his would put strings on any money they parceled his way. They never gave out anything without getting something back in return. How Roy turned out to be such a decent human being was beyond her. She shouldn't have gone off on him the way she had. But *he* should have talked to her before he agreed to bring the kid back. Then again, what choice did he have? She gave him an earful on the phone that he didn't really deserve.

The bottom line remained that she'd have to make the best of it. *And* she had to sort out how to explain it to the girls before he got home.

"Does the doctor have toys I can play with?" Janie Ray asked from the jump seat behind her in the truck.

Rosalind had been too distracted by Roy's absence and then the fire to remember to set up someplace for Janie Ray to go. She had no choice but to bring the child with her to the doctor and then to her first day at the grill.

"I'm seeing that doctor who comes to the health department twice a week, sweetie. They have that room where you play, remember. The nice lady takes care of you until I'm done."

"That other boy smelled bad last time I went there," Janie Ray halfheartedly complained. "And all the toys are broken."

"Well, I can't do anything about the toys, but I bet that boy won't be there today. This won't take long and then I'll take you to my new job with me and let you have French fries at the grill, okay?"

"Okay," the girl said.

She was a good child. Rosalind worried sometimes that she accepted things too easily. She wanted both her daughters to expect a lot from life.

She turned her thoughts away from her youngest and toward Lola. Roy and the boy were already across the Virginia line when Roy called. She told him not to bring this Luke person directly to the house. To call first and to not plan on arriving before five o'clock. She didn't know how Roy and the kid would bide their time until then, but she had to have a chance to talk to Lola. She'd cut things short at the grill when Lola got out of school.

She saw the county health clinic building just down the road. The parking lot was full. It was always full on the days when the doctors visited, but it seemed even worse than usual. She had an appointment, but still, it could go long, and she worried that she wouldn't make it to the grill for her training session with Mae Rose. She parked on the street, not even bothering to negotiate the parking lot. With a reluctant Janie Ray in tow, she went inside.

* * *

"Sorry I'm late," Rosalind said to Mae Rose as she arrived at the Linton Grill.

"Settle down, darlin'." Mae Rose smiled at her. The woman had ten years and twenty pounds on Rosalind, but something from a bottle kept her hair a deep velvet black. "Take a second to breathe," she said. "The lunch crowd hasn't picked up yet. We've got plenty of time.

"Hey, Miss Janie Ray." Mae Rose squatted to eye level with the girl. "You know what I just happen to have at that back table over there?"

"What?" Janie Ray looked more wary than excited.

"Come see."

Rosalind followed as Mae Rose took her daughter's hand and walked with her to the back of the dining area. On the very back table sat a new box of crayons and several books. A coloring book, a paper doll book, and a trace-the-picture book with a perfectly sharpened pencil lying alongside. Lined behind the books, several cans of Play-Doh sat, still in the packaging, and there was an egg-shaped container of Silly Putty beside them. Janie Ray grinned but didn't move.

"Go on." Mae Rose gave her a gentle push. "Have at it."

Janie Ray scrambled into the booth. She stacked all the books and laid the box of crayons on top. Then she took a can of blue Play-Doh, and after opening it, began her work in earnest.

"You're something else," Rosalind said to Mae Rose. "What do I owe you for that stuff?"

"I keep a few supplies around for the little guys," she said. "Helps them stay distracted while their parents eat."

"Yeah," Rosalind said. "That's why all those things are brand-new."

"Everything's brand-new at some time or other." Mae Rose waved her hand in a dismissal of the conversation, walked back toward the front of the grill.

Rosalind looked at Janie Ray, happy and engrossed in play, and forced her shoulders to relax. The constant ache in her joints eased a little with that conscious effort. She followed Mae Rose back behind the counter.

"You may want to wear something a little cooler in here," Mae Rose said, looking at the loose, bell-shaped sleeves of Rosalind's linen blouse. "Even with air-conditioning, it gets warm behind the counter with the griddle and the fryers all going at once."

Rosalind thought of making up an excuse, then decided keeping up any ruse would be too much effort.

"I've got marks on my arms I'd rather not show," she said. "The doctor here says he thinks I have a condition that causes something like bruising, but it looks more like a rash to me. I've got a few loose blouses like this one. I'll be okay."

"Is it serious?" Mae Rose asked.

"Not contagious," Rosalind said, thinking she'd get right to the point.

"That's not what I asked." Mae Rose leaned with her elbows on the counter. "Are you okay?"

"I'm fine," she said. "They just have to keep an eye on it."

That wasn't what the doctor told her. In fact, he said that she needed to see a specialist right away. Her immune system had been compromised by a blood disorder. She made herself memorize that impossibly long name he threw at her. Idiopathic thrombocytopenic purpura. ITP for short. It sounded like something that should have killed her already, but he said if that's really what it was, there were different options on how to manage it. He knew of a public hospital in Gastonia that would take her, but they were always pretty backed up. Options ranged from medicine to surgery. He said something about her spleen and she was embarrassed to even ask what that organ was exactly. By the time she went to get Janie Ray from the playroom, she was shaking, frightened out of her mind.

"I'm a little tired here and there," she said. "You can see the things on my arms."

She raised her sleeve.

Mae Rose ran a finger over one of the places. "I've never seen anything like that before," she said.

"Me either," Rosalind said. "Not until it showed up on me. Like I said, it's not catching."

"I'm not worried, darlin'. You just tell me if the job gets to be too much."

Kindness of that variety was a rarity, Rosalind thought. Even in a small town where most people were good by nature, true charity couldn't always be counted upon.

"Thank you," Rosalind said. The emotion she felt embarrassed her and she had to look away from the older woman. "Where do we start?" She turned her attention to the equipment behind the counter.

"First, let's get you acquainted with the soft-serve machine here." Mae Rose took her cue and ended the disease discussion. "Greg's out back having a cigarette before the rush, but he'll do the cooking. You need to feed him the orders and keep them straight going out. You can make milk shakes and serve up cones. That and the drinks, plus the orders, will be your job."

The instruction went on. Most of it seemed no more complicated than her own house when a crowd of her relatives visited. If she could keep her strength up, she'd do fine.

Janie Ray had stretched out on the back booth and fallen asleep. Rosalind wished she could join her. She had been working only five hours, but near exhaustion had set in. She couldn't let on. She needed the job, and independent of that, she didn't want to let Mae Rose down.

She glanced up to see Lola walking through the front door,

arms weighed down with books. The girl stopped to talk to Preacher Reeves, one of the regulars.

"Hey, there's the other one," Mae Rose said, looking toward Lola. "Both your girls are just beautiful."

"I won't disagree with you there," Rosalind said. "I'll run both of them home in a bit if you don't mind, then I'll put in a full day next time." She didn't want to explain about Roy's return if she could avoid it.

"That'll be fine." Mae Rose nodded. "Listen, before you leave, do you mind walking across to the bank for me? Everybody and their cousin seem to be paying with a twenty-dollar bill today. I could use a stack or two of ones to get through the evening."

"Sure thing," Rosalind said.

Mae Rose went to the cash register and pulled out a few twenties. She put them into a bank pouch and handed it to Rosalind. "Thanks, hon."

On the way out, Rosalind passed Lola. The girl had put her books on the table, obviously resigned to a lengthy conversation with Preacher Reeves, who wasn't a preacher at all—although he was a bit of a town institution all to himself.

"I need to run to the bank for a minute," Rosalind interrupted their talk to tell Lola. "Your sister is asleep in the back booth. See if you can rouse her a little. I'll drive you home as soon as I get back."

"Okay," Lola said.

"Oh," Rosalind said, turning back around. "How was your day? I didn't even ask."

"Good," Lola said.

But Rosalind didn't believe it. Still, she let it go at that, heading out into the baked air to run her errand before she melted into a puddle of fatigue.

Twenty

Lola looked out of the grill's glass storefront to the street outside. She wished she could politely get away from Preacher Reeves, but he showed no signs of letting her go any time soon.

After her mother's brief interruption, the old man launched back into the story he was telling about a fish he caught that had two heads. She wondered if there was a head on each end or if there were two heads and one tail, but she was afraid to ask because she didn't want to encourage the yarn to go on any longer than it already had.

"That's your mama, right?" He stopped his narrative mid-sentence to ask the question, and motioned his head toward the door where her mama had just exited out toward the street.

"Yes, sir," she answered.

"You favor your mama," he said, adjusting the baseball cap on his head. "The little one looks like your daddy, but you . . ." He shook his head. "Looks like Rosalind Vines spat you right out. What's your name again?"

"Lola, sir." She tried not to be distracted by the unlikely image he conjured of her mother spitting. "That's what people tell me," she said, still trying to figure out a way to get away from him without acting mean.

With a direct look, like he knew her mind as clear as his own, he stood up and gestured for her to go on by. People said he was crazy, but she didn't think so.

"Preacher Reeves?" She smiled at him.

"Yes, Miss Lola," he answered.

"Will you do that thing with your hat?" she asked.

He grinned. A few teeth, but mostly gums, greeted her request. Then he stepped into the open space between his booth and a table, putting his finger up for her to wait just a second. He took off his cap, and without any hurry, tossed it backward. The hat arched lightly, made two somersaults above his head, and landed fully on his crown. He hadn't even adjusted the position of his head to make it land right. Daddy always said it was the damnedest thing. Preacher Reeves could do that trick twenty times in a row without missing once.

Lola clapped and so did the few other customers scattered around at the various tables. Preacher Reeves kept his mouth closed, but a smile stretched full across his face. Then he motioned his head for her to go on back to her little sister.

"Your mama said to wake her up," he added.

She smiled at him and turned to go back to where Janie Ray still slept. When she glanced back in his direction, she saw him sitting again in his booth, directing a blank stare toward Main Street as he sipped on his coffee.

"Hey," Lola said as she passed Mae Rose at the counter.

"Hey, darlin'," Mae Rose said. The extra skin on her upper arms wiggled as she leaned forward and rested her elbows on the counter. "Your little sister wore herself out entertaining the customers all afternoon. Between her and the Reverend, we ought to charge admission."

Lola laughed, was about to walk on when the look on Mae Rose's face changed. She was staring toward the front entrance.

Lola turned to see what was there. She recognized her daddy standing inside the door, backlit by sun coming through the storefront window. He looked to be ringed with fire, and she wondered for an instant if he was a ghost. Maybe the ghost she'd tried to conjure that night.

"Lola?" he called out, breaking the spell. "What are you doing here, sugar?"

She walked to him. It seemed as though she ought to hug him, but given his absence and the strange circumstance of the reunion, she just stood there, staring.

"Lola?" He said it again, this time with more concern. "Are you okay?"

She started crying. She couldn't help it, and the embarrassment brought by her own breakdown untapped a reservoir of tears.

A few people quietly slipped by her to leave the grill. Preacher Reeves laid a hand on her shoulder while Mae Rose brought her a clean dishtowel to dry her eyes.

"Where did you come from?" Lola managed to ask. "Mama said you have parents still alive and you went to see them. When did you get back?"

"Just now," he said. "We stopped to get a bite and I was going to call your mama from here and tell her I'm on the way home."

He didn't know Mama was working at the grill. That much came clear to her. But something else was wrong. What was it? *We*. He'd said, *We stopped to get a bite* . . . She looked behind him. Standing near the door was a boy about her age. He looked so much like her daddy, it was like seeing a picture from Daddy's high school yearbook. Only this boy wasn't a picture. He was a frowning, breathing person. A person who didn't look very happy to be where he was at that moment.

"I'm Lola." She wiped her eyes with the dishtowel, put it on a table, and stuck out her hand to the boy. The gesture was as much a challenge as a greeting, she realized, but it was the best she could manage under the circumstances.

"I'm Luke," the boy said. Even his voice had a familiar quality. "I guess I'm your brother."

At that moment, Lola realized Mama had walked through the front door. In her hand, she held the bulging, zippered bank pouch. She and Lola's daddy made eye contact, a look so strong and fierce, Lola felt like she could rub a finger along a line connecting the two of them.

Mama wore a Linton Grill apron on top of her dress, but Lola wasn't sure Daddy had noticed.

Brother. Did that boy say he was her brother? But then, looking at this Luke, she couldn't imagine he'd be anything else. She felt more tears pushing through and she clamped her jaw tight, trying to hold them at bay.

Janie Ray had crawled out of the back booth, wandered sleepy-eyed over to Daddy, and as if out of habit, he reached down and lifted her up to hold her.

"I reckon this ought to be a moment of private time," Preacher Reeves said, as he stood up and calmly exited the grill.

Glad for the distraction, Lola let her eyes follow him as he left, and she watched as he turned onto the sidewalk outside. She saw the bright sun swallow him up before the door had even closed all the way.

Twenty-one

L uke couldn't help but go over it again in his head. If he'd turned left instead of right—if he'd gone on to school instead of going to Kendra's—he wouldn't be in this mess. He wouldn't be standing in some greasy dive looking at a girl who'd grown up with the daddy he should have had.

He stared at Roy who was now holding a little girl who had his exact same shade of red-brown hair. While Luke's hair ran a little darker than those two, they all shared the same features. It was weird.

Judging from the resemblance of the girl, Lola, to the woman who'd just walked in, Luke surmised he was looking at Roy's second wife. Roy stared at the woman—Rosalind was her name—as she stood just inside the door, and Luke had to admit she was beautiful. Even for someone who had to be old enough to be his mama, she would have gotten his attention walking into a room. Dark hair and creamy skin. Small, but strong-looking.

He thought of his own mama, what he remembered clearly anyway, along with what he'd seen in pictures. She'd been pretty enough, but nothing like this woman. He felt bad, disloyal, even thinking it, but it was true. No wonder old Roy had dropped everything in the world, including his own son, and run after her. Rosalind, he'd called her. He thought of Kendra again. Maybe the nut didn't fall so far from the tree.

But that didn't let Roy off the hook. Luke was pissed as hell about being abandoned in the first place. He was pissed as hell about being kicked out of his real life because of something that wasn't even his fault. And most of all, he was pissed as hell about being dragged to this godforsaken town and forced to stand there with these people while they tried to figure out what to say to each other.

"Are you all right?" Roy asked the woman. "You seem tired."

"Hello to you, too," she said, still looking at him like he was the only person in the room.

The little girl squirmed in Roy's arms and the big sister, *his* sister, was crying again, and no one was trying to deal with that at all. He walked over to Lola. That's what her name was. Lola. He picked up the dishtowel that she'd put on the table beside her and handed it in her direction.

"Thanks." She took the towel.

"This sucks," he said.

"Yeah." Both of them were looking at the adults.

In spite of himself, Luke felt a certain alliance with the girl and it surprised the hell out of him. If Roy didn't feel anything like family to him, why should this half sister be any different? But they'd both gotten a raw deal in this one. None of it was her fault.

"I think I might be sick," Lola whispered to him. "I had school pizza at lunch and I don't think I can hold it down."

"Come on." Luke took her wrist and gently pulled her toward

the front door. On the way out, he grabbed a pack of cigarettes and a lighter that one of the customers had accidentally left behind when making a hasty exit. The overweight woman who ran the place still stood behind the counter. She saw him take it, but she didn't say anything.

The heat outside felt like a pillow somebody pushed against his face. Gray's Hollow was in the mountains and ten degrees cooler midday than this hellhole. But Lola didn't seem to notice. She bent over and propped her hands on her knees. At least her color had come back and she looked a little better out in the fresh air.

"How can you be my brother?" she managed, once she could take a deep breath again. She stood back up.

"Half brother," he said. "Your daddy was married to my mama for about five minutes, I guess. He met your mama and took off. That's all I know."

Her forehead wrinkled up like she couldn't match up what he was saying with the Roy who stood inside that place holding the little girl and talking to his wife. Truth was, he couldn't, either. Even the little bit of time he'd spent with Roy since the day before had showed him nothing but a fairly decent man. Nothing like what he expected to find when he finally met his son-of-a-bitch daddy. But regardless of what things seemed like, they were the way they were. All the facts matched up, even if the personalities didn't.

"Where's your mama?" Lola asked.

"She's dead," he said, putting a cigarette in his mouth and lighting it. "She died when I was nine."

"Who raised you?" She had gone to looking pale again.

"This smoke bothering you?" he asked.

She shook her head. "I feel sick," she said, "but the smoke's got nothing to do with it."

"I know what you mean," he said. "Anyway, my grandparents . . . your grandparents, Nanny and Pap Taylor, took me in. Mont's been around, too, and his wife, Della. Della's not the sharpest tool in the shed, but Mont's a pretty good guy."

"What are our grandparents like?"

"Nanny and Pap?" What was there to tell her? "They're both real religious, spare-the-rod types. He owns a hardware store. She's home most of the time. They've done their best, I guess."

"And who's Mont?" she asked.

Damn. She's been duped worse than I have. "Mont's your daddy's twin brother. If you put the two of them side by side in the same clothes, I bet you couldn't even tell them apart."

"Holy shit," she said. Her voice was barely there and the words came out as a single expelled breath.

"Mont's got a daughter—your cousin—Nell. Nell's already in college, although they must have paid Sweet Briar a shitload of money to take her 'cause she's even dumber than her mother." He was on a roll, spilling all the family secrets. "I guess we've got a lot of catching up to do, little sister."

"I guess we do," she said, still looking stunned.

Both of them stared inside the storefront. Behind the glass windows, Roy still held the small girl who wouldn't look up and wouldn't let go of his neck for the world. But he wasn't seeing anyone but this Rosalind woman. The two grown-ups had stepped close to each other, and even though they weren't touching, Luke felt as if he was watching something that he ought to be embarrassed to see. The moment looked that intimate.

"They always like that?" he asked.

"Anytime they're in the same room with each other," Lola said.

"My poor mother," he said. "She never had a fucking prayer."

He took a drag off his cigarette, a brand he didn't know that tasted raw and barely filtered. It burned at his lungs and he didn't mind, took another drag just to feel it again. He wondered when Roy would remember he was there. Lola must have been wondering the same thing, because she couldn't take her eyes off her parents. She looked just like her mother, and he looked like Roy. The two of them were junior replicas of the authentic items inside.

"We should go back in," Lola said. "We ought to just get this over with."

Girl or not, she had balls, this little sister of his. He half smiled in spite of his misery, and followed her inside the door.

Twenty-two

"Y ou can't just take on Mont's problems for him," Rosalind said to Roy.

"He's not a *problem*, he's a boy, Rosie," Roy said, defending himself. "He's got no other options at the moment. I know what it feels like to get thrown away by those people."

"I thought this was about the money we needed," she said. A horrible thing to say and she knew it. She acted as if the boy was some kind of livestock to get traded around. But a panic came up inside her, and it brought out every mean bone she had.

"I know you, Rosalind," he said. "You don't think that way. We *do* need the money, but it's more than that now. As much as I would never have offered to take him, he's here—pretty much against his will, and we've all got to figure out how to live with it for a little while."

"What was it like?" she asked. "Seeing your folks again."

"They're a bunch of hyenas up there." Roy shook his head. She could almost see inside his thoughts, feel what it had been like for him in that house. "Luke got into a little trouble and they talked about him—decided things about him—like he wasn't even there. Who knows, I might be just like them if it hadn't been for you. They're my own flesh, but I'm not sure what they have running through their veins. Not the same stuff that runs in mine—and yours."

Roy's blood kin had betrayed him, but her actual *blood*, the stuff that ran through her heart and back out, had betrayed her. The thought of blood, her own blood, brought back the panic she'd felt as she sat and listened to the doctor that morning. Low platelet count. Medication. Possible surgery. All of it ran together and she couldn't think straight. The family had hit a breaking point before Roy took off for Virginia. His trip was supposed to make things better. Not worse.

"Rosalind?" Roy was waiting for her to say something.

He was right. She had turned selfish, and that wasn't an option with children involved. Even this Luke fellow was a child still, in spite of the fact that he looked full grown. Still, she had such a hard time even looking at him.

"I'm sorry, Roy." She honestly didn't know what she meant by the words. Was she apologizing? Or was she telling him that her first response was the best she could offer? That she couldn't be any better, any more charitable, toward Sherry Vines's son than she'd already been? "We'll figure it out."

The boy Luke dropped his cigarette just outside the door and put it out with his foot. Then he walked back into the grill with Lola. If Rosalind had seen him in a crowd, she would have thought the ghost of Roy's younger self had been conjured up just to mess with her mind. He looked exactly the way Roy had looked in that church reception hall on that first night. For that reason alone, she couldn't hate him. But not hating him was a far cry from treating him like family.

"Lola," Roy said. He still held Janie Ray, but he put out his free arm to hug his other daughter.

Rosalind watched her go to him. Lola accepted his embrace. But Rosalind also saw her stiffen as she leaned against him. Lola refused to act like everything had gone back to normal, and Rosalind knew just how she felt.

"Everybody," Roy said, "this is Luke."

"Is he my brother?" Lola asked.

Rosalind's stomach dropped at the question and she was glad it was directed at Roy and not her. But underneath her discomfort, she registered a certain amount of pride at her daughter's willingness to meet the issue head on.

"It's complicated," Roy said.

"It shouldn't be," Lola told him. "A brother is a pretty easy thing to define. He says his mama was your first wife."

"That's true," Roy said.

Rosalind saw the pain on his face. She wished she could take some of it from him. He didn't do anything to deserve the way Lola looked at him. She'd have to intervene, but that time would come later. In private.

"And I've got living grandparents?" The words were more of an attack than a question. "And some uncle who's your *twin*?"

"I'll explain everything to you girls a little later," Roy said, looking around the grill at the few remaining astonished faces. "But for now, why don't we get a bite to eat and settle down. Then we'll all go home."

"Roy," Rosalind said, gesturing at the apron. "I'm working for a little longer. I'll get you a little something to eat, then you take everybody home. I'll meet you there before dinner."

Roy stared at her. She couldn't believe that he hadn't noticed what she was wearing earlier. But then he'd been distracted with delivering his own revelations.

"Mae Rose has taken me on part-time," she said. "I'll be here four days a week during the lunch shift. Then I'll help with dinner setup and head home."

It was Roy's turn to go silent. She couldn't tell if he was mad or not. Most likely he was, but she wouldn't let that change anything. Even with the fatigue of her condition, she felt a new pride, a new energy at taking some responsibility for solving their problems. Even if he got money from his family, they could use more, especially with a teenage boy in the house to feed.

"Have a seat, ya'll," she said, taking on a lighter tone. "French fries and Coke?"

She watched her entire family—plus one she refused to include in that bunch. They all nodded in agreement and made their way back to the booth where Janie Ray had been.

"I'll see if I can't rustle up some onion rings, too. Okay?"

Again the nods. Not a word came out of anyone. Lola set to work gathering all of Janie Ray's art supplies. Books and crayons, Play-Doh and scissors, scattered over the table like debris from a wreck.

"Mont wrote me a check," Roy said.

Rosalind sat with Roy on the porch swing after dinner. She felt his arm around her, and for the first time in days, believed she might be whole again. The illness had been an alien presence, taking part of her against her will. She'd felt something similar when she was pregnant with Lola, only she'd welcomed the intrusion, and all the fatigue and the energy that her body gave to Lola had a purpose. The illness—this ITP—took and would give nothing back. The point was to fight it, to overcome it. Not to endure it for the promise of a miracle at the end of the struggle.

"I'm sick, Roy," she said, because they had to talk about it.

"I know," he told her, "but Mont wrote me a check. He said he'd be able to write another one and send it in a couple of days. It'll be okay."

He hadn't gone beyond the barest of inquiries into her doctor's appointment. He seemed to think that money would fix it, no matter what the doctor told her. He had this solid vision that the money equaled her good health. How could she tell him that, even with all he'd done, all it had cost him going to his parents, they had a struggle ahead of them?

"It could be worse than we thought," she said. "Even with the money and a specialist, I may end up needing surgery or—"

"Don't say it, Rosie," he stopped her. "We'll get you in over at Winston-Salem and they'll know what to do. We'll do whatever they say."

At both her appointments, the local doctor explained that health department referrals went to the public hospital in Gastonia. Implied in his tone was that this hospital, like the health department, was overwhelmed and understaffed. If she could afford private care, the hospital in Winston had specialists who worked with her kind of problem. Roy had pinned his hopes on that.

"I don't want to get the notion that this is simple, Roy. From what they tell me—"

"Stop, Rosalind." The look in his eyes told her that he knew. He wasn't kidding himself. "We'll get you the best, and then we'll deal with what they tell us."

"They gave me a number to call," she said. "I'll do it tomorrow and find out how to get an appointment at the medical center in Winston-Salem." She knew he was right about one thing. No point in preparing for the worst without hoping for the best. She'd try to see it through his eyes for a while. His attitude rested upon ideas and intentions put into practice. If the big problems seemed too hard, he'd tackle the smaller ones, one at a time. Like dinner.

When she got home from the grill, she discovered Roy had dinner started. He'd thawed some fish he'd caught earlier in the spring. He'd already put it in the pan to fry and opened a can of corn, so she didn't have to sort out how to feed everyone on top of everything else.

At the table, they'd relied on Janie Ray's chatter to keep silence from settling in. No one else knew what to say. Lola was clearly angry at both of them.

Too many things couldn't be said without the commitment to either an argument or, at the very least, a long discussion. So Janie Ray and her talk of the afternoon adventure at the grill sufficed and they were all grateful for it. After dinner, Luke and Lola relented to Janie Ray's endless whining for a game of Go Fish, and Rosalind motioned for Roy to follow her to the porch.

"I can't get used to looking at that burned-out place down there," Roy said.

Rosalind followed his gaze toward what was left of the Thomas house.

"She was here, in that kitchen making her cakes and such when I left for the mountains," he said. "And she's gone when I come back. Life shouldn't be easy to lose. It's everything we have. The only thing we have, really—then gone so fast."

Rosalind knew that he thought a lot of Mrs. Thomas. But she also knew that the older woman wasn't the one he was thinking about with all his musings on mortality.

"I'm not dying, Roy," she said, taking care to keep her voice gentle. "Or at least, no more than we all are at any given minute. I don't know all the details about this thing I have. Let's don't worry too much until I find out more."

He looked toward the Thomas house again. "What's he going to do?" Roy asked. "How's that old man going to go on?"

"You'd be surprised," she said. "People are more resilient than you think. He'll find something to live for. Just you wait."

"I heard in town that the fire started after he was burning in the yard," Roy said. "What would he have been burning this time of year?"

"I don't know what marijuana smells like, but Vicky Benson said that's what it was."

"Dope?"

"That's just what Vicky said," Rosalind told him. "Half the time she doesn't know her head from a hole in the ground. I don't know."

Janie Ray let loose a squeal of delight.

"Somebody won." Roy smiled.

It bothered her that the girls had taken a liking to Luke so quickly. Her most selfish impulses told her they were being disloyal. She couldn't give in to that.

"Janie Ray has a way of making you let her win just to put an end to the game," Rosalind said. "I know that much from experience."

"If Luke's figured out that much," Roy said, "he's conquered half the battle with his new living circumstances."

Roy, too. She wished she could talk easily about Luke with her husband. But old resentments died hard and the boy's presence rubbed every raw nerve she had. As much as he looked like Roy, she could only see Sherry when she studied him. Sherry, who shared Roy's bed first. Sherry, who took his name first. Sherry, who would have kept him with a baby that wasn't even his if she could have managed it. Rosalind had no reason to still let that bother her. She had Roy, and Sherry was dead. But it did bother her, and the result left her mean-spirited and wrong.

Rosalind didn't like herself very much when she thought about Luke.

"Luke has to sleep somewhere," she said, steering the conversation toward more practical ends. "Any ideas?"

"A crazy one," he said.

"I'm all for crazy," she told him.

"The back porch." He looked at her as if pleased with himself, as if the boy could sleep in a screened-in room that inside of a month would be no better than eighty degrees at night. "Hear me out," he continued.

She raised her eyebrows. "All right." She pictured the back porch, just off the kitchen. It was already covered and screened in. A wood-paneled wall came up waist-high with screens rising above that.

"It has that part of a wall already," he said. "I can cover the screen sections with plastic on the outside," he said, building momentum as he described it. "I'll rig up some curtains on the inside that he can pull for privacy and to keep the sun out. The kitchen window unit is our biggest one. If we seal off the porch and leave that kitchen door open, it ought to cool two rooms pretty easily."

"That's quite a plan," she said, trying not to sound discouraging, but the kitchen represented a sanctuary of sorts for her. Living on the porch, he would intrude even more on her life, her space. Roy had no idea the war that was raging inside her. She'd tell him if it would change anything. But it wouldn't.

"It's got those smooth, wood floors," he was saying. "I bet you could even find an old rug to put down and make it more like a room."

She could feel him willing her to catch his enthusiasm. He was trying to make the best of it. "It's not perfect," Roy said, "but I think it'll work."

"A sleeping porch," she said. Her parents talked about the

old houses having screened porches for sleeping on hot nights. Before air-conditioning, people made do any way they could.

"A sleeping porch," Roy echoed.

She forced a smile. "I think it'll work," she said. She said it for him. She'd do anything for him. God, she loved that man. Every problem had an answer somewhere. He believed it and then made it true. "I'll make up the couch for tonight," she said. "You can start rigging that up tomorrow."

He kissed the top of her head. "Thank you," he said. He was as much a victim as anyone and he wanted to make the best of things. "Hey, the other good thing about it," he said, pulling back with a sudden smile, "Vicky Benson can see our back porch from her yard. It'll drive her crazy. What are those gypsies doing now?" Roy imitated Vicky's high-pitched screech.

Rosalind laughed. A real laugh for the first time in days. He brought her close with both his arms. In spite of being bone tired, she wanted him, couldn't wait to have him in their bed again. She wondered if she would ever grow tired of his body, or if, even when they were old, every nerve in her body would still yearn for him. Then the larger question came unbidden. Would she get old, or would he be the one left alone in their bed? The thought of it made her worry more for him than she did for herself. Death was death, but one of them living without the other . . . that would be hell. She shook her head, literally tried to shake the image of her own absence away.

"What?" He pulled back, the question lingering on his face.

"I don't know," she told him. "Nothing. Hey, is that car you drove here staying with us?"

"I think so," he said. "It was sitting in the old garage at the back of Mont's property. Luke said he'd never seen anybody drive it. Ever. I got under the hood and Mont got a temporary license for it. It runs a little rough, but I'll take it to the shop tomorrow and get it tuned up."

"So can I take the truck to work tomorrow?" She braced herself for his argument. They hadn't talked about her job at the grill. She felt his arm stiffen. There were too many conflicts for her to keep up, and she had to have him with her, they had to be a team, or they would never get through the summer. She was ready to back down, to say she'd quit when he took a deep breath and turned to her.

"You don't *have* to work, Rosie." He said it low and the words had a tone of concession. He was going to give in without too much fight.

"It's something for me, Roy," she said. "Not just the money, though God knows that's why I called Mae Rose in the first place. But I like the feel of it. I know it's only been one day, and I may get more knocked down if my health doesn't hold up. But right now, work is something different. Something new to tackle."

"People are going to say that it's a shame I can't support you. Can't take care of our family without putting you to work. When word gets out about your medical business, the talk will get worse."

"That bother you?" She sounded defiant, hoped he would respond in kind.

"Yes, it does," he said, not qualifying his words with an apology for his feelings. "I'd lay down my life for you, Rosie. And shallow as it may be, I can't stand to have anybody think otherwise."

"Can you get over it?" she asked. "Can you do that for me?" It was his turn to bend.

"I'll try," he said. "But you've got to promise me you'll quit when it's time. When it starts to take the energy you need to fight this thing. You promise me that?"

"I promise," she said. "And Roy, a little extra money won't hurt."

"It won't hurt," he agreed.

Restless sounds from inside made them end their private time. Lola came to the door.

"Should I give Janie Ray a bath?" she asked.

"You've taken on too much of the mothering over the last few days," Rosalind said. "I'll bathe her. You take some time and do something you want. Go visit Charlotte if you like. Daddy and I will take care of your sister and the kitchen."

"Thanks, Mama," Lola said, going back inside.

Roy leaned over and touched his forehead to hers. "It'll get easier, Rosie."

"I hope so," she said.

They stood up together and went inside.

Twenty-three

Roy felt better after some sleep, but he had to check on the garage. He couldn't neglect his business any longer. The boy, Jerry, had been running things for three days. Hell, he wasn't a boy. He had a wife, with a kid on the way any day. But he couldn't seem to change a twenty without making a mistake. Still, he'd been pretty solid and he knew his way around engines. Roy just hoped the business end of things held together while he was away.

It was Saturday. Rosalind had been asleep when he got up, and he left her that way. He'd planned to go by the garage the day before, but his world had unexpectedly gone haywire when he got to the grill with Luke. Since arriving back in Linton Springs, he'd barely thought about the business. Now he couldn't think of anything else.

He pulled up and parked beside the building. Helen Atkins's

car sat in front of the garage door that opened to the largest bay. He got out, looked around for Helen and spotted her husband, his friend Nate Atkins, across the street at the funeral home, sitting in one of the chairs on the front stoop. Nate looked up and saw Roy. He immediately got up and crossed the street.

Nate must have been at least fifteen years older than Roy. He'd worked in the office at the textile mill during most of his life, but he'd left that job a few years back and opened up his own business—keeping the books and filing taxes for a few small businesses in town.

"Everything okay?" Roy asked. "You got somebody in the funeral home?"

"No, no," Nate said. "I was just waiting over there because there was shade. Minnie Thomas is in there though. The viewing is tonight. A shame what happened." Nate shook his head.

"I know it," Roy said, unlocking the door. Jerry should have opened up already and Roy wondered if his wife went into labor early. "I was away in Virginia on some family business, so I wasn't around when their house burned. Rosalind said it was awful. Poor old Alva. I don't know what he's going to do."

Nate came in behind him, shuffled around in one spot like he had something to say, but didn't know how to come out with it. Roy gave him a few seconds, and when it didn't look like they were going to get anywhere he said, "What's on your mind, Nate?"

Nate looked at him. "It's your boy here," he said. For a second, Roy thought Nate was talking about Luke, then he realized Nate meant the *boy* who worked for him.

"Jerry?"

"Yeah, Jerry." He stopped, looked around, then back at Roy. "He had some kind of meltdown, Roy. I was here yesterday afternoon. I had an appointment to bring my car in. He was here, but he acted nervous as a squirrel, said he couldn't do the work right then. Something unexpected had popped up, he said.

"I asked where you were and he said he didn't know. I left, came back around an hour later, and he'd already closed up. Two people—old lady Jones and that blond fellow from up Stone's Creek way—they were both here. The blond guy, Fred's his name, I think . . . that's his car there. It was supposed to be ready, he said. It's still locked up in there."

Roy glanced in the smaller of the two bays. Fred Dandy's car sat up on the lift. It shouldn't have been left up like that and Jerry was supposed to finish working on it the day before.

"Miz Jones just wanted to drop her car off," he said, "but nobody was around. I called out at your house, but didn't get an answer, so I got a little worried."

"Yeah," Roy said, his mind running crazy with the possibilities. "I got back yesterday afternoon and was tied up most of the day with family stuff. I can't explain Jerry. He's not the smartest fellow in the world, but he's always been pretty reliable."

That was when Roy saw the cash register. The drawer was open slightly, less than an inch. He went over and opened it up. Empty. Not even a penny in the change trays. He lifted up. A few checks, but no larger bills underneath where they kept them. Looked as if Jerry had left early and cleaned out the money when he went.

"Damn it," Roy muttered. "The son-of-a-bitch took every penny in the drawer. What the hell is wrong with that boy?"

"I am sorry, Roy." Nate looked at the floor as if he felt embarrassed for his friend. "I was afraid something had happened. I wish I'd had some idea of what he was planning when I was here."

"I knew I shouldn't have left him here in charge," Roy said. "I could have just closed up for a couple of days. I don't know what

I was thinking. I was just down the street yesterday when I got in and I didn't even ride this way to take a look."

"Don't blame yourself, for heaven's sake," Nate said. "He's the one that took off with your money. You're acting like you handed it to him and then got surprised that it's gone. You left the boy in charge. He's your employee and had keys to the place. He could have come in whether you closed up or not. Besides, you ought to be able to leave somebody in charge without worrying about them robbing you blind."

"I know," Roy said. But he didn't really know anything. All he could sort out at that moment was that he was out three days' worth of cash from the register. Thank God he'd made a deposit with all the receipts just before he left. He would have to make a call or two, just in case he was wrong about Jerry. But there weren't too many explanations out there. The boy had planned the whole thing. He'd worked for three days and built up the cash on hand, then cleared out before Roy came back. Roy's bet was that Jerry was well out of town with his wife and that baby on the way. Unless Jerry took off without her. Either way, the story was the same for Roy. He flipped over the "Open" sign on the window.

"I told him I'd be a couple of days," Roy said. "I guess by yesterday, he was beginning to get nervous that I'd come back." He turned back to Nate, who looked as if he still had something on his mind. "So you still need work on your car?" Roy asked.

"That's just the thing," Nate said, again looking at the floor. "I left it here yesterday, and I don't see it anywhere around."

Roy closed his eyes and took in a full breath to calm himself. "I'm so sorry, Nate. Let me see what I can find out." Nate drove a newer model Buick. He'd only had it a little over a year. "You need something to get around in at the moment? It's not much, but I can loan you that old Chevy Nova I'm driving."

Nate glanced over at the ill-used car parked by the side of the building. "That's okay, Roy," he said. "I've got Helen's car there, and she doesn't need it much, we live so close to town. We can get by with one for the time being. But thanks."

"You're a good man, Nate," Roy said. "I'll see what I can do about your car. In the meantime, you might as well file it as stolen with your insurance."

Nate nodded, offered a weak smile, then turned to go toward his wife's sedan.

"Thanks for coming by to tell me," Roy said as the older man left.

Nate didn't turn around, but lifted his hand and waved back at Roy as he walked down the stoop.

Roy washed up and changed clothes in his office at the back of the garage. He was closing up early to walk over to the funeral home and meet Rosalind, Lola, and Janie Ray for Minnie Thomas's viewing. He looked across the street and saw Alva Thomas going inside with a blond fellow who looked to be in his early twenties. Must be the grandson, Roy decided. Roy hadn't seen the boy in a couple of years. He'd almost grown into a man.

"Hey, Roy." Dan Richfield, wearing a dark suit, but a ready smile, greeted him as he crossed Main Street. Dan stood on the level cement porch that went flush into the front yard of the funeral home. If Roy didn't know the man, he'd never in a million years peg him for an undertaker. He didn't have the look.

"You're early," Dan said. "Nobody but the family's inside at the moment."

"I'll keep you company out here for a bit, then," Roy told him. "Mind if I smoke?"

"No, sir," Dan said. "I'd join you if I wasn't working."

Roy lit up. The first drag calmed him enough to keep still in one place without fidgeting. The Jerry thing had him edgy. He'd called the guy's house and gotten no answer. Then he'd called the sheriff's office and filed a report. They said the best chance they had was locating him through Nate's car. As bad as it was to have a customer's car missing and his own cash box emptied, those things weren't what bothered him the most. Getting stabbed in the back by somebody he tried to help. *That* made him feel sick. And that wouldn't change, whether they found Jerry or not.

Even standing outside, Roy could smell the funeral home. What was that odor? Part flowers, but something else. Maybe the chemicals they used when embalming the bodies. Roy didn't want to think too much about that.

Dan turned to give instruction to one of his guys, another dark-suited fellow Roy didn't know well, and Roy stared out across the street at his business. It seemed tainted after Jerry's betrayal. Why would the boy do that to him? Roy had never been anything but fair and the two of them had gotten on really well.

"Hey, Dan," Roy said when his friend had finished with the other guy. "Did you happen to notice anything at the garage over the last couple of days?"

"Like what?" Dan looked around, then reached over to sneak a drag off Roy's cigarette. He handed it back, then stuck his hands in his pockets and looked down the street.

"I don't know," Roy said. "I was out of town. Did Jerry have anybody coming around or did anything seem strange?"

"Don't think so." Dan wrinkled his forehead. "He walked over one day—must have been a week or two ago—and asked if we did the yard here or if we paid somebody to do it. I thought he wanted some extra work, but I told him we don't have that much to take care of here, so we do it ourselves. He asked if he could borrow some yard tools."

"Yard tools?" Roy was really confused. Jerry and his wife lived in a garage apartment at Ted Wilson's house. Jerry joked all the time that he went from one garage to another day and night. He wouldn't have a yard unless it was Ted's. But then Ted would have his own tools.

"I can't remember what all he took."

"Did he bring it back?" Roy asked.

"Not that I know of," Dan told him. "Somebody else could have took it back though. I didn't think any more about it."

"Well, I'd count your tools gone," Roy said, feeling his stomach sink again.

"Why's that?"

"Jerry cleaned out the cash register yesterday, and best I can tell, skipped town with my money and Nate Atkins's car." Roy hated even saying it. He felt as if he'd brought some disease on the town by hiring Jerry, giving people a legitimate reason to trust the guy.

"Holy moly." Dan shook his head. "You sure?"

"Yeah. 'Fraid so."

"Oh, man, I'm sorry. What a thing to happen. You were good to that boy." Dan looked at Roy with a certain amount of pity. Roy was glad no one else was around to see.

"What can you do?" Roy shrugged his shoulders, trying to dismiss the subject.

People were going into the funeral home. Minnie Thomas's viewing had begun in earnest. Roy saw his family getting out of the truck and went over to join them.

"Thanks, Dan," he said as he walked away. "I'm sorry about your tools."

"You've got other things to worry about," Dan said. "Don't give that one a second thought."

As Roy kissed Rosalind hello and picked up Janie Ray, he moved to greet Lola, but she stepped away before he reached her. Lola looked at the funeral home as if something serious was on her mind, and he wondered if she felt sad over the older lady's passing or something else entirely. He wished he could read his daughter. But telling her at the age of sixteen that she had a brother—and that being a lie on top of everything else— was not the way to get closer to a girl her age.

"Everything okay at work?" Rosalind asked him.

"Not even close," Roy said, deciding he would wait to fill her in on Jerry's departure until they were home and on the porch alone. "We'll talk later," he added in low tones, and she understood. Without any more words, *she understood*—and he realized that the fact of that alone just might save him from the crazy things the world had laid on him.

Twenty-four

Lola tried to get Luke to come to the funeral home with them. Even though he didn't know Mrs. Thomas, she didn't want to hurt his feelings by telling him to stay home. Still, in her heart of hearts, she was glad he hadn't agreed to go. She told Charlotte about him that morning, but she dreaded explaining him over and over until everybody knew who he was. *Daddy had a wife before Mama.* She couldn't get that idea to make sense.

As pissed as she was at her dad, she had to admit that the brother thing was the most exciting event she could remember happening in their family. Discovering that he existed made her feel far less ordinary than she had felt before. At the same time, she could barely speak to her daddy. How could he have gone all that time without telling her? These feelings conflicted with each other and she knew it. That didn't stop them though.

"Hello, Lola," Dan Richfield, the undertaker, greeted her, smiling, as they went into the front door. Mr. Richfield stood just inside the door with his hands clasped behind his back. His round middle that spilled out to his sides made it hard for him to keep his hands together, but it didn't seem to bother him. Lola had never seen him less than cheerful, which made his profession seem like an unusual choice for him.

"Hey, Mr. Richfield," she said. The rest of her family lagged behind, so she hurried past him so as not to get caught in conversation.

"Please take a moment to sign the register." He seemed to say this to no one in particular.

She veered right toward the viewing room. She wanted to get her encounter with Mrs. Thomas's dead body over with. As she stepped into the large room, she saw a line of people moving slowly by the casket. Those near the front were quiet. Some cried. But the farther away from the body the line got, the more people talked and laughed just like they were at a picnic.

As Lola stood in line, she heard one woman saying that since Mrs. Thomas had died breathing smoke and not burning up, the body was in pretty good shape.

"That's lucky for her," the woman said.

"I know it," the other lady said. "It's easier on the family when the bodies look natural. That's what I would want."

Bunches of flowers made a frame around the coffin. A big wreath in the front had plastic letters stuck on it that read "Mother." The flowers looked plastic, too, although they were probably real. Mrs. Thomas had kept a nice flower garden, and Lola thought it was a shame that none of the flowers sent to her were as pretty as the ones she grew herself.

Lola could see into the greeting room. Mama and Daddy had gone in there first, Daddy dragging Janie Ray around by one hand. Watching her family, she almost lost track of what she was doing in line and before she knew it, she was staring down at the pale form of her neighbor.

Mrs. Thomas's mouth was pulled tight, her lips thin and drawn on with lipstick. None of the old lady's humor or kindness was left. She'd been dressed in a heavy, navy-colored suit dress that overwhelmed her small body. Jewelry, old-looking stuff, had been stuck on her fingers, ears, and neck. The result made her look decorated—more like one of the cakes that came out of her oven than the woman who baked them. Mrs. Thomas seemed pitiful with all that stuff she never wore piled on her.

Looking at the older woman, Lola felt unexpected tears, an occurrence that left her horrified. Lola just wanted Mrs. Thomas to go back to the way she'd been. Lola wanted her own self back the way she'd been not too long before. Mrs. Thomas ought to be in her kitchen baking, while Lola picked up eggs from her and ate samples of her cake. Lola took a tissue from a box sitting on a small table nearby and moved quickly to join her family in the other room.

There were chairs lined up along the wall, but the Thomas family, three of them, stood together at the side of the room. Mr. Thomas wore a gray suit with a skinny tie. People moved by him, talked to him, but he didn't seem to understand. He said nothing back and only half looked at them, staring mostly off to the side.

Beside him was a large woman who looked about his age, maybe his sister or sister-in-law. Then there was another woman who looked about the age of Lola's parents. She was the most uncomfortable-looking woman Lola had ever seen. Beauty-shop done up, she looked too teased to move. But her face had a nice way about it, almost sweet. It was exactly the same face as the grandson/fireman Duncan. This had to be his mama. No doubt about that. Duncan wasn't with them; she didn't see him anywhere in the room.

"Hi, I'm Vicky Benson," Charlotte's mama was saying to the

older woman beside Mr. Thomas. "We live next door and we're all just sick about Minnie. She was a good neighbor."

Except for the peacocks, Lola thought. At least Vicky Benson could manage to behave when she needed to, Lola decided. Besides, she hadn't seen the peacocks around since the fire. The flames either killed them or drove them away because you normally couldn't go two days without at least hearing them.

When Lola reached the family, she introduced herself to the older woman as a neighbor from up the street. "I'm their daughter," Lola said, and pointed to her family across the room. The elderly woman put her hand on Lola's cheek. She smelled old—oily creams and snuff on the sly, just like Grandma Simsy.

"I'm Alva's sister, Cara Ann," she said. "You favor your mama." She turned toward Mr. Thomas. "Alva," she said, using an inappropriately loud voice to get his attention. "Alva, this young lady lives by you. You remember her?"

He turned his gaze toward her. Enormous eyes surrounded by fallen skin. As he looked at her, his focus cleared. He seemed pleased and less confused.

"Sure, I know her. You came to the house sometimes," he said. "I remember when you sat on the piano stool in the kitchen watching my Minnie work." He took her hand between his, and pressed it like sandwich meat between his long, cool fingers.

"Yes, sir," Lola answered. "I liked her cakes a lot. She was a terrific cook."

"She sure was that. Lucky the both of us were skinny by nature, or we'd of been enormous a long time ago." He cut his eyes over toward his sister—a not so subtle gesture. He smiled and seemed tickled with himself. His shoulders bobbed up and down a little, and he still had hold of Lola's hand.

"Daddy," the younger woman said. "Don't get too excited."

"She liked you," he went on, still talking to Lola. "Enjoyed you and that other little girl coming around."

Mama and Daddy both waited for her to get free. Daddy, especially, had begun to fidget.

"She said you looked like our Ruthie here." He looked over at his daughter. "Like our Ruthie before she got the big head and stopped coming back to see us."

"Daddy, that's enough." Grown-up Ruthie shot a look at her daddy, but her teased-up hair stayed right with her head, molded to her scalp like a plastic wig. Lola hoped she didn't grow up to look anything like their Ruthie.

Lola thought it was funny that he said she got the big head. With that hairdo, it was literally true.

"Dr. Barber gave him something to relax him," the older woman whispered in Lola's ear. "Don't pay him any mind."

Mama came over and put a gentle hand on Mr. Thomas's shoulder, and with the other she lightly tugged Lola out of the receiving line. He extended his hands that were still holding Lola's until she got too far away for him to keep them any longer. People were backed up behind them, almost to the door.

After they exited the room, Mr. Richfield saw them collecting themselves in the hall, and he pointed to the other room, as if it might be a complicated maneuver to figure out how to get from the family room to the viewing room without instruction.

"I think it's that way," Mama said, joking.

"I've already been by," Lola said. "I don't want to go in again, so I'll go outside and wait."

"Take your sister," Mama said. "She might start chatting away at the body."

Lola took Janie Ray's hand and led her toward the double doors that went to the side patio outside. As she went out, she saw *him*. Duncan stood by himself, smoking. He had on a brown suit that hung loose, like a hand-me-down. The blond stubble was gone, but his hair, loose and over his ears, looked barely combed. When she got close enough, she could make out the beginnings of the scar at the edge of his hair.

"Hey," Janie Ray called out, pulling Lola toward him. "You were at the fire. Is Mrs. Thomas your mama?"

"My grandma," he said. "And what's your name?"

"I'm Janie Ray Vines," she said.

"Well, hello, Janie Ray Vines. I'm Duncan Randleman Cranford." He shook her hand.

"I saw your grandma in there. Mama wouldn't let me go in the room with her, but I saw her from the door. I know she's dead, but she looks like somebody who's asleep. I wonder if dead people dream?"

"I don't know," he said. He seemed to take the question seriously. "If she does, I hope it's a good dream she's having."

Lola wanted her sister to stop talking, but he didn't seem to mind.

"I fell asleep once at my own birthday party," Janie Ray said. "I woke up and I was mad at what I missed. Do you think she's sad about what she'll miss?"

The pained look on his face made Lola jerk on her little sister's arm. Lola shot her a look and shook her head no.

"I'm Lola," she said. "We live up the street from your grandparents' house. I met you the other night."

"Yeah," he said, "I remember you." He dropped his cigarette on the ground and put it out with the toe of his shoe.

A bold heartbeat rose and pounded in her neck, higher than her real heart could have been. It threw her breathing out of whack, and for a slow, scared moment she thought she might lose the use of her legs. The patio was covered with a roof extension supported by two columns. Duncan leaned against one column, a round cylinder of white cement.

"I'm really sorry about your grandmother," she said. "I liked her a lot."

"Thank you," he said.

Janie Ray spotted an overweight cat in one of the wicker patio chairs and peeled off to investigate. That left Lola standing in front of Duncan by herself.

"Did you know it was her house when you were on the way to the fire?" Lola asked.

He nodded. "A buddy of mine from Linton Springs knew I volunteered with the Creston crew. That's one reason they called us for backup."

"What started it?" Lola asked. She thought of the odd-smelling smoke the afternoon before the house went up in flames. She wondered if he knew that his granddaddy had been burning something all afternoon.

"It was my fault." That was all he said.

"You weren't even there," she said.

"Doesn't matter," he said, lighting another cigarette. He looked at the glowing tip. "I might as well have been."

She waited, thought he might elaborate, but he didn't. She struggled to figure out where to go next with the conversation. In front of the funeral home, cars on Main Street slowed for the light, the only stoplight in town. The four corners at that light held her daddy's garage, the funeral home, the courthouse, and the grocery store. Just about any kind of business essential to life or death could be conducted at that intersection. All that was missing was a church.

"That fellow who works across the street with your daddy," he said, "is he here by any chance?"

"Jerry?" Why would he ask about Jerry? "I haven't seen him. Is he a friend of yours?"

"No." Duncan took a long drag and looked across at her daddy's garage. "I just know him, that's all. He helped me with my car sometimes."

She got the feeling he was lying, and she also decided that he wasn't very good at it. She figured it was better not to press him on the subject of Jerry.

"What do you drive?" she asked.

"A sixty-seven Mustang. I bought it when I turned eighteen. It's the best thing I own."

"When did you turn eighteen?" she asked. Too late, she realized what a transparent question it was.

"A year and a half ago." He smiled.

"So you graduated from high school already." She hated to be obvious, but what the hell? There wasn't much way around it if she wanted information.

"Yeah," he said, "then spent last fall at Wake Forest before I had to drop out."

"What happened?"

"I was on a baseball scholarship. Only way I could afford it." He shifted his weight to lean on the other shoulder. "Over Thanksgiving, I wiped out on a friend's dirt bike and messed up my hand." He held up his right hand. Lola could see that the index finger and the one next to it were misshapen, like somebody had put the bones in the wrong order. "They let me go back and finish the semester on scholarship. But I can't pitch anymore. Turns out they won't pay my way just because I've got such a pretty face."

He was joking, but the irony was he *did* have a pretty face. Prettier than a lot of girls. But he didn't look like a girl or anything. Her feelings got jumbled up and confused again. She had the absurd impulse to touch his hair, but stopped short of actually following through with it. What was wrong with her?

"Anyway," he continued when she didn't say anything, "it's not like I would have ever made the majors or anything. I just figured I'd at least get college out of it. But what can you do?"

"That's too bad," she managed. "You think you'll ever go back?"

"Not sure."

A fine mist of rain had set in, bringing the smell of damp tar and pavement to the humid air. Rain smells changed so much depending on what was around. The ones in town were nice enough, but her favorites were at the lake. Mud, fish, moss, and bark, mixed up like soup. She brought her mind back from the rain and the smells and found him looking at her. It was like she'd come into focus for him all of a sudden and it made her feel self-conscious.

"So," she said, "a Mustang." Better to return to the original topic. "That's a great car. You work on it yourself?" She knew a little about cars. Being around her daddy, there was no way not to learn a few things.

"Yep. That's what I've been doing this spring," he said.

"Working on your car?" She figured that must leave him with a lot of time on his hands.

"No." He laughed. "Working with *cars*. Stock cars. I met a fellow in Winston and I've been working on his crew since the start of race season this spring."

"Has he won anything?" she asked, not knowing if that was even the right question. She didn't know anything about racing.

"He places pretty well," Duncan said, letting it go at that.

She had no idea if that meant yes or no. She felt out of her element all of a sudden, and she found it hard to breathe.

"What's wrong?" he asked.

"Nothing," she said. "I'm fine." She walked over toward the opposite column and leaned against it, a mirror of his stance at the opposite side of the patio. She decided he'd have to come to her. Either that, or to end their conversation. One way or the other, she wanted him to choose. She didn't want to be the eager one.

He did come over. She could hear Janie Ray making noises at the cat. She could hear her own heart where it had picked up the pounding again.

"So I told you I'm nineteen. How old are you?" he asked.

She wanted to lie and jump straight to seventeen. She would be in two months and that sounded so much better. But she'd look foolish if she got caught in the lie, and it would say too much about her feelings. "I'm sixteen," she said, looking him in the eye when she said it.

He took a moment, as if considering that information. He stepped back, almost as if by instinct. "Sixteen. Those were the days." He said it as a joke, but he seemed genuinely disappointed.

"Yeah, nineteen," she said. "I bet you take your teeth out at night."

"Fair enough," he said, laughing. "It's just that you seem older. The way you talk and everything. Sixteen is younger than I expected."

She kept her face as blank as she could manage, hoped he couldn't read her real feelings. "Well, I'll be seventeen in two months," she said, trying not to sound defensive. "And I guess it all depends on what you have in mind, anyway." It would have been easy to cry, but she would never let that happen in front of him. "There's no age limit on most of the things I do. I should go."

She didn't wait for him to say anything else. She went over to her little sister, and without looking back at him, took Janie Ray's hand and led her off toward where they'd left the truck parked on the street. Her hand trembled—her arms and shoulders with it—and she hoped Janie Ray wouldn't announce that fact as they walked. At least the misting rain had stopped.

When she did allow herself the small luxury of glancing back his way, she saw him leaning against his column again, watching her still. To his credit, he didn't look smug, pleased with himself like boys her age tended to be.

He looked sad and she remembered that his grandmother had just died. She remembered that he said it was his fault. What did that mean? And in spite of herself, she wondered when she might see him again. For pride's sake, she hated to admit just how much she wanted to.

As she came closer to the truck, she saw Daddy sitting on the tailgate. He'd taken off his tie and loosened his collar. His legs dangled off the end of the truck bed and he almost looked like a kid.

She glanced back to see if she could still see Duncan, but a big hedge blocked him from her view. She and Janie Ray reached the truck, and the smaller girl jumped up to sit beside their daddy.

"Mama's still inside," he said. "She got caught with Tom Janeway's wife. It could be a while. That woman can *talk*." He picked up a brown paper sack sitting beside him and opened it. He reached inside and brought out bottles of Coca-Cola and Moon Pies.

"Where'd that come from?" Janie Ray squealed in delight.

"I walked across and got them at the garage," Daddy said. He handed each of them a snack cake, then used a bottle opener on his key chain to take the top off a Coke. He handed it to Lola, then did the same with another one for Janie Ray. Mama was going to kill him. If the sugar didn't keep Janie Ray up all night, the full bottle of Coke would.

For Lola's money, Moon Pies were better than ice cream. Marshmallow and cake dipped in chocolate. She put Duncan and Mrs. Thomas out of her mind. For just a few minutes, she would let go of all her anger at Daddy for keeping Luke and the rest of his family from her for all those years. Being mad took effort, and she needed a rest from it.

She bit into her snack cake and the gooey middle stuck to her teeth. Like a song or a smell, the taste reminded her of things; it reminded her of long afternoons with her daddy. She'd go with him on warm spring days into the woods, and she'd play around while he worked on building a deer stand that he could use during hunting season the next fall. He brought Moon Pies and Cokes then, too, and he said not to tell, because Mama would fuss at him for spoiling supper.

For the first time since he got back, Lola grinned at her daddy. She felt the chocolate and crumbs on her lips and licked them away. Then she drank deep, her Coca-Cola still cold enough to make her throat ache. The cool bubbles tickled inside her stomach and felt almost the same as being nervous. It felt almost the same as expecting, or at least hoping, something good might happen.

Twenty-five

Luke thought he'd like being by himself in Roy's house, but he didn't. The truth of it was, he didn't much like being by himself anytime, and they'd been gone awhile. Still, the last thing he'd wanted was to go view some dead lady he never met.

The television seemed too loud, so he turned it off and went to his "room." The sealed-in back porch was pretty comfortable, but with plastic all around the outside, it felt a little like living in a greenhouse. It was the best they could offer. He knew that. But damn. He'd had a room and a life and friends in Virginia. At Roy's, he barely had enough air to breathe.

The overhead porch light was too dim for reading so he turned on the lamp they'd run out to the porch with an extension cord. He picked up a fishing magazine Roy had put out there for him. He always considered Gray's Hollow boring, but it was nothing compared to Linton Springs. Shit. If things stayed like they were, he'd blow his brains out just for something to do by the end of the summer.

Beside the daybed he slept on was the stack of work he had to finish so that he could graduate with his class. Mont had called his physics teacher the morning he left Virginia and gotten him to go around and gather any makeup work he still had to do before final grades went into his record. He'd already had his exams, and so there wasn't much. A paper in English he'd never turned in and one due in history. Two worksheets, one in physics and one in math.

He pulled out the work and started in on one of the math sheets. Out in the backyard, a mist of rain had come and gone, and the moon, better than half full, lit up Rosalind's garden. Other than that staked-out patch, the grass and trees were pretty much left to their own devices. An old swing set tilted slightly to one side. Once green, it had become mottled with rust. Janie Ray still played on it, but he noticed that one corner lifted and bumped when she went too high.

Hell, if he was going to be bored, he might as well do something productive. He'd spent his whole life hanging around Pap Taylor's hardware store. He knew how to fix things.

He went down the back steps and over to the swing set. The structure seemed pretty sound. If he anchored it with something inside a hole in the ground, then painted it, the whole set would look pretty decent.

Roy didn't have a garage, but he had a little storage house off to the side of the duplex. Luke went inside, flipped on the light, and found the treasure of work materials. Mostly stuff for cars. Parts and touch-up paint. Oil and vinyl shine. After he finished with the swing set, he could do some work on the old Chevy Mont sent them off in.

In one corner he found a small bag of cement mix. That would get things started. He wagered he could find some sandpaper lying around, and if he was lucky, a can of rustproof paint. A few minutes later, he had everything he needed, including a bucket that looked like it had been used before to mix up the cement.

With the backyard lights turned on, plus the light the moon offered, he could manage. He took everything out back, found the spigot and the hose, and set to work.

"Hey."

Luke heard the girl's voice, but the porch light blinded him to the shadows around the periphery of the yard.

"Hey yourself," he said. He'd finished sanding down most of the rust from the metal frame of the swing set. Then he'd put the loose leg back into the hole, and filled in around it with wet cement.

He'd also discovered that Roy kept cold beer in a small refrigerator in the storage house and he had one open beside him. The voice sounded young, not likely to be anyone who would object to him having a Budweiser while he worked, but all the same, he put it out of sight behind the cement bucket.

"What're you doing?" the girl asked.

She came into view, and the closer she got, the more interesting she became. She had on shorts—really short shorts—with a sleeveless gauzy kind of top that was cut low enough to get a full view of the tops of her breasts. Damn.

"I'm fixing the swing set." He stated the obvious. "Who're you?"

"I'm Charlotte," the girl said. "I live down there. Lola and I are best friends. Are you the long-lost brother or just some kind of freak who sneaks into people's yards and fixes things at night?"

"Luke Vines," he said, extending his hand. "I'm Lola's half brother."

"Holy shit," she said. "I knew you were here, but somehow it just didn't seem like it could be real. Lola and I didn't really talk about it, but I guess that means Mr. Vines and your mother . . ." She shook her head, as if it just couldn't be true.

"Yep. My mother was Roy's first wife."

"Wife?" Not even the obligatory profanity for that one. The little sexpot was speechless, but her eyes had gone the size of inner tubes.

"I don't believe you," she managed. But her voice sounded timid. "Lola didn't say anything about another wife."

He lost his interest in messing with her head. "She had all of it thrown at her yesterday," he told her. "I was kind of sprung on everybody. I've been living in Virginia with my grandparents. Roy's folks. But I got in some trouble and they shipped me off for the summer. I'm not real happy about it, but I guess Lola's family isn't all that thrilled, either."

"So they told you that you had to fix stuff if you were going to stay here?" She seemed genuinely confused, and he laughed. "Why is that funny?" She had a pout thing going on. She was really pretty, this Charlotte.

"I'm sorry," he said. "It's not funny." He picked up his beer and took a sip, then handed it to her.

She looked at the can, shot him a grin, and said, "Okay, I forgive you. Don't tell Lola I drank this."

"Don't tell Lola I gave it to you."

Again, the grin.

"Charlotte!" Another voice from the dark edge of the yard. "Mama told me to find you. What the hell are you do—" She stopped.

Luke could make out another girl's form, but not her features. She, too, wore shorts, with a shirt that he could tell was half-way unbuttoned. Underneath the shirt, a bikini bathing suit top covered her breasts. From what he could tell, not as large as the other girl's, but still nothing to dismiss. Man, ten degrees hotter than Gray's Hollow and half-naked girls were everywhere. Luke figured he could get used to the heat if that was the silver lining of the thing.

"Who are you?" the second girl asked. It sounded like an accusation.

He started to speak, but Charlotte beat him to the explanation. The new one didn't seem all that shocked or impressed with the news.

"This is my sister, Shelby," Charlotte told him.

"Go on home, Charlotte," Shelby said. "Mama says it's your turn to do the dishes."

"Come on, Shelby," Charlotte argued. "I'm here visiting with Luke. Leave me alone."

"Go home." The Shelby girl's voice managed to sound both bored and unrelenting at the same time. Charlotte rolled her eyes toward Luke and mouthed the word "bitch" while her head was turned away from the bossy sister.

"See you later," Charlotte said. She turned and walked toward the larger house down the street. For reasons he couldn't name, he felt sorry to see her go. Her assessment of the other one seemed to be pretty much on the money, and he'd had enough lately of controlling, manipulating girls.

"Is there more where that came from?" Shelby pointed to his beer.

"Last one," he lied, picking up the putty knife and prying off the lid of the paint can.

"Like hell," she said, but didn't press him further. "I've got something better anyway." She walked toward him and unbuttoned her shirt the rest of the way. She took it off and tied it by the arms around her waist, the tail flapping over her butt as she moved. Then she pulled out a joint from the pocket of her cutoffs.

As she came fully into the light, he saw that she wasn't wearing a bathing suit top at all. *Damn.* It was a bra and a pretty sheer one at that. *What the hell was he supposed to do?* Good sense told him that this sort of thing got him into a shitload of trouble before.

"Luke! You here?" Roy's voice echoed out from the house.

Luke stood frozen. There was nowhere to go. Holy shit, it was happening again. At least he saw the girl stuff the joint back into her pocket, but still . . . In the split second that it took Roy to make it through the house to the backyard, Luke had gone from panicked to resigned. He could see the entire scene as if he floated above it. There he stood, with a girl in her see-through bra, lit up by a pool of light from the house and a too-bright moon. He wondered if Roy would ship him away somewhere even worse.

In his hand, a half-empty beer can, and in his jeans, the monster of all erections. For the life of him, he couldn't figure out why his embarrassment and horror didn't make that last one go away. But there it was, still announcing his intentions when Rosalind followed Roy down the steps and over to where he stood with Shelby.

"Mama! Daddy!" Janie Ray called from the house. "Lola won't let me turn on the TV."

"Go on inside with those two," Roy said to Rosalind. "Shelby," he said, not looking at the girl as she worked on buttoning up the shirt she'd mercifully put on again. "You need to go home too. And Luke," he said, shaking his head, "let's take a walk."

So much for productivity and good deeds. Luke was screwed all over again. And again, it wasn't his fault. He didn't like the patterns that were forming in his life. At least, along with the girl, the boner had made an exit, and he felt himself shriveled and emasculated as he took off around the house with Roy.

Only as they were walking did he realize that Roy wasn't acting royally pissed. He'd started talking with Luke about how he understood the impulses that were there, especially when you were a teenager. He talked about them being natural, but at the same time, having to control them. To learn how to be an adult. None of the living-under-my-roof, follow-my-rules, beg-Jesus-to-forgive-you-or-you'll-end-up-in-a-fiery-pit-of-hell bullshit he'd gotten from Mont, Nanny, and Pap over the years.

This is what a father's supposed to sound like. The thought surprised him, but inside his amazement at Roy's response, he registered an anger that Roy hadn't claimed his place as a parent when he should have—long before circumstances forced the issue.

"You listening, Luke?" Roy's face looked clear in the moonlit night as they got to the end of the street and turned back around.

"Yes, sir," Luke said, torn up with feelings that wouldn't, *couldn't* exist inside him at the same time. He was more pissed at Roy than he would have been if the man had raged on him.

"You'll apologize to Rosalind for all that out there and then we'll move on," Roy said.

"Yes, sir," Luke said again, reining in his words to keep them free of the emotions he felt.

They left the night outside and went back into the house. Roy went down the hall and into the bathroom, and Luke found himself alone in the kitchen with Rosalind. He'd been told to apologize to her, but he hadn't done a damn thing and couldn't bring himself to say he was sorry for it.

"What in the world was that all about out there?" Rosalind asked. There was astonishment in her voice, but nothing in the way of a scolding.

"Hell if I know," he answered truthfully. "She came up and started to undress for no reason. Honest to God, I didn't do anything."

"That one's just like her mother," Rosalind said. "Bad news

from the word go. Charlotte's like her dad. Good-natured. I don't know how they all live together down there."

She looked pale, and Luke remembered that she had some kind of illness. That was why Roy had gone all the way to Virginia in the first place. Roy's arrival at Pap and Nanny's had nothing to do with him. None of these people had anything to do with him.

"What were you doing in the backyard?" Rosalind asked, almost as an afterthought.

Luke remembered the swing set. Put back in the ground, but not yet painted. The effort seemed tainted and he wasn't sure why he'd even felt compelled to do it in the first place.

"Nothing," he said. "I just needed some air."

She looked at him, waited for him to say more, but there wasn't anything else to tell her. Not really. After a moment, she went back to wiping down the counter. He went through to the makeshift space they called his room, and from there he could see the can of paint he'd left open sitting on the ground outside. He walked out to close it up so that the paint wouldn't be ruined. Then he went back to the porch to lie down and try for a little sleep.

Twenty-six

More than anything, Rosalind wanted to crawl in bed. Janie Ray was down for the night and Lola had gone to the front porch swing to read. The boy was off to himself again. There was more going on than he showed. A little part of her felt sorry for him, the way he'd been thrown into the situation with them. But he was Sherry's son. And even though Sherry was gone, that didn't make him Rosalind's business.

"Hey there." Roy came into the kitchen. "Why don't you leave that for the morning? Come sit with me outside."

"Lola's out there on the porch reading," Rosalind told him. "Everybody's looking for a little corner of space to themselves in this place." Her words came out hard and she didn't have it in her to apologize.

"I know it," Roy said, settling down at the table. "I'm sorry,

Rosie. I don't know what else to say." He squeezed his eyes together like he had a headache. "Where'd Luke go?"

She motioned her head in the direction of the back porch. The door between his space and the kitchen was closed.

"He shut the door when he went out," she said. "It's got to be hotter than hell out there without any air from the house coming through."

"He'll be all right," Roy said. "Not too long ago, nobody had air-conditioning and it didn't kill us. Come here." He motioned for her to come and sit on his lap.

She put down her dishrag and went over to him, and he pulled her down. She drew her knees up and curled into him as his arms held firm around her. The children all used to love sitting on Roy's lap. There could be no safer place, it seemed. Under Roy's protection, Rosalind felt that her illness might even begin to subside.

She thought again of Luke; she couldn't help it. Had he ever sat on anyone's lap when he was little? Sherry had always seemed to be in motion, too nervous to sit and hold a child for long. And if you gathered Mont, Taylor, and Lydia in a room, you wouldn't find a comforting lap among the whole lot of them. No, Luke had never had that, she was pretty certain. And she should feel worse about it—more compassion for the boy—than she did. But all she could feel was that he'd come as an intrusion when she could least handle it.

"You smell like tobacco." She made a face.

"Never bothered you before," he said, teasing her as he nuzzled his nose into her neck. He worked at being playful, but she could tell his heart wasn't in it.

"There are at least three reasons in this house for us to stop this foolishness," she said, getting up from his lap and going back to the sink. "What's on your mind, Roy? You've been a little off all night."

She watched his face change. He leaned back in the chair as if bracing himself against the words that would follow.

"Roy?"

"I didn't want to bring this up at the funeral home," he said, "but it's Jerry."

"What did he mess up this time?" she asked. It couldn't come as a surprise that holding down the business was too much for the boy.

"Sometime yesterday afternoon, he cleared out all the cash in the register and took off in Nate Atkins's car," Roy said. "I feel just awful for Nate."

"Oh, Roy . . ." She felt the breath go out of her.

"I talked to him on the phone before I got into town. I didn't pick up on anything then, but I guess he'd planned it. Three days' worth of cash . . . A few people paid by check and he left those. Best I can tell, he only took money and the car."

She walked over to him again, ran her fingers through the lock of hair that fell across his forehead.

"Nate tried his house yesterday and got no answer. Same for me today. He's gone and I guess his wife with him. I don't know why he did it."

"Did you call the sheriff's office?" she asked.

"I had to." He looked pained even saying it.

He'd tried to give Jerry a chance to learn the business. Rosalind didn't know which was worse for her husband, being betrayed by his employee or calling the law on the boy.

"So what happens next?" she asked.

"I open up on Monday." He'd lost all pretense of playfulness.

"How is it," she asked, "that our world stayed the same for so long, and all at once everything changed? I get sick, Minnie gets killed, Luke is here, now this thing with Jerry . . ."

"We'll get through all this," he said.

She had other things on her mind, too many things. She wanted the long summer to stretch ahead of her with none of their new worries getting in the way.

"Roy, how long's Luke going to be here?"

He looked at her as if he didn't understand the question. "I told you that he goes to Washington and Lee in the fall."

"And he's here until then?" She wasn't sure what she wanted to know. Sometimes it seemed as if she couldn't stand to think of a day or two with Luke in her house, much less several months. Other times, she felt purely sorry for the boy.

"This isn't the way I wanted it, either, Rosie."

She didn't answer. She didn't know how to explain it to Roy. She couldn't even explain it to herself.

"Sherry couldn't come between us, even when I was married to her, and she's gone now. The boy isn't a threat to us. He never was." Roy got up and motioned for her to go into the den with him. Even with the door closed and the AC running, it was too easy to hear through the thin walls of the duplex.

She sat on the couch with him, but felt lost for words.

"Come on. Talk to me," he pressed. "We can't do this if we don't talk."

"I know you did this for me," she said. "That almost makes it worse, like I brought it on myself by getting sick or by not being stronger."

"That makes no sense," he said. "You didn't *want* to get sick."

"I know," she said. Her feelings felt all jumbled.

Roy leaned his head forward, as if straining to understand. "I don't know what you're saying."

"When you look at Luke," she said, "you only see *him*. I wish I could do that. I see all of it. I see her trying to use this baby to keep you."

"But she didn't . . ."

"I knew you were married, Roy. I knew you were married and I wanted you anyway."

"We both knew it," he said. "And we kept ourselves from each other because of it."

"That's what we said we did." The thoughts were forming in her mind, thoughts she kept in pieces most of the time because when she put them together she didn't want to be the person who stepped forward in her memory. "But you made up some excuse to come to my house every chance you got and I waited for you. I thought about you all the time. You sat and talked hunting with my daddy, but you were watching me. And when Daddy left the room, and you would touch my arm or say something low to me . . . We might as well have been making love. That's what it was, even though it was just in our minds. We both knew it, Roy. It was probably a matter of time if we'd kept on like that."

"Sherry cheated on me," he said, his jaw set in a hard line.

"With someone who looked just like you." She couldn't let it go. She'd started the conversation; she had to let it run its course. "You pulled yourself away from her. Even sleeping beside her in the same bed, you might as well have been in the next county. She was desperate for you and she turned to Mont."

"You think that makes it right? That my own brother got my wife pregnant? I'd be lying if I said I wasn't relieved when I found out. But that doesn't change anything. She made the choice. Not me."

He had to keep it up. He wasn't ready to live with it any other way. But Rosalind couldn't do it anymore, not with Luke on the other side of her kitchen wall every day. "What choice did we give her?" she asked.

He had a look of pleading and she wished she could chime in with everything he wanted to hear.

"Looking at Luke," she said, holding firm, "reminds me of a person I don't like."

"He doesn't even look like her," Roy said.

"I don't mean Sherry," she went on. "I mean me. I'm the person I can't stand when I look at him. It doesn't help that he's the spitting image of you twenty years ago. He looks exactly the way you looked on the first night I saw you. It makes everything too confusing. That was the day I decided I'd have you, the day I became someone who would take another woman's husband regardless of the damage."

"But look what we've built," he said.

"I know. It's just that no matter how we tell the story, the facts don't change. I love you with every inch of my soul, Roy Vines. And I've been able to feel that and put the rest of it out of my mind most of the time for over seventeen years. But I look at him, and I can't put it to the side anymore. I can't pretend to care much about the rest of your family. But even I have to admit that Luke didn't do anything to deserve the things that have happened to him. I go between those feelings and resenting the hell out of him being in my house."

"I don't know what to say, Rosalind." Roy looked away from her. "I can't turn back the clock. And I wouldn't if I could. And I can't turn him out with nowhere to go." Then he shifted back to her, leaned in close. "You wouldn't want me to. That wouldn't solve anything. At the very least," he said in lowered tones, "he's my nephew. And Mont may be his daddy, but that hasn't done him much good. He thinks I'm his father. I can't send him out. Maybe you're right. Maybe we do own some responsibility for what happened back then. If that's true, we owe something to the boy now. Maybe we owe it to Sherry, too."

"I'm not saying you're wrong. Of course we can't turn him out." She couldn't make her thoughts settle down. "I just don't know how to make it right."

"Step back and look at the family we've built," he said. "Lola and Janie Ray are proof of the good that came of all this. And get to know Luke. Let's both try. Let him become a person to you, so that he isn't a reminder of me twenty years ago—or you twenty years ago for that matter."

"I'll try," she said. "I promise I'll try." And she would. But that didn't make accepting the situation any easier.

She looked at Roy, thought of how he loved her. The certainty of that made up the foundation of her entire adult life. He stood up, and she suddenly felt that she didn't have the energy to walk to her own bed. As if reading her mind, he bent over and picked her up. She felt the lightness of her own body measured against the strength of his arms.

"I'm home now, Rosie," he said, "and I'll take care of you. Everything will be fine again. It'll be just fine."

She put her head on his shoulder and closed her eyes and felt the relief that with no effort at all, she would soon be able to sleep.

Twenty-seven

Lola stood behind the door in the hall bathroom. She'd come in to pee and was heading back out to the front porch when she heard her parents walking into the den. They were talking about Luke, and then they were talking about themselves. She knew she shouldn't have listened to them, but she couldn't help it. And the more she heard, the more some things made sense.

When she heard them getting up, she went into the bathroom again to keep from being seen. She felt guilty hiding from them, but she knew she'd feel worse if they found her there and knew what she heard. So she stayed tight in the shadows against the bathroom wall.

They'd turned off the lamp in the den when they left, and then one of them turned the light off in the hall. Lola relaxed a little with the cool dark surrounding her. Then she heard their bedroom door close. She stepped out quietly, but her mind felt busy and loud with everything they'd said. *Luke isn't my brother.* She couldn't tell from her own feelings if the news was a relief or a disappointment. He was still a relative. A cousin. That would have been big news on its own two days before. And the real dilemma? He didn't know. What was she supposed to do with that?

She looked down at the empty hall and slipped through the dark den and into the still-bright light of the kitchen.

"Hey." Luke spoke up as he opened the door from the porch and came into the kitchen. "I thought I'd go for some privacy out there, but it's like a sauna with that door shut."

Lola felt her heart racing. What should she say to him?

"You just see a ghost or something?" he joked.

Yeah. The ghost of parents past. "You startled me, that's all." She took in a deep breath.

"You hungry?" he asked. "I'm making myself a sandwich with some of the leftover barbeque your mom brought home from the grill."

"I'm good," she said, trying and failing to keep her voice casual.

"Your dad told you, didn't he?" Luke stood up and slammed his open hand against the side of the refrigerator.

Lola jumped at the outburst.

"Damn it to hell. Doesn't anything stay a secret in this family?" he said.

He knew? Why would Luke have lied to her about being her brother if he knew the truth?

"I didn't do anything with her." His voice calmed a little as he tried to explain. "I was in the backyard when the sister—that friend of yours—comes up and starts talking to me. Then the older one shows up and chases her off. Before I know it, big sister's down to her bra. I didn't do a damn thing to get her to do that. *Not one damn thing!*"

"Okay, okay . . ." Lola's mind raced. Bra? Backyard? "Daddy didn't tell me anything. I overheard him talking with Mama, but I just got bits and pieces. Tell me what happened."

He exhaled, closed his eyes for a second. "Have a seat," he said. "Let me finish making my sandwich and I'll tell you." Then he added, "Sorry to sound like I was mad at you. It's just . . ."

"It's okay," she said.

He went back to preparing a snack for himself, and she waited. She still didn't have a clear answer to the big question. Should she tell him what she'd heard? But at least he hadn't been lying to her like her parents.

"Shelby," he said, sitting down at the table across from her. The way he said it, the name itself sounded like an indictment. "That's her name, right? The older girl down the street?"

"Yeah," Lola said, "Shelby." He didn't really need to say much more, but Lola let him finish.

He launched into his story about the backyard and fixing Janie Ray's swing and Charlotte coming up first and then Shelby, well, being Shelby.

"I mean, she's good-looking and all," he said. "But I've gotten into enough trouble with girls lately, and one thing I've learned is that the ones like Shelby come with a high price tag. I figured out that much before I left Virginia and I'm not falling for it again."

Lola felt glad to hear him say it, but not totally convinced. Plenty of guys said that Shelby was "too damn much trouble" and then ended up going out with her anyway. She pulled her mind back to something he was asking her.

"Your friend," he said. "The younger one. What's her story?"

"Her story?" Lola asked.

"She's pretty cool," he said. "I didn't talk to her long, but I liked her a lot better than the Antichrist in her underwear."

He liked Charlotte. The conversation kept taking strange

turns and she wouldn't have predicted that one. But why not?

"Charlotte's great," Lola told him. "We've been best friends since we were little."

"She have a boyfriend?" he asked, wiping barbeque sauce from his chin with a paper napkin.

"No. She did, but she broke up with him." "Broke up" and even "boyfriend" were pretty loose terms to describe Charlotte's relationship with Trey Blankenship. Making out at basketball games in junior high segued into making out at football games in high school. Charlotte decided he was a moron and stopped talking to him over a year before. But Lola wanted to put it in the most flattering light possible. "I know she's not interested in anybody right now."

"That's cool," he said, taking another bite of his sandwich and washing it down with iced tea. "So, how about you?"

"What about me?"

"Any guys I need to intimidate?" He grinned. His smile looked just like her daddy's. "I don't have any practice, but I could probably pull off a pretty good big brother routine."

Big brother. He seemed to like the role. No need to spoil things until she thought more about what she'd overheard.

"I'm a nerd," she said. "Too busy with school stuff to date." She'd had boys who were interested, but no one she liked. The really good-looking guys were mostly jerks. That didn't leave many options. In her mind, she saw Duncan Cranford leaning against the column at the funeral home, then told herself she should aim for somebody in her league. "I'll keep you posted, though, if circumstances change."

"Sounds good," he said. "Are you all right with it if, you know, I ask your friend out to a movie or something?"

"Yeah," she said. Was she? "Charlotte's great." She put the two of them side by side in her mind. She could handle that.

"Okay," he said, standing up. He took his plate to the sink and rinsed it. Then he put it in the dish drainer. His grandmother—*her grandmother*—had trained him pretty well.

"I'm going to bed," she said, standing, too. "I'll see you tomorrow."

"Night." He went back out to the back porch. She wondered if sleeping out there made him feel like the family pet.

"Night," she called to him. What had his room been like at her grandparents' house? She'd have to ask him more about them. As she left to go to her own shared room, she decided that the back porch wouldn't be so bad if she had it to herself.

With the grandmother she'd never met still fresh on her mind, she dried the plate Luke left to drain, then put it away. She heard music coming from the porch. She'd loaned him the small transistor radio she took to the pool with her, and he had it on.

Brother? Cousin? Did it matter so much? Maybe it didn't have to matter at all.

Twenty-eight

Roy got up early. He left Rosalind quietly, knowing she had to be tired. They'd both slept instantly after going to bed, but in the middle of the night—with a little rest behind them—they found each other. The dreamlike lovemaking took up a good chunk of the night and left them exhausted. Exhausted, but satisfied. That part of their world had been put to rights again, and in spite of the interruption of his sleep, Roy woke just after dawn, feeling that he could handle whatever the day brought him.

He looked in on Luke. The boy's lamp was on and static noise from a radio suggested the dying battery had been at it all night. Roy turned off the noise and the light.

Luke slept without fear—sprawled and vulnerable, his sheet in a tangle. He was naked waist-up, but still wore his jeans from the day before. They had something splattered on them. Paint.

He smelled paint, too, and when he looked out at the first light hitting the backyard he saw why. Janie Ray's swing set, a ramshackle setup left over from Lola's younger days, looked nearly new. All four legs were in the ground and the color looked the same as the blue metal of the front porch glider he'd painted earlier in the spring.

"What's wrong?" A groggy Luke squinted and looked up at him from the daybed.

"Did you fix the swing set?"

"Yeah." Luke raised himself up on his elbows. "I thought she'd like to use it again without having that one leg thump up and down."

"You painted it?"

Luke shrugged. A no-big-deal gesture. Roy recognized it as a way to deflect attention. He did the same thing when he felt self-conscious.

"Thanks," Roy said. "I appreciate that."

"Sure." Again the shrug. But Roy saw something else. Just a shade of a smile. Luke hadn't gotten much in the way of praise in his life. Probably next to none since his mom died. Roy would put money on that one.

"We're going to church this morning," Roy said. "You up for it?"

"I'm not sure I'm ready for my *debut* at church yet," Luke said, sitting up. "How do we explain me?"

"We tell them I was married to your mother before I moved here," Roy said. "They'll gossip. They already are, I guess, after our little scene at the grill. No way around it. But you're here and I won't pretend you're not. I'm not ashamed of you, Luke. This isn't easy on anybody, but you're a good kid." He sat on the edge of the daybed. "When everybody settles down, that's what they'll start noticing."

"You caught me in the dark last night with a half-naked girl," Luke said. "I'm not sure that makes me any kind of Boy Scout."

"Rosalind tells me that the half-naked girl in question probably had a lot more to do with it than you did," Roy said. "Is that right?"

"Yes, sir." Luke looked grateful.

"Just be careful," Roy said. "You know as well as anyone that you're not just held accountable for what you do, but for what it looks like you've done. I know it all too well myself. And while the Good Lord probably knows the difference, that part doesn't always seem to matter to most folks here below."

"It matters to you," Luke said. He looked like he might say something more, but didn't.

"Yeah, it does." Roy knew he wanted answers. Luke wanted to know why Roy hadn't been around for his whole life. He could tell him why, but would that make things easier or harder for Luke to handle? Harder probably, knowing the truth about his mom and Mont.

"I didn't know your mother had died," Roy said. "I would have stepped up sooner to see what I could do for you if I'd known." As the words left his mouth, Roy wondered if they were true. He liked to think they were. "I have reasons I can't explain for not showing up in your life before. I can't go into them now, and I'm sorry about that. But I'm happy to be here in your life now if you can accept that."

"I'm working out everything in my mind," Luke said. "It's all happened pretty quick."

"I know. It's like that for all of us."

"I used to hate you," Luke said, the words rushed out as if they'd been stored and spring-loaded for a long time. He stopped there, but still seemed to be searching for what he needed to say.

Roy didn't say anything. He didn't know any more than Luke what to feel. When he looked at the swing set in the yard, it really got to him. All the effort it took to fix it. Somewhere deep down, Luke had to want their approval.

"I don't hate you now," Luke said, finally. "You've been decent. More than I would have guessed. I don't know what to make of it."

"Of what?" Roy asked.

"The difference between the way I thought you were and the way you really are," Luke said.

Roy thought again of the truth behind it all. Unburdening himself would offer such relief. But for the second time, Luke would be stuck with a father who hadn't claimed him. Only this time, it would be a man who'd been there all along.

Luke looked up to Mont, and as much as Roy would like to be vindicated, he knew nothing good could come of taking Mont down. Not to mention Sherry. To hear that his mother had slept with her brother-in-law wouldn't really be the whole story anyway. Like Rosalind said, they held some responsibility. The waters had calmed some on the surface. Better to leave them that way.

Luke stared at him, the questions still showing all over his face.

"You think we might let the past go for the time being?" Roy asked. "I'm not saying you're wrong to have questions. I wouldn't insult you like that. But if we could take the here and now and just see what happens, I think something good could come of it."

"Okay," Luke said. "I guess."

"And Luke," Roy added, "be patient with Rosalind. She's been knocked sideways with all this and a lot of other things lately."

Luke nodded, but didn't comment one way or the other.

Roy looked again at the backyard. The sun had come up fully

and he could see that Luke had done a good job. "When did you actually do all that work out there?"

"I got the post in cement before the girl caused such a ruckus last night," Luke said, grinning. "Then I couldn't sleep in the middle of the night, so I got up and started painting."

Roy wondered if Luke had heard him and Rosalind, if that woke him up. Not something he could ask the kid.

"Well, that's really something," Roy said. "You'll be one little girl's hero, for sure." He turned to go back into the house. "Let me know if you change your mind about church."

Luke shook his head. "Don't think so."

On his way through the kitchen, Roy turned the AC unit on high so that things would stay cool enough for Luke out there. In spite of everything wrong that had happened, Roy felt he might have just done something right.

Twenty-nine

For the second time in as many days, Luke found himself at Roy's house alone. By this time, though, he felt curious about the new family he'd stumbled into. He walked through the empty house and went into Roy and Rosalind's room first. He didn't want to snoop, he just felt like getting a clear picture of the place and these people. The bed was made and a stack of magazines sat on the floor by one side. Judging from the kind of magazines, Luke knew it was Rosalind's side. *Better Homes and Gardens*, *Woman's Day*, and *Life*.

He went out of the room. A window in the hall looked out at the backyard, but the view was blocked because they'd put an air conditioner like the one in the kitchen inside that window, too. The unit hummed on low, keeping that end of the house livable, if not cool. The rest of the house consisted of the girls' room and the other parts he'd seen. Overall, there wasn't much to the whole place, not compared to Nanny and Pap's house.

Stem to stern it was only four rooms, if you didn't count the two bathrooms or the makeshift bedroom they'd rigged up for him on the back porch. The washer and dryer sat in a closet at the back of the kitchen.

It seemed funny to him that he'd begun to wonder what it would have been like to grow up in Linton Springs. He didn't want to be disloyal to the memory of his mom, but she had enough trouble looking after herself, so he'd begun to take care of himself early on. When she died, he was really sad, but he thought at least Nanny and Pap might seem more like real parents to him than his mom. Turns out they did, just not in any of the ways he wanted. They were good at discipline. *Keeping him in line.* But Nanny did feed him and wash his clothes. Pap let him drive the old Buick. That was something, he guessed.

But one thing he'd realized in the days since leaving Virginia—Roy was the kind of parent he'd wanted back then. He couldn't think about that too much or he'd get sad, or worse, mad, that Roy didn't come get him sooner. He wanted to be done with feeling both of those things.

A knock at the front door made him jump. When he opened up, a young guy, about his age, maybe a little older, stood on the other side of the screen door.

"Hey," the guy said, "I'm Duncan Cranford. My granddaddy and I are moving in next door and I thought I'd come by and let everybody here know what we're up to so the noises don't take anybody by surprise."

"Hey, I'm Luke Vines," Luke told him. He opened the screen door and let the guy in. "I'm the only one here. The rest of the family's at church."

"Oh, right," Duncan said, shaking his head, "it *is* Sunday, isn't it? The place that burned down was my grandparents' house. Ever since the fire, all the days have run together. My grandma died in the fire. Her funeral is this afternoon."

"I heard about that," Luke said. "I'm really sorry."

"Did you know her?" Duncan asked.

Something about the way the guy asked the question made Luke wish he could say yes. Truth was, she was already dead by the time he set foot in Linton Springs.

"No," he said. "I just got here. Roy's my daddy, but I've been living with his folks, my grandparents, up in Virginia. I don't know anybody yet."

"Well, you know me now," Duncan said. He stuck out his hand and Luke shook it. "I haven't been here much, either," Duncan went on. "I've been living with my mama in Creston. I'm just moving out here to help Granddaddy. Grandma's passing has been hard on him. Hard on all of us. She was a terrific old lady."

Luke didn't know what to say. He'd already said he was sorry about the accident. He'd been on the other side of similar conversations after his mom died and, even though he'd been real young, he remembered he'd just wanted the subject to change every time.

"Is that your car out there?" Luke asked. Through the front window, he could see a blue Mustang in the duplex's shared driveway.

"Yeah," Duncan said. "Nice, huh?"

"Damn!" Luke stared at the car. "It's beautiful."

"When I bought it," Duncan said, "the thing was a mess. I've spent two years and every dime I can get my hands on fixing her up."

"You in school?" Luke asked.

"I was for a semester," the guy told him. He looked out the window as he talked, and Luke got the feeling he'd been asked that question a lot. "I had a baseball scholarship to Wake, but I hurt my hand. Couldn't pitch anymore. Since then, I've been working in the pit crew for one of the Winston franchises."

"That's better than college," Luke said. He wasn't just trying to make the guy feel better. He meant it.

"I should get back to Granddaddy," Duncan said. "We've only moved one chair and a television in so far and I left him sitting there, staring at reruns. We're getting beds and a few other things in tonight after the funeral, then we'll go from there, I guess."

"You need any help," Luke said, "let me know."

"Thanks, I'll do that. And hey," Duncan added, his face breaking into a smile, "if you want to go for a ride sometime, I'll let you drive her."

"I'll take you up on it," Luke told him.

In a moment, Luke heard noises from next door, and he found it comforting. He didn't feel like being alone anymore, and he didn't have to hide from the whole town. Roy had said so himself. He went into his room where his things still sat piled on top of the suitcase he'd brought from Virginia. He found his best pair of pants—permanent press khakis—and a polo shirt that, while not exactly clean, wasn't too wrinkled and didn't smell. After he dressed, he went in Roy's room and found the keys to the truck lying on the bureau.

Careful to lock the door as he left, he got in the truck and fired the engine. Except for that first, awkward encounter at the grill, he'd kept himself pretty well hidden from Roy's larger world. He thought of Lola, heading back inside the restaurant to face down her family, not to mention the few customers who'd stayed. In spite of the shock at finding out she had a brother, she pulled herself together and went inside to deal with the situation. *Might as well get this over with*, she'd said. Nerve. That's what you needed to get by in this life. He'd take a page from his little sister. *Might as well get this over with.*

He pressed on the gas and felt the truck's momentum change, and when he came to the stop sign, he made the turn that would take him into town.

Thirty

Preacher Harlow talked about the Prodigal Son, a fellow who asked his daddy for his inheritance up front, and then blew it all immediately and had to eat with pigs just to stay alive.

Lola sat with her family near the front of the church. It was their pew. Four rows back from the pulpit. They sat there every Sunday.

"And not many days after the younger son gathered all together," the preacher chimed as Lola struggled to keep her eyes open, "he took his journey into a far country and there wasted his substance with *riotous* living."

Lola suspected that way down deep, the notion of riotous living sort of appealed to Preacher Harlow. The minister moved at a good pace and she knew he was building steam for the part about the feast. The reverend was rail thin, but he ate like a linebacker. He always got long-winded when he talked about food.

But just as the preacher had gotten to the part about killing the best calf to celebrate the foolish son's homecoming, Lola heard a movement in the pews behind them and a general mumbling from all around the sanctuary. Lola figured that Annie Lawson, who was as old as Jesus, had probably had another spell. Lola looked around to see if the old lady had fallen off the pew again.

Beside Lola, Janie Ray rose up onto her knees and turned backward to see what was going on. She started grinning and waving. Mama, determined to keep her focus on the preacher, slapped lightly at the younger girl's leg and whispered for her to sit down, but Janie Ray began motioning at someone in the back of the church.

Lola followed her little sister's gaze and saw what had caused the commotion. Luke stood in the entryway. Her throat caught a tight sound before it came out of her mouth. She heard the low mumbling of people around her grow into agitated bits of whispered conversation.

Luke caught sight of Janie Ray and stepped forward into the aisle. Lola watched him in those nervous moments. As he came toward them, he grew in her mind's eye, like a shadow grows when light comes in sideways and stretches a body out for miles. Lola wondered if other people were seeing him like that. He seemed larger than the entire room.

She glanced around the church. The Benson family sat in the very front pew. Charlotte and Shelby turned in unison to see him and they both looked as if they'd just caught sight of a new pony on Christmas morning.

Preacher Harlow pushed on with a valiant effort at regaining control of his congregation, but it soon became clear that his cause was lost. He wrapped up with an abbreviated platitude that Lola had heard a million times before. Something about

Jesus' rejoicing at finding the one lost lamb. Sheep always stood for something other than livestock in the Bible.

"Hey," Luke whispered as he sat down at the end of their pew beside Lola.

Lola glanced at Mama, who wore a look of pure horror. Daddy just seemed confused at Luke's untimely arrival. Lola fought to overcome her own embarrassment at being the focus of the entire gathering. Mostly, she felt sorry for newfound-sort-of-half-brother who seemed to catch on pretty fast that Janie Ray was the only one in the family happy to see him.

"Let's stand for hymn number 167." Preacher Harlow sounded entirely defeated.

As the hymn built in earnest around them, Luke bent down toward Lola's ear and said, "This was a mistake, wasn't it?"

"Yeah," Lola said in low tones, "but don't act like it. After church, compliment people. If you get them talking about themselves, they'll love you. It'll be okay."

He glanced down the pew at the rest of the family.

"Your mama's going to have my ass." He looked as if he might be sick.

"Not till we get home. Turn on the charm and you'll be fine," Lola said. "Start with the big lady wearing blue up there." Lola nodded toward Mrs. Lytleman. "If you win her over, the rest of them will melt like ice cream."

He nodded, mouthed the word "sorry" toward Lola's mama and daddy. Daddy gave him an encouraging nod, but Mama held her hymnal in an iron grip that might as well have been Luke's throat. She sang as if her life depended on it.

"Pride's got her back up at the moment. She'll settle down before we get home." She didn't believe it for a second, but he needed all the courage he could muster for coffee hour, so she did her best to build him up.

* * *

"So who is your mama exactly?" Vicky Benson wasted no time getting to the point with Luke.

Lola stood near enough to hear. She planned to jump in and help if Mrs. Benson got too obnoxious.

"Her name was Sherry Vines," Luke told her. "She died when I was little and I lived with my grandparents after that." He didn't say how little he was when she died, but Lola knew that he hadn't been a baby. Still, he seemed to be trying to protect Daddy by keeping it vague. "It makes me sad to think about her dying so young," he added. "I don't really talk about it much. You have a beautiful home." He changed the subject. "I walked by and saw all your flowers. I bet it takes a lot of effort to keep it like that."

Smooth. Lola was impressed.

"You wouldn't believe what it takes." Vicky Benson was off and running, talking about watering schedules and the sort of dirt necessary to keep the plants healthy. She wouldn't remember until she got home that she'd intended to pry deeper into Luke's story.

Later, she heard him telling Mrs. Lytleman that he had a favorite aunt who wore that color of blue and he thought it was just about the prettiest color in the world. As a compliment, Lola thought that one might be too obvious, but the old lady bought it.

"It takes skin that's never been in the sun to wear this color," she said, holding up a hat that could have doubled as an umbrella. "Anything other than porcelain skin will make this bright blue look too cheap. My Harvey, God bless him, used to say that when I wore this dress, it looked like blue water against white sand."

There's an ocean of water in that dress, not to mention more than a beach full of sand in her arms alone. The thought flashed through

Lola's mind and she felt bad at being so mean in the church reception hall.

"He's doing okay," Lola said when Mama brought her coffee over and stood beside her. "Everybody likes him."

"Especially those Benson girls," Mama said, pointing to where Luke now stood, flanked by the sisters.

Shelby leaned in and touched her shoulder to his arm while she talked, but Lola saw him smile at Charlotte.

"You ought to warn him off that older one again," Mama said. She'd relaxed a little. "Shelby's too much like her mama to be good news for any boy. He ought to know that after the other night."

"I told him," Lola said. "I don't think he's interested in her. He likes Charlotte, though."

"That'd be okay. Charlotte's got sweet ways." Mama took a sip of her coffee.

"You're starting to get used to him, aren't you?" Lola asked. She kept her voice casual, but she wanted to hear how Mama would answer.

"I've never thought ill about him," Mama said. "Nothing that happened is his fault. He just brings to mind difficult times. That's all."

"What happened back then?" Lola asked. "Nobody will tell me the whole story. Luke won't say much of anything." Lola thought of what she'd overheard the night before. She wondered if they ever planned to tell Luke the truth.

"It's not my story to tell, really," she said. "Contrary to what your daddy's parents think, I didn't go with your daddy while he was married." She looked around to make sure no one else could hear the conversation. "Luke's mama did some things that left Daddy no choice but to leave her." She spoke in barely a whisper to make sure. "I won't go into any more than that. But your daddy wasn't a terrible person to Sherry, or anyone else."

Lola saw Daddy looking over their way, and Mama motioned her head toward the door. Mama's color had grown pale. "Are you feeling bad?" she asked.

"Just tired," Mama said. "I've got food ready at the house and after we eat, I think I'll get a little nap in before Minnie's funeral this afternoon. I need to rest up a bit for work tomorrow."

"When's your next doctor's appointment?" Lola hadn't asked much about her mama's medical problems.

"Daddy's going to drive me over to my doctor's appointment on Thursday," she said. "The specialist—a hematologist—there knows everything there is to know about my problem. He'll fix me right up." She talked about it like it was a cavity in her tooth, but Lola knew better.

"Hey, you ladies ready to go?" Daddy walked over. Luke followed carrying Janie Ray.

Luke's presence had gone from unbelievable to almost normal in just a couple of days. He'd even turned his terrible decision to show up in the middle of the service into a chance for people to see that he was okay.

"Oh, I forgot to tell you," Luke said as they went out of the church hall and across the lawn to the parking lot, "the old guy who lost his wife in the fire is moving in next door with his grandson."

"That makes sense," Mama said. "Alva would want to be near his house as they sort through what's left down there."

"Duncan's going to be next door?" Lola asked no one in particular, her voice high and off pitch. Daddy gave her a funny look.

"Duncan," Luke said. "Yeah, that was his name. Works part-time with a pit crew for some guy's outfit. So he must know his way around cars pretty well. Drives an old Mustang he fixed up himself. Anyway, he seems like a great guy."

"Minnie doted on him," Mama said as she slipped into the

car's front seat. "She didn't mention her daughter, that mother of his, all that much, but she talked about the grandson all the time. I think he's in college somewhere."

"He was," Lola said, trying to sound casual. "He had a baseball scholarship to Wake Forest, but then he hurt his hand and had to drop out. He wants to go back when he can afford it."

"Wake Forest," Mama said. "That's right. Too bad about his hand."

Lola could barely keep her thoughts on the conversation. All she could think about was Duncan living right beside her. Sixteen years and she'd never counted on anything of consequence happening in her life. Not one damn thing out of the ordinary. Then suddenly she had nothing but surprises. How could she get homework or anything else done, just *knowing* that Duncan was walking around on the other side of one thin wall?

"Your color's up, child," Mama said, smiling. "What's on your mind?" She looked way too pleased with her own teasing.

"Hush," Lola said, followed by "Ouch!" as she got in the back seat and the hot vinyl interior burned her legs. "We ought to get cloth seats." She felt fully irritated with her entire family.

"Come on and ride in the truck with me," Luke said, putting Janie Ray down.

She got out of the car and followed the boy who would be her brother, but her thoughts returned to the boy now living next door. Let her family make fun of her. It didn't matter. Regardless of all the ups and downs of the previous days, the fact remained, Duncan would only be a couple of layers of sheetrock away.

"What are you smiling about?" Luke said as they got into the truck.

"Nothing," she said.

He rolled his eyes at her and let it go.

Thirty-one

The blue Mustang Luke had mentioned was in the driveway and it got Rosalind's attention. She thought Lola and Alva's grandson might be a cute pair, but the car gave her a whole new perspective. Did she want Lola riding off with a boy in a car like that? She didn't think so. But it was possible the train had already left the station on that one. Clearly, from Lola's perspective, it had.

"I'll have food out in a few minutes," Rosalind said when they all got into the house. "I ought to take something over to our new neighbors, although I expect they're elbow high in casseroles at this point. The funeral's this afternoon. You going with me, Roy?"

"I'd rather not," he said, "but I won't make you go alone."

"I'll go," Lola said. She worked at sounding offhand, but Rosalind knew better. "Daddy can stay with Janie Ray."

"That's what we'll do then," Rosalind said.

Lola went out back. Luke stood near the newly resurrected swing set, pushing Janie Ray. They couldn't keep their youngest off the swings for another second, but Roy said the quick-dry cement seemed to be holding.

"Sounds like Lola's got a crush." Roy poured himself a glass of tea and sat at the table.

"She's got it bad," Rosalind said.

"Isn't he too old?"

Rosalind smiled. Roy still saw Lola as a child. "He's barely nineteen," she said. "I chatted a bit with his mama at the funeral home. Seems like a nice family. And Lola will be seventeen in two months. Although that car worries me a little."

The phone rang.

"The car's the only thing that doesn't worry me," Roy told her, getting up to answer it.

Rosalind pulled out the pork roast she'd already cooked and put it in the oven to heat through. She'd get out the potato salad next.

"Hello." The smile faded from Roy's face, replaced by a scowl when he heard the voice on the other end of the phone. "What's on your mind?" he said.

He listened for what seemed to Rosalind like a long time. She made iced tea and put rolls in the oven to warm. Out back, Lola and Luke took turns pushing Janie Ray, who'd stay there all day if they didn't tell her it was time to stop.

"It'll be up to him," Roy said finally, with the grim demeanor holding its course. "He's not a damn yo-yo, Mont. The three of you can't order him out of town, then tell him he has a summons to return. He's got feelings."

Mont wanted Luke to come back and not stay the whole summer with them as planned. Rosalind should have been glad after all he'd stirred up. But something in her balked at the notion. Part of it had to do with the fact that she couldn't stand for Mont to have his way with one phone call, but that wasn't all of it. She'd warmed a little toward Luke. His efforts with the swing set touched something in her. If she felt it even a little, Roy felt it more, and the girls treated Luke like the brother they thought he was.

"I know I didn't want him at first, but that's not the point here," Roy said, his voice rising.

Another pause, and Rosalind saw the color come up in Roy's face. She rarely saw him mad, and it always surprised her when it happened. "I'm not working any angles." Roy defended himself against whatever accusations Mont had hurled. "The money we agreed on will ease things for us, but I'm not asking for or expecting anything more. I don't want your damn fortune, Mont. Take whatever Mama and Daddy signed over to you and make yourself president for all I care. I don't give a damn what you do, just stop jerking me around. And most of all, stop jerking that kid around. He deserves better."

Roy looked spent. Rosalind went to him, laid an open hand on his cheek. He quietly kissed the top of her head as he listened to his brother.

"I didn't mean to lose my temper, Mont," he said. "I just think that, at some point, you have to acknowledge that Luke is a person with feelings."

Mont must have been good and alone, because even Rosalind could hear him as he declared loudly into the phone, "He's my son, Roy. I can work this out any way I see fit."

That was a new one. Mont using his paternity to *help* him win an argument.

"Why don't you ask him whose son he is?" Roy stayed surprisingly calm as he said this. "That's the answer that matters, don't you think? You let him believe things about me his whole life, and now he's getting to know me and you can't stand it." He glanced around to make sure no one else had come into the kitchen, and Rosalind motioned outside to let him know that the kids were still out of the house.

Rosalind couldn't make out Mont's response, but the whole conversation left Roy looking as if he'd had the wind knocked out of him.

"We're sitting down to Sunday dinner right now, Mont," he said. "I'll talk to Luke and have him call you later." After a moment he said, "I'm not trying to play a game, Mont." A weary resignation had come over him. "I know he's only seventeen, but you're not his legal guardian, either, Mama is. She made that clear when all of you forced him to go with me. Maybe she agrees with you about bringing him back, but I don't hear her making this phone call. I'll tell Luke straight up that you want him to come back. I think we ought to let him make up his mind what he wants to do."

Roy hung up the phone. Rosalind put her arms around his waist, and she felt him tighten his grip around her. She was used to feeling shielded by him, but this time, he seemed to be the one in need of protection.

"Do you think Luke wants to go back?" she asked.

"Two days ago, that's all he wanted," Roy said. "Now . . . I don't know."

"You don't want him to go," she said.

Roy sighed. "I'm sorry," he said. "None of this has been fair to you. If having him go back is best for you, I'll just tell him he needs to go."

She kept her face against his chest, listened to his heart inside thin walls of skin and bone. Something tugged at her. The thought of Luke in that house in Virginia. Luke, the spitting image of her husband as a much younger man. But it wasn't just the outside of him that seemed so similar. He had some of Roy's tenderness in him, too.

"See what he wants," she said. "But that house up there can't be good for anybody with a fully functioning heart. He can stay if he wants."

Roy pulled her tighter against him.

"Hey, both of you, cut it out!" a smiling Lola said, coming in from the backyard, just ahead of Luke and Janie Ray. "You've got a room to yourselves for that sort of stuff."

"If we didn't like *this sort of stuff*, Miss Lola, you wouldn't be here," Rosalind said, laughing. Only when she saw the strained look come over Luke's face did she realize how hard her words would be for him to hear. If Lola was conceived in love, where did that leave him?

"Grab a plate and serve yourselves," she said. "The roast should be warm and there are potatoes and rolls on the table." No need to backtrack. The damage could not be undone.

Luke picked up a plate from the table, but stood back and waited for the girls to go first. Rosalind was impressed with his thoughtfulness, especially considering the pack of wolves that had raised him for over half his life.

"Help yourself, Luke," she said. "Hope you like pork."

"Yes, ma'am, I do," he said.

Roy's uncharacteristic silence unnerved her, and she dreaded the toll his coming talk with Luke would take on him. Maybe he shouldn't tell the boy the whole truth about his mother and Mont. For the first time since Roy had arrived home with him, she understood what that news would do to Luke. If he deserved any small amount of goodness in his life, her family might be his only hope.

As they sat down, took hands, and bowed their heads for

grace, Rosalind felt her fingers around Luke's hand. She offered a small squeeze, and to her surprise, he returned it, which for reasons not even she could explain, brought tears to her eyes.

As Roy petitioned for God "to bless this meal and the hands that prepared it," Rosalind sent up her own silent prayer for God to help her do right by all the people sitting around her table. Luke included.

Surprises were everywhere, it seemed.

Thirty-two

What the hell was Mont up to with that phone call? Roy went outside to smoke on the front porch after he'd finished eating. He could hear his family inside, talking and doing the dishes, but he was too agitated by his brother's change of direction to joke around.

Mont never did anything without a reason.

"Things have blown over here faster than I expected," Mont had said. "The deputy and the sheriff gave the impression that Luke was brought in for trying to pull off a senior prank. Nothing much came of the whole thing. You can put him in that car I loaned you and just send him back. He can finish up school like he planned."

He'd clearly expected no resistance from Roy and became angry and insulting when Roy balked. Why wouldn't Roy want Luke to go back to his old life? The boy had been gone only a couple of days. What Mont suggested wasn't that outrageous. The outrageous part was that they'd sent him away in the first place.

"Hey, Roy." Alva Thomas came down the steps on the other side of the duplex. He wore suit pants with a dress shirt opened at the collar. He paused at the bottom of Roy's stairs. "You mind if I come up and sit a minute?" the old man asked.

"Not at all, Alva," Roy said. "Come on up."

Alva's features looked ragged. Roy couldn't imagine what the old guy must have gone through in just a few days' time. He sat on the glider beside Roy's chair. The porch swing looked empty and forlorn, but it wasn't a day for rocking leisurely back and forth. Not for either of them.

"I guess you've got a hard afternoon ahead of you," Roy said. No use pretending that the funeral wasn't on the widower's mind.

"I guess so," Alva said. "My Minnie seems right here, though. Seems she can't be gone. I know it's true, but I can't get it straight in my head."

"I'm sorry I wasn't around when it happened," Roy said. "I was in Virginia on family business. I don't expect I could have done anything to help, but I would have tried."

"I appreciate that, Roy," Alva Thomas said. He bent forward and rested his elbows on his knees, as if sitting straight took too much out of him. "It was my own fault. I had a pile burning. I didn't take proper care to put it out and there was enough wind to spark the house. I'll never forgive myself."

Roy had obvious questions. It was spring and there were no leaves to burn. He didn't want to pry, but old Alva seemed to want to talk.

"Things happen, Alva. Minnie wouldn't have you blaming yourself. You know that."

Alva stared off into space and Roy wondered if he'd even heard him. The older man looked toward his property, and the grim set of his mouth seemed like something chiseled in stone.

"You've got children," Alva said, without explanation for the change of topic.

"Yes, sir," Roy said. "That's a fact."

"They're a joy," he went on, "but sometimes . . ."

Roy waited, sensed that whatever it was, Alva Thomas needed time to say it.

"I haven't been close with my daughter." He spoke up, finally. "She pulled away from me and Minnie both. Married a fellow over in Creston with more education and money than she came from and that seemed to be reason enough to leave us behind." He paused, took a breath, and sat back up in the chair. "Duncan, her son—the one who's over there with me now—he's stayed close. Kept coming even when she barely sent a card for the holidays.

"He's a good boy. In spite of everything that happened, he *is* a good boy." Alva spoke as if to convince himself. "He started growing some things out on my property. Way out to the side of my regular fields in a clearing just through the woods."

"Growing what?" Roy said. He remembered Rosalind saying that the smoke smelled funny. Suddenly, things were making more sense.

"That stuff they all smoke these days."

"Marijuana?" Roy asked.

Alva made a face, closed his eyes, and nodded. "He didn't have much land committed to it, but it got away from him. He had help. I guess you ought to know this, because it concerns you, too. I was planning to tell you when it was over and done with and then let you decide what you wanted to do."

What could that mean? Lola? Not possible. But the fear took hold of him anyway.

"Duncan met that fellow who works with you," Alva said. "Jerry."

Relief ran through Roy like blood through his veins.

"How'd they know each other?" Roy asked. He'd never seen Duncan around the garage.

"They met out here one time when the young guy dropped off something from work at your place. Duncan was here and they got to talking. Before long, this Jerry fellow was in on it with him. He wanted to make it a bigger deal. What Duncan tells me is that he was just growing it for himself and a few friends. Jerry wanted to clear a bigger piece of land out there and grow it to sell for a profit."

Good Lord. Roy felt weak. All this had been right under his nose and he never suspected a thing.

"I can't tell you what to do," Alva said, "but Jerry is bad news. I don't plan to turn him in because that would take my grandson down with him, but I'd take him off my payroll if I were you."

"He's already gone, Alva." Roy rubbed his eyes, tried to put the whole picture together in his head. "While I was in the mountains, he cleared out the register and took off in a customer's car. He had a pregnant wife, so I'm guessing she went, too, because nobody's seen either of them."

Alva nodded. It was his turn to put the rest of the puzzle together for himself, it seemed. "I guess I'm not surprised," he said. "I wouldn't have known about any of it. Not a thing. But about two weeks ago, when Duncan wasn't even around, I heard something going on over on the other side of those woods. I found Jerry out there in that patch where all that stuff was growing. I knew him from the garage. Confronted him. He came clean about what the two of them had been doing."

"Good God, Alva," Roy said. "I had no idea. I'm awfully sorry."

"Not your fault," Alva said. "These young ones, I don't understand what they're thinking. Maybe it's the times we're living in, I don't know. I'm just sorry I didn't tell you before. You could have fired him before he took your money and that fellow's car."

"So what did you tell him when you confronted him?"

"I threatened to call the law on him," the old man said. "I was mad as can be. It was an empty threat, but I guess he didn't know it if he took off on you like that. He must have been sitting there sweating, waiting to hear the sheriff's car in his driveway."

"When I went out of town for a few days," Roy finished the story, "he saw his chance."

"That sounds about right," Alva said. Then, almost as an afterthought, he said, "I pulled all that stuff up. I think he might have taken some with him from the looks of things, but what was there, I put in a pile to dry. Duncan came to see me and I guess to tend to his garden. I read him the riot act. Told him in no uncertain terms that I was doing away with what I found and there would be no more of it. Not on my property, and if he had any sense, not anywhere. He promised he was done.

"When it was good and dry, I put it in a pile to burn." He stopped there, didn't need to explain any more.

Roy looked at the old man and could feel the ache that went through his whole body. It was worse than a physical pain. Roy had felt a small piece of that ache when Rosalind said she'd had some bad news from the doctor. Alva's hurt had taken over. It had won, and there was no way back to where he'd been in life with his precious Minnie.

"I should get back over there." Alva stood up. "We need to leave for the church soon. I'll ask you to keep our talk in confidence for my grandson's sake. I was angry, but in the end, what happened was more my fault than his. He's what I've got now."

"I'll talk with Rosalind," he said. "I don't keep secrets from her, but that will be the end of it. You have my word."

"I appreciate it," he said. "I owed it to you since your work fellow was involved, but I've been dreading even saying it all out loud. I'm sorry I didn't come to you sooner when I first found him out there."

"Don't apologize, Alva," he said. "What I've lost is an inconvenience. Your whole life has been taken from you. I'm going to be keeping my youngest here, but Rosalind and Lola will be there to pay all our respects at the funeral."

"That oldest girl of yours," Alva said. "Lola? She's a special one. I can tell."

"She is that."

Alva Thomas stood up and started down the stairs, but midway on the first step, he stopped and turned around. "Are you alone at your place up there now?"

"What place?" Roy asked.

"Your work. If that Jerry took off, you're by yourself, then?" Alva seemed to be thinking while he talked.

"For now," Roy said. "But it's okay. With the interstate and business slowing down, I kept him on more for him than for me." Roy felt a shot of anger go through him just thinking of his foolishness in trying to do the right thing by Jerry.

"Duncan's good with cars," Alva said. "Real good. He works with those fellows that race sometimes in the . . . Oh, what does he call it? The pit crew. Seems to me he owes you for starting this whole mess. And he'll do anything for me. I know that much. Why don't you plan on having him give you a hand with whatever you need up there."

"Alva—" Roy began to protest, but the old man put up his hand.

"It'll help him work off his guilt," he said. "Let him do it. He's not a bad kid. And I believe him when he says he's done with that other mess. He gave me his word, and you have mine."

Roy nodded. He went over and put his hand on the old guy's shoulder. "Okay, Alva," he said. "Thank you."

Without saying more Alva went down Roy's stairs and up the other identical set to his own porch. Roy watched him go into his place, ready to offer some final gesture of sympathy, but the old man never looked back.

Thirty-three

From his porch room, Luke could see the house where those two girls lived. One of them, he couldn't tell which one, had stretched out to sunbathe on a lounge chair in the backyard. Luke strained to make out her features. But the plastic Roy put up to keep the cool air inside made everything look wavy, so he walked outside on the top step to get a better view.

It was the one he liked. Charlotte, the one who was friends with Lola. He wanted to go talk to her, but wondered if it would be weird to just walk over there. Hell, she was outside. He decided not to analyze the whole damn thing and just go talk to the girl.

"Hey," he called out when he was still a good distance away. He didn't want to sneak up on her.

She sat up and held her hand over her eyes like a visor. When she saw him, she grinned and waved.

"Mind if I sit with you for a few minutes?" he asked. How stupid was that to say?

"Sure," she said. She wore sunglasses, so he couldn't tell where she was looking exactly. It made him nervous. "I'm bored out of my mind, so you came just in time." Her hair color fell in between blond and brown. A description could go either way and not be wrong. She wore it in a ponytail, but stray pieces fell out of the band. She looked really good.

As he got closer, he saw that her body was even better than he'd thought at first. He had some friends who were into skinny girls and this one wouldn't do the trick for them, but for his money, a little bit of round in all the right places made a girl perfect—and this one was just about perfect. The tiny bathing suit didn't leave him wondering about much of anything.

"My mama and daddy are at Minnie Thomas's funeral," she said. "I think Shelby must be with them, so I'm here by myself." She stopped to take a small breath, then started up again. "I should have gone to Mrs. Thomas's funeral, but I get really creeped out by those things. I figure I'll visit Mr. Thomas when he's lonely someday and that'll make up for it. She was a really nice old lady."

"That's what everybody says." He couldn't get his eyes to stay on her face when she was talking.

"She did nice things all the time," she said. "And she baked better cakes than anybody. People loved her."

What he had to remember was that the bitch of a sister had a good body, too—he'd gotten an eyeful without even asking—but he liked this one because of other things. He had to take his time and talk to her instead of acting like some horny fourteen-year-old. But damn, it'd be easier if she was wearing something other than those tiny little pieces of blue cloth.

"So keep me company," she said, standing up. "I'll get you a chair." She walked across the patio and dragged another lawn chair over to where she'd angled hers toward the sun.

"Want something to drink?" she asked.

"Sure." A little recovery time. That would help.

"What do you like?"

"Whatever you have," he said. "I like anything." He focused on a corner of the house where a gutter had come loose from the roof. It'd be pretty easy to fix that.

She went inside and he sat down. A small vegetable garden took up a patch of yard near the back. Green tomatoes hung on the vine, but nothing else planted had grown much.

"Here you go," she said, coming out with two glasses of what looked like Coke and handing him one. She had put on a sheer cover-up that helped a little, but her tanned legs gave him plenty to appreciate.

"So you and Lola have been friends since you were little, huh?" he asked.

"Forever," she said. "It's weird she didn't know she had a brother. You look just like her dad."

"Yeah, it's crazy," he said, unsure about which part of her observation he was supposed to respond to—his resemblance to Roy or his existence in general.

"Did you graduate already?" she asked.

"I go back to graduation in a week and a half," he said.

"Really?" She made a face. "Why didn't you just stay until then?"

"There was some family trouble in Virginia," he said, "so I came here while they're sorting it out. I've lived with my grandparents since my mom died when I was nine."

"Yeah," she said. "That's the other bizarre part. Lola thought those guys, your grandparents, were both in a cemetery somewhere already. All this time and she didn't know they were still kicking. I always thought I was the one with the screwed-up family. Hers always seemed like nothing but normal. Man, when you told me her dad was married before . . . Holy shit."

The girl talked a lot. He wanted to get her off the subject of his situation with Roy, but that was all she knew about him, he guessed. And in some ways, he liked the fact that she said what she was thinking. She didn't dance around stuff like everybody else. Besides, what she said was true. Why not get it out there? Maybe he could even play it for a little sympathy.

"My grandparents are good people," he said. "But I always wished that I had a dad around."

"It's sad," she said. "I think Mr. Vines missed out, too."

"How's that?"

"Lola told me once—a long time ago—that she thought he would have liked to have a boy, along with the two girls," Charlotte said. "If he knew about you, and if he wanted a boy, he must have thought staying away might be better for you or something. I mean, he's a really nice man. I've never seen him do anything to hurt anybody. He and my daddy are good friends. They're a lot alike that way."

Luke's head hurt. Maybe he'd gotten too much sun or maybe he'd just gotten too worked up over Charlotte, but he felt like hell. A little dizzy. He braced his elbows on his knees and lowered his head a little, looked up at her, and managed a weak smile.

"Are you okay?" she asked. She took off her sunglasses, and her forehead had a faint line of pink sunburn above where the glasses had been.

"I don't know," he said. He couldn't get his thoughts straight. "Yeah, I'm fine. I get light-headed sometimes. My mom used to do that once in a while and I guess I do it, too."

"I'm sorry," Charlotte said, leaning over and putting a hand on his arm. "I run my mouth too much sometimes. I guess I'd make anybody dizzy."

"No," he said. "It's not that. I promise."

Her hand felt soft against his skin. As turned on as she got him, what he felt with her hand there was something different.

It was comforting. It reminded him of the way he'd felt at lunch when Rosalind squeezed his fingers before Sunday dinner, or when Roy talked to him and didn't get mad after the Shelby thing. It made him feel safe. He knew Nanny and Pap cared about him. Mont, too. They had their own ways of showing it. But he hadn't felt safe like that since his mom died. With the rest of them up there in Virginia, things could always turn.

He looked up at Charlotte's face again. He took in her expression, and it occurred to him that even with everything else she had going for her, those eyes were the prettiest part of her.

He smiled and she smiled back. He knew he could have kissed her and it would have been okay, but for the first time in his life, he wanted to do everything the right way with a girl. His head had cleared a little, so he took a deep breath and straightened up.

"I should go back," he said. "I didn't tell anybody I was leaving."

"Okay." She nodded, took a sip of her drink. His glass of Coke sat sweating on the patio table beside his chair and he hadn't even picked it up yet.

He took a sip, more to be polite than anything else, then he looked at her again. "Would you like to do something some-time?" he asked. "Get something to eat or go to a movie?"

"Yeah," she said. "I'd like that. The only movie real close by is a drive-in. My mama would freak out, but if we kept it quiet that'd be okay. Shelby goes all the time."

"That's okay. We can get some food somewhere," he said. "I don't want to end up on your mama's bad side if I can help it. Maybe this weekend. Saturday or something?"

"Saturday's good."

"Okay." He felt a surge of energy, but tried to act normal. "Good. I'll talk to you before then and we'll figure out where. I don't know what's around here."

"Okay," she said again. "That sounds good."

As he walked back across the stretch between their houses, he resisted the urge to turn around. She'd already said yes and he could only hurt himself by getting too eager. But he felt her back there. The breeze picked up behind him, and for the first time in a long time, everything seemed good.

Roy was sitting on the back porch steps when he got to the house.

"Visiting Charlotte?" Roy asked.

"Just walked down to say hi."

"Pretty girl." Roy shielded his eyes from the sun.

"Yes, sir," Luke said. "She is. You didn't go to the funeral?"

"I offered to stay home with Janie Ray. She's too little to sit through it without making noise," he said. "And Rosalind's better at that stuff than I am, anyway. Lola went with her."

"I could have kept Janie Ray for you," Luke said as he sat down on the stair beside Roy.

"Yeah," he said. "I thought of that, but Rosalind didn't, so I didn't bring it up." Roy was smiling. "I thought the world of old Minnie Thomas, but I think she'd forgive me for sitting this one out and paying my respects from here."

"Where is Janie Ray?" Luke asked. The little girl made a habit of hanging around him when she was awake. He'd gone a whole hour or more without seeing her.

"Bass fishing show is on television," Roy said. "For some strange reason, the child loves to watch men fish. She'll sit there as long as there's a man in a boat throwing a line. Get her talking about lures and you'll get an earful."

"Really?" Luke shook his head. "I'll be damned."

"She's a funny little thing, all right." Roy smiled.

A silence settled, and Roy's face went serious. Luke could hear the high, tinny sound of Charlotte's transistor radio from across the way, and he waited for Roy to bring up whatever might be on his mind. After a few minutes, Luke started to worry. He knew Rosalind had some kind of medical problem, but she couldn't have heard any bad news on a weekend.

"Is everything all right?" Luke asked, finally.

Roy shifted his weight, leaned back on the screened door, his forearm resting on one knee.

"Yeah . . . yeah. But I need to talk to you about something," Roy said. "I waited until the girls left so we'd have some time to ourselves."

"What is it?" Luke asked. "Did I do something? I told Rosalind I was sorry for making a scene at church like that. I wasn't thinking. But it turned out all right, didn't it?"

"No, it's not that," Roy said. "That all settled out fine. No, what I needed to tell you is that Mont called earlier today." Roy kept his eyes focused out into the yard, and he didn't look over at Luke, not once as he relayed the reason that prompted Mont's call. "Mont said that they all overreacted," Roy told him. "He said that he wants me to send you back. Said you could drive the Nova by yourself."

"When?" Luke asked. Questions raced through his head, but they wouldn't slow enough for him to put them into words.

"He called just after we got in from church," Roy told him.

"No, no," Luke said. "When would he want me to come back? I'm going back for graduation, you said. He wants me before then? For how long?"

Roy picked up a twig lying on the step beside him. He twiddled it in his fingers, still looking away from Luke.

"He said that if you come back right away, you won't have missed more than a couple of days of school. He's talking about you moving back, picking up where you left off."

Roy's mouth was set in a grim line. Luke couldn't tell what

the man was thinking. Damn it! When were they all going to stop fucking with him?

"What'd you tell him?" Luke asked.

"I said I'd tell you. It's up to you."

Maybe this was a relief to Roy. After all, daddy or not, Roy clearly hadn't been thrilled about bringing him to Linton Springs in the first place. Hell, Luke for sure hadn't been happy about coming. He thought Roy's feelings had softened over a couple of days, but it didn't sound like that was the case. Why wouldn't Roy and Rosalind both want him to leave? They were strapped for cash and he ate like a horse. And they had no room, for God's sake. He slept on a screened porch.

"Okay," Luke said. "I could go back."

Why didn't he want to? His whole life had been in Gray's Hollow. He'd known Roy Vines less than a week. Why did he feel like his world was crashing and burning when he was getting his old life back? He'd have summer with all his friends. Wasn't that what he wanted?

"Yeah," he said, his resolve settling in. "I guess I could leave tomorrow morning. I'd want to say good-bye to Lola and Janie Ray. And Rosalind. I know she wasn't real keen on me when I got here, but it's been decent of her to put up with this."

Roy nodded, glanced over and then away again. "Well, you know you have a place here as long as you want one." Roy's voice sounded flat. Obligatory. "I'm sorry we didn't have a better setup for you."

Luke felt like an idiot for reading more into his interaction with his newfound daddy. Roy wasn't the son-of-a-bitch Luke had always considered him to be, but he also wasn't the full-fledged father Luke had fashioned him into in such a short time. Clearly Luke had made Roy and the whole damn family into something *he* wanted them to be. Suddenly Luke felt sick. Literally, stomach-churning, puking sick.

"I think I might take a walk," he said, standing up.

As his head tried to sort through what had just happened, memories of a kid in grade school named Little Glenn came to mind. Little Glenn had foster parents instead of real ones, and one time he told Luke about his foster daddy punishing him by burning his arm with the end of a cigarette. He showed Luke the scab.

"It's okay, though," Little Glenn had said. "Most of the time, he's nice. It's just his temper gets the best of him sometimes."

Luke had met the man a lot of times. He seemed normal in every way. But clearly he could turn without much warning.

Luke didn't have scabs or scorched flesh as a result of his conversation with Roy, but he felt wounded all the same. He wondered how Little Glenn had lived with the uncertainty.

In the hot afternoon air, Luke set off. He hoped the nausea would subside before he hurled within eyesight of Roy. From a distance, Charlotte's radio whined like an insect over the short stretch of field between houses. Saturday. He'd told her they'd go out on Saturday, and now he'd be long gone by then. He thought of her hand, her small fingers, on his arm, and a sound caught in his throat. He was a few feet away from the back steps and Roy looked up.

"What's that?" Roy asked. "You say something?"

"No," Luke called back to him, but didn't turn around. "A gnat flew in my mouth."

Without another word, Luke headed toward the road. He'd walk away from the direction of Charlotte's house. He'd walk away from all of them, and he'd be damned if he'd ever look back.

Thirty-four

The air-conditioning unit at the church had given out sometime between the morning service and the funeral. The men from the funeral home distributed paper fans, the advertisement for their services becoming a wild blur as the fans moved in the hot air.

Lola listened to the preacher. She tried to conjure images of Mrs. Thomas and think sad thoughts. But the frenzy of the fans, coupled with a clear view of the back of Duncan's blond head, had her thoughts in all the wrong places.

By the time they all stood for the last hymn, "In the Sweet By and By," Lola's pulse raced at the notion of talking to Duncan again.

The music ended and the pallbearers rose and surrounded the casket. Lola thought of how sad Duncan must be at the thought of his grandmother, not only being gone, but being in that box. He'd said it was his fault and Lola still didn't understand how he could think that. He wasn't around when Mr. Thomas fired up all that dry brush, and during the fire, Duncan was the one who'd gone inside and pulled her out. It was too late, but still, he'd done all he could.

Lola filed out as her row emptied. Everyone followed the casket to the cemetery below the church. It hadn't rained in a while, so the ground felt solid, not muddy like she'd seen it before. She navigated around tombstones, glancing at names that nobody used anymore. Hester, Cleo, Bessie, and Fan. Pretty names, some of them. Lola wondered why they went out of style.

She settled at the back of the crowd with her mama a few feet away. From in front of her, she heard Annie Lawson whispering to Mrs. Lytleman loud enough for the words to carry beyond church property.

"The daughter, Ruthie, said she doesn't know what she's going to do with that young boy, the grandson," the old lady said. "Alva won't talk about it, but somebody said that the burning he was doing before the fire had something to do with getting rid of marijuana the boy was growing on Alva's property. Ruthie, his mother, I knew her when she was a little thing. She's beside herself."

Lola wished she would shut up. Everyone could hear her. She projected better in a whisper than the guest preacher from Ruthie's church in Creston did in his normal voice. The minister had been invited to say the graveside words, and Lola thought he looked too young to be a full-fledged preacher.

"The boy is living with Alva in one of those dinky rental units just up the road from the Thomas place," old lady Lawson continued. Lola's ears fired hot as the blood rushed to her face. "That can't be a very good idea. If he's hopped up on drugs, Alva can't control him. No telling what could happen."

Lola looked at Duncan, sitting with his mother and Mr. Thomas in the row of chairs lined up in front of the grave. If they heard the whisper shouts of Annie Lawson behind them, they didn't let on.

"That stuff takes you out of your mind, you know," Mrs. Lytleman added, in a still audible but slightly more appropriate range.

Lola felt Mama move past her and gently make her way up to the two older ladies. She whispered something to the women, and from the looks on their faces they weren't happy about what she said. Annie closed her mouth, her lips pressed in an angry pucker. Lola could see only the substantial back of Mrs. Lytleman, but her shoulders were squared in a defiant posture.

Mama made her way back to Lola, and the only sound, once again, was the slight breeze through the trees and the timid preacher extolling the virtues of a woman he'd likely never met.

After the graveside part of the service ended, Lola looked around for somebody she could talk to while she kept an eye on Duncan. She was mad at Charlotte for not coming. Shelby was there with Mr. and Mrs. Benson and that did Lola no good at all.

"Hi there, Lola." Mae Rose stepped up beside her. Lola almost didn't recognize her in church clothes. She'd never seen her in anything but the waitress-type uniform she wore every day at the Linton Grill.

"Hey, Mae Rose," Lola said. The woman was one of the few grown-ups that all the kids called by a first name. Lola never knew why, but that's just the way it was. "It was a nice service, huh?"

"It was nice," the woman said. "But I could bake chickens in that sanctuary."

"Yeah, I know," Lola said, relaxing. Mae Rose always said exactly what she thought. "I was afraid somebody might pass out from the heat before it was over. Did you know Mrs. Thomas pretty well?" she asked. Mae Rose didn't go to the Baptist church with them—or any church that Lola knew of.

"She made all those cupcakes I sell in the bakery case," Mae Rose said. "Best damn cupcakes in the state if you ask my opinion. She never would tell me what she added to give the icing that flavor, but I think it was almond extract. I ate more than I sold."

Lola smiled. She'd had the cupcakes herself, but never knew Mrs. Thomas made them. Mae Rose was right, they were the best.

"You need to rescue me." Duncan's voice, low and in her ear, startled her.

She turned her head to see him and found her face an inch or so from his. "What's wrong?" He smelled good. Aftershave or some earthy-scented soap.

"Those old ladies are on some kind of mission to drag me kicking and screaming toward redemption, best I can tell," he said. "That big one got in my face and asked if I wanted to hold hands and confess my sins. Who the hell just pops up and asks you to do that at your grandmother's funeral? It freaked me out."

Mae Rose smiled and gave Lola a pat on the arm along with a small wink Lola hoped Duncan didn't see. "I'll see you soon, Lola," she said, making an exit toward Mr. Thomas.

"Those two gossiped all during the graveside ceremony," Lola told him. She didn't say they'd been talking about him, and about the subpar living quarters that her family now shared with him and his grandfather.

"I just don't get some people," he said. "My grandma couldn't stand it when people butted their nose in her business."

Lola thought about Mrs. Thomas. Her friendly kitchen. That kitchen wasn't there anymore. It was kind of fitting that it went at the same time she did.

"Why didn't I know you growing up?" Lola asked. "We've lived where we are now since I was six. I guess I saw you some when you were younger, but I can't believe we never really talked before."

"I used to go all the time when I was a little kid," he said. "Until I got to be about eight or so. Then my mama had a big fight with them because they wouldn't go in with my daddy on some investment project. They didn't like him much and it turns out they were right. He ran off with a woman who worked in our eye doctor's office when I was fifteen. But anyway, Mama stopped going down there or taking me to visit."

"Were you mad at your grandparents, too?" Lola asked.

"No." He shrugged. "I always missed seeing them. After I got my license, I'd slip off sometimes and visit. Then this past winter, when I didn't go back to school, I started hanging out down there a lot. Mostly on weekdays, so I guess you were at school."

"I guess," she said. His cheeks were pink from standing in the sun. "Where is your family going after the funeral?" Lola asked. Usually family and close friends went back to the dead person's house, but the Thomas house was too damaged and the duplex too small.

"The church ladies set up something here in the reception hall," he said. "People got together and brought food here instead of the house." He closed his eyes for a second, took in a deep breath. "I gotta get out of here," he said. "I feel like I'm going to come out of my skin if I have to stand here and talk to people any more. Mama can drive Grandpa Thomas home. I just can't stay here."

Lola didn't know what to do. Had she said something wrong?

"Want to go with me?" he asked before she had time to say anything else.

"Right now?" Lola had a hard time not smiling. She wanted to be in that Mustang with him more than anything in the world. Would her mama let her? She had to handle it just right.

"Let me tell Mama," she said. "You better tell your family, too," she said. "You can't just leave or they'll worry about you."

"You're right," he said. "See, I need you around to keep my head on straight." This last part sounded like a flirting remark, but he didn't say it like one. Before she could decide, he'd gone off to tell his mama and grandpa he was leaving.

Lola presented the suggestion to Mama as casually as she could manage, but Mama wasn't fooled.

"This isn't just a ride home and you know it," Mama told her. "This is an older boy you like. I'm not saying that's bad, but you need to call it what it is. Judging from that car he drives, you can bet he's had a bit more experience with dating than you have."

"I'm not going on a date with him." Lola's voice went high and she looked around for whoever might have been in earshot. "I'm riding back to our house. It also happens to be his house. His grandma, who was a sweet lady I liked a lot, just died. He needs a friend."

Mama's eyebrow went up. Still not buying it, Lola thought. "I don't like gossip," she said, taking Lola's cue and lowering her voice. "But Lola, you heard those women as clear as I did. What if there's something to that business with the marijuana? Have you thought about that?"

"Miss Annie had everybody at Vacation Bible School thinking Janie Ray had lice," Lola said. "And all because Janie Ray kept scratching a mosquito bite on her head."

Mama had been furious with Annie Lawson the summer before. Mama told the old woman that if she didn't stop spreading things about her child, she was going to take her complaint to Preacher Harlow and suggest that he counsel her on the evils of idle gossip.

"I don't know, Lola," Mama said, clearly wrestling with herself over what to do.

"Head lice, Mama," Lola said. "The woman makes up half of what she says. And Mrs. Lytleman is worse. Don't you trust me? He's a good guy."

Mama looked over at Duncan. He had his hand on Mr. Thomas's shoulder and was saying something into the old man's good ear. Mr. Thomas nodded, offered a sad smile to his grandson.

"Okay," Mama said. "You're old enough to use your judgment. But if something seems off when you're around him, I have to trust you to keep yourself clear. Is that understood?"

"Yes, ma'am." Lola could barely keep still. In just a few minutes, she would be sitting in a car with Duncan Cranford. She knew she should feel worse about the circumstances. Mrs. Thomas had been laid in the ground, and all she could think about was Duncan's voice so close in her ear. But the old lady had liked her. She would approve. Lola felt sure of it.

"Hi, Mrs. Vines." Duncan came up beside her and said hello to her mama. "It's good to see you again."

"Tell your granddaddy to call on me anytime," Mama said, and Lola relaxed a little when she realized he wasn't going to get grilled about his driving or about going straight home.

"You ready?" He turned to Lola.

"Yeah," she said. "Should I say good-bye to your grandpa?"

"You'll see him at home," he said. "He's not hearing half of what people are saying to him at the moment anyway."

Lola said good-bye to her mama and they walked toward the graveled area where all the cars were parked.

"So," he said when they were away from the crowd. "I guess I'll be helping your dad out at the garage starting tomorrow."

This was news. "Daddy offered you a job?"

"More like my grandpa offered me for the job." He laughed,

but sounded a little nervous. "Not really a paying job. I'll just be giving a hand."

"Why?" It didn't sound like Daddy to let somebody work for free.

"I have some things to make up to my granddaddy," he said. "This is what the old guy wants, so this is what I'll do."

She waited for him to explain in more detail, but he'd finished, it seemed, and they'd reached the cars, so she let it drop. His Mustang sat in the shade and it looked out of place among all the sedans and trucks. He opened the door for her and the blue color made her feel as if she was sliding into a swimming pool.

"Hey, Duncan! Are you leaving? Can I get a ride back?" Shelby hurried from the edge of the cemetery to catch them before they drove off.

Lola had never liked Shelby, but she'd never really hated her before. At that moment, she purely despised Charlotte's big sister. Duncan shot Lola a look, but there was nothing they could do.

"Whew!" Shelby reached the car. "I'm dying to get out of here. Can I hop in?"

Poor choice of words at a funeral. Duncan either didn't notice or decided to ignore it, because the next thing Lola knew he'd agreed to let Shelby's slutty self get in with them. Lola had to get out and put her seat forward for the older girl to get in the back. For a second, Shelby hesitated as if she expected to take the front seat herself, but Lola put an end to that by motioning for her to get on in.

Once under way, Shelby leaned forward so that her head separated Lola and Duncan. "Thank God you were leaving," she said. "You got a cigarette? I'm dying for a smoke."

Dying again? What was it with her?

"Sure." Duncan pulled a pack of Newports out of his pocket and handed it to Shelby. He pushed in the cigarette lighter.

Lola tried to put Shelby's intrusion out of her mind. She closed her eyes for a second and let the wind rush at her through the open window.

"You got anything else to smoke?" Shelby asked. A teasing grin took over her smug face.

Duncan handed her the glowing lighter. "Nope," he said without elaborating or even looking back in her direction.

Lola glanced at her in time to see Shelby shrug in an offhand way that suggested she had to at least ask. "Too bad," she said. That's when Lola realized what she'd wanted. Maybe there was something to what old Annie Lawson had to say after all. Lola grudgingly took the lighter from her and put it away. As Shelby sprawled out, her smoke swirled in the open air of the car.

Lola had the notion that she looked all too comfortable there. She wondered if that was because of her experience with back-seats in general, or if Shelby had more intimate memories of this particular car.

"Hey," Shelby said, sitting up again, "I'll be at UNC-G next year. You ought to go back to Wake Forest. Even if you're not playing baseball, you could get a work-study scholarship, I bet. I know lots of people doing that from my class. Plus Winston-Salem and Greensboro are so close. We could hang out together."

"I've thought about going back," Duncan said, sounding intrigued at the notion. "I don't know. Maybe I should look into something like that."

Lola thought of him on a college campus with Shelby falling all over him.

Her first car ride with Duncan hadn't turned out the way she'd hoped, but at least he'd asked her to go with him and she hadn't glommed on to a ride like some slimy leech.

"Hey, Lola," Shelby said, "Charlotte says your daddy walked out on all of you, but then he came back and brought that brother you didn't even know existed. What was that about?"

Lola's face burned. She didn't know if she felt more embarrassed or just plain angry. Duncan looked down at his lap for a second, then back up at the road.

"Yeah," Lola said. "It's kind of nice to have a big brother to talk to. You know, someone my age and all. And by the way, Luke said you looked pretty in your underwear the other night, but he just wasn't in the mood."

Shelby's back stiffened, and for a second, Lola thought the girl might reach up and slap her. She almost wished it would happen. That would be perfect. If Lola could make her totally lose her shit in front of Duncan. But the older girl restrained herself, slumped back again, and went silent for the first time in Lola's memory.

Lola looked over, and Duncan had his face turned partially away from both of them, but from her seat beside him, she could see the smile on his face. She turned her own face toward the window and felt the air wash over her again as Duncan turned up the radio. David Bowie's "Young Americans" overwhelmed the possibility of more uncomfortable conversation for any of them.

About half a mile from the road that turned off toward their houses, Lola looked out her window and saw someone swimming alone in the pond that belonged to Mr. Haywood. The old man and his wife kept a few black-faced cattle on the property and Lola had never seen anything but cows get in the pond.

"Who is that?" She sat up and pointed.

Duncan slowed the car, pulled over to the side of the road.

"Looks like your brand-new brother," Shelby said.

Lola squinted against the sun. It was Luke. He swam over to

the shallow edge and stood knee-deep in the pond. Lola watched him brush his wet hair off his forehead with both hands. He'd taken off his T-shirt, but wore the khaki shorts she'd seen him in before she left for the funeral.

"Hey look," Lola said. "He took his shirt off. Now you two are even."

"Kiss my ass," Shelby said.

Lola cut her eyes back at Shelby. She'd never stood up to Charlotte's sister before. It felt good.

Duncan pulled off the road, stopped and Lola leaned out of her window. "What are you doing?" she called out to Luke.

He emerged the rest of the way from the water, his bare feet muddy from the bottom of the pond. He came over, dripping wet, and stood beside Lola's car door. "I went for a walk and decided to jump in and cool off."

"Is that pond good for swimming?" Lola asked. She'd swim in the ocean or in the lake, but no way would she get in a cow pond—she didn't care how hot she felt.

"It's actually pretty clear," Luke said. "Come on in."

"No thanks," she told him.

"He's right," Duncan said. "It's spring-fed. A great place to swim. I used to come up here with Grandpa when I was a little kid."

"So what's stopping you? Come on," Luke urged. He was grinning, but it didn't look right.

Lola had been around him for only a couple of days, but he looked so much like her daddy, she felt she knew him inside out. The way he was acting was the way her daddy acted when something had him upset and he didn't want to let on.

"No way," Shelby said. "I can walk home from here if I have to."

"I need to get to the house," Duncan said. "Grandpa's going to be a mess when they get him home. I don't think this has really hit him yet."

Everyone nodded, gave the comment a respectful pause. Lola didn't know what to do. The last thing she wanted was for Shelby to have Duncan to herself, but something was up with Luke. It felt strange to read him so clearly, like understanding French when you hadn't had any classes. She wondered if the connection between her and Luke had been there forever, just waiting for them to meet. Even if he wasn't her brother, he *was* family.

Was that what he was upset about? Had her daddy told him the truth? In a lot of ways, Luke ought to know, but something in her hoped he didn't.

"You two go on home," Lola said to Duncan and Shelby. "I'm going to stay here with Luke for a little while."

Duncan looked a little surprised, then, to Lola's delight, a little disappointed. "All right," he said. "See you later, I guess."

Shelby seemed all too pleased with that turn of events, but Lola couldn't worry about Charlotte's evil sister.

"Why'd you blow off golden boy there?" Luke walked over and sat on a rock the size of a VW Beetle. "I know you like him."

"Am I that obvious?" she asked.

He shook his head and started to say no, but stopped. "Yeah," he said. "Actually, you are. But not in a bad way. It's good for a guy to know you're at least interested. The whole aloof, bitchy, hard-to-get thing gets pretty old."

"You don't say." She sat beside him, staying clear of the little rivers of water running from his wet shorts.

"I don't get what goes through girls' minds." He shook his dark curls like a dog, spraying her with the suspect pond water.

"Stop it," she said. "I'll leave you here by yourself."

"I *was* by myself," he said. "And doing just fine."

"Not doing just fine." Lola decided to be direct. It worked with Daddy. Maybe it would work with Luke. "Something's wrong. I can tell. What is it?"

The smile left his face. He looked at her as if deciding whether to let his guard down.

"I'm family," she said. This much was true, at least. "You can trust me."

"Those two things don't have anything to do with each other." His tone took on a bitter edge. "But I do trust you," he added.

"What happened?" she asked.

"Roy's sending me back to Virginia."

The words moved slowly into her conscious thought. She hadn't expected a concrete pronouncement that would undo everything that had happened since her daddy got back.

"That doesn't make sense," she said. "You just got here. I thought you were going to stay all summer."

"So did I." He pushed his hair back off his face again. "Guess we're both wrong. Mont called and said I could come back, and your old man was only too happy to have me packing."

"That's not true," she said. She'd seen Daddy with Luke. He'd gotten attached to him, too, the same as Lola and Janie Ray. Even Mama had shown signs of coming around. "Daddy wouldn't do that. Not unless he thought it was what you wanted. Did you tell him you want to stay?"

"Who says I want to stay?" he said, prideful bluster winning out.

It made Lola want to scream. What was it with boys? They made everything so hard.

"All my friends are in Virginia," he went on, "and I'm graduating in a week. I didn't want to get hauled off here in the first place. So why wouldn't I want to get in the car and drive home?"

"Just stop it," she said. "You can pull this bullshit with everybody else if you want to, but I know you don't feel that way."

High color came to his cheeks. Anger? Sadness? She couldn't tell.

"So now you read minds, too?" he countered. "You've known me for like three days."

"You're right. I don't know what you're thinking," she said, keeping her voice calm, "but I know how you're feeling. You like being here with us. You can say it. I won't tell anybody if you don't want me to, but at least be honest with me."

He dropped his head, giving up the pretense, she hoped. She waited on him. If she waited Daddy out, he always settled down.

"I thought I wanted to be in Virginia," he said. "I thought that the whole ride down from there. I was mad as hell that they made me leave. But I fit in with your family somehow. I never felt that at Pap Taylor and Nanny's house. I owed them for taking me in and I never got to forget it. I didn't feel that way after even a little while at your house.

"I just thought Roy, maybe—" He stopped. "It doesn't matter. He was just being decent, that's all. Hell, it's not like any of this matters. I'll go to college in September and I don't have to think about any of this shit anymore."

"Did you tell Daddy that you want to stay?" she asked again.

"No."

"Come on," she said. "That's the next thing we need to do."

"No," he said. "It was pathetic enough getting suckered into caring in the first place. Your daddy ran out on me. How stupid was I to think he'd really want me now? He got the money he needs to look after your mama. That's the only reason he brought me here."

"Daddy cares about you."

"Your mom's sick with something," he said. He said it with too much animation, as if firing bullets back at Lola. "Your dad just needed money to look after her and Mont gave it to him."

How awful for her daddy. But she couldn't think about that. She had to stay with Luke's problems.

"Luke," she said with a sternness that took both of them by surprise. "Forget my daddy for a minute and think about this. I care whether you go or stay."

"What?"

The pronouncement had stopped him, at least. "I want you to stay here and be my brother for a whole summer. I want you to come back for Thanksgiving and Christmas. I feel like that's the way it's supposed to be. Don't you?"

He pressed his jaw tight. Stubborn. She knew that trick, too.

"Luke Vines," she said. "If you're too good for us and you want to go back to your cool Virginia friends, just do it. I've laid everything out there for you. I've told you I like you being part of this family. I can tell you that Daddy and Janie Ray feel the same way. And Mama . . . Mama actually likes you, which is pretty damn amazing considering everything. If all this has happened in just three days, I'd think you might want to stick around, but I'm finished trying to convince you. Go ahead and be an asshole. Drive off and don't come back. I'm done with you."

She stood up, didn't look at him, and started walking. This is exactly what Mama did. Lola had seen it enough to know the drill. You say the truth and leave. Let them stew on it.

"Lola," he called out. "I'm sorry."

Wow. That wasn't much stewing. He was a pushover. She'd have to teach her almost big brother to have a little backbone now and again. She turned around. He looked so damn helpless. Daddy hadn't meant to, but he'd cut that boy to the quick by acting like he really wanted to send him off.

She went over and hugged him, soggy shorts and all. She hadn't done this before, but he let her do it, then, after a moment, returned the hug, tentatively at first, and then with the surrender of someone who is relieved to have lost.

Minutes later, after they'd walked nearly all the way home, she looked up and saw what she had dreaded. Shelby stood on the porch with Duncan on his side of the duplex.

Luke shook his head. "He's an idiot."

"It's okay," Lola said. "I don't even know him, really. Besides, Shelby's trying to get him to go back to school in Winston-Salem so they can hang out together next year. I might as well give up."

"He ought to go back to school," Luke said. "Not because of Shelby, but because he should."

"Thanks a lot for taking her side," she told him.

"Shelby's a selfish bitch," he said. "But that doesn't mean she's wrong. Hell, you'll be in college in two years. You want him to still be hanging around here?"

That much made sense. Two years left for her. Maybe only one. She thought about Mrs. Jessup's throwaway alternative to the Graham School. Graduating early. She might even be able to get into Wake Forest.

"I'm on your side," Luke said. "You know that, don't you?"

"Yeah," she said. "I'm just being stupid." But her spirits sank as she watched Duncan and Shelby from the road. Shelby touched his arm. For the first time, Lola noticed her skirt—a slim number that barely covered her ass. As Shelby stood, she shifted her weight from one leg to the other so that her hips moved from side to side.

Shelby was all skinny hips and long legs. She told Charlotte once that the reason she did drill team at school was that it helped keep her butt firm.

"Guys are just stupid sometimes," Luke said. He was watching them, too. "I speak from painful experience."

"Maybe she's the kind of person he likes." Lola felt like crying. Shelby took off one shoe and shook it upside down, emptying—or at least pretending to empty—a rock out of it. She stood on one leg as if her tender foot had never touched the ground bare and as she faltered slightly, Duncan reached under her arm and put his hand on her ribs to steady her.

"God, she makes me want to throw up." Lola looked away from the two of them.

"Don't worry about her." Luke nudged Lola with his elbow. "She's temporary fun. No one wants to be with a girl like that for long. When a guy starts with a girl like Shelby, he's thinking with something other than his brain. And that something will always go away—eventually."

Lola laughed in spite of herself.

"I'm sorry." He laughed, too. "I shouldn't have said that."

"It's okay," she said. "You made me laugh."

"Anytime." He messed up her hair with his hand, something she'd seen him do to Janie Ray. "Come on," he said. "Let's bust up their party."

"Okay."

They went toward the house. In the distance, Lola heard church bells start in on a hymn. They did that before the five o'clock service. She didn't know how it had gotten so late. Mama would be worried.

"Tell me I'm right about something," Luke said, out of the blue.

"What's that?"

"Charlotte's nothing like her, right?" He nodded toward Shelby, who had both her shoes on again, but had maintained her proximity to Duncan all the same.

"Nothing," Lola said. "Charlotte's one of the best people I know."

"That's what I thought," Luke said, and left it at that.

When they reached the duplex, Duncan greeted them with a wave and an enthusiastic smile. He had no idea that the display on the porch would bother Lola. Or maybe he just didn't care. It was all so confusing.

"You're right," she mumbled to Luke. "Guys are stupid."

"Sometimes," he corrected her. "I said *sometimes*."

"Hey," Duncan said, clearly addressing Luke. "You ought to come up to your dad's garage tomorrow. I'm going to be working with him for a little while since his guy quit. I'll show you what I've done to the Mustang."

They launched into talk about engines. Other than standing at about the same height, the two were a study in contrast. Luke's reddish curls. Duncan's straight blond hair. Lola leaned on the porch rail and watched them. Shelby, sensing her moment had passed, said she needed to get home and started off toward her house.

"Yeah," Lola said. "I should go, too."

She was suddenly too proud to hang around and wait on Duncan after watching him with Shelby.

"You want to come back later?" Duncan asked when he saw her leaving.

She looked at Luke, thought she saw just the barest shake of his head, telling her to say no.

"I can't tonight," she said. "Thanks for the ride, though."

"No problem," Duncan said, clearly perplexed.

"Tell your granddaddy that I said the funeral was real nice," she said. "Mrs. Thomas would have liked all the things people said."

"I'll tell him," Duncan said.

She started down the steps and then stopped. "Luke," she said, "you need to have a talk with Daddy."

"I know," he said. "I will soon. But I don't want to go in yet. I'm going to walk around for a few minutes."

She watched him go, then went on her own porch and sat on the swing. She'd lived in that house for a long time and never thought that anything was missing. But if Luke left it would feel that way—like something got started and was never seen through. She needed to tell Mama and Daddy that very thing. She needed to make them see that whether he was or he wasn't Daddy's boy, Luke should stay part of their family. That was the one thing she felt with any certainty. Everything else came out as a jumble of questions—questions that not even her parents seemed to know how to answer.

Thirty-five

Rosalind, home from the funeral, felt shaky from standing so long in the cemetery. She went into the bathroom and splashed water on her face, then sat on the edge of her bed. She could sleep so easily if she put her head down. But she couldn't give in like that. After a few minutes, the feelings passed, and she felt better. She got up and went in search of her family.

Janie Ray sat at the table with a Q-tip. She had some yarn that she attempted to wind around the stick between the cotton ends. A variety of items that seemed to be part of her project—glue, feathers, sequins, and paper clips—cluttered the table.

"What are you doing?" Rosalind asked.

"Making a lure." The girl remained focused on the Q-tip and didn't look up when she answered.

"Daddy let you watch the show with the bass fishermen again?"

"Uh-huh." Again, her eyes stayed trained on the "lure."

"Where's Daddy?" Rosalind asked.

"Out back on the steps," she said. "He's been there a long time." Janie Ray's tongue pressed against her top lip in concentration.

Rosalind had to smile. She'd always thought that Janie Ray would have to stand in for the boy she and Roy never had. She liked outside better than in, fishing better than dolls. Now that Luke was in the picture—for better or for worse—it seemed her husband had the real deal.

She walked through the back porch. She'd seen Luke up the road with Lola as she drove home, so in his absence, she took a minute to look around his space. He'd made an attempt to straighten the covers on the daybed. Underneath it, his two suitcases lay side by side. They served as drawers for the few clothes and possessions he brought with him when he left Virginia.

On the small night table they'd moved out for him, he had a Hershey's bar, a magazine about cars, and a wooden game with a clown face in the middle. The game was the kind with small, metal balls that roll around until you fit them all into a hole. For some reason, the sight of his things made her sad. Such a kidlike collection. Little boy things. Boy smells. She hadn't had that before.

What had Roy told him about Mont's phone call? She hoped the two of them had worked it out while she and Lola were at the funeral.

She walked out back. As Janie Ray said, Roy sat on the steps down near the yard. He had a cigarette in his hand, his elbows resting on his knees. From the back, she couldn't tell what kind of mood he was in, but when he heard her and turned around, her spirits fell. It hadn't gone well.

"What happened?" she asked.

"He's going back to the mountains," he said. "I think he'll

probably leave tomorrow. I haven't called Mont yet. Luke went off walking after we talked, so I figured I'd wait until he comes back to make the call."

"I saw him up at Haywood's pond with Lola when I drove in," she said, sitting down beside him on the step. "The two of them were tight in conversation, so I didn't stop. Was he excited when you told him? Did he *want* to go back?" She couldn't imagine that Luke wouldn't feel conflicted at least. He'd been with them only a few days, but a lot had happened in that time. Just seeing the way he and Lola got along should have given him a reason to at least *think* about staying.

"He sounded like he wanted to," Roy said. "I don't know. He kinda pulled back, getting polite and agreeable, but not really saying anything. I guess it makes sense he'd want to go back to his life. All his friends are there and my parents have raised him for the last eight years. I feel all torn up inside about it, but I don't want to let on. I don't want to make him feel guilty about leaving. He's entitled to his own life."

Roy took a drag of his cigarette. Rosalind leaned in and he put it to her lips so that she could take a puff. She'd done that all the time when they were first married, but she hadn't done it in years. They needed to go back to being more playful with each other. Raising the kids and solving money troubles kept them from being young. And they weren't old. Not yet.

Roy stared out at the backyard and Rosalind tried to imagine what he would do if something happened to her. She couldn't. The two of them together made a new and better whole.

"You can find out what he's thinking without making him feel obligated to stay," she said. "You owe it to yourself and him to get below the surface with that boy."

"Mont's right. He's not mine," Roy said. The way he said it, she knew that for the first time in their lives together, he wished that Sherry's son *was* his child.

So much inside her rose up against that thought, but she knew that the feelings had nothing to do with his first wife. Luke had gotten to Roy without even trying, really.

"He's not anybody's, Roy," she said. "He belongs to himself. We all do. Find out what he's really thinking and let him decide."

Roy looked up at her with a mixture of astonishment and gratitude on his face.

"Mont's selfish," she said, "and your folks are cold, distant people. I'm not saying they're bad, but they don't know how to show love. Not our kind of love. I'm sure Sherry doted on him, but my bet is that not one of them has treated him as anything special since she passed."

"I know it," Roy said. He took a last puff and put the cigarette out under his foot. "That good sense of yours . . ." He smiled. "First thing I loved about you."

"The first?" She smiled.

"Maybe the second," he said.

"When you show that boy the least little bit of generosity," she said, "he drinks it like water."

"You've seen it, too," Roy said.

"Can't help but see it," she said. She didn't go any further. She didn't say that Roy's twin and his mama were capable of more than neglect. They could do harm. But she thought it. And believing that made it a sin to throw that boy back in their direction.

They both turned when they heard Lola come through the back porch. Luke came around the side of the house at about the same time. The would-be siblings stared like deer stranded in the road when they saw her and Roy on the steps. Luke's shirt was dry, but his shorts had been soaked through.

Lola walked down and stood beside him. "We need to have a talk," she said.

Luke winced as she spoke up, but, once again, Rosalind was proud of her daughter for diving in headfirst.

"Yes, we do," Rosalind said. "Come on out here. Let's have a family discussion."

Roy took her hand as they waited for the teenagers to come. Rosalind decided she couldn't let sickness win out. Her family needed too much from her.

"Say exactly how you feel about Mont's phone call, Luke." Rosalind gave him no time to fashion what he thought they wanted to hear. "Do you really want to go back to Virginia now? If you do, that's fine, but if you have any doubts, we need to hear about it. Everybody's tiptoeing around too much."

He hesitated, and Rosalind feared he'd never get it out. When it came to trust, he was shy his portion. They could help him with that.

"Luke," Lola said, "tell them the things you said to me. You need to do it."

"Let me start," Roy said. "Before you say a word, know that I want you here. I won't blame you if you go back to the life you've had, but that's not what I want. We didn't start out headed in that direction, I know. But that's where I am now. Like I said, you need to know that before you decide anything."

Rosalind saw that Lola was fighting tears. Fighting a losing battle, as a drop ran down the perfect young skin of her cheek. But she wasn't the only one. Luke's eyes had filled. He might look like a man sometimes, but Rosalind thought of all that stuff by the bed. He was really just a boy. Good Lord, had Mont, Lydia, or Taylor ever let him be one?

"I want to stay here," he said, the words choked in his throat as he fought not to openly show his emotions.

A small smile of relief came to Roy's face.

"Let's go make a phone call then." Rosalind stood up before the moment became too awkward for any of them.

"Right now?" Luke said, his voice suddenly cheerful.

"Right now," Roy said, standing also.

The kids went inside and Rosalind leaned in to whisper to her husband. "Mont's going to be madder than a feral dog when you tell him." The delight she took in that represented the one mean sliver in an otherwise worthy response to the family crisis.

"Ain't it the truth," Roy said, grinning in spite of an obvious effort to stop himself.

She was tired. Bone-tired. But the situation with Mont and Luke had given her an unexpected push of energy. She would ride that until after supper, when, God willing, she'd have a restful night, and for the first time in five days—she hoped—an uneventful day to follow it.

Thirty-six

I t seemed impossible that his world had turned around again. He'd been all set to go back to Virginia. He thought he had no choice. In his experience, people who had the authority to say no usually did just that. But Roy and Rosalind sat there together and said he could stay, that he *should* stay if he wanted to. Both of them said it.

Luke changed into jeans and went into the kitchen where the rest of them waited for him.

"I can't believe I still know Mont's number by heart," Roy said. He went to the phone. Rosalind sat down in the kitchen with Luke and Lola. Janie Ray's supplies littered the table's surface and the girl showed no signs of tiring in her efforts to create Q-tip lures. But she was the only one at the table not watching Roy. To Luke, it seemed that the three of them might have been waiting for a show to start.

Roy stood for a minute before dialing. He seemed to be bracing for the unpleasant words he and his brother would exchange. But the fact that he dreaded the phone call and he was still going to make it meant that he really wanted Luke to stay.

Maybe Lola had been right. Maybe Roy thought Luke wanted to go back to Pap Taylor and Nanny's house. He thought of the place he'd lived for the last eight years and wondered why he didn't want to return to his old life. He had his own room. They'd never been exactly mean to him. He got spanked some-times when he was younger, but Pap Taylor had never hit him in anger. Some kids he knew went through that shit with their folks.

But ever since his mom died, he'd had the feeling that Nanny and Pap saw it as their obligation to keep a roof over his head and a plate of food in front of him. They were his grandparents. Mont was his uncle. So he guessed there would be some family responsibility there, no matter what. But he got the feeling there was more to it than that. Especially with Nanny.

He'd heard Mont talking to her one time when he was on the stairs and they were in the kitchen.

"I can usually get my way about most anything," Mont said. "But Della won't stand to have him living in our house."

"We care for the boy," Nanny told Mont. "You know that. But at our age, it's hard to raise a child."

"I'm sorry, Mama." Mont sounded five years old. "But if Della runs to her daddy, I won't get elected as dog catcher anywhere in this state. You're the only one who's ever really understood my ambitions, Mama."

"I know, son," Nanny said. "We'll do what we have to do. You know we'll look after him." After hearing what they said, Luke took care to pick up after himself and not talk back. That lasted pretty much until the mistake that got him booted out with Roy.

Luke had always thought that he'd like to be like Mont, but

he didn't really think that anymore. Della was always setting up some luncheon with the mayor's wife or some fund-raising dinner. Mont's decision to run for the state legislature had consumed the whole family for the last couple of years and it made Mont seem important. But Luke had seen something different in Roy's house. Everybody was important.

Mont and Della never really seemed all that married except when they were at some fancy dinner together. Luke got trotted out for those sometimes, along with their loser daughter, his cousin Nell, before she went off to college. In front of people, Mont always made a big deal about how he took Luke under his wing since his parents weren't there to raise him. Luke felt like a special project or something.

"You're a good man to step in and be a role model for the boy." People always said something like that when Luke was around. Sometimes at those events, and sometimes at Mont's house, Luke would see Della's daddy. The Judge, everyone called him. Nanny and Pap were cuddly compared to that son-of-a-bitch. Even Della jumped halfway out of her skin when he spoke up. Then again, Della jumped halfway out of her skin when Casper said, "Boo."

"It's busy," Roy said, putting the receiver back on the hook.

"Let's eat a bite of supper and then we can try again," Rosalind said.

"I don't think I can enjoy a meal until I get this over with," Roy said.

Luke felt relief when he said that. Swallowing would not come easy for him, either. He dreaded Mont's reaction to Roy's call, but not as much as he'd dreaded going back.

Rosalind got busy doing a few dishes and Lola went to help dry, but Roy and Luke sat and stared at nothing in particular.

"You think he's going to be mad?" Luke asked.

"Yeah," Roy said. "Mont likes to get his way." He got up to

dial again. After a few seconds, Roy sat down in the chair by the phone. He looked to be bracing for a physical hit.

"Hey, Della," Roy said. "Is Mont home?"

Roy waited. Luke could hear his breath go in and out. A funny thing occurred to him. Roy felt as skittish around Mont, Pap Taylor, and Nanny as he did. It was like he and Roy were cut from the same piece of cloth. They were different from those three. Luke looked at Roy's face, so much like his own. *Exactly* like Mont's. Except not. Side by side, he could tell Roy from Mont now. Mont wasn't a bad person, but Roy had something gentle in him that Mont didn't.

That's why Luke didn't want to go back to the mountains. It had gotten so that he didn't even expect much in the way of kindness, but at Roy's house, he had it coming from all directions, even from Rosalind, who he knew was ready to skin him alive when he first got there.

"Hey, Mont," Roy said. "I've had a chance to talk to Luke and—"

Mont must have started in saying something because Roy stopped.

"No," Roy said, finally, "he's not." Then after another stretch of silence on his end, he said, "No, Mont. He's decided not to come back. He's decided to stay around here for the summer. We'll be back up for his graduation. He can get more of his things then."

Roy listened again. Whatever Mont said, it was an earful. No one in the kitchen breathed except Janie Ray. She had a pile of long, thin sticks from the yard that Roy had brought in for her and she put the lures on the end of strings and taped them to the sticks.

"I'm not trying to pull anything, Mont," Roy said, finally. He motioned for Lola and Luke to take Janie Ray outside.

"You three go out on the front porch," Rosalind said. "Let Roy handle this without an audience."

"Let's go outside," Lola said to her little sister.

"I'm not finished with all the poles yet," Janie Ray whined.

Roy put his finger to his lips for her to talk more quietly.

"You've got three finished," Lola coaxed. "That means we can all fish off the porch. Come on."

Janie Ray agreed and they all went through to the front of the house.

Outside, Luke saw Duncan lifting a box of kitchen things from the trunk of his car. Mr. Thomas knelt on the ground at the edge of his steps. He picked up dirt and let it run through his fingers.

"You okay, Mr. Thomas?" Lola asked.

"Good as I can be under the circumstances, I suppose," he answered her.

She talked to the old man, but her eyes were on Duncan as he came toward the house with the box in his arms. Duncan seemed like a decent enough guy, but Luke knew what went through his mind with girls and he hoped Duncan would be careful around Lola.

"Anything I can do?" Lola knelt beside Mr. Thomas so that her face came level with his. He looked up at her and tried to smile. Poor old guy, Luke thought. Luke never knew the wife, but she must have been everything to him.

"Thought I might plant some geraniums here for Minnie," Mr. Thomas said. "She couldn't stand a summer without her geraniums. Had them in hanging pots and flowerbeds all over the property."

"That's nice." Lola looked up at Duncan. He stood over her with the box still in his arms. She shrugged her shoulders with an expression on her face that asked, *What do I do?*

Duncan just shook his head. They were all at a loss.

Still on the porch beside Janie Ray, Luke took one of the girl's fishing poles and dropped the yarn and lure over the side of the porch. Lola stood and walked up the stairs to join them.

"Mr. Thomas?" Janie Ray spoke up out of the blue.

"What is it, missy?" Mr. Thomas looked up.

"You know how to fish?" the girl asked, swinging her pretend lure back and forth, enticing all the imaginary fish that sailed through the air around the porch.

"I've dropped a pole or two in the water in my day." He smiled. A real smile.

"Will you take me sometime?" she asked.

He seemed to think for a second, then he nodded. "How about right now?"

"Now?" Janie Ray practically squealed her response.

"Why not," Mr. Thomas said. "I've got a couple of poles in the shed by the house down there and there are worms galore in this dirt here." With some effort, he stood up from his kneeling position. "We can walk up to Haywood's pond up there and see what's biting before the sun goes down."

"Granddaddy," Duncan said, putting the box down on the porch. "You've had a long day."

"And I think fishing is just the ticket for the end of it," he said. The old guy had launched into a mission.

"I don't mind walking to the pond again," Luke said. "Sounds like fun."

"Let's all go," Janie Ray piped in. "Please." She looked from Lola to Luke and back.

It was hard to say no to that kid. "All right."

"Walk down to the house with me, Lola," Duncan said. The guy's eyes had a lock on Lola's, and Luke felt almost embarrassed watching them. "We'll grab the poles and be back in a second or two, Granddaddy."

"We'll be putting worms in this bowl." He reached up into the box on the porch and pulled out a plastic mixing bowl. The dead lady might have objected to that kind of use—or abuse—of her kitchenware, but no one there would deny the old man his moment of pleasure.

Luke watched Lola set off down the road with Duncan. Janie Ray put a bear hug around one of his legs. "Thanks, Luke." She closed her eyes and squeezed hard. Family was confusing and messy . . . and he craved it like a drug. Luke wondered what was going on inside with Roy's phone call to Mont. He imagined a power of wills between the twins and worried that Mont had the advantage in that department. Overthinking it wouldn't change anything. Until Roy came out to get him, there was nothing to do but wait.

He stood at the porch rail with his little sister. The thought of having two siblings still seemed unreal. Janie Ray had dropped her pole over the side of the porch again. He couldn't help but smile as the two of them fished for some invisible catch that only hope, yarn, and Q-tips could coax out of the air.

Thirty-seven

"What have you told that boy about me, Roy?" Mont had calmed down enough to talk, at least. "Three days ago I had to practically hog-tie him and throw him in the car to get him to go with you. Now you're telling me he won't come back?"

Roy's head hurt deep behind his temples. He rubbed his eyes, but it didn't help.

"I didn't tell him anything," Roy said. "Fact is, we haven't talked about you or Mama and Daddy at all. He's been working on getting to know the family here and I think he'd like to hang around for a while. He likes the girls."

"Hell, that's what got him into trouble to start with."

Mont was smart, but sometimes he was a damn idiot. "Not girls in general, Mont. *My girls.* Lola and Janie Ray. He likes having family his own age."

"He had Nell here," Mont said, "and he never seemed to give a crap one way or the other."

The last time Roy had seen Mont's daughter, she'd been small, and she'd been a strange, quiet child even then. From what little Luke had said about her, she'd only gotten worse over the years.

"Nell's older," Roy said, trying not to insult his niece. "I think he likes being the oldest."

"Well, that's all well and good," Mont said, "but I need him here now."

"Need him? Why?"

Rosalind handed Roy two aspirin and a glass of water. Grateful, he took them from her and mouthed out "Thank you" as Mont launched into some explanation about a fund-raising dinner Luke needed to go to in the coming week. At first, Roy only half listened. It sounded like typical Mont bullshit. But something about Mont's words didn't sound right and it nagged at him.

"I'm sorry, Mont," Roy said, putting his focus back on the phone call. "I got distracted, what did you say?"

"Three of the big commerce organizations in this section of the state are having a dinner for me on Friday to raise money." Mont spoke slowly as if Roy might be a child. "They've decided to honor my work with kids who need role models. I've made that a campaign issue. I need Luke there with me."

Again, Roy felt a rush of anger rise inside him. What a hypocrite. Mont saw Luke as some kind of animated prop. Nearly two decades had passed and Mont hadn't changed. Roy forced regular breathing to keep his feelings at bay. He needed to stay even and in control. "You should have thought about that before you shipped him off, Mont."

"Don't get on your high horse," his brother said. "I have these dinners all the time." Mont sounded tired of talking, almost bored. He thought he'd won. Hell, knowing Mont, he assumed he'd have his way before he made the first phone call. "I've got so much going on, you can't possibly understand. I never even look at my calendar until a few days before," he said, as if it provided some justification for his demands. "That's why I only put this together today. Just get him in the car, Roy."

"Can't do that," Roy said. "He's a human being for God's sake. Not a life-sized campaign poster. Besides, what happened to all your worries about his run-in with the law?"

"Like I told you before. That died down faster than I thought it would. Word got out that he was hauled in by the police on some senior prank. No one's thought twice about it. He's fine to come finish out the summer here with his friends and his real family. Just tell me what this is about, Roy. You want more money?"

If Mont had been in front of him instead of a disembodied voice on the phone line, Roy would have slugged him. He felt the impulse as his fingers tightened into the makings of a fist. Good God, what was he? Ten years old again?

"Luke gets to decide where he wants to be," Roy said, although he was beginning to think he'd hog-tie Luke himself, if he had to, to keep him away from Mont. Rosalind was right, his family was toxic. It took all his effort to keep his voice steady. "I asked him and he said he wants to stay here. Just because he's gone from being a liability back to being an asset to your political career doesn't have anything to do with what's best for him."

"What'd you get him for his birthday when he was twelve, Roy?" Mont suddenly became the taunting bully of their teenage years. "How about when he turned fifteen? Did you take him to get his learner's permit?"

"So trot out the home movies," Roy said. "You and all those self-righteous assholes at your role model dinner can have a

great time patting each other on the back. Just leave him alone."
Roy took another sip of water. He wished to God the aspirin
would kick in. He didn't want to lose his temper. "The fact of
the matter is, I asked Luke plain and simple what he wanted to
do. I don't have a gun to his head and we both know I've got
nothing to bribe the kid with. He said he wants to stay and I'm
backing him up. That's where it ends, Mont."

"Mama's down as his legal guardian." Mont sounded so
sure, but Roy knew the last part was a bluff. Getting Lydia
involved in some kind of legal mess wouldn't get Luke there by
the weekend.

He had a hand to play, too. He could threaten to expose what
Mont and Sherry did. But that would hurt Luke more than
anyone else, he realized. "You'll see him at graduation, Mont," he
said. "Not before. Get Mama involved if you want to. You really
want to drag him back with a court order? He's seventeen, a year
shy of making all his own decisions anyway. Leave him be."

"You're really going to do this, Roy? Go up against me on
this one?"

"I'm not against you," Roy told him. "I'm for him. Somebody's
got to look out for him."

"What the hell does that mean?" Mont clearly hated losing,
especially when it came out of left field. "I've mailed that last
check to you, but you know I can still cancel it."

Roy glanced over at Rosalind. She'd hate it if she knew her
illness gave Roy's brother an ounce of leverage.

"Yeah, that'll get him excited about going back to Virginia,"
Roy said, enjoying the sarcasm spent in every word. "You can
try and force him, brother, but you can't make him *want* to be
with you."

"Where is he?" Mont asked. "I want to talk with him."

"He went out." Technically true, although Roy could hear
him laughing with Janie Ray on the front porch.

"I want *him* to call me," Mont said. "I want to deal with the boy myself."

"I'll give him the message." Roy looked at Rosalind, closed his eyes, and let out a long breath. It was almost over.

"I don't understand why you're doing this, Roy," Mont said. "I just don't get it. You never cared about Sherry."

"And you did?" Roy said, his voice heavy with sarcasm. "My mistake."

Mont didn't respond, but Roy could hear him breathing on the other end. He waited for a response. "Mont?"

The line clicked. Mont had hung up. All the insults they'd hurled and Mont stayed on the line to argue, but Roy's passing dig about his first wife ended their discussion without so much as a good-bye.

"What was that about?" Rosalind came and sat on his lap. He still held the phone in his hand and only hung up when the obnoxious signal reminded him that it was off the hook.

"Damned if I know," Roy said.

He pulled Rosalind to him, her thick hair soft against his face. And he felt sorry for Mont. In spite of all his problems, Roy realized that *he* was the fortunate one.

"So Luke stays?" Rosalind asked.

"I think so," Roy said, suddenly eager to tell Luke the news. He kissed Rosalind full on the mouth and grinned. He couldn't believe he'd held his ground.

"You think you could put a little food out for the kids?" she asked. "There's plenty in the fridge left over from earlier. I'm going to have to lie down."

"Sure," he said, his victory slipping away as he made note of her pale color. "Go on. I'll call Mae Rose and tell her you're not feeling well, and I'll get the kids settled for the night."

"I'm going to work tomorrow," she said, standing up. Her voice had an edge, and he knew what it meant. She'd use energy she didn't have to go head-to-head with him if necessary. The woman was stubborn. "I just need some rest now. I'll be fine in the morning." Her face softened. "Don't worry," she said. "We've got that appointment Thursday in Winston. Everything will be fine."

He didn't press, just watched her go, then he went out to tell Luke about his conversation with Mont. The triumph, any triumph, had a hollow core if Rosalind didn't share it. It occurred to him that loving people made you both strong and weak at the same time. Luke didn't know that yet. Neither did Lola or Janie Ray. And that's the way it ought to be, he thought. His job was to keep that knowledge from reaching them for as long as possible. Long enough for them to claim love and depend on it before learning to fear it.

He stepped onto the porch to join his younger daughter and the boy who, for the time being at least, would stay part of their family.

Thirty-eight

Lola walked beside Duncan. Late afternoon light fell on the side of his face and she got a good look at his scar. The line of it skirting in and out of his hairline made him more gorgeous somehow. Past mistakes, visible scars, even his weakness when flirting with Shelby . . . All that made him human. Hearing some of this from Luke's perspective made boys, even older ones like Duncan, less frightening. More manageable.

"How'd you get that scar?" she asked, surprised that the question had traveled through her brain and come out of her mouth. They were halfway to the old Thomas property, had just passed Charlotte's house. She could hear Pinball barking inside the Bensons' house as she and Duncan went by.

"I'm sorry," she said when he didn't answer right away. "It's rude to ask something like that." But she wasn't really sorry. She knew that there wasn't a thing he could tell her that wouldn't make her like him even more.

"I haven't talked about it in a long time," he said, looking ahead to where they were going and not over at her. "When I was fourteen, my brother and I took the car—"

He stopped. She didn't know if that was all he planned to say. If she was supposed to imagine the rest.

"You've got a brother?" She didn't remember another grandchild at the funeral home and had never heard Mr. or Mrs. Thomas mention another boy. "I thought you were the only one," she said. "The only grandchild they had."

"I am," he said. "My daddy's older than my mama. They're not together anymore anyway, but he had a family before her. His first wife died of cancer when my brother was two."

"What's his name?" In her mind, she pictured an older, smoother version of Duncan.

"Jarrod. His name's Jarrod," he told her. "Anyway, when I was fourteen, we took the car. He'd gotten his license the year before and he took me out almost every day with him. Sometimes with friends. Sometimes just the two of us. We'd go to the parking lot at the country fairgrounds and cut up. Do doughnuts and stuff like that. Jarrod taught me how to drive."

She could feel the bad part of the story approaching. Nothing good came of cars in empty fairground lots. Not when the story ended in a scar.

"That day there were three of us. Me, Jarrod, and a boy named Farley. Jarrod was supposed to be at basketball practice, but he skipped."

They came to the edge of the Thomas property. She saw the shed where the fishing poles would be, but he walked to the side in a different direction. She followed, still listening for the rest of his story. She didn't ask where he was going, or why.

"Off to one side of the parking lot, an old billboard had fallen down," he said. "Farley got the idea that if we used some bricks and stuff to prop up the billboard, we could build ourselves a jump ramp. He said we could jump like the big trucks on TV.

"We set it up, and Farley said since it was his idea, he got to take the first run. Jarrod argued that it was his car, but Farley won the argument, and Jarrod got out to mark the distance when we came down. It went pretty well. We went about one car length. The landing felt pretty rough, but we thought it was fun."

Duncan stopped to take a breath. He pulled out a cigarette and lit it. "I can't smoke in the house with Granddaddy because it bothers his breathing. You mind if I smoke here?"

She shook her head no. Waited for him to finish his story.

"On the second run, it was me and Jarrod in the car and Farley outside. We came up on the ramp, the same as before, only something underneath must have shifted on the first jump. As soon as we hit the ramp, I felt the car lean over to the right and the support gave out from underneath. We were going so fast and we were already on the ramp. Jarrod tried to push through to the other side, but the car went up on two wheels, rolled over and then back upright. Problem was, it rolled over Farley."

He raised the cigarette to his lips and she saw his hand shaking. She wanted to pull him over to her. She wanted to tell him she understood how he felt. But she didn't. How could she?

"Farley's arm got caught on some part of the car and he ended up on the hood, draped down over the broken windshield. Maybe he broke it with his body, I don't know. He was dead from the second it hit him, I think, 'cause he never moved. Not that I saw."

Lola let out an involuntary gasp. She could see it all. Two dumbstruck boys inside and the dead one lying over the front, blocking the light from their faces.

"How'd you get help?" she asked, trying to move the story away from the horror of that scene.

"Somebody passing on the highway saw us," he said. "Two men stayed while another drove to get the police."

"You were only fourteen, Duncan. Your brother was older and made the decision to do it. Him and his friend."

"Yeah," he said, a bitter smile taking over his face. "That's what most people said. That's what my mama told me. But then, I was okay except for the slash on my face. Her *real* son was okay. That's what my daddy used to say to her if he'd been drinking at all. Other times, he didn't say much of anything to either of us."

"What happened to Jarrod?" She almost hated to ask.

"He got the sense knocked out of him. Most of it didn't come back. He managed to stay in high school. Teachers felt sorry for him and found ways to move him through the classes he needed to graduate. Then he got out and tried to work at one of the mills, but with all those machines around, he almost got himself killed too many times. Nobody could watch him twenty-four hours a day, so they finally put him in a place in the mountains. I go see him every couple of months."

"It must have been rough on your parents," she said. She didn't know what else to say.

"Daddy accused Mama of being glad it wasn't me. He thought there was nobody but him who cared about Jarrod. Wasn't true. Mama never saw any difference between the two of us. Jarrod was just a little three-year-old when she married Daddy and she raised him the same as me. They fought about it all the time, and finally Daddy took up with that other woman and moved out. The two of them eventually moved near where Jarrod lives. I see them once in a while."

They were standing at the edge of a clearing. Dirt had been newly turned out and pieces of dead plants were mixed in with the clumps. Duncan looked out over the bare patch. Smoke hung around his face like a veil.

"Your daddy couldn't blame you for what happened," she said.

"He always said he didn't," Duncan said. "Same as Granddaddy says he doesn't blame me for Grandma dying like she did."

Lola looked around. She didn't understand what he was saying. "Why are we standing here?" she asked.

He picked up a dead piece of plant. The dry wilted leaf looked familiar. She'd seen boys at school drawing a leaf shaped like that on doodles when they were bored in class.

"You planted pot here?" she asked.

He nodded, took a last drag on his cigarette, and dropped it by his foot to put out. "A little patch," he said. "Just for me and my buddies so we wouldn't spend all our money buying the shit. One of them got greedy, but I don't want to go into that, really. But the bottom line is Granddaddy found out. I was out of town for a couple of weeks working with the race circuit. A friend of mine said he'd keep an eye on it for me. Granddaddy followed him. He scared the shit out of my buddy, saying he was going to call the law. Then he dug it all up and let it dry out."

Smells like old Mr. Thomas just fired up the world's biggest bong. Lola remembered Charlotte's comment the day of the fire. Turns out, that's exactly what it had been.

Lola looked at Duncan. Those had to be the two worst stories of his life. Why had he told both of them, one right after the other?

"That's it," he said. "That's as bad as it gets with me." He looked at her and seemed to want something. What was he looking for? Did he want to see if she couldn't stand him after everything she'd heard?

"Why tell me both these stories now?" she asked.

"Because I like you," he said. "I haven't liked anybody . . . felt like I could talk to a girl, in a long time. You're about as real as any person I've ever met. But if you can't look at me the same way after hearing the truth, I might as well know it now. Save us both the trouble."

She felt it inside her. She'd been turned on by boys before. Dancing. Making out a little. But standing by Duncan, she felt a current carrying her—like she was in a river and warm water pulled her toward places she ached to go. She reached up and touched his scar. She ran her finger along his skin, tracing it. He still didn't kiss her, and she wanted him to. So she took a step toward him, closing the distance between them.

And then he bent forward, bringing his lips down on her. His mouth felt soft, inside and out. Then her whole body felt soft, inside and out. If he'd tried to touch her, if he'd laid her down and asked to have her, she might have let him. But he didn't. He just kissed her with a need that left her as weak as a new bird. The urgency of it made her wonder how they would ever manage to stop. Maybe they would just die of old age, standing there and still kissing.

"Oh, God, I'm sorry." Charlotte's voice came out of nowhere.

Lola felt naked even though her clothes were fully on.

"I saw y'all walking this way and thought I'd come out." Charlotte grinned, her eyes wide and smiling at Lola.

"It's okay," Lola managed. "We came down to get fishing poles so Mr. Thomas can take Janie Ray up to the pond."

Duncan looked shaken for a moment. Then he caught Lola's eye and glanced over at the ravaged field beside them. He didn't want Charlotte to see it and realize what had been there. Lola began walking back toward the burned-out house and Charlotte followed her. They got to the shed and as Duncan rummaged for poles, Charlotte said, "Hey, Luke's taking me out this weekend. Y'all want to double date?"

Balancing three cane poles in the crook of his arm, Duncan said, "It's up to her."

"Yeah," Lola said. Her brain couldn't stop racing, screaming, *Yes, yes* . . . "That'd be great."

On the way back up to the duplex, he held the fishing poles

in one arm and put his other arm over her shoulders. Charlotte gave her a thumbs-up and Lola waved her away, hoping Duncan didn't see. With his fingers touching the bare skin of her arm, Lola felt claimed, somehow, and entirely happy.

Even when they got to the house and Daddy was on the porch talking with Luke, she couldn't bring herself to leave Duncan's side. Curious as she was about what happened with Daddy's phone call, she wanted to stay with Duncan more than anything she'd ever wanted before.

"I'm going to go with Janie Ray up to the pond," she said as casually as she could manage.

Janie Ray put down her pretend pole and ran down the steps. Mr. Thomas came from the other side to join them, carrying a mixing bowl full of dirt and worms.

"Don't be gone long," Daddy said, clearly distracted by his conversation with Luke. "Mama's not feeling well, so I'll put some supper out when you get back."

"Okay," Lola called to him as she made headway toward the road. She took her little sister's hand and pulled her alongside. Duncan walked behind. She didn't look back, but she felt him there. She wondered briefly if it was a sin to be so happy on a day when such a nice woman had been buried.

She glanced back toward the duplex and saw Duncan's mama standing on the porch. She had a new respect for someone who'd been through all that Duncan had described and then kept on going. Some scars were on the outside and some stayed in, but what all scars had in common was that they didn't leave. If you got lucky, they faded and smoothed out into skin that still fit you—skin that still felt like yours after everything else in your life had changed.

Thirty-nine

For four nights straight, Rosalind had gone to bed just after dinner, her earliest bedtime coming the night before. She'd been in bed for something like fourteen hours by the time she got up. She woke feeling like some fairy tale character who'd fallen asleep in winter and come to in the spring while everyone she loved went about their business.

By the time she got up, Roy was dressed and making coffee. Everything in the kitchen looked clean, but the room smelled strongly of fish.

"What happened in here?" she asked wrinkling her nose.

"Janie Ray caught three brim at Haywood's pond," he said. "She begs Luke to take her every day. Last night, they walked up there after dinner. Luke and I cleaned the latest ones out back last evening and put them in the freezer."

"Were they even big enough to eat?" Nothing bigger than a goldfish seemed to come out of that pond.

"She was so proud," Roy said. "There were more bones than

meat, but we'll add all of them together and make a stew. She won't know the difference."

"Where is everybody?" she asked.

"Luke offered to drive Lola to school," he told her. "Janie Ray rode with him. He said he'd look after her today so she doesn't have to go to the doctor with us. Duncan will cover things at the garage."

She still didn't understand why that boy was working for free. Roy said he'd explain when things settled down. About that time Luke came in with Janie Ray riding piggyback, and Roy had fried up eggs for all of them before the two of them had to take off for the doctor's appointment in Winston-Salem.

Rosalind got up off the table in the exam room after the doctor left. She took off the cotton gown and threw it in the basket by the door, then she found her clothes and put them on again.

The doctor and his nurse poked, probed, and listened to her for what seemed like forever. They'd taken her temperature and then taken her blood. They pressed on her neck and her belly until she was sore. Just as well. She wanted to know everything. She could fight what she knew.

The doctor had talked to her in his office before she went to change. He looked too young to have gotten all the degrees on his wall. But she trusted him. Her gut told her he knew what he was doing. He said to meet him back in his office after she got dressed. Roy had been with them before, but he'd gotten restless and gone out to get some air. She suspected that thinking too much had left him panicked.

But she didn't feel any panic for some reason. She felt strangely calm, as if everything would be okay. She'd get better or she'd deal with the worst of it. The doctor kept calling her condition *manageable.* That sounded less dire than she'd feared when she first learned about everything.

"Ready?" The nurse popped her head back in the door.

"You bet," Rosalind said, and followed her down the hall.

"Is your husband here?" she asked.

"He's walking around," she said. "Send him in when he comes back."

"They're strong until they're not." The nurse smiled.

"That's about it." But Rosalind knew she was Roy's only real weakness.

"We'll get all the final tests back," Dr. Packard told her after she'd settled into a chair in front of his desk. An empty chair waited for Roy to join them. "I'm pretty certain about what we'll find, but we need to rule out things like lupus. I'm going to start you on something called prednisone. That's almost always where we begin with ITP."

Prednisone. It sounded lovely. She doubted that would be the case.

"I have to be honest with you," he said. "You might not like it much."

"Is it like chemotherapy?" she asked. She'd known people who had cancer, a few others who'd had heart attacks. She had no point of reference for blood disorders.

"No," he said. "This is a type of steroid. It's different. You might have mood swings. Irritability. Maybe trouble sleeping."

"That ought to make me popular around the house," she said. She tried to stay calm, but a panic rose inside her.

He looked apologetic, as if the side effects might be his fault. She liked this doctor. "But the thing that often bothers people the most is the physical changes they have while taking the drug."

"Like what?" She imagined hair falling out or her skin going pasty.

He handed over some pages. On them were pictures of people, men and women, who looked as if someone had inserted a straw into them and blown them up. They'd become balloon figures.

"I'll look like that?" Looking at the pictures made her want to cry.

"People react differently," he said gently. "Most have this sort of swelling."

"This is more than swelling, Dr. Packard."

"It's very effective," he said. "We wouldn't use it otherwise."

"And if it doesn't work?" After what she'd heard, she almost wished they could skip to Plan B.

"A splenectomy," he said. "Taking out your spleen. As operations go, it's not a bad one, but no operation is good, really. And it leaves you with a compromised immune system. We may need to resort to that, but let's take it one step at a time."

We? He wasn't the one who was going to look like a cartoon character. But she understood that he only wanted her to feel that he was invested in getting her better. From the sound of it, *better* was the best outcome. No one talked about curing her.

She looked down at the pictures again, then at the door. Roy might walk in and she didn't want him to know. But then, he would know. He'd have to look at her every day. He would always love her, but would he still want her if she looked like that? She thought of the operation. Just taking part of her out would solve her problem. That almost sounded preferable. She glanced at the pictures again. How shallow was it to be more afraid of losing her looks than of going under the knife?

The picture at the top of the stack had two people together. Both women. Even in their altered states they looked just the same.

"Twins with this disease?" She held up the picture so that he could see the one she meant. She wanted to distract herself for a moment, take a little time to process what she'd just heard.

"I have others," he said. "Other twins I've worked with. A while back, I was involved with testing on a number of twins,

trying to sort out the increased risk to family members if someone is diagnosed. I published papers on those studies. Twins are
fascinating."

"My husband's a twin," she said.

As if on cue, Roy opened the door, knocking only after the
fact. "Sorry," he said. I shouldn't barge in."

"No secrets in here." Rosalind tried to smile. She looked at
the pictures still sitting in her lap and began to cry.

Rosalind took off her apron and sat down at a corner booth
with a cup of coffee. The lunch crowd had been well under way
when she came in after her appointment, but now most everyone had cleared out of the grill. She felt tired, but still okay,
better than she would have expected given her early morning
appointment, not to mention the level of fatigue she'd reached
the night before.

She looked out the glass storefront of the grill. Kids passed
by and a few came in and sat at the counter. She thought of
how embarrassing it would be for Lola if her mother looked
like those people in the picture. *A limited time.* That's what the
doctor said. If the last test results showed what they expected,
they would try the drugs for a short while and avoid surgery,
and hope that the disease went into remission. That's what she
should concentrate on.

She'd never thought of herself as that vain before, but she'd
never had to consider what she looked like one way or the other.
Her looks, her energy, they'd always been there. Only when they
would be taken away did she realize how much they defined her
self-image. Roy said it didn't matter. But it did matter. To her,
it mattered.

"I'll get these guys," Greg told her. "You sit for a minute." The
scruffy-bearded chef nodded toward the kids who'd come in. He
never seemed to get agitated.

"Thanks, Greg." She strained to see if Lola was with all the others. She'd start to worry if she didn't see her soon.

In the back office, Mae Rose talked on the phone. Greg finished helping the teenagers and then closed up a large Tupperware container full of sliced onions and put them in the refrigerator. His white apron was splattered with grease from turning dozens of burgers for the lunch crowd. Rosalind would need to slice more tomatoes but it could wait.

She pushed the disturbing notions of her treatment aside for a moment and thought about his experiments with twins. Funny, she never thought of Roy as a twin. She never thought of him as a son or brother even. They'd been on their own for so long, it seemed like they'd never belonged to anybody else. Listening to the doctor, it struck her that Roy and Mont didn't just look alike, but their cells carried the same codes for not just eye color, but diseases as well.

Much as she had pushed it out of her mind, Roy came from somewhere, and in just over a week, they would drive back there to watch Luke graduate. She couldn't imagine seeing Lydia, Taylor, and Mont. She thought she'd never have to.

"Hey." Lola sat down in the booth across from her. She put her books down. "How'd it go this morning?"

"I didn't see you come in. It went fine," Rosalind said, showing her the inside of her arm. "If I lose this job I can get work as a pincushion." The joke sounded flat, even to her own ears, and Lola didn't laugh. She just looked more worried. "I'm okay," Rosalind said. "Really. You wait, I'll be better than I was before. Nothing to worry about."

Mae Rose came out of the back office and waved to Lola. Rosalind took the moment of distraction to change the subject. "So, you and Duncan . . . Daddy says every time you so much as catch a glimpse of him you turn all pink in the face and happy."

As if on cue, color rose in Lola's cheeks. "I didn't think Daddy even noticed things like that."

"Daddy always notices it when a boy is hanging around his girl," Rosalind said.

"What's going on with you two? He drove you home from the cemetery, then you go off walking."

"I really like him," Lola said. "I felt like I knew him the first time I saw him at the fire. Is that crazy?"

"No," Rosalind said. "That's exactly how I felt about your daddy. It doesn't happen to most people. Just be careful. Don't hand over your heart too fast. There's plenty of time to get to know him."

Lola looked down at the table and Rosalind wondered what she was thinking. Had she already gone too far with the boy?

"Lola? You haven't done anything you regret, have you?" Being somebody's mama got too hard sometimes. You had to ask questions even if you didn't want to hear the answer.

"No!" Lola looked horrified. "I just don't know how to talk about this, that's all. I just like him a lot and I don't even understand exactly why."

"It's okay, sweetie," Rosalind said. She glanced around to see if more customers had come into the grill. Things seemed under control.

"You felt something about Daddy the first time you saw him?" Lola asked.

Rosalind remembered arriving at the church fellowship hall. It had been like a part of her very own being sat right across the room from her.

"Yes," she said. "Before we'd even been introduced. I can't tell you why, but it's as true as my name."

"Was he married to Luke's mama?" Lola looked her straight in the eyes.

That's my girl. Take it head-on. "Yes," Rosalind answered. "We didn't act on our feelings for that reason. Not until his situation changed. But we felt it all the same."

"And you're the reason Daddy left her?" Lola looked at her, not with judgment, but with earnest effort. She wanted to know and Rosalind had to tell her.

But how could Rosalind explain something so complicated?

"Daddy never so much as held my hand when he was married to Sherry," she said. "But that being said . . . He felt the same way about me that I felt about him. From the very start, we both knew we felt it without ever saying so. And that made him pull away from her. So yes, it was my fault. I could have told him to stay gone from me. But I didn't. Even standing in the same room together, having a casual conversation, everything we did was an act of infidelity because of what we both knew about our feelings. I haven't admitted that to myself until this thing with Luke happened. But it's true and I have to live with it."

"Is that why Luke's mama went to bed with Daddy's brother?" Lola asked. The words had a tenuous quality, as if she could barely speak them out loud.

Rosalind felt her pulse quicken. "How on earth do you know about that?"

"I heard you and Daddy talking."

"Does Luke know?" Rosalind's mind raced forward to what that would mean, but Lola shook her head no. She hadn't told him.

A week before, all Rosalind had wanted was for him to know the truth and go back to his real father. But the boy had a basic good nature that deserved better than Mont Vines. Better than Lydia and Taylor. And if she was really honest, part of her needed to make up for the wrong she'd done Sherry Vines. Helping her son was the only way.

"Sherry felt desperate, I'm sure," Rosalind said. "She most

likely turned to Mont for comfort. I can only guess that's why. I don't know for sure. The truth is, all those years ago, I was so happy to have a reason for Roy to leave her, that I didn't care why she'd done it. I'm ashamed of that now."

"I understand . . . sort of," Lola said. "Something picks you up and carries you away, whether you want it to or not."

"You're talking about Duncan, now. Right?" Rosalind had to remember that Lola was her daughter, not her confidante, and the girl needed a mother.

"I guess."

"That's why you have to be careful, Lola," she said. "Careful with your heart and your body. You understand?"

"Stop it, Mama, I know all that." Lola looked down at the table. Color flamed in her cheeks.

"I just don't want you to make mistakes, sweetheart." Rosalind reached over and put her hand on Lola's arm, but the girl still didn't look up.

Enough. The child was thoroughly embarrassed and Rosalind felt drained from the effort of dragging all that old baggage up to the surface.

"More people are coming in," Rosalind said. "My break's over, I think. What's up with you and Charlotte this afternoon?"

"Since Luke's got Janie Ray at home already, Charlotte wants the two of us to go lie out in the sun at the lake." Lola looked at her again. Her relief at the change of topic made her seem giddy.

"How're you going to get there?" Rosalind asked.

"She said her mama would meet us here with the car. Mrs. Benson can get a ride home with Mr. Benson, and we'll take the car. I brought my bathing suit to school with me. Is that okay?"

"How much homework do you have?" Rosalind asked. The question was a formality. Lola could do the work they gave her in her sleep.

"Not much. It's so close to the end of the year. We're just reviewing for exams now," she said. "We won't be late anyway. We'll lie out for an hour or two."

"Okay."

Charlotte came out of the bathroom and sat down beside Lola. Rosalind felt such genuine affection for the child. She and Lola had been close for so long, Charlotte seemed like another daughter.

"So Lola tells me you and Luke are going out," Rosalind said.

Charlotte either blushed or beamed, Rosalind couldn't tell which.

"Yeah," she said, "he's different than anybody I know."

"Well, I hope you have fun," Rosalind said. "You girls get some French fries if you're hungry. I'm going to get to work now."

Vicky Benson stood at the counter. Rosalind hadn't seen her come in.

"Hey, Vicky," she said. "You want to sit down, or can I get you something to go?"

Vicky looked at her, but didn't answer right away. She looked up and down at the apron Rosalind wore. "When did you start here?" she asked, finally.

"Last week. I'm helping Mae Rose through the lunch shift."

Vicky nodded. Rosalind wanted to be done with her interaction with her neighbor. The woman was unpleasant under any circumstances. But when Rosalind had to be nice to her—had no option of walking away—the minutes seemed painful.

"I'll have two orders of fried chicken with regular mashed potatoes," she said. "To go." She looked around as if sitting down in the grill was the last thing she'd lower herself to do.

"Anything to drink?" Rosalind asked.

"You're not writing this down?" Vicky looked suspicious.

"Chicken and potatoes," Rosalind repeated. "I think I have it. Drinks?"

Vicky shook her head. "I'm meeting Hal at the dealership," she said. "He's got Cokes there."

Just wanted an answer, not an explanation, Rosalind thought. She relayed Vicky's order to Greg, then went to the register to check on change and small bills. If she needed to make a run to the bank, she'd have to go before the grill got inundated with the after-school crowd of kids ordering milk shakes and hamburgers.

The cash drawer looked to be in good shape.

"These are for your girls over there," Greg said, putting a paper boat full of fries on the counter.

Rosalind smiled and took them over to Lola and Charlotte.

"You two be careful at the lake," she said. "Don't go in without looking out for each other."

"Yes, Mama," Lola said, rolling her eyes.

Rosalind glanced over and saw Mae Rose at the cash register with Vicky's order. She was glad not to have to deal with the woman again.

"Will you be home for dinner?" she asked Lola, "or are you calling these French fries your meal for the day?"

"I'll be home," Lola said.

Rosalind turned to see if any customers waited to give their orders, and just as she did, Vicky shot an accusing glance in her direction.

"I never said gravy on these mashed potatoes!" Vicky's shrill exclamation suddenly rose over all the other sounds in the grill. "Why can't anyone ever listen? I told her to write it down."

Rosalind walked over. "What's the problem, Vicky?" She held her temper by a hangnail.

"I don't want *gravy*." Her face twisted into the most unattractive grimace Rosalind could recall in the woman's long history of unpleasant expressions. "You think I want my family to get fat like everybody else in this town?"

Preacher Reeves sat at his usual spot near the door. He got so tickled at this that he switched sides at his booth in order to get a better view of the show.

Rosalind took the Styrofoam containers from Mae Rose, began scraping the potatoes into the trash.

"Don't just scrape 'em off," she said, nearly growling the words. "I want whole new plates of everything."

Rosalind wondered how Hal Benson sold cars to anybody in town after his wife got through pissing them off.

"Calm down, Vicky," Mae Rose said. "We'll get you new plates if that's what you want."

"I know Rosalind here is new, but you've got to tell her to pay attention to what the paying customer wants."

Rosalind looked over at the girls, mainly to avoid looking at Vicky. Lola was about ready to spit fire and poor Charlotte had her eyes so far down, nothing but the top of her pretty brown head was visible.

"Vicky Benson." Rosalind turned back to the woman. Enough was enough. "We've been neighbors for going on fifteen years, and in that time I've learned not to expect a casserole to arrive at the door when I'm sick. But damn it, do you have to be such a bitch?"

Rosalind glanced over in time to see Preacher Reeves slap his knee in pure delight. Vicky's face turned from red to purple, and Mae Rose took a step toward Rosalind.

Rosalind would either get herself fired or not, but she would not take this sort of garbage from a woman who wasn't worth the price of the damn mashed potatoes she ordered.

"Why don't you take a smoking break outside for a minute," Mae Rose said, her voice gentle. Rosalind saw that she was fighting a smile that threatened to turn into a grin.

"I don't smoke," Rosalind said, suddenly afraid she might laugh just looking at Mae Rose.

"It might be a good time to start." Mae Rose picked up a pack of Salem Lights and matches from behind the counter and offered them to her.

"That's okay," Rosalind said. "I'll just take a walk." She didn't dare look Mae Rose in the eye again. Vicky would go crazy if she saw them openly laughing at her display.

Rosalind walked out, followed by Lola and Charlotte, who couldn't escape the grill fast enough, it seemed.

"What is your mama's problem?" Lola aimed the words at her poor friend.

Rosalind was about to intervene on the girl's behalf when Charlotte said, "My mama *is* the problem." She was clearly fighting off tears. "She's everybody's problem, but especially mine."

"I'm sorry," Lola said. "It's not your fault."

"That's okay," Charlotte said. "I deserve it just for being related to her."

"Listen," Rosalind said. "You girls go on to the lake and enjoy yourselves. Charlotte, don't worry about your mama. She flares up and settles down. No one thinks anything about it."

Charlotte looked grateful.

"You okay?" Lola asked Rosalind.

"I'm fine," Rosalind said. Not true, but her problems had little or nothing to do with Vicky Benson.

Lola and Charlotte walked off toward the Benson car, and Rosalind looked through the glass to see Vicky Benson paying for a new order of chicken and potatoes. She did not want to be standing there when the woman walked outside.

Instinctively she headed for the garage. Roy would calm her down. He'd laugh as she regaled him with Vicky's outburst, and things in her life would right themselves momentarily.

The street was quiet. A dull, mid-afternoon lull settled over everything. Rosalind had heard that in some countries, all the stores shut down for people to take afternoon naps. Then they opened up again for the evening. That seemed like a good idea to her, especially in the heat of summer.

As she approached the garage, she saw Roy and Duncan hunched under the hood of a truck. Both of them smiled, looked as if they were enjoying the work and each other. Lola's instincts about the boy seemed right. He was a little old for her and there were some troubling rumblings about his activities, but Rosalind had a gut feeling about him overall. He came from good stock. People didn't come any better than Alva and Minnie Thomas.

"Yeah," Roy was saying to Duncan as she walked up behind them, "I think you nailed this one. I don't know why I didn't see it. We can fix this up in no time."

She smiled as the two of them caught sight of her. Then out of the corner of her eye, she saw what they could not. The raised hood shielded from view a car that pulled in and parked in front of the garage door. The window was rolled down and she could see the man inside the Cadillac as well as her own husband in front of the truck. It was a view she hadn't seen in over fifteen years. Her husband's face in duplicate.

Mont Vines got out of the car. It took her breath away to regard the two of them at once. So alike and yet, she knew, so different.

"You've got a visitor," she said to Roy.

He and Duncan both stepped out from behind the hood, and while Duncan's face registered confusion, Roy's fell into blank resignation. Rosalind had no idea what would play out in the moments that would follow, but she silently thanked Vicky Benson for putting her there. Whatever happened, she could help her husband through it. She walked over to his side and prepared to get reacquainted with her brother-in-law.

Forty

Roy shouldn't have been surprised to see his brother standing in front of the garage. If he'd thought about it, he could have predicted that Mont would get in his car and drive to Linton Springs. But since he hadn't once considered it, the sight of the new model Cadillac with Mont standing beside it caught him off guard. Thank God Luke was at the house. As far as he knew, Mont had no idea how to find the duplex.

"Been a long time, Mont." Rosalind spoke up first.

"How are you, Rosalind," Mont said. It was a greeting, not a question, and without waiting for a reply, he turned toward Roy. "Where is he, brother?"

"Not here," Roy said.

"I see that," Mont said. He walked over to where Roy and Duncan stood by the truck. "I asked where he is."

"I told you over the phone that Luke made his own decision. You've wasted a day for yourself driving here. Go home."

Mont put his hands in his pockets, looked up at the sky as if gathering strength from the Almighty, but Roy knew better. Mont had certain tactics for dealing with conflict. One was to go silent and let the other person second-guess his own decisions until he gave in. *Not going to happen.* Not since falling for Rosalind had Roy been so sure of his own mind.

"You two are the spitting image of each other," Duncan mumbled, as if Roy might not have known this. "Never seen two people, even twins, look so much alike."

"Their looks are where it ends," Rosalind said to Duncan, but she thought of the doctor's twin pictures and wondered where it *did* end, exactly.

"If you're planning to stay for any length of time," Roy said to his brother, "you need to find a room. We're flat out of space at the house."

"Stop this game, Roy. I swear, if you won't . . ."

An ambulance went by, drowning Mont's sentence in a siren wail. The sight of Mont mouthing his response seemed almost comical and brought his color up in frustration. Mont might have been a child stamping his feet for all the good his words were doing him.

"What was that?" Roy said, unable to keep the grin off his face.

"Nothing." Mont took a deep breath and came a few steps closer to where Roy stood. "I went by your house and nobody was there," he said, regaining some composure. "I don't know where you've got him hidden, but he can't stay there forever. Just tell me where he is."

The first part of Mont's statement puzzled Roy. Luke should have been at the duplex with Janie Ray.

"How'd you find out where I live?" Roy asked. Maybe he'd gone to the wrong place.

"I stopped at a quick-mart and asked. That's all it takes to get that kind of information, brother," Mont said. "And it doesn't take much to convince anybody I'm your brother, now does it?"

"How long ago were you at the house?" Rosalind asked. Roy went to stand by his wife.

"Twenty minutes," Mont said. "Maybe a half hour. Listen, I'm getting tired of—"

"Duncan," Roy said, ignoring Mont's new line of protest, "do you and your granddaddy have a phone line set up yet?"

Duncan shook his head. "They're coming to put it in to-morrow."

"I'm sure everything's all right, but I'd just as soon check on those two," Roy said. "Can you watch things here for a few minutes?" Luke didn't have the car or the truck, so he couldn't go anywhere far with Janie Ray. If Mont knew how to find the duplex, he'd just camp out there until Luke came back.

Duncan nodded. "I'll be fine," he said.

"If you're going back out there," Mont said, already getting in his car, "I'm coming, too."

"Suit yourself." Roy said. He wondered if Luke saw Mont coming and decided to hide.

Rosalind got in the truck beside him. They drove off, and she put her hand on his arm. "You're not worried about the kids, are you?" she asked.

"Not really," he said. "I just think we ought to get this done on our terms. Mont's not going away until it's settled. Let's see if we can give Luke some warning. He's probably up at the pond with Janie Ray."

"You're right," she said.

Roy saw Mont in the rear mirror. "Luke's been used for too long now. This is where it stops."

He drove past the city limits and out in the county. He and Rosalind didn't talk for much of the ride.

"How are you feeling?" he asked finally, unable to keep the

subject of her health off his mind for five straight minutes at a time.

"I'm not bad," she said. "Everything will be okay. Even the doctor said—"

"Rosalind stop," he interrupted her. "You can save that speech for the kids. Tell me what you're really thinking."

"I'm thinking—" She stopped. She stared out the side window and he didn't know what to do or say to help her.

"I'm thinking," she began again, "that I won't really know who I am if I look like the people in those pictures. If I look different and I'm getting crazy moods. I know it's vain to think that way, but I can't help it."

Roy was scared, too. He could deal with almost anything if she was getting better. Changes in her looks, having to wait on her more. But if she didn't act like herself, if the changes in her made her feel like somebody different . . . He couldn't live without the Rosalind he knew.

"Could you fall in love with Mont, Rosalind?" he asked.

"Good Lord, no!" She looked at him as if he'd lost his senses.

"He looks just like me."

"Roy, I don't know what—"

"Inside," Roy told her. "I'm different inside than Mont. You love me, you *need* me because of things that have nothing to do with my face."

She looked down at her lap, offered a small nod.

"It'll be hard, Rosie," he said. "But don't leave me. Don't take away the wife I need because some medicine makes you doubt who you are. *I know who you are.* I'll remind you every day, if you let me."

"Okay," she said. Her eyes were wet. She didn't cry often and it always got to him.

He took her hand and they rode in silence until they slowed to turn off the main stretch and onto their road.

"Look," Rosalind said, "but don't pull over." She was smiling again.

He glanced over and saw the two of them—Luke and Janie Ray—sitting with their backs to the road on a rock by Haywood's pond. They held fishing poles. Janie Ray had her head resting on Luke's shoulder.

"Like I thought. She wore him down again," Roy said. "He says he's so damn sick of cleaning fish, but she won't let up."

Roy turned right onto their road, and continued toward the house. With any luck, Mont would follow without looking at the pond.

"I'll try to slip off and get to the two of them at the pond," Rosalind said. "You need to take some time and talk to Mont."

They pulled into the driveway of the duplex, Mont's car right behind them.

Minutes later, inside the empty house, Roy looked around and saw his home for the first time through his brother's eyes. Old furniture and worn rugs. The new coat of paint Roy had put on the walls a few months before kept it from appearing completely run-down. But still, it looked nothing like Lydia and Taylor's sturdy farmhouse, and it seemed pitiful next to Della's old home place that the Judge had given Mont and Della as an anniversary present a few years after they got married.

"Where do you think he went?" Mont asked, apparently unconcerned that Janie Ray was part of the equation as well.

"I expect he's close by somewhere." Roy glanced over at Rosalind.

"I'll check around outside," Rosalind said. "You two have a seat in the kitchen here where it's cool."

She left, and for the first time in well over a decade, Roy sat in a room alone with his brother. He didn't know where to begin. All the starting points led to conflict, and in spite of all that had happened between them over the years, Roy wished he had a single common thread on which to hang their beginning words. He couldn't think of a thing.

"You prefer bourbon over iced tea?" Roy asked.

"I would be dearly grateful for that option," Mont said.

"Come on out to the back step then. Rosalind doesn't like for me to have it in the house."

Mont nodded. "Della's the same way."

Roy put a couple of ice cubes in two glasses. Out on the back porch, Luke's "room," he retrieved the bourbon from a toolbox that sat behind a planter full of greenery. He poured a generous amount in each glass, replaced the bottle in the toolbox, and then the two of them proceeded out to sit side by side on the back steps.

It wasn't much, Roy reasoned, but it was a beginning.

Forty-one

He's here?" Luke tried to reconcile the new with the old. Rosalind had walked up to the pond just moments before to warn him that Mont had arrived in town.

"Roy told him I don't want to go back," he said. "Not until graduation. Why is he pushing this so hard? He's the one who wanted me gone in the first place after I screwed everything up in Virginia."

Janie Ray pulled her line out of the water for the umpteenth time in five minutes to check the bait. The fish weren't biting, and try as he might, Luke couldn't get her to stay patient and let bait sit there long enough for the newly lethargic fish to take notice.

"Leave it in there, Janie Ray," he said. "You won't catch anything if you're yanking it in and out all the time."

"Who's Mont?" she asked, dropping the line back in the water.

How did they plan to explain that to the kid? Luke didn't want to be part of that one. Lola had been surprised enough by the news that her daddy had a twin. The four-going-on-five-year-old would be completely confused.

"That's something we need to talk about, sweetie pie," Rosalind said. "But let me talk to Luke for a minute now."

Luke didn't want to talk. He didn't want to deal with Mont. Why couldn't he fucking decide where he wanted to be without Mont, Pap Taylor, and Nanny making a federal case out of it?

"Do I have to go back right now?" Luke asked.

"As a matter of fact," Rosalind said, "I think it's better if you don't."

"What do you mean?"

"Let's give Roy a chance to have a talk with him," she said. "The more he gets ironed out before Mont sees you, the less you'll have to deal with."

"I'm all for that," Luke said. Things had been pretty uncomfortable with Rosalind when he first met her, but she'd turned out to be all right. Nothing about his real dad and his real dad's family turned out to be the way he thought.

"You think we can convince her to give up for the day?" Rosalind whispered to Luke as she gave a nod toward Janie Ray.

"Maybe if you throw cookies before dinner into the offer," he said.

Rosalind laughed. She had a really nice laugh. She and Roy had fallen in love, and the more Luke was around her, the less he could blame Roy. Nothing that happened was his mom's fault, but he couldn't really bring himself to say Roy and Rosalind were awful people for what they did.

Still, he felt bad for his mom. He felt bad that he couldn't remember as much about her as he thought he would, and then he felt even worse about that. He thought of math class. There were exponential layers of possible shitheadedness, and he'd reached an astounding number of them.

"Something took my worm," Janie Ray whined, pulling her line out and dropping it onto the dirt bank beside the rock.

The two fish they'd caught—one just large enough to eat and the other only big enough to keep it company in the bucket—looked unhappy in the water that had been warmed by the sun.

"We need to clean these things pretty soon," Luke said, pouring out half the water and replacing it with a fresh supply from the pond. "You did pretty well, Sweet Jane," he said. She smiled. "How 'bout we call it a day?"

He turned when he saw a car pull over by the side of the road. Lola and Charlotte got out and walked toward the pond. They wore cover-ups, but he could see their halter top bathing suit straps around their necks.

"Hey!" Charlotte came over and sat down beside Janie Ray. She grinned up at Luke, and he wished more than anything that Saturday would come sooner.

"You're back early," Rosalind said to Lola. "Did you go to the lake?"

"We changed into our suits at the grill after Mrs. Benson left," Lola told her. "And we planned to still go. But once we got in the car, we realized we weren't in the mood, so we decided to ride home. What are you doing up here?" Lola asked. "You hate fishing."

"Oh." Rosalind sighed. "What am I doing? That's a very long story. And before I explain, let's figure out where we're going to take these fish that our Miss Janie Ray caught. I want to stay clear of our house for a little while."

Lola gave her a look. "What's going on?"

"Your uncle Mont paid us a visit."

A look of understanding came over Lola's face.

"We can ride down to my place," Charlotte said. "Daddy's probably home by now and he has that table out back for cleaning fish."

"And your mama?" Rosalind shot a look at Charlotte that meant something more than she was saying.

"She said she just had to do something to calm down," Charlotte said, still smiling, "She said after she dropped Daddy home, she was going to drive to the mall in Gastonia with Aunt Rae. She won't be home until after the stores close."

"Praise Jesus," Rosalind said.

Luke would have to get the story behind all that sometime.

"Can we have the fish for dinner?" Janie Ray asked.

Luke looked in the bucket. *Not unless that same Jesus steps in and does some snazzy loaves and fishes trick.*

"Not tonight, peanut," Rosalind told her. "We'll put these in the freezer with the ones you caught yesterday and I'll fry them up one night this week. Okay?"

The girl nodded.

"So." Rosalind stood up. "Let's go to the Benson house. Lola, remind me to call Mae Rose. I walked out after that tussle with Vicky and never went back."

"She said to tell you to call it a day," Lola said.

Luke saw Charlotte look down at the ground. He'd never seen her be anything but open and bubbly. He didn't know what was wrong exactly, but it didn't take a genius to figure out that her mother had been even more of a bitch than usual.

"Hey," he said quietly, bending low to look at Charlotte's downturned face. He put his hand on her shoulder. "You okay?"

She shook her head.

"Anything I can do?" he asked.

Again, she shook her head, but this time she looked up and attempted a smile.

Saturday. He mouthed the word and gave her a thumbs-up.

She nodded.

"Come on, Miss Janie Ray," Rosalind said. "Time to leave these fish be."

With reluctance, Janie Ray pulled her pole out of the water and the entire ragtag bunch of them headed off to Charlotte's car.

Luke hoped that he wouldn't run into Mont along the way. He realized, with some surprise, that if he never saw Mont, Pap Taylor, or Nanny again, he would feel very little sadness. Did that make him a bad person? Hell, he was who he was, and Roy seemed to get that about him. That was reason enough to stick around Linton Springs for as long as he could.

Forty-two

M ont had gotten loose. Not drunk, but not entirely sober, either. Roy felt so tightly wound that the booze barely registered. He looked out over the backyard. The newly restored swing set reminded him of all that was at stake.

"Look," he said to Mont, "I'm not trying to undermine what you have with Luke, but I do think it's been good for him to be here. He's enjoyed getting to know the girls, and truth be told, Rosalind and I have grown fond of the kid. I didn't expect that, but more family to count on never hurt anybody."

"You haven't been there, Roy." Mont stared out at nothing. "I've seen him every week of his life. Bought him birthday presents. Paid his speeding tickets."

It was true. Nothing Mont said could be disputed. But even the way he said it spoke of distance. Of boundaries he'd set with Luke.

"You ever talk to him, Mont?"

"What the hell kind of question is that?" Mont made a face—a kind of derisive sneer—that Roy hoped his identical features never replicated. "I just told you, I've been around him for his whole life. You think I've had some vow of silence going that whole time?"

"I mean ask him things," Roy pressed. "Have you ever talked to him about how he feels? You don't seem all that interested in Luke. Why are you doing this? Is it because you want to parade him out at some damn political dinner when it suits you?"

"Shut the hell up." For such angry words, Mont's tone was oddly calm, and Roy wondered if he was even more drunk than he appeared. "You don't know anything. You don't know what the kid means to me, so just shut up about it. It's none of your business."

Roy took another fortifying sip of his own bourbon. "What are you saying, Mont?"

"Nothing."

"Okay, Mont," Roy said, losing patience. "Stop all this. Tell me what he means to you. You're dancing around everything like there's more to it than I know. Why is this so important to you? You're the one who made me bring him here."

"That was a mistake." Mont looked at him. "I panicked. He belongs in Gray's Hollow. He belongs where I can see him and . . ."

Roy waited. He looked at his brother, refusing to look away until Mont answered him. Through the woods at the back of the yard, he could hear the low rumble of trucks passing on the interstate less than a mile on the other side of the trees. Birds had gone quiet for the day and the cicadas were just beginning. He'd wait all night if he had to. He felt a mosquito on his arm and slapped hard at the insect, still keeping his eyes locked on his brother's face.

"I told you before, Mama is his legal guardian," Mont said,

getting back to a less emotional approach. "If we have to force the issue, we can. He's gotten his head turned around here for some reason, but once he's back with us, with all his friends, he'll understand who his real family is. Mama's in charge of all the money Sherry had set up for his college. I put in most of it. That's enough reason for him to do what I say and get his ass home."

Mont's words ran together a little and his eyes had lost clear focus. Time to cut him off. No telling what kind of abuse Mont would lay on the boy if he got drunk.

"He just needs to do what I say," Mont repeated.

"You plan to threaten him?" Roy wondered how they could possibly share the same blood. How could they have lived in the same womb for nine months and then become so fundamentally different from each other? "If you want the boy's love, that's not the way to play it."

"The boy's love?" Mont said, letting loose a bitter laugh. "After all these years, I deserve his love *and* his respect." He stopped. The day hung there between them. "You want to talk about love. I loved *her*," he said, finally, then stopped again, as if voicing the last part, putting it out in the air between them, had taken him by surprise. He closed his lips for a moment, then seemed to make a decision. "I loved her, Roy. You never did. And even if Luke doesn't know it, he is mine."

Loved her? Sherry? "What are you talking about, Mont?"

"She was Luke's mother," Mont said, "and she was the woman I loved. She was always the one I loved. He's the only part of her that's left. I didn't realize how important that was until he wasn't there anymore."

It sounded maudlin. Entirely unlike the pragmatic Mont that Roy had known all his life. Everyone had a secret life, but this was almost more than he could buy.

"She turned to you," Roy said. "She was trying to keep her

marriage to me going. That's not love, brother. You've got a wife. A family. You made a mistake."

"No." Mont cut him off. "You don't understand. You never understood. You were so damn stupid. And you screwed everything up. That's all you ever did was screw everything up." Mont sounded more pathetic than mean. Roy half expected to see tears in his eyes. He moved the bourbon out of easy reach for Mont.

Roy didn't know how to respond. The breeze shifted and the smell of grilled meat came from somewhere. Roy thought of people having a pleasant barbeque on a normal weekday evening. He wanted a regular life again.

"Just tell me what you're trying to say, Mont," he said with as much kindness as he could muster. To his recollection, he'd never before had a soul-baring conversation with his brother. Ever. At least Mont was making some effort at honesty—even if he had become insufferable. "When did you decide you loved Sherry?"

Mont turned to him. The rims of his eyes had grown slightly pink, so that he almost looked to be in pain. "Before you ever laid eyes on her."

It took a moment for the words to sort themselves out in Roy's brain, and when they did, he felt the old familiar anger toward his brother creeping into consciousness. "What do you mean?"

"In college," Mont said, "when I was engaged to Della. I met Sherry toward the end of junior year. I'd been engaged to Della forever by then, it seemed like. Her daddy had been making plans for me from the minute I proposed. Then Sherry was there and I didn't know what to do. I'd gotten myself trapped by then. I loved her, but I couldn't do anything about it."

The sound of cicadas had been replaced with the sound of Roy's own blood flooding through his vessels. His neck and ears went hot and he wondered if his skin might burst in the rush of it. An entire portion of his life began to rewrite itself in his mind.

"I met her at a party senior year," Roy said. "You were there. You met her that night too."

Mont shook his head. To his credit, he looked like misery incarnate. He reached past Roy to pick up the bottle and managed to get a little in his glass before Roy took it away from him. He shot Roy a look, but let it go, then took a sip.

"God, Roy. This has weighed heavy on me for so long. It's time I told you. I had Sherry come to that party," he said. "Della was in Charleston for the weekend and I knew she wouldn't be around. It was such work. Always making sure that Sherry and Della were never in the same place. Sherry got emotional. I didn't think she could pull it off. She knew how it had to be from the very start. I never lied to her about my circumstances."

"How what had to be?" Numbness began to balance out the anger. Roy calmed himself enough to finish the conversation.

"With us," Mont said. "She knew that I had to marry Della. My career depended on it. My future. So we had to make some kind of plan that would put us together without raising suspicion." Again, Mont turned to Roy and looked him in the eye.

Mont seemed to be asking for some kind of absolution, but Roy found himself inching closer toward hatred than forgiveness.

"Why are you telling me this now?" Roy knew that his brother never did anything without a reason, and he couldn't see anything to be gained by Mont's abrupt confession.

"I don't know," Mont said. "Honestly, I don't. I guess I want you to understand why Luke is more than a mistake I made eighteen years ago. And I guess I'm just tired of carrying it around with me. It wasn't right, what we did. But I felt so desperate."

"What did you do exactly?" Roy ran through a reel of his

time with Sherry. How did he not know how she felt about his brother? Had he sensed something? Was that why he'd opened himself up to Rosalind? No, he decided. He couldn't claim that. He hadn't known a thing.

"We decided that if she got with you, we could be together. It made sense. You didn't have anyone. She really did care about you. I guess, after a while, she loved you a little, and that bothered me. But she was never *in love* with you. That was only for me. And it all worked out fine until you went crazy over Rosalind." Mont shook his head and smiled. But it wasn't a smile. "And now you want to take the one little bit of Sherry I have left." His expression faded into a hard, thin line.

"Luke's not a souvenir, Mont," Roy said. "He's a human being. And he doesn't want to go home with you." Dead nerves had overtaken his body and his brain. He felt nothing. If he had, he might have wanted to kill his brother. Instead, he responded as if Mont told him that he'd lost Roy's favorite rifle. Had a fender-bender in his car. "You need to get some perspective on this thing, brother."

"He hasn't seen me yet," Mont said, undeterred. "He'll change his mind when he sees me."

Roy shook his head. He wondered how he had lived through all that misery with Sherry and not known that she loved his brother. He thought back to the party where he met her. A pretty girl, laughing with him. Slightly drunk. That's all he remembered.

"The entire time I was married to her," Roy said, still stunned beyond feeling much of any recognizable emotion. "That whole time—you kept on sleeping with her?"

"From the time I met her until she died," he said. "I never stopped. God help me, Roy. It's weighed on me. From the very beginning, it did."

"When I finally take all this in and get as furious with you as I ought to be," Roy said, "what makes you think I won't tell Della?"

The sad nonsmile smile returned to his brother's face. "What makes you think she doesn't know?"

"Oh, sweet Jesus, Mont. When did you tell her?"

Mont put his glass down on the step. He put his hands together and made a steeple with his fingers. "Della found out about the two of us before we ever got married."

"What did she do?" Roy tried to imagine Rosalind finding out about something like that. She'd leave him and probably take a knife and separate him from his privates before she went.

"She'd watched her daddy have women over the years when her mother was alive," he said. "I don't think she was all that surprised about me. She cried a lot at first. But then she told me that I was stupid to be so obvious. She said she'd marry me, but if I couldn't be discreet about the other women, she'd have her daddy ruin me. She expected a string of women, I guess, but it was only Sherry. When Sherry died, I turned into a faithful husband. You'd think Della would be glad, but I don't think she cared by then what I did. She only cared about how it looked."

How the hell had Luke grown up with any shred of humanity?

"I don't know what to say to you, Mont." Roy had finished the bourbon in his own glass and thought of pouring another, but decided against it. "Luke will come back for graduation and not before, and he's got a home here for as long as I'm drawing breath. I don't even know how I feel at the moment, but I'd appreciate it if you would sober up enough to drive back to Virginia where you belong and leave the boy alone. Leave all of us alone."

"I'll see the boy," Mont said. "And then I'll go. But this isn't over. I meant what I said about Mama. She knows what he means to me and she'll use her status as his guardian if she has to."

Roy was about ready to tell him that'd he'd use anything and everything he knew to keep Mont away from Luke when they both heard voices and looked up to see Luke, Lola, Janie Ray, and Rosalind coming through the yard from the Benson house. Roy slipped the bourbon bottle just under the stairs.

It didn't matter that his conversation with Mont was now over. He didn't know what more he could have said anyway. Mont didn't seem to care whether Luke *wanted* to be around him or not. He simply needed to control the kid. Maybe the only way he knew how to love somebody was to control him. He'd certainly controlled Sherry. How could that have happened?

"Hey there." Rosalind spoke up first. "Look what we have here. A couple more fish from up the street to add to those guys in the freezer. Janie Ray talked Luke into getting the poles out again."

Her cheerful tone sounded forced, but Roy knew she was doing her best. Luke looked as if he might be sick and Lola just looked purely stunned. Janie Ray was the only one in the bunch smiling.

"You look just like my daddy," the little girl said, addressing Mont. "Do you have the same mama and daddy?"

"Yes," Mont said. "We certainly do. You must be Janie Ray. I heard you're smart as a whip."

"You don't sound like my daddy," she said.

Mont had gone into politician mode and Janie Ray, with a look of suspicion on her little face, was having none of it. *Good for her.*

"So Luke, my boy," Mont said, turning to the older kids, "Roy here seems to think you don't want to come back to Gray's Hollow. That didn't make any sense to me, so I rode down to tell you face to face how much we miss you at home."

Roy wanted to do something, anything to end the boy's misery. The look on his face told the whole story. He might not have it in him to go against Mont. Old habits died hard and

Luke had been ordered around by Mont, Lydia, and Taylor for most of the life he remembered.

"My big brother and I are just getting to know each other, Uncle Mont." Lola looked Mont straight in the eyes. "He's promised to go out this weekend with some of us. I don't imagine he was raised to break his promises, now was he?" She made the last part teasing and sweet. Just the right tone.

Roy made eye contact with Rosalind. He saw the hint of a smile come across his wife's face.

"If everybody always kept their promises," Mont said, made bold with bourbon, "you likely wouldn't have been born, little missy."

Roy shook his head. How could he be so self-righteous after everything he'd just admitted to? "That's enough, Mont," Roy spoke up.

Mont suddenly stood. "You're right," he said. "I have had enough of all of this. Come on, Luke. It's time to go home."

Luke remained in place with Rosalind and Lola flanking him like sentries. Lola reached out and touched his arm, and this gesture seemed to give him what he needed to speak up.

"I've made some commitments here, Mont," Luke said. "I believe I'll stick to the original plan and drive back up for graduation next week."

"And after that?" Mont's eyes narrowed.

"I honestly don't know," Luke said, keeping eye contact with Mont even though it clearly pained him to do it.

"Your grandmother won't be happy," Mont countered, making his threat clear to Roy if not to Luke.

"Yes, sir," Luke said. "I expect she won't. Please give her my apologies, but I need to finish some things I've started here."

Mont bit his bottom lip. He might have had more in mind to say, but for whatever reason, decided to keep it to himself. He stood up. "Good to see you again, Rosalind, and nice to meet my nieces."

"You might not want to drive at the moment." Roy kept his voice low. "Wait it out for a bit, Mont."

"I'll be fine," Mont said, turning toward the driveway. "My head's all too clear at the moment." Then he turned to Luke, "I'm disappointed. I misjudged you, boy."

"I'm sorry, Mont." Luke didn't look up. It took everything he had, and then some, Roy wagered, to stand his ground.

Roy watched his brother walk around the house and disappear. Moments later, the new model Cadillac—nicer than any car Roy had ever driven—pulled out and headed down the road.

"Well, that was uncomfortable," Rosalind offered, to break the silence.

"You don't know the half of it," Roy mumbled.

As she and the girls walked up the stairs to the house, Roy went over to Luke. The boy had a blank look, but his shoulders twitched slightly as if spasms racked him from within.

"It's okay, son," Roy said. "You did good."

"What?"

"I said you did good," Roy repeated.

The gratitude that came into the boy's eyes told Roy he hadn't heard those words often enough in his life. He put his arm around Luke's shoulders and guided him. Together, they followed the others into the house.

Forty-three

After a week of nonstop surprises, two full days passed without anything new, and Lola wondered if that would be it. Maybe the explosion of excitement, both the good and the bad, would have to last them a while. She'd gone to school—her last week of sophomore year—while Mama went to the grill. Luke split his time between looking after Janie Ray and hanging out at the garage with Duncan and Daddy.

He seemed like someone who'd been away on a trip, but had finally come home. It felt that natural to have him there. She tried to imagine him in his other life, living with that man Mont and the old people who were her grandparents. When she started to see it in her mind, she got sad, because it didn't strike her as a good life for him to have had. He didn't say it exactly, but the way he talked about "Nanny" and "Pap Taylor," she knew they weren't the kind of grandparents who loved you to death.

And Mont . . . Good God. Rosalind had warned Lola, "He looks just like your daddy. It'll throw you at first."

Lola thought she was prepared, but when she saw him she almost fell over. Listening to this Mont person, however, brought Lola back to herself. He didn't have her daddy's soul. He opened his mouth and became an actor in Daddy's skin. That was when she spoke up. Luke didn't know it because he never had the distance to figure it out, but Mont was a bully, and bullies didn't know what to do when you weren't scared.

"Hey there," Duncan stood on the front step of her porch. It was Saturday and she'd gone outside to read, but had lost track of her book when her thoughts took over.

"Hey," she said, smiling.

"You looked like your mind was off somewhere else," he said. "Hope I'm not bothering you." He walked up the steps and sat beside her on the swing.

"No. I was just thinking about Luke," she said, "and how it's weird that I only met him a week ago."

"So you never had any idea that you had a brother?" he asked.

She thought about telling him the truth, telling him what she'd heard from her parents. But she decided against it.

"Surprised the hell out of me," she said, and left it at that.

In fact, in spite of what she knew, she'd begun to think of Luke as a sibling. She wanted him to be and he was—as long as one of the adults in the mix didn't screw things up. Mont was married and had a whole political career to worry about. Her daddy and mama seemed to be intent on leaving it alone.

"I thought you were working with Daddy today."

"It was slow," Duncan told her. "Roy told me to come on home."

"Are we still going out tonight?" Lola asked.

"Unless you've changed your mind," he said.

He rocked the two of them with his feet. She liked the sway and pull of the motion. He smelled faintly of motor oil and other garage smells that she counted as familiar. Having it linger the way it did with her daddy made her feel safe. She wondered how long it took before you could really be in love with somebody instead of just thinking that you felt that way. Was there a difference?

He looked off toward his grandparents' house. The section that had burned looked like a picture Janie Ray might have drawn with black crayon—a barely recognizable shape with uncertain edges.

"Granddaddy's hurting so much," he said, still staring at the remains of the old place. "I am, too, but nothing like what he's going through. I'd go back in a second and make it right if I could."

"I know you would," she said. She wanted to comfort him, but sensed it was out of her reach. She felt shy, but even so, had to work not to move toward him. The pull was that strong. Maybe he'd be the person she would be with forever, like her mama and daddy. Her heart raced ahead of her at that thought, and she made herself come away from that idea and think about the swing and the warm air, the feel of the book still in her hands.

"You know," she said, changing the subject, "as much as I hate to admit it, Shelby had a point when she told you to think about school."

"Never thought I'd hear you give Shelby credit for anything." He grinned.

"Just this once."

"I'm thinking about it," he said. "I went to the library and got information on the work-study programs. We'll see."

She didn't mention that she was thinking about finishing

high school early. There would be time for that later. Who knew what would even happen with the two of them anyway?

"I'll come over and get you at seven or so, okay?" he asked.

She nodded because suddenly her voice failed her.

"Luke and Charlotte are talking about a movie," he said, "but your daddy told me to stay away from the drive-in or he'd follow us there and make a scene nobody wants to see."

She laughed like she thought it was funny, but inside she could kill Daddy for talking about her with Duncan when she wasn't there. He didn't have much sense or experience with her dating. She didn't, either, but she surely knew that much ought to be off-limits.

"Seven, then," he said, standing up.

She nodded again and stood up, too. She felt stupid for having gone mute, but for the life of her, she couldn't come up with a single word to say.

"Jeans okay?" she managed before he rounded to the other side of the duplex.

"I've only got jeans and church clothes," he said, "and I don't plan on hearing a sermon tonight."

He was gone before she could think of anything clever to say back to him. Dull as a cucumber. That's how she acted around him. As she turned to go into the house, she saw Janie Ray standing on the other side of the screen.

"Hey," Lola said to her little sister.

"Are you going to get married to Duncan and have babies?" Janie Ray asked.

"Not that I know of." She opened the door and went inside. It seemed her whole family had to be involved in her love life.

"I say it's okay if you do," the girl said. "As long as I get to throw flowers in the aisle like Sarah did when her cousin got married."

"You bet," Lola said, losing her irritation with her sister. She tugged lightly on Janie Ray's ponytail as she walked inside.

"Tell him to marry you instead of Shelby," Janie Ray said.

"Why do you think he'd marry Shelby?" she asked. She sat on the arm of the couch.

Janie Ray shrugged her shoulders, then looked at her feet.

"Tell me," Lola said, her voice harsher than she intended.

Janie Ray came over and leaned against her leg. The girl looked up at Lola with an expression that aged her beyond her four years. "I listened to them talking on Duncan's porch today," she said. "Shelby thanked him for letting her ride home in his car and she said she liked having lunch with him. It sounded like they kissed, but I couldn't see for sure."

Lola worked at not crying. She didn't want to make Janie Ray feel bad for telling her. And so it was a relief when the anger took hold, pushing any hurt and sadness off to the side.

"What's up?" Luke said, walking into the room.

"Mama and Daddy will be home soon," Lola said. "Can you stay with her a minute? I need to go talk to Charlotte."

"Sure," he said. "Anything wrong?"

"Everything," she said. Without bothering to explain, she got up and went outside.

She could see Charlotte sitting on the grass in her front yard. Pinball retrieved a dog toy of some sort and brought it back. Walking along the road toward the Benson house, Lola watched Charlotte throw it again and again. Each time the dog responded with the same enthusiasm.

As Lola came near, Charlotte looked up. "Uh-oh," she said. "What kind of bug flew up your butt?" she asked.

Lola sat beside her. Pinball jumped all around, scratching Lola's legs. She brushed the dog aside and looked at Charlotte— a direct stare that demanded eye contact. "Did you know that

Shelby's still been after Duncan?" she asked. "That she had lunch with him this afternoon?"

Charlotte looked down and scratched the dog's ears. She bit her lip, which signaled the worst kind of guilt. "It wasn't his fault." She looked up again. "He was sitting by himself at the Burger Spot and she plopped herself down across from him."

"Were you there?"

"Daddy took her car away," Charlotte said, "so Mama dropped us at the library. We just walked over to get some food and he was there. I guess he'd been working with your dad and went for a late lunch. It was only a ride and he didn't even offer. She asked." She looked at Lola hopefully.

"Did you go with them?" Lola asked.

Charlotte grinned. "Yep. Shelby got so pissed. She looked like she was going to melt right down like the green witch in *The Wizard of Oz*. It was beautiful."

Charlotte seemed pleased with herself, but Lola didn't feel much comfort from anything she said.

"Janie Ray said they kissed," Lola said. "At least, she thinks that's what she heard."

"I didn't have any excuse to stick around when she went on the porch with him," Charlotte said. "Sorry, I don't know what happened."

"Where is she now?"

Charlotte shrugged her shoulders, gave an apologetic look.

"Why didn't you call me?" Lola asked. "God, Charlotte. I'm so sick of your sister."

"He likes you," Charlotte said.

"Yeah, well, I have a rule. My mouth doesn't go where Shelby's has been," Lola said. "That one's not negotiable."

"You don't know for sure that he even kissed her," Charlotte said. "And he's going out with you tonight. Not her."

"I don't think so," Lola said, standing up.

"Oh, come on," Charlotte protested, "we've got it all planned."

But Lola didn't turn around. She just walked back up the street. She didn't even know him and she was acting like a freak. She wouldn't do this. Better to let it go before it even got started. She'd send somebody to the door when he came.

Mama and Daddy had driven with Janie Ray to Kmart in Gastonia. She'd outgrown all her summer clothes and needed shorts and T-shirts for the warm weather. They bribed her with the promise of a new plastic blow-up pool if she was good while picking out some clothes.

Lola stayed in her room. She'd enlisted Luke to tell Duncan she wasn't coming out. But, as it turned out, seven o'clock came and went and he didn't show anyway. And to think she'd been giving Shelby credit for her ideas about school. She was glad she didn't mention her own plans. She wouldn't follow Duncan Cranford across the street, much less to college.

"Want me to go over and see what's up?" Luke asked. He was anxious to go down and get Charlotte. Lola knew he was trying to be helpful, but he wanted to get on with his date, even if hers was going to be a bust.

"You go on," she said. "If he shows up, I'll just tell him myself."

"I think he's a better guy than this," Luke offered. "He wouldn't just ditch the whole thing without saying anything. There's probably a reason."

"Yeah," she said. "I think that reason is blond and skanky."

"Stop it, Lola."

"Just go," she said. "Please."

"I don't want to leave you sitting here," he told her. "Come on with us, at least."

She raised her eyebrows. God, how pathetic would that be? He obviously thought better of it, too.

"Sorry," he said. "I'll call Charlotte and stay here with you."

"You'll get your butt out the door," she said, forcing a smile. "Go. Have fun. I'll be fine. Mama and Daddy will be back soon. I'll watch *Lawrence Welk* with them."

He looked just shy of horrified. "You are joking, aren't you?"

"Yeah," she said. "Of course I'm joking."

The truth was even sadder than that. She'd sit in her room and read. Books were better than ice cream at providing comfort. She wouldn't tell him that or he'd stay home for sure just to keep her from being that much of a loser. But all she wanted was to see him head out the door. She wanted to be by herself.

"Go," she said again.

This time, he complied.

She sat in her room. Mostly she stared out at the empty yard and the street beyond. No sounds came from next door—or anywhere for that matter. She thought about two more years of the same view out her window. Duncan or no Duncan, she'd find out how to finish high school in a year. But even after she graduated, what would she be able to do? Get a scholarship, she hoped.

She heard a car engine down the street, and seconds later saw Luke and Charlotte drive by on their way to what should have been a double date. It was after seven, and Duncan hadn't shown up. Had he heard that she was pissed? Maybe Shelby had gone over there and he had no intention of picking Lola up. She at least wanted the satisfaction of telling him to screw off.

By seven-thirty, she was so mad she couldn't think straight. Her stomach growled because she hadn't eaten anything and she decided to act halfway normal and go make herself a sandwich. She walked into the den on her way to the kitchen and jumped back when she saw Duncan standing at the screen door.

"Sorry," he said. "I didn't know whether to call out or knock with the door open."

"How about neither one," she said. She wanted him to go away. She didn't want to be in the room with him, or to follow through on all the arguments she'd run through in her head. She barely knew him and he'd shown himself to be a total shit. That was that. "I don't feel like dealing with this," she said.

"What?" He seemed honest in his confusion.

"It's seven-thirty."

"I'm sorry I lost track of time," he said.

"You lost more than that," she said. "You lost your date for the night when you decided to get cozy with Shelby earlier today."

"Shelby?" He looked toward his side of the duplex, seemed distracted. "Shelby shows up, I don't ask her. I didn't do anything . . . Listen, I'm just worried about my granddaddy right now."

If he was lying, it was a new low—blaming an old man. He looked really worried. She went to open the door.

"What happened?" she asked.

He stepped in, walked to the couch and then back toward the door before he stopped. "He's talking kind of out of his head," he told her. "Sometimes he makes sense and then he doesn't. I'm afraid to leave him for long."

"You want me to go over there with you?" She was halfway to believing him about Shelby, and even if she didn't, she wanted to help Mr. Thomas.

"If you don't mind." He stopped moving, looked at her for the first time. "I'd really appreciate somebody else seeing it. I keep thinking maybe I'm the one going crazy. He hasn't done this before."

She walked out with him. Having a fit over Shelby felt small and stupid all of a sudden. At least she'd had her little hissy fit by herself and hadn't gone storming over to him.

They walked down her porch steps together. Duncan stopped on the last step. He motioned for her to be quiet and then pointed toward the road. Across the street, in the high grass, stood a deer. It looked like the same one she saw the night she walked down to the Bensons', but beside it there was another movement in the grass. A small fawn with matchstick legs stood by its mama. They grazed, and both their heads angled down like they might be praying. It looked like a painting.

Then out of the blue, a deafening crack broke the air. Lola jumped and grabbed Duncan's arm. In the same instant, he'd folded his torso around in front of her, putting his whole body between her and the source of the noise. She smelled gunpowder and realized somebody shot a gun. The deer were long gone, and Lola looked over Duncan's shoulder to see what the hell happened.

"Damn varmints!" Mr. Thomas walked out from his steps into the yard. "Big rats if you ask me. They eat up half of what I plant every year."

"Granddaddy!" Duncan sounded out of breath. "You scared the living shit out of me. What're you doing?"

"I may be an old man," Mr. Thomas said, "but I'm a good shot. I didn't plan on hitting those deer or anything else. I just wanted to scare them onto somebody else's property."

"Sweet Jesus," Duncan said, walking toward the old man. "Don't ever do that again."

Mr. Thomas didn't answer him. He turned and walked back into the house. At that moment, the truck pulled in and Mama and Daddy got out with Janie Ray piling out behind them. They had plastic bags from Kmart and Janie Ray held her pool, still small in its packaging.

"What's going on?" Mama asked. "I heard a shot."

Lola and Duncan both shook their heads, still too stunned to explain.

"Are you two okay?" Daddy asked.

"Yeah," they said in unison.

"I thought you were going to dinner tonight," Daddy said, looking uneasy.

"We haven't left yet," Duncan said.

Lola wondered what that meant. She hadn't agreed to go anywhere yet.

"Then again," he added, "maybe we'll just stay here and grill some venison."

Lola looked at Duncan, and in spite of herself, she got tickled. They both got tickled. Nervous laughter fed on itself and it seemed like they'd never stop.

"Have you two been drinking?" Mama asked, her voice low to keep Janie Ray out of earshot.

"No, ma'am," Duncan managed.

"Duncan," Daddy said. "Can I talk to you for a minute?" His expression fell somewhere in between perplexed and angry.

"I just need to check on Granddaddy," he said.

"I'll check on him for you," Lola told him. "You talk to Daddy." She turned to go into the Thomas side of the house for the first time.

Inside, a small table sat by the door. A crystal candy bowl sat on the table filled with white butter mints. She stared at the bowl. It seemed out of place with everything else in the room. Nothing hung on the walls and the couch looked to be secondhand. In the middle of all that, the delicate bowl stood out like an altar, something elevated and worthy of better.

In the corner, the television played. Low chords of accordion music came from the small set perched on a rickety stand. *Lawrence Welk*. Mr. Welk held a thin stick in his hand. He moved it when he talked, conducting his own words. She stepped closer as Bobby and Cissy, the dancing couple, came onstage.

"I like those two." Mr. Thomas was suddenly in the room with her. "They dance like they're both made of cotton candy."

"I like them, too," she said. She did, even though she laughed with her friends about the show. Janie Ray said once they must be rich because they dressed like Cinderella and the Prince every week. That made Lola wonder what they ate for breakfast. What kind of laundry detergent they bought. What did famous people do when they weren't on TV?

"I'm sorry if I scared you before," the old man said.

"That's okay," she said, still looking at the couple on the screen. "Did you put the gun away?" she asked. He didn't answer, and she turned to find him gone again.

"Damn it," she muttered to herself. She looked in the kitchen and down the hall. "Mr. Thomas," she called. No answer. On the television back in the den, Bobby's and Cissy's smiles took up the whole screen. The camera closed in on their faces and Lola could see that only their mouths smiled, not their eyes.

"Mr. Thomas!" she called louder.

She walked through the kitchen and onto the back porch. Outside, the yard merged with her own. A wind came up, moving Janie Ray's swings. Beyond the yard, Mr. Thomas stood in grass that reached up past his knees. He stared out toward his own property down beyond Charlotte's house.

"Mr. Thomas?" She spoke quietly so as not to startle him. He seemed to be concentrating on something, but there was nothing remarkable as far as she could see.

"Come out here." He turned to her. "You've got to listen to something."

She walked toward him, and when she reached him, he took her arm and led her deeper into the high grass.

"Listen," he said. "You'll hear 'em in a minute."

She stood still, an awkward quiet thick between them. She heard the faint noise of cars moving on the interstate. The sound of all that travel made her feel anxious. She wanted to go inside, but he seemed intent on whatever he'd heard. Just when her patience began to give, she heard the sound, eerie and small.

Everybody thought they were gone—driven away by the smoke or, worse yet, burned when their majestic feathers caught fire. But the peacocks were alive and now called out to Mr. Thomas, who received them like a blessing.

"You hear them?"

"Yes, sir." She smiled. Their survival seemed proof of something, but she had no idea what.

"It's like Minnie talking to me," he said. "She loved those birds, especially the boys with their tails flashing like a stained glass window. Treated them like babies, she did. She even gave them names, but I can't remember any of them now."

Lola heard them again, and he took a few steps toward the lingering call.

"You always said they'd last longer than we did," he said. "I guess you were partly right, anyway," he said. "I wish it wasn't true."

He was talking to Mrs. Thomas, Lola realized. She felt she was somehow eavesdropping.

The wind picked up again and she thought she heard the birds, but couldn't be sure. Maybe there were no birds at all. Maybe Mrs. Thomas *was* calling out to him. Who knew what souls could do when they passed through?

"It feels like it might rain," she said. "You want to go inside?"

"I suppose so." He turned back to her.

"Are you okay, Mr. Thomas?" she asked.

"Sure I am. I haven't felt this good since my Minnie passed."

She believed him. He'd lost, at least for the moment, the pull of grief in his face.

"Matter of fact," he said, "I'm hungry as a wrestler."

He started toward the duplex, and she wondered if she should stay with him. He really seemed okay. When he reached the back porch door, he turned toward where she stood in the yard.

"You heard them, too, right?" he asked. "You weren't just humoring me. They're out there."

"Yes, sir," she said, putting every ounce of conviction possible in her reply. "I promise. I heard them, too."

That seemed to satisfy him. He went in and the screen door slapped and rattled, leaving her in the yard alone. Between the wind and the highway sounds there were no more peacocks. But she *had* heard them. She was sure of it.

She wondered if she and Duncan were still going out. Did she want to? Shelby didn't seem to matter anymore, and Lola felt ridiculous for blaming Duncan when the whole thing was nothing more than one of Shelby's stunts.

She walked around the house and saw her daddy still talking to Duncan in the yard. She'd seen Shelby at work before. Maybe she'd overreacted.

Both Daddy and Duncan held cigarettes and seemed deep inside important talk of some sort. Daddy leaned toward him, said something, and then listened for Duncan's response. Lola realized that her daddy had been drowning in girls for so long, he must have been starved for a little of his own kind. And then in a snap second, he had Luke and Duncan, and even old Mr. Thomas to balance things out.

Her uncle Mont's arrival had threatened it. That part wasn't over yet and she worried that the truth about Luke and the intentions of Daddy's family in the mountains would be too much for them. And Duncan. He wouldn't stay at the duplex forever.

She watched the two of them, Daddy and Duncan, and barely let herself breathe. It was too fine, that balance, too fragile to last. And she wanted to hold it in place for as long as she could.

Forty-four

Roy inhaled, letting the smoky calm of the nicotine fill his lungs and then seep out into his shoulders, his arms, and even to the tips of the fingers that held the cigarette. He would quit, but not before the next trip to Virginia was behind them.

"So you think you can handle the garage while I'm gone?" he asked Duncan for the second, maybe third time. The boy was barely older than Lola, but he handled himself well and knew his way around an engine better than most men three times his age.

"I don't mean to sound like I don't trust you," he said, "but that buddy of yours, Jerry, cleaned me out the last time I left town. I'm a little skittish. I was going to just close up, but I can't really afford to."

"Mr. Vines," Duncan said, "I know you have reason not to trust me. I know Granddaddy was up front with you about everything that happened. But I promise, I'm done with all that

and I'll do my best for you. It means a lot to me that you'd consider putting me in charge."

Roy didn't plan to tell Alva, but after working with Duncan
for three days, he'd begun paying the boy some by the hour.
Not a lot, but as much as he could afford. Truth was, Duncan
turned out to be the best help he'd ever had. That business of
marijuana . . . He believed to his core that the kid had learned
his lesson in the hardest way possible. Hell, he even trusted him
with Lola. His business was nothing compared to that.

"I know you'll do just fine," Roy said. "When I get back, if
you're interested, we'll talk about getting you on salary."

"Yes, sir."

Roy sensed some hesitation. Maybe the kid had other plans.
But having him around took care of his short-term problem of
keeping the place covered while he went to Luke's graduation.

"What's it like having a twin?" Duncan asked out of the blue.
"That fellow who showed up the other day . . . It was spooky
looking at the two of you standing there together."

What *was* it like? He saw Mont and he knew they were the
same. He looked at pictures where the two of them were together. So he knew what other people saw. But he never had
the experience of *seeing* himself side by side with his brother in
the flesh. Mirrors and pictures weren't the same. From Roy's
vantage inside his own head—especially if you factored in their
thoughts, their view of life—Mont could have been a different
species.

"You get used to it," he said, because it seemed too complicated to explain. "I've never been all that happy having my
face walking around doing the things Mont does. But I can't
change it."

"Why didn't Lola know about him?" Duncan asked. "About
all those people in Virginia?"

Did Duncan have the right to ask him that?

"I'm sorry," Duncan said, sensing he'd overstepped. "I just want to know all I can about Lola, about your family. I like her a lot, Mr. Vines. Granddaddy said that Grandma used to say Lola had an old soul for such a young girl. I feel that way when I talk to her."

"It's okay. I don't mind you asking," he said, not entirely sure that was true. "My family—that family up there in Virginia— they did more harm than good. To me, I mean. I realized early on that if I planned to get what I needed from a family, I'd have to make a better one than I came from. Until recently, I didn't have a reason to risk showing those people everything Rosalind and I have built. I don't want to go into it any more than that. But I will say I'm glad I got Luke here. I think he's been living what I lived up there. He needs to know there's more to hope for him than what's been offered so far."

Duncan took a last drag of his cigarette, then dropped it in the dirt by the road. After a minute, he said, "Listen, I should mention, I'm worried a little about Granddaddy. He's been going off a little here and there. Most of the time, he's fine. But tonight, he got worse. And he scared the hell out of me with that gun."

Duncan had told him about Alva shooting at the deer. It was kind of funny until you thought about it. And then it wasn't.

"If he has a bad day while you're away up there . . ."

"Close up," Roy said. "Stay home with him. Or bring him up with you. Whatever you need to do. That goes without saying."

"Thank you," Duncan said. "I appreciate your understanding on that."

Roy nodded. The boy had things straight in his head. That was good. It made him feel like he could trust his gut feelings about the kid.

Roy looked over toward the duplex. Lola stood on the porch looking at them. She wanted to go off with Duncan. They'd planned to have a date, but Duncan had gotten sidetracked with his granddaddy.

"I'm going to invite Alva over to watch some TV with us tonight," Roy said. "We'll have some dessert and see if there's a rerun movie on some channel. You go out with Lola and have fun."

Duncan stood there for a moment without responding. He kept his head down, looking at the ground. When he looked up, Roy saw relief in his expression.

"Thank you," Duncan said. "That makes me feel a lot better. Lola and Luke, they're lucky to have you."

Roy wondered what he'd been through in his life. Everybody had something to get over, it seemed. While Roy was still trying to decide what to say next, Duncan looked up, his expression showing nothing of what had been said seconds before.

"How does barbeque sound to you?" Duncan called out to Lola. "You still willing to go out with me? We can try to catch up with Luke and Charlotte."

Lola hesitated for a minute, and Roy wondered what was going on. "Okay," she said, finally. "I'll put on a different shirt." She went in the house.

"I better change, too," Duncan said, looking down at the holes in his T-shirt.

"You behave with my girl," Roy said, only half joking. "You might be twenty-plus years younger than I am, but when I get riled, years don't mean a thing."

"I hear you, sir," Duncan said, not sounding all that worried. He walked off toward the house.

Roy lit another cigarette. He'd take a few minutes to enjoy watching the sky around him that wasn't quite day and wasn't quite night. The moon would be up soon, but he saw no sign of it in the strange light.

He'd have to get his thoughts ready for the trip to the mountains, but that could wait. His quiet life had turned into a series of days where one thing followed too closely on the heels of another. He glanced toward the house and saw Rosalind step out onto the porch. The steel edge of the moon peeked over the horizon that stretched behind the house. The constant moon, and his wife, just as steady. He'd be okay, he reasoned. They'd all be okay.

Forty-five

ancin' Pigs BBQ sat on a flat piece of land in the middle of nowhere. The sign had two pigs, a boy and a girl, in square dance clothes looping arms in a jig.

"Why the hell do they always show happy pictures of the things you plan to eat when you get inside?" Luke opened the door for Charlotte to go in. "It doesn't seem right."

She rolled her eyes. "Smells great, doesn't it?"

Before the girl came over to seat them, Charlotte ran off toward the far corner of the place, so he followed her. A fish tank set into the wall gurgled and hummed, and near it on a shelf, a birdcage sat high and away from the seating area. It didn't seem like a good idea to have a live animal in the dining room. The bird inside, a large, black thing, cocked its head to regard them.

"Pretty bird," Charlotte cooed.

"That is a damn ugly bird," Luke said.

"Hush," Charlotte snapped, as if the thing might be offended. "It's a mynah bird. It can talk."

"That doesn't mean it understands what we're saying," he told her.

Next to the birdcage, a small plaque hung on the wall. Four cloven feet had been mounted, coming straight out like somebody had punched the animal through the wall, feet first. Luke read the inscription.

First hog served at Dancin' Pigs BBQ, June 12, 1962.

Luke's appetite threatened to abandon him. He looked again at the bird. Mean, pebble eyes judged him.

"What's his name?" Charlotte asked a passing waitress.

"The owner grew up in Asheville, so he named him Thomas Wolfe, after the famous writer from there," she said. "But we just call him Tom-Boy." She delivered large glasses of tea to a table nearby.

"Hey, Tom-Boy," Charlotte said. "Look here, Tom-Boy."

"Hey, toots." The bird suddenly sprang to life, startling everyone in the room. He squawked again, "Hey, toots!"—louder the second time—and moved from side to side on the perch in a manic little two-step. "Go home. Go home," he said.

"Hush up, Tom-Boy," the waitress yelled over to the bird. "They haven't even eat nothin' yet." She came back over to where Charlotte and Luke stood. "Hoyt, the owner, got it in his head to teach Tom-Boy the names of some of that writer's books. He got as far as the one everybody knows best, *You Cain't Get Back Home Again*, or something like that, and all the dang bird will say is 'Go home, go home.' And sometimes he says 'Eat face,'" she added. "We don't know how he learned it, but we figure it might be Hoyt's nephew. That's what the kids call kissing," she added, as if they weren't teenagers themselves.

The bird settled back down and the waitress took them to a table. After they ordered, Luke felt in his pocket for his wallet.

It was a reflex, anticipating the bill that would arrive at the end of the meal. He hoped he had enough cash to pay for the dinner. He had some money with him when he left, and he hadn't spent anything all week. But Mont usually slipped him money every few days and Roy didn't have anything to spare.

"I need to use the bathroom," Charlotte said. "I'll be right back."

The waitress brought hush puppies before Charlotte got back and he put one whole in his mouth. The salty grease burned his tongue. Then he waited for Charlotte, feeling conspicuous alone at the table.

"Sorry," she said when she finally returned. "There was a line in there. There's always a line for the girls."

"Speaking of girls," he said, "what was up with Lola?" The shift in topic was a stretch, he knew. But he'd been curious about his sister all night. "She stomped out of the house cussing about your sister, and then Duncan didn't show up and she wouldn't let me go over there and ask him why."

"All I know," Charlotte said, "is that Shelby threw herself at Duncan again. He's too smart to fall for that, but I don't know what happened with the two of them. Shelby wasn't home all afternoon, but she's usually not home, so that doesn't mean squat."

He hoped Lola was okay. It felt strange to worry about somebody like that. To worry about a *sister*. He liked feeling connected to Lola and Janie Ray. They'd been family all along. How weird was that? It seemed to him that the impulses had been inside him all along, too. Meeting Roy's family turned on a switch that put those feelings in play.

"You with me, Luke?" Charlotte leaned over the table toward him.

"I'm here," he said. "I was just thinking about how weird it is to be around family I didn't know until a week ago."

"That's what Lola says, too. I've lived with my sister all our lives and I don't care about her as much as you two care about each other."

She looked sad about this revelation. He thought he should move the subject along.

"I just don't know what's going to happen," he said. "Mont's pushing for me to still be part of the Virginia family. But the truth is, I don't want to. I mean, I'd like to visit them and all sometimes. But they don't feel like my real family. Roy, Lola, and Janie Ray . . . hell, even Rosalind . . . they do."

"Well, you've only got the summer to worry about," she said. "Then you're in college, right? At that fancy school in Virginia?"

"You don't stop having family when you go to college." He hadn't thought much about that part until the last week, but it was true. "You go home sometimes on weekends and you spend Christmas and summers somewhere. I'm worried that they're going to make me do all that in Gray's Hollow."

"They can't *make* you do anything, can they?" she asked.

"It seems like they can," he said, trying to think of why that was. "They raised me after my mama died. It's hard to let go of what I've been used to for so long. It's funny, when they first sent me off with Roy, all I wanted was to stay. But now I'm kind of scared about going back for graduation next week." An uneasiness crept in now when he thought of Gray's Hollow.

"Why?" She leaned over and touched his arm. Again, her touch soothed him, something different from feeling horny— although she made him feel that, too. But her fingers on his arm, it was nice. He hoped she'd keep her hand there.

"I don't know why," he said. This was the truth.

"Eat face!" Tom-Boy called from across the room.

Charlotte laughed, but the bird seriously creeped him out. Just then, the waitress arrived balancing plates of barbecue on one hand and another basket of hush puppies in the other. Charlotte pulled her hand away from his arm and he felt the absence of it.

At the door, he saw Lola and Duncan. They must have just walked in. Lola's hair was wet, so the rain had finally come.

"Hey!" Charlotte waved them over.

His sister's arrival reassured him, set things right. He stood up, his food getting cold, but he didn't care.

"Everything all right?" He leaned down to ask Lola quietly when she was beside him.

"Yeah," she whispered back. "I think so."

Maybe it was, he thought, switching sides of the booth to sit by Charlotte.

Forty-six

The phone rang in the kitchen. Roy sat on the couch in front of the TV with Rosalind, Janie Ray snuggled in and asleep between them. Beside them, in Roy's usual chair, Alva Thomas sat, smiling at Jimmy Stewart, who bumbled his way through a courtroom monologue on the screen. The old man didn't seem to hear the phone.

"I'll get it," Roy whispered to Rosalind. He transferred the limp form of his younger daughter to Rosalind's lap and got up to go to the other room.

"Hello," he said into the receiver.

The other end of the line was silent except for the sound of a baseball announcer on a radio in the background.

"Hello," he said again.

"Roy?" The woman's voice sounded familiar, but he couldn't place it.

"Yes," he said. "Who's speaking?"

"It's Della," she said. "I'm sorry it's so late."

His sister-in-law spoke in hushed tones. He could almost hear the radio more clearly than her words.

"Is something wrong?" he asked. He thought of Mont, of his parents. In spite of everything that had gone on, the fear that something bad had happened still gripped him. Feelings about family could be the damnedest thing.

"Mont fell asleep listening to the game," she said. "He'd be mad if he knew, but I thought I ought to call you."

"What is it?"

Again, the silence. Roy waited. "Della?" he said after nearly a minute passed.

"I think he's going to tell him the truth," she said, then let out a long breath as if the pressure behind the words had become unbearable. "He's talking about telling Luke everything."

The words were cryptic enough, but he had no doubt what they meant. He didn't know what to say to her. The news didn't really surprise him, not really. Mont couldn't stand to lose anything. Not a bet. Not a dollar. Why would he stand for losing his son?

"His career," Roy said, "his campaign . . . Has he thought about what he'll be doing to all that?" Roy's heartbeat pounded in his neck. He didn't give a damn about Mont's career, but that's what he had to fight with if he wanted to stop this. "Della? Has he thought about that?"

Roy knew a confession like that would destroy the kid. It would make him question his memories about the only decent parent he'd had growing up. Not to mention finding out that he hadn't had an absent daddy, just one who was there all along but didn't claim him. Didn't his brother realize that? Mont had always thought he could have everything he wanted by force of will, but this was different.

"I've known about it," she said. "You've known. Even Lydia.

He'll find a way to keep Luke quiet, too. He'll turn it around so that it sounds like the right thing to do."

Of course he would. Della understood better than anyone how it would all play out. She'd lived with that game longer than Roy could imagine.

"How do you feel about it, Della?" How did Della feel about anything? He'd never really known.

"When he first said it," she said, "it didn't seem like it made much difference. That was yesterday. But it bothers me. It bothers me a lot. It's like she's back again in the middle of our lives. And he's never once considered how it will make Nell feel. He's never given much thought to Luke before and now that's all he talks about. It's like he's obsessed. It seems like the last straw for me."

"Did you tell him that?" Roy asked.

She fell silent again. "Yes," she said, finally. "I don't think he believes me. Daddy's getting too senile to bully him. That's the only thing that ever got to him."

It was the most sincere conversation he'd ever had with Della. Certainly the most honest. Suddenly he felt for her. In all of it, she'd drawn the short lot. She had nothing to show for her life but a "Mrs." in front of her name.

"Maybe you could talk to him," she said. "When you get here. Before he does it. Maybe you can convince him that it's too much of a risk, or threaten to go public with it if he tells him."

Roy just wanted it to go away. He wanted his brother to go away. He hadn't brought himself to tell Rosalind yet about Mont's full confession. He didn't know why. It would only serve to ease her conscience about their past. But something about it . . . It was too humiliating still. He had to get over that part and talk to her. But first he'd have to deal with this new crisis.

"I'll do what I can, Della," he said, "but I've never changed

Mont's mind about much of anything. Mama might be a better bet."

"I thought about that, but I hate to go to her. She'll act like it's my fault just because I'm the one who told her. She might even agree with him, and that would make it worse. She always takes his side eventually. You know that."

Who knew how Lydia would react? Governed by stubbornness, a convenient sort of religion, and a blind ambition for at least one of her sons, she couldn't be predicted. The possibilities ran the gamut.

"He has another night or two to sleep on it," Roy said without much conviction. "Maybe he'll change his mind."

"Maybe," she said, absent any notion of hope.

"Della?"

"Yes."

"You said it's the last straw," he said. "Will you leave him?" If Mont thought she would really go, he might listen to her. Roy waited for her to answer.

"No," she said after too long a pause for there to be any other answer. "He knows that as well as I do."

Both of them let her words settle. Suddenly there was nothing left to say.

"Good night, Roy," she offered.

"Good night, Della." He hung up the phone and went back to his family and Alva Thomas. He sat down to finish the movie, a story that he knew well, one that would turn out okay in the end.

Forty-seven

Rosalind felt as if they were leading the boy to slaughter. She rode in the truck with Roy. Janie Ray sat in the small jump seat behind them. Luke followed in the car with Lola. They'd agreed to ride up on Tuesday, with his graduation the next day. Roy hadn't slept much in the three nights since Della's phone call. He'd been up taking antacids and pacing around. Luke had sensed that something was off and asked her about it.

"Roy's got a lot on his mind," she'd told the boy. This wasn't a lie, but it wasn't the truth, either. The truth was going to kill both him and Roy. She was sure of it.

"Hills are pretty." Roy made conversation.

"Green," she said.

They'd left so early, it was barely eight-thirty when they reached the foothills of the Blue Ridge mountains. Rosalind could see the close layers of the low hills, rising one right after the other. Janie Ray said they looked like brown puppies up next to their mama.

As they climbed gradually in elevation, she realized that the interstate sliced straight through the hills ahead, leaving underground creeks to bleed out of the high solid bands and hit open air.

"We need to stop for gas pretty soon," Roy said. "Keep a lookout for an Exxon station. They haven't gone up as much as everybody else on their prices. Not yet anyway."

Rosalind knew Roy worried about the oil shortage. If people drove less, that was bad for the garage business. She overheard Hal Benson tell Roy that the Arabs had our country by the balls. She couldn't imagine what countries like Iraq and Iran would look like. She'd barely left her own backyard in her entire life. Would she ever feel like going out and seeing the world? She couldn't picture what the rest of her life might be.

"Remind me to call the doctor's office when we get to your folks' house," she said. "The last of my results are supposed to be in today, and he wanted to talk to me over the phone. We can pay your parents for the long-distance. I won't talk long."

"They can afford it," he said. "Seems they owe us that much at least. They gave Mont the whole damn business."

She hadn't talked much to Roy about his family's business. He'd given up so much when he walked away with her all those years ago. Mostly he seemed okay with it, but there were bitter edges left over from learning that Mont now had it all in his name.

"Maybe that doctor will give us some good news," Roy said, forcing a lightness she knew he didn't feel.

Good news was relative. She was already taking medication that would change her. Her looks. Her moods. She purely hated the idea, but Roy's words came back to her. Looking and feeling different didn't take away who she really was. Her family needed that person. If medicine could keep her body from turning on itself, vanity would have to take a backseat. Already it was easier thinking about it without wanting to cry.

She thought about another part of the conversation she'd had with her doctor. Another idea had been forming, and she had a few questions for this doctor when she called him later—and not all of them about her health.

"How much money do you have on you?" Roy asked. "I need to fill up the tank for Luke, too, but I forgot to go by the bank before I left."

"I think I've got enough," she said, looking in her purse. "Yeah, we should be fine. I cashed my paycheck from the grill after work yesterday."

Maybe it was best to just live and not think too much about illness, oil, or the rising cost of gas. Maybe everyone should just hold on tight to what they love and live minute by minute. Get along as best they can.

She looked back at Luke and Lola following close behind them. They were laughing at something, riding with their windows down. How would it change for them if Mont told Luke he wasn't really Lola's brother? It hadn't made a difference to Lola, so maybe that part wouldn't matter to him, either. Sister or cousin—she was still family. But deep down, Rosalind knew that it *would* matter. It would change him to know the truth—and not for the better, she feared. She might have a chance to spare him all that. She'd have to think on it, though.

"Is Exxon the one with the tiger?" Janie Ray asked from behind them.

"Yes, ma'am," Roy answered.

"I see one up there," she said, staring between the two of them.

"Her young eyes are better than mine," Roy said, slowing down. "She's right."

He pulled over at a place called the Trading Post. Exxon pumps sat out front. The building looked like a log cabin and had a wooden Indian standing beside benches made of split logs. The bottom half of the benches were round tree trunks with bark still on them. When they pulled up to the pump, Luke stopped at the one behind them. A skinny boy with a big mole on his neck came out to pump gas for them.

"Look at that Indian," Janie Ray said, hanging over the seat between them. "Can I touch it?"

The place would have barrels of penny candy, plastic viewers with scenes of the mountains inside, and toy tomahawks. Rosalind didn't have the energy for Janie Ray's begging. Best to keep her occupied with the Indian.

"Sure, pumpkin," she said. "Go see it if you want."

After both cars were filled, they got back on the road again. Rosalind couldn't get Luke off her mind, or the idea she had to help the boy. She'd have to talk with her doctor first to get her facts straight, and then it would take swallowing every ounce of pride she had in her, but she thought she could do it.

She made a decision. It wouldn't come without cost, but if she could, she would do everything in her power to spare that boy any more hurt and confusion than he'd already had. He might be Sherry's son, but he was a good kid, with a good heart. He deserved better than he'd had.

Forty-eight

Luke had gone quiet and Lola didn't know whether she should fill the silence with mindless chatter to distract him or give him some space. She'd seen a sign that said Gray's Hollow was nine miles away. She didn't blame him if he felt nervous. She was anxious, and she didn't have everything at stake the way he did.

"What are they like?" she asked. Might as well talk about it if he could, she figured. "Nanny and Pap Taylor. I still can't believe I've got a grandma and grandpa on Daddy's side. It doesn't seem real."

Tall trees closed in thick on either side of them, causing the day to seem dark even though the sun was shining.

"They're all right," he said. "Strict, I guess. Especially compared to the way you've grown up with Roy and Rosalind."

Lola was glad that Luke still called her daddy Roy. If he'd switched to Daddy that would have been weird, even if she didn't know everything she knew.

"Will they hate me because of Mama?" she asked.

"Maybe. Nanny is especially hard that way. She won't let anything go. Pap Taylor can be a little softer sometimes."

"How should I act?" She hadn't thought much about it. The trip had been on her mind, but not the arrival. With just miles to go, the reality of meeting her grandparents came down hard in front of her. She couldn't go around it anymore.

"Polite," he said. "Don't say much unless they ask you. Don't try to win them over or anything. It doesn't work like that with them. Bring up church any chance you get. If they know you've been raised Christian it might help. I don't know. Hell, I don't even know how I'm going to act yet. It's weird."

Weird. That summed it up. They rode for a while without any more talk, and after a couple of miles, the trees gave way to pastures. Farmhouses appeared here and there, well back from the road. All of them painted white. Lola wondered if her granddaddy's hardware store sold any other color. She imagined shelves full of paint cans in varying shades of white. True white, ecru, ivory, pearl . . . All seeming to offer choice, but looking the same from a distance.

"How much further?" she asked.

"Two miles," he answered, drumming the steering wheel with his fingers. "Town's over that way, but we don't go through it to get to them. My high school's just down that road. I'll go over for graduation practice later today, I guess."

"It'll be good to see your friends again, won't it?"

"Yeah," he said, without much enthusiasm. "Yeah."

Lola had heard Mama and Daddy talking. Mont's wife had called, but she didn't know what it was about. Whatever it was, they hadn't shared it with Luke and they didn't seem happy. She closed her eyes, sent a quick thought to Jesus for good measure. *Let Luke have a good graduation. Don't let them mess it up.*

She felt the car slowing and opened her eyes. Ahead of them,

Daddy turned the truck onto a smaller road and Luke made a right turn following him. In the distance, she could see a house sitting up on a small rise. She stared at it, and as they got closer she decided that it looked just like a house in some Christmas movie about coming home. A big porch and wide shutters, a lower one-story section off to the side. It looked perfect, even better than Charlotte's house. How could the people inside not be perfect, too? But they weren't. The look on Luke's face as they neared the driveway reminded her of that.

"Here we are," Luke said, pulling the car alongside the truck in a flat graveled area beside the house.

Under the shelter of a carport, a big pickup sat alongside an Oldsmobile wagon. Everything around her seemed like a place normal grandparents would live. But if they were so normal, she would have memories of them going back to when she was little. For Daddy not to mention them, for them not to find her . . . They weren't like any grandparents she knew. Even when Ruthie had a falling out with Mr. and Mrs. Thomas, they kept up with Duncan.

Lola looked up. On the front porch, an older couple stood side by side. She was thin and small-boned, while he stood a foot higher, at least. The woman's gray hair was pulled back, but her face didn't have as many wrinkles as Grandma Simsy. The old people didn't smile or offer loud greetings, so the five of them in a line—Daddy, Mama, Janie Ray, Lola, and Luke— approached the porch as if granted an audience with royalty. They stopped short of coming up the stairs.

"Roy," the old man said. "I see you made it."

"Mama, Daddy," Lola's own daddy said, "these are my girls, Lola and Janie Ray."

Nanny and Pap Taylor walked down the stairs instead of welcoming everyone up, and Lola wondered if they'd all be sent away. Nanny stopped about a foot in front of Lola.

"You look like your mama," she said. Judging from the woman's expression, this was not the compliment most people meant it to be when they said it. Then Nanny glanced down at Janie Ray. "At least you look like you have some Vines in you." She took a step over toward Luke. "We've missed you, son," she said. "After Mont called down to Roy's, we all thought you'd have been back up here before now."

"I had some things planned already this week," he said, looking down. His voice shook a little.

"Must have been important," she said.

Lola had yet to see anything resembling a smile cross the woman's face. She wanted to slap the ole biddy.

"Lydia." Pap Taylor came up beside his wife. "These girls are here for the first time. I bet they'd like something to drink. Luke, you must be thirsty, too, after the drive." He awkwardly put a hand on Luke's shoulder, then took it away.

"Yes, sir," Luke said.

"We have some iced tea or something in there," Pap Taylor said to his wife.

She nodded and turned to go inside the house. They were to follow, Lola guessed. No one had acknowledged her own mama. This had to be the weirdest family reunion ever. Lola glanced at Daddy for some guidance. He motioned for her to go on into the house behind her grandparents.

As she walked into her grandmother's spotless kitchen, she thought of Mr. and Mrs. Thomas. The warm, messy counters crowded with cakes and batter bowls in the house that had burned. Lola wished she could blink her eyes and substitute the Thomases for these nasty old people. That wasn't quite fair. Pap Taylor seemed more standoffish than anything else. But Nanny . . . There was a mean streak a mile wide in that one.

"I'm hungry," Janie Ray whispered to her.

Lola made a shushing face at her sister. "Later," she whispered back.

They stood in the middle of the room, no one venturing to sit down. Lola held Janie Ray's hand and took hold of Luke's arm with her other hand. Luke didn't belong with these people. Not them or that uncle who looked, but didn't act, like her daddy. Whatever happened after Luke walked that procession and graduated, he needed to be heading back to Linton Springs with them.

"We're your family now," she whispered to him. "You're staying with us."

He nodded, but his eyes were fixed on Nanny.

"Mont's on his way," Nanny called over her shoulder as she got glasses down for iced tea. "When he gets here we can have a visit before we go to your graduation practice."

"You're going?" Luke asked.

"They said families can come take pictures if they want," she told him. "Everybody, have a seat." She put glasses with ice on the table.

They all obeyed. Even an oddly quiet Janie Ray, who, for the first time in her life, seemed to know a stranger when she saw one.

They all sipped their tea and waited, but Lola had met Mont. If anything, his arrival would make the gathering more uncomfortable.

She stared out the kitchen door, and prayed for time to pass.

Forty-nine

Roy sat on the bleachers of his old high school stadium. Beside him, Mont took off his tie and opened his collar in the heat. People stared openly at the two of them. A lot of the kids—the ones who hadn't heard about Luke's adventure at the police station, at least—didn't know that Commissioner Vines even had a twin. The older people in the crowd hadn't seen them together in nearly twenty years.

On top of that, there were the whispers—Roy had overheard a few of them—about Luke's absence. His name had been mixed in with all of that talk, as well. It made for an unusual amount of interest in the Vines family at the stadium where the kids had gathered to do a practice run through the graduation ceremony.

"Remember when we were doing this?" Mont asked.

"Yes, I do," Roy said. And he did. He hadn't been in the high school stadium since his own graduation day, but it all came back with unexpected clarity.

Lydia and Taylor Vines sat on the other side of Mont. They

kept their eyes on the field where the kids milled around and joked with each other. Roy had his wife and two daughters beside him. It looked as if they'd gathered into teams, or battalions, depending on how things went. All Roy knew for sure was that he had to manage a serious conversation with his brother before Mont had any chance to talk to Luke.

Roy hadn't been able to get Mont alone. He'd hoped to speak again with Della, to find out if Mont knew about her phone call. But she didn't come to the house or the high school. Lydia asked about her, and Mont said she felt under the weather. His hushed conversation with her had occupied his mind for two straight days, but still he had no idea how to talk his brother out of tearing Luke's world to pieces.

"There he is." Rosalind leaned toward him and pointed toward Luke where he'd taken his place at the end of the last row on the risers. Vines. He came near the back alphabetically, but they'd gotten lucky with him on the end. He was close enough to get some good pictures.

Mont had a newer Kodak model, of course. The film went in as a cartridge. But Roy didn't mind using the ancient box of a camera he'd had for years. They both pointed and snapped, Roy's camera making enough noise to draw attention.

"Is he all right?" Lola voiced the question.

Roy looked closely at Luke. She was right. He'd lost all color in his face and had a slight sway to his stance. Lydia was on her feet before anyone else. She stepped down through the people sitting in front of them to get closer to the risers on the field. Roy followed her. At the railing that separated the stands from the field, they were maybe ten feet from Luke.

"Sweet Lord," Lydia said, mumbling the words in a breathy panic. "That's just the way his mama looked before she fell and died."

Roy climbed over the rail and jumped down.

"Somebody get him," Lydia screamed from behind him. "He's going to fall!"

Roy reached the edge of the risers just as Luke's knees gave. The boy beside Luke grabbed his arm as he slumped down, and Roy reached up and got a hand on his shoulder in time to stop him from toppling. Luke lay crumpled on the riser floor. From below, Roy kept a hand on him to keep him from falling off the edge.

"Luke," he said. "You with me? Luke."

Several teachers ran over, and two of them, tall men like Roy, helped him pull the boy off the risers and lay him flat on the field. By that time Luke was coming to. He looked up at one of the men, his eyes gaining focus. "Hey, Coach," he said, as if greeting him in the hall at school.

"Hey there, Luke." The coach smiled. "You scared us there for a second."

Luke sat up, shook his head like a dog shaking off water.

"Have you ever done that before?" one of the other men asked. "Passed out?" He sounded suspicious, and Roy figured he thought Luke might be on something.

"No, sir," Luke said.

"His mama had a history of pass-outs," Roy offered. "They're not dangerous unless you hit something on the way down. He comes by it naturally. He ought to be fine. Mainly, we just needed to keep him from hurting himself in the fall."

"He's right." A man came down from the stands and walked over to the crowd around Luke. "I'll take a look at him, but his color's good now. I bet he's okay." The man wore casual clothes, but clearly had some authority to make the judgment.

"Thanks, Doc," the coach said to the man.

Roy stepped away and gave the doctor his place by Luke.

After ten minutes or so, the practice continued, but they rear-ranged the rows. Luke was no longer anywhere near the end.

Back at home, they sat on the porch that wrapped around the corner of the house. Chairs and gliders, most of them dating back to Roy's childhood, offered seating. Standing out from the rest, a newer patio table made of tempered glass occupied the corner. Lydia had pulled out cushions that went on the chairs. Around the table, a game of Go Fish occupied Janie Ray, Luke, Lola, and Mont's daughter, Nell, who had shown up with Della after the practice at the school. Nell played under duress only after her mother threatened to take her car away if she didn't interact with her new cousins.

Rosalind came out to the porch from the house.

"Did you reach your doctor?" Roy asked her.

She nodded.

"Everything okay?"

"It's what he thought," she said. "The news isn't any better, but at least it's nothing worse."

Roy saw the look on her face. He knew she was thinking of herself transformed into someone different in the mirror. They had work ahead of them. They'd have to live with this thing that had invaded her body. But then, they were a team. He'd keep telling her that until she believed it.

"We'll deal with whatever comes," he said.

She nodded. "I have to go in next week to get my blood levels checked again."

It seemed they were taking more blood than her body could spare. If she could be okay, he could handle everything else. That's what he had to keep telling himself.

"I need to get some food out for everybody." Lydia stood up. "Taylor, put that mosquito candle on the table to keep those kids from getting eaten alive."

Roy sat in the corner, off to himself. He kept a close eye on Luke at the table, and Mont across the porch. Mont smoked a cigar and seemed intent on reading some papers he pulled out of a briefcase. Roy planned to step in if Mont tried to get Luke off by himself. Something nagged at Roy. Something he thought he ought to remember, but couldn't. *What is it?* He looked around, hoping to jog up the answer, somehow. Nothing but the smoke of Mont's sweet cigar came over him.

"Roy," Lydia said, "I need some serving dishes off a high shelf. Will you help me?"

Was she innocently asking, or did she have some agenda? God, there were too many things going on for one family. He didn't want to leave the porch, but he had no choice. "Watch Mont," he whispered to Rosalind as he went by. She was sitting near Della, but Roy didn't think Mont's wife had heard. Rosalind nodded, and he went to help his mother.

He had told Rosalind just about everything. Everything but Mont's revelation about the length of his relationship with Sherry. Maybe it was because she'd always thought—hell, *he'd* always thought—that he'd made the grand gesture of leaving Sherry and choosing Rosalind. Turns out, his first wife was never really his to abandon. He knew it was foolish, keeping it from her. If he expected her to trust him with any changes that came to her, he'd have to trust her, too.

"Hurry up, son." In the kitchen, Lydia waited by the counter.

"Up there," she said, pointing toward one of the cabinets. "I need the two long Pyrex dishes on the top shelf."

He reached up to get the dishes.

"Your brother's going to make a mistake," she said as he settled the glass baking dishes on the counter. She stood close enough to him to keep her voice low. "He's got his mind set on telling Luke that he's his daddy. He thinks he can control that genie once it's out of the bottle, but I think he's dead wrong on that one."

"For once, Mama, we agree," he said.

She crossed her arms, leaned back against the counter. "It's up to you, then," she said.

What did that mean? It was up to him. No one had less influence on Mont than he did.

"I've racked my brain on that one," he told her. "I can speak to him until I'm blue, but I've never been able to talk him out of something when his mind is set. You're more likely to succeed on that score than I am."

She shook her head. "I can't get anywhere. And that wife of his is worthless. Always has been. If it wasn't for what her daddy did for him, I'd say he'd thrown his life away with that woman."

In fact, Della was growing on Roy. He'd seen more humanity in her lately than in the rest of the Virginia lot put together.

"If we're going to stop this, it has to be through the boy," she said. "If you talk Luke into coming back here for the rest of the summer and making this his home again—the home he comes to by choice—Mont will drop this other business. I'm sure of it." Her mouth was set in that hard line that used to scare the bejesus out of him as a kid. Matter of fact, it still did.

"He needs to be able to make his own choices, Mama." Roy shifted his weight, tried to buy some time while he thought of a good argument to make. Something other than *He flat-out likes us better than he likes you.* Inside his head, that unknown something still nagged at him. He tried to pin it down. Was it something Mont said or did? Something he'd seen?

"Sherry intended for him to be here with us," she said. "If nothing else, Roy, you need to respect his mother's wishes. Talk to him."

Sherry. He thought of Luke, on that riser. Pale and losing himself. Poor Sherry. She'd had no one to catch her on that final fall. A cold chill went through Roy's arms, his chest. He literally felt the shudder travel the length of him. *That's just the way his mama looked before she fell and died.* Those were his mother's exact words before Luke collapsed.

"You were with her," he said, more to himself than to his mother.

"What?" Her forehead gathered in a bunch. She'd been caught in a lie and she didn't even know it yet.

"In that department store bathroom," he said. "You were with Sherry. Good God, Mama. What did you do?"

Her mouth had a slight tremble as if she might cry. But she wasn't going to break down. She didn't have that kind of weakness in her. She had the stomach to stand and watch a woman die. But why?

"You saw Luke today. You knew he was going to pass out. You were with Sherry when she fell and died. Why the hell didn't you get help for her? What are you?"

"She would fall sometimes," she said. "You knew that. I was just remembering how she looked . . ."

"You said *before she died.* Stop lying to me, Mama. Tell me what happened."

She steadied herself on the counter, but he knew that, too, was for show. She had her ways of garnering sympathy, of becoming a distressed woman, when it suited her. But she had more steel in her than Mont's Cadillac.

"Answer me, Mama," he said.

She crossed the room and sat down at the table. It was the same table where she'd served him breakfast when he was Luke's age, but the whole room seemed foreign at that moment. Even the air felt different.

"It was God's will," Lydia said, everything about her suddenly steady with resolve. "We were talking. I looked in my purse to get a tissue and when I glanced up she didn't have a thimble of blood in her face. Then she was on the floor. The edge of the counter cut the side of her head and she had more blood than I've ever seen pooled all around her right away. I've seen cows slaughtered. Pigs, too. I've never seen that much blood so fast. They said it wasn't that bleeding that killed her. It was the bleeding inside her head, against her brain. But I don't think I believe that."

She had started rambling and it seemed to be the narrative of some distant third party, not the mother of her grandson.

"Mont told me she'd been down for twenty or thirty minutes when somebody got to her," he said. He struggled to remember the particulars of what his brother told him, but he was sure of that much. "Where were you?"

"Like I said. God struck her down. I went out to get help. I looked and didn't see anybody. Then it was like God spoke to me, and I knew what I had to do."

"What was that?" He felt like a little boy listening to a horror tale.

"I had to stop and listen until He was done," she said. "There's no blame in that. Maybe it was half an hour before I heard the commotion and they brought her out. I honestly don't know. God took me to someplace that didn't have time or space. My body may have been in that department store, but my soul floated free in His presence. They took her to the hospital. She was there for a couple of days, but she never opened her eyes. When she passed, I knew it was His will."

She believed it. For the first time, he realized how truly unstable his mother had become since he left. She'd always been a zealot, but this delusion of spiritual ecstasy at the cost of a woman's life went beyond any argument for normal.

"Sherry never did anything to hurt you. What made you think God wanted her to die?"

"Because it was going to destroy him," she said.

"Him? God?" He didn't know if he could possibly get a coherent answer.

"No." She sounded annoyed. "Mont. She was in the bathroom looking to see if she'd got a period. She said it had been almost three months. I didn't know then, not until that very minute, that she'd been manipulating Mont all along. Kept him going with her, and him a good family man. She sounded upset that there might be another baby, but I knew it would only be a matter of time before she used it to get him all to herself. That notion would come to her and he'd be sunk. Men are weak when it comes to women."

Roy thought of his own feelings for Rosalind. His mother had never made such excuses for him. Then again, he wasn't one election away from becoming a state congressman.

"I liked Sherry. I did," she continued. "But that would never do. I told him time and again not to get too mixed up with her. The one child—Luke—that could have wrecked your poor brother's chances, but it didn't. Another one, especially if she had to explain it . . . who the father was . . ."

"I wasn't around to blame it on." Roy saw it all too clearly. He felt sick to his stomach.

The air around him seemed stale all of a sudden. His own mother. He'd always known she had a hard shell, but he never thought of her as evil. Looking at her, at the lack of concern on her face for all that she'd just told him, he wasn't so sure. What was evil, if not willful and unrepentant harm to another human being?

"You should be locked up," he said. "Do you know that? You essentially murdered that poor woman."

She looked at him, made full eye contact. Her hands rested calmly on the table, not a tremor in sight. "You put everything in motion, son," she said. "You were the one who went outside your vows with that woman. And you have the nerve to question the way the rest of us cleaned up your mess? You left poor Mont with two women depending on him. You have to answer for that. I don't think you have it in you to bring more trouble to this family. I certainly hope not."

She believed what he had believed all those years. She thought that Sherry had met Roy first and turned to Mont after Roy found Rosalind. Only he, Mont, and Della knew the real story on that one. His mother sat so smug in her self-righteous delusion. But she was right to some degree. What did he want to bring down on his family? Who would believe him? Even if Lydia confessed, she'd give the same crazy spiel he'd just heard and she'd land in a mental hospital. What in heaven's name was he supposed to do? What leverage did he have?

He couldn't pull the rest of the family out of that hole they'd dug for themselves down in the middle of those mountains. But he could get Luke out.

"Mont has no idea about this, does he?" Roy said. "He doesn't even know Sherry thought she was pregnant at the time." These were statements of fact, not questions. He turned them over in his mind. What was he obligated to do? Who was he obligated to tell? Only after he mentioned his brother did he see the first sign of fear on her face. "It's too late for a lot of things, Mama," he said. "But maybe Mont has a right to know what you did for him."

"Leave Mont out of this," she said. She pressed her flat palms against the pale Formica table. "Taylor would understand, but Mont had a blind spot over that woman. Don't you hurt him with this."

He had his leverage.

"Give me control of Luke's guardianship," Roy said. "All the money his mama left him for school and everything else."

"Mont gave her that money for him," she said. "And Mont

would have handled it, but we all thought it would look better for me to do it. Mont makes the decisions."

"I'm making them now," he said. "Convince Mont, somehow, to leave him be. And give me control of his money."

"Why?" she asked. "So you can use it for that wife of yours? Those girls?"

"It's Luke's," he said as calmly as he could manage, "and it will stay that way."

"I can put your name on the money," she said, "and I want Mont to let that boy go as much as anyone, but I can't stop him from telling Luke the truth. Destroy me if you want to, but I don't have that power."

Through the door, he saw Lola come into the den from the porch. She walked through toward the kitchen, smiling at him.

"Make arrangements for the money," he said quickly, before Lola arrived in earshot, "and Mont and I will never have that discussion."

She gave him a look that should have sent him low, but it didn't. He smiled at Lola as she came into the room. With Lola came his ability to breathe again. He had his family. By some miracle, he'd gotten it right when, all those years before, he'd left these miserable people behind.

"Mama says she needs you," Lola told him. "Right away."

"She okay?" he asked.

"I guess," she said. "She looks all right, but she made me get up and come tell you instead of coming in here herself."

He leaned over and kissed Lola on the head, then headed to the porch as fast as he could. Mont was up to something and he had ten, maybe fifteen, steps ahead of him to figure out what to do about it.

Fifty

The kids tired of card games, and Rosalind had watched Mont take this opportunity to go over and sit beside his daughter. Luke looked out over the Vineses' back property. The sun wouldn't be gone for an hour or so, but it had already dipped behind the ridge. She looked toward the kitchen, hoping Lola would send Roy out soon. She wanted to give him some idea of what she planned to do.

Roy stepped out of the house and onto the porch. At that moment, she heard Mont over her shoulder.

"Listen, Luke," he said, "let's walk out in front for a few minutes. I want to have a talk before supper."

Luke shot a desperate glance in Rosalind's direction. He saw Roy behind her and included him in his silent plea.

"Before you do that, Mont," Roy broke in before Luke had to answer, "I need to touch base with you on a couple of things."

"Maybe later would be better," Mont said.

"I think maybe now." Roy held firm, but Rosalind could tell from his expression that he was flying blind and making things up as he went along.

Mont nodded his unhappy agreement. He got up from the table and walked down the porch stairs toward the backyard with Roy behind him. Rosalind took in a full breath and went after the two men. She hoped she could go through with it. What she had to say galled her, but she couldn't think of any other way.

They went deep into the property, beyond the groomed edge of the yard where no one on the porch could hear them.

"I thought this was between me and my brother," Mont said when he saw her joining them.

Roy gave her a confused glance. He didn't understand, either, but he soon would.

"I'm part of this, Mont. What Roy and I have to say needs to be said together. Long ago, we came to terms with things that happened. I need to be by his side now."

Roy's forehead became a map of wrinkles as his face formed unspoken questions. She gave a slow nod and he returned it. He'd let her take the lead. That was all she needed.

"What is it you plan to do, Mont?" she asked.

Mont glanced at Roy, waited for him to send her away. When that didn't happen, he shook his head as if to clear it, and said to both of them, "I think you've heard. I know Della called you and she shouldn't have. But it doesn't matter. I've made up my mind to tell him the truth. This is his home. Mama is his guardian."

"Mama has agreed to sign over guardianship and control of Luke's trust fund to me," Roy said.

"Why would she do that?" Mont asked, clearly caught off guard.

This was news to Rosalind, too. She couldn't wait to hear how that came about.

"You'll have to ask her about that," Roy said.

"Well, I'll believe it when it happens," he said, "but it doesn't matter. Once I tell him the truth, and especially after the election if I feel like I can make it public, all that will revert to me."

"What makes you think you'll get to choose how and when this comes out?" Roy asked. "If you do this, if you tell him this, I'll make it public myself, Mont."

"Of course it would be best if this stayed among family until after the election, but I can weather it, I think. I've got strong backing. I plan to gradually come out with the truth after I'm in office, anyway. Once I have a record of service, it won't do that much harm. But if you choose to try and hurt me before that . . . I'll deal with it. I've always dealt with things and come out okay." Then he added, "I don't believe in your heart you are a spiteful person, brother."

Mont had lost all perspective, even all his usual warped perspective. He was obsessed with Luke, even if it destroyed everything else in his life. And he wasn't even doing it because he loved the boy. It was about *winning*. It was always about winning. He'd just never had to think about winning Luke before.

"And Della's daddy . . ." Roy added; he was grasping.

"The Judge has been a wonderful mentor to me," Mont said. "But he has seen some decline, I'm afraid."

"So you plan to tell Luke you're his daddy." Rosalind stated the obvious.

"I do," he said. He looked ready to go back to the house, as if that declaration settled the matter.

"And you don't think he'll resent you for not telling him before?" Roy asked.

"I would have thought so before, but look how he took to

you. He all but hated you until you showed up in the flesh. All of a sudden, he was willing to see you as his daddy. Well, that's wrong, I've decided."

"The trouble is," Rosalind broke in, "we don't know that."

Roy looked at her. She kept her eyes locked on his. He would understand. All he had to do was fall back and let her talk.

"What the hell is going on with you two?" Mont said, his impatience getting the upper hand.

"Roy thinks I've been through enough," she said. "And he doesn't want to make me relive such a painful time. But it's important."

"What in the devil are you talking about?" Mont asked.

"Roy explained to me all those years ago," she began. She'd rehearsed the words in her head, but saying them was harder than she thought it would be. "That while he loved me from the very start, he cared for Sherry—felt some obligation as her husband to at least try to have a marriage. I, of course, was terribly hurt by this. Knowing that he shared a bed with her . . ." She paused and looked at Roy. ". . . in every sense, long after he fell in love with me. I know it's different for men than it is for women."

Roy shook his head slightly, almost imperceptibly, but she caught it. He would know what a story like that cost her—even a fabricated one about intimacy with his first wife. He wouldn't have asked it of her, but she would not let him or Luke suffer because of her pride.

"This isn't going to work," Mont said. "This ploy you two have dreamed up."

"Years ago, Roy and I came to terms with it," she pushed through. "It's difficult to think about, but I know he loves me and we've moved beyond it."

Mont laughed. It sounded forced and ugly.

"I'm sorry you think this is funny," Roy spoke up.

"I don't just think it's funny," he said. "It's futile, *brother.* I'll get the best doctors and lawyers in the state involved if I have to. I've met most of them, as a matter of fact. I have deep pockets and I'll empty them if I have to. You won't win this."

"It's interesting," Rosalind said, "that I've had a conversation lately with one of the best doctors in North Carolina." She paused. "You know about my difficulty," she said, "and I appreciate the assistance you've given us to ensure that I get the best care. This leading blood doctor, it turns out, did a lot of work years ago with families. Twins, in particular."

"Twins." Mont sounded dismissive.

"Trying to figure out if one twin got a blood disorder, would the other one be more likely to have it. That sort of thing." She looked again at Roy, saw the beginnings of a smile on his face.

"And how did that turn out?" Mont asked, still humoring her.

"I don't know," she said. "I was more interested in other things."

Roy and Mont both looked at her. For the first time, Mont, too, seemed to get an inkling of where she was going.

"I asked him . . . this doctor," she said, "how I could get an answer—through a medical test of some sort—" She stopped there. In all her dread of the conversation, she hadn't anticipated the sheer pleasure of watching her brother-in-law's face. "If I wanted to find out for sure whether Roy was or wasn't Luke's daddy, how could I find out? That's what I asked him."

"And what did he tell you?" Mont asked. His lips barely opened as he spoke.

She looked directly into her brother-in-law's eyes, beyond the shape and color and into the depths of them. They looked nothing like Roy's to her. Not a trace of similarity. "He said he was sorry. He said that, unfortunately, I'd be out of luck. That as far as any tests could determine, you and Roy might as well be the same person."

Mont didn't take his eyes off Rosalind. Malignant eyes that repulsed her, but she would not look away.

"This doesn't change anything," Mont said, although Rosalind saw in his eyes that it did. "I'll tell him I'm his daddy. I am his daddy and you both know it. I don't care what fairy tales you make up."

"He might hate you, Mont," Roy said. "You don't know for sure how he'll see it. And even if he doesn't, you'll hurt him to the core. All these years, so close and not telling him. What about how he sees his mama? Do you really want to destroy that? And we'll hold to this story, Mont. To the dying breath we take. He'll never know for sure, no matter what you tell him." Roy took a deep breath. "At best it will be a draw. He'll always have doubts." He'd given every reason he could think of and he was spent. "He's a good boy, Mont. Don't do this to him."

"He is," Rosalind said. "It's hard for me to admit it, but he seems to share Roy's nature. Even you have to see that. What do you think he'll believe?"

Mont looked from one to the other. Rosalind felt the invisible cord of love and years that connected her with Roy. No one, least of all Mont Vines, had a prayer of breaking through. Still, they both waited to see if it was enough. Mont's face went hard. Before he opened his mouth, Roy took a step toward his brother.

"Mont, the boy's accepted me as his daddy. He's happy. He loves Lola and Janie Ray. Think about it. Anything you do won't be for Luke. It'll be for pride or spite—maybe both. And it won't get you anywhere. You'll put a shadow on his memory of Sherry and you won't accomplish more than treading water. At best, he'd have to choose between us."

That last statement seemed to get to Mont. Maybe in his gut, he knew what choice Luke would make. Rosalind stepped back. Roy's shoulders relaxed a little, and she knew he sensed the same thing she did, that the wind had shifted in their favor.

"You'd let this lie stand, Roy? Hell, both these lies. You can live with yourself doing that?" Mont asked, his voice still mocking, but thick with defeat.

Roy paused, and a look of contentment came over him, something Rosalind hadn't seen in a while.

"After the last eighteen years, brother, do you even have to ask?"

Fifty-one

Mont walked past Luke and didn't stop. He'd apparently forgotten about whatever talk he wanted to have. Luke felt like he'd dodged a bullet. From the looks of things, he had Roy and Rosalind to thank for it. They'd gone out of sight into the yard with his uncle, and after they came back, whatever Mont wanted to say to Luke got blown all to hell.

Nanny called them in to supper, and Luke picked up Janie Ray and went into the house. He'd been afraid that Mont would put pressure on him to come back for the rest of the summer. He didn't know why, but he had the feeling all that was behind him. It had been good to see his friends again at the graduation practice. Passing out like that was weird as shit, but that didn't spoil it for him. Not really.

He'd enjoy walking in the procession and hanging out with people for a while after. But what he really wanted was to get back to his makeshift room on the porch at Roy's house. He wanted to kiss Charlotte again. They'd made out in the car after going to the restaurant. Mild stuff compared to what he'd done with other girls. But things were different with her. He felt different with her.

"Hey, Luke." Pap Taylor stood behind him in the den. "You feeling okay after that spell at the stadium?" Nanny had dishes of food lined up along the counter. The others had gone into the kitchen to fill their plates, and he put Janie Ray down to go with them.

"Yeah, Pap," Luke said. "I'm feeling okay." He'd kind of miss the old guy. Pap had tried to help him sometimes, but he didn't seem to understand what Luke needed. Not like Roy. "I guess I'm going back to North Carolina with all of them tomorrow."

"I guess so," Pap said. "You sure that's what you want? This has been your home for a long time, son."

Luke nodded. "I appreciate everything here, Pap. I really do. But I like getting to know my real daddy before I go to school. To spend some time with Lola and Janie Ray, too." He didn't mention Rosalind. Rosalind didn't sit well with Nanny and Pap Taylor. He wished that was different, and it surprised him to feel that way. But in his gut, he felt his own mama would understand. "I've even met a girl down there," he said. "Her name's Charlotte."

Pap shook his head. "Son, girls are your downfall. You know that."

"A nice one, Pap," he said. "Honestly. You'd like her. Maybe you'll meet her."

"Maybe," Pap said. He sounded sad.

Luke felt sad, too. Pap Taylor would never come to Linton Springs. He'd never meet Charlotte.

"We should get some food before it gets cold," Pap said. "Your grandmama'll be fussing at us in a minute."

"Yes, sir," Luke said.

He followed Pap Taylor into the kitchen. He looked at Rosalind standing with Roy and he thought of his mama. *I'm not forgetting you. I promise.* He sent up the words to float free and find her, he hoped. But when it came to his mama, it was all hope and thinning memories. That was all he had.

Fifty-two

The mountain air seemed older than air in other places, gathering smells inside the valley like a light summer stew. Earth, new leaves, and evergreens, along with a faint, lingering wood smoke from cold days long past.

Lola sat in the high school stadium on the end of the row beside Janie Ray. Down the bleachers, her family stretched out, taking up nearly the entire bench. At least half of them she'd only met the day before. And after she got home, she might never see any of them again. She wished she could put Mr. Thomas, Duncan, and Charlotte in the place of all of them. That would be the gathering Luke deserved.

"Where is he?" Janie Ray asked, squinting toward the aisle where the graduates would come in.

"He'll be here soon," she said. "They'll play a special song and they'll walk in with their robes on."

"Is he going to fall down again?" Her little face screwed up in worry.

"No," Lola told her, "they're putting him in the middle this time."

The first notes of "Pomp and Circumstance" sounded and everyone stood. All the teachers and coaches sat in folding chairs on the field and the seniors filed in and walked in the aisle between them. Families snapped pictures from the bleachers. Luke would come in near the end.

Lola thought about her own plans. She could finish early and be doing this next spring. It would mean she didn't walk with Charlotte. There was a cost to every single decision in life. But graduating early would give her one less year of wasted time. Nine less months of the mind-numbing boredom. There was no one but Charlotte at the high school she would miss. And Charlotte would be in her life forever.

She would do it. In the time it took for Luke's procession, her decision had been made.

Luke came in and immediately looked in their direction. He found her face and smiled. Janie Ray squealed, "There he is!" and people around them laughed. Lola looked at her sister and down the row to Mama and Daddy. They both smiled, too. But beyond them a sober group finished out the row. The Gray's Hollow Vines might as well have been at a funeral. Were they always like that? Or did they feel a real sadness that Luke didn't want to stay with them?

Lola decided they weren't a cheerful bunch to begin with, and her daddy had broken free just in time. He'd been able to keep that essential part of himself. She waited and watched as senior after senior walked up. Their whole names sounded like the names of senators or famous writers, not just a bunch of kids wearing church clothes under their robes.

"Lucas Ezra Vines." The principal called Luke's full name.

Lola watched him walk across the stage. When the music started again, she watched until he disappeared into the locker rooms where they all filed out. She leaned over to her daddy. "Where does 'Ezra' come from?"

"Sherry thought she might have twin boys and she came up with Lucas and Ezra," he whispered. "Since there was just the one, she gave him both names."

Lola guessed that made sense. "Where are his other grandparents?" she asked, suddenly aware that he should have another family somewhere.

"They were old twenty years ago," he said. "They had Sherry late in life. My guess is they're both dead, but I couldn't say for sure."

She felt the weight of being among a chosen few, the ones that Luke could call family. She wondered for the thousandth time if she should tell him what she'd overheard. Did he have a right to know who his real daddy was? And she decided for the thousandth time that he couldn't get a more real or loving daddy than Roy Vines. She looked down the row at his alternative, and her mind was set. She wished she'd never heard it, but the next best thing was putting it in a little box in her head and letting it stay there.

Later, as they all congregated on the field to visit and take more pictures, Lola again took in the strong mountain air and let it clear her head. Daddy stood with Luke, talking to one of the coaches, and Mama had gone off with Janie Ray to find a bathroom. She didn't know or care where the rest of the Vines had gone. No one bothered Lola, and she felt free to stand back and look at people around her.

Her daddy had played football on the very place she stood. And while she didn't think much of her relatives, she did like having a history on Daddy's side for the first time. It gave a pleasant weight to her own life.

She heard Janie Ray call her name from a distance and looked up. Her sister was small, but unmistakable, running down the bleacher steps. Mama moved fast behind her, keeping up, both of them laughing as they came onto the field. Janie Ray would be across the broad reach of green in no time.

Lola walked over to stand with Daddy and Luke.

"Hey, sugar," Daddy said. Luke put an arm around her.

"How about, before we get back to the house," Daddy said, "we stop off and get Moon Pies and a cold drink somewhere?" He was already squatting, arms out, ready to gather Janie Ray as she ran to him.

"Sounds good to me." Luke grinned.

Lola smiled at Mama just across the field. She leaned against Luke and watched Janie Ray arrive at Daddy's arms. In an instant, her little sister was rising tall, fearless, as Daddy lifted her high above the crowd.

A⁺
AUTHOR INSIGHTS, EXTRAS & MORE...

FROM

JEAN REYNOLDS PAGE

AND

AVON A

Q&A with Jean Reynolds Page

With every book, there are always natural questions that arise out of the narrative. My first inkling of what questions readers will ask comes from the comments of my early readers—my Texas writers' group, my agent, and my editor among them. I decided that these author discussion pages are a good place to address some of the questions that have already come up during the editing process of this book.

If you, as readers, have any other questions about different aspects of the storyline, the setting, or the medical issues addressed within the book, let me know. My Web site has an e-mail address and I'd love to hear from you.

Are pass-out spells, such as the ones experienced by Sherry and Luke, a dangerous occurrence, and if so, shouldn't Luke's episode be treated with a higher level of concern among his family members?

At the age of fifteen, I stood in line for a roller coaster at Carowinds amusement park in Charlotte, North Carolina. Six of us had been waiting for over forty-five minutes to get on the ride that simulated a runaway train in an old abandoned mine. The day was stifling, no breeze at all, but we had only another five minutes to go before we were on the ride. That's when one of my friends went down. Without warning, she dropped like a sack of potatoes to the hot asphalt of the amusement park. The rest of us struggled to grab her, and while it must have been seconds, it seemed like hours before she revived. She was pale, clammy, and thoroughly embarrassed.

Other than the panic of the moment, I remember clearly the responses the rest of us had to her episode. Four of us struggled to get her over to a place where she could lie down, while one particularly practical girl remained firmly in line, saying, "We've been in line for almost an hour. If we can just get her sitting down on the ride, she'll be fine!" Needless to say, that lone voice lost out in that debate and we got our fallen friend to a shady bench.

And she *was* fine. This happened to her again a few years later at a local standing-room-only performance of the *Messiah*. She was one of the people standing . . . And then she wasn't. I knew by then that these spells were only dangerous if she hit something on the way down (which never happened, thank God). But I didn't know the explanation until years later after I married a cardiologist. My friend was a "sinker," the very unscientific term for someone prone to pass-out spells called syncope.

Characterized by nausea, sweating, and light-headedness, syncope is a vaso-vagal response that can be brought on by heat, prolonged standing, stress, or some underlying illness like a stomach or cold virus. It can even be a reaction to the sight of blood or the sensation of pain.

I took all this knowledge for granted when incorporating the fainting spells of Sherry Vines and Luke Vines into the narrative of *Leaving Before It's Over*. But my agent looked over the manuscript and registered concern at the lack of rigorous medical attention for Luke ("Shouldn't people be more concerned about Luke when he passes out at graduation?" she asked). It was a good question: I realized I needed to clarify these episodes a little better within the story.

In the book, Sherry, Luke's mother, has the misfortune of hitting her head when she falls. The other members of the Vines family know of her history and are aware that they need to protect Luke from a similar fate when he gets that pale, clammy, wobbly look at the graduation practice. I went back and put more explanation into the dialogue and even added a local doc who checked him out on the field and offered his assessment.

And then it occurred to me that, as the good wife of a cardiologist, I should probably use these pages to distinguish between these relatively benign pass-out occurrences and the more threatening variety that signal a dangerous arrhythmia or a full-on heart attack. So, here goes.

As mentioned, a person with a vaso-vagal response (nonthreatening pass-out spells) will often have a history of prior spells and will feel light-headed and perhaps nauseated and clammy. "Vaso" refers to the vascular relaxation that contributes to the lowered blood pressure and secondary loss of consciousness. "Vagal" is a medical term referring to the vagus nerve and the involuntary nervous system that relates to relaxation and digestion (the opposite of an adrenaline response associated with "flight or fight." Vagal tone also lowers the blood pressure and slows the heart. It is the nervous reaction associated with lower blood pressure and heart rate that causes the blood pressure drop and loss of consciousness. As soon as the person is flat, blood returns to the heart and brain, and he or she regains consciousness.

The more dangerous varieties of syncope can be associated with palpitations and a history of enlargement of the heart. Passing out while exercising is often a signal of an arrhythmia, and any family history of sudden death is a big red flag. Also, heart palpitations without any warning can be a sign of a dangerous problem. Especially in these cases the person should get to a doctor and have it checked out (sooner rather than later).

So, the bottom line is, in Luke's instance, his family isn't acting in an irresponsible manner after he quickly regains consciousness on the field at graduation practice.

One interesting coincidence occurred as I pulled together my notes for this A+ section of the book. My husband and I were on a plane home after visiting our two youngest kids in college. In the middle of the six-hour flight, a series of unusual call button dings on the airplane was followed by a flight attendant urgently removing an oxygen tank from overhead.

"A medical problem?" my husband asked, already getting up.

"A woman in the back," the flight attendant told him.

Half an hour later, he came back and sat down.

"She's fine," he said.

"A sinker?" I asked.

He nodded. "Vaso-vagal."

The notes about Sherry and Luke were literally in my hands. With my writing, realism and credibility rank high on my list of priorities, and it has always been my hope that life and fiction appear interchangeable. But sometimes they get a little *too* close to each other.

Anyway, if you would like more information on pass-out spells or the more life-threatening events of dangerous arrhythmia and heart attack, the Heart Rhythm Society has a terrific Web site at www.HRSonline.org that details all the symptoms and the appropriate responses to these episodes.

Where is Linton Springs, and are the people based on anyone you know?

This question always comes up, first with early readers, and later when I attend book clubs and other events. Since my books center on small-town Southern life, people who knew me growing up are particularly interested in the answer to this one, I find.

So here is the answer, as honestly as I can give it, although with the disclaimer that not even I know where many aspects of my stories originate. It's a mystery. But I do know for sure that Linton Springs, North Carolina, is an entirely fictional town. In my mind, it sits somewhere off Interstate 77 north of Charlotte, and it is well to the west of the place that is nearest and dearest to my heart in my home state. Go due east through the Uwharrie National Forest and you'll come to my hometown of Troy, North Carolina.

And while Linton Springs will not be found on any map, people who live in or have driven through Troy will recognize certain similarities in the makeup of the town and my fictional setting. The funeral home sits across the street from what used to be my dad's Texaco station (in the book, it is a garage). The courthouse and the grocery store are indeed nearby, although not situated exactly as I have it in the book.

This often happens. Living so far away, I love to travel "home" when I'm writing, and the landscapes and streets in my imagination take shape as places I love. So I have to thank my North Carolina home for giving me such rich imagery to draw upon when I give my characters their surroundings.

As for the second part of the question, rest assured that I have not populated Linton Springs with any actual people from my present or past. (There is no real Vicky Benson from my years growing up. If you knew me all those years ago, don't even speculate. I promise, she doesn't exist! Ditto for Mrs. Lytleman and Annie Lawson.)

A few true "characters" in the book did exist in my memory, however. "Preacher Reeves" will be familiar to many in Troy. Also the peacocks. I grew up listening to the call of those lovely birds. Neighbors across the way kept them. Unlike the neighbors in the book, no one was ever irritated by them, as far as I know. I heard them far more often than I saw them, but they always seemed to be part of the soundtrack of my daily life.

While I always pull images and places from the past in my writing, the physical descriptions in this book are—more than in any other book I've written, I think—a tribute to the wonderful town where I spent my first eighteen years. So my gratitude goes to Troy for lending me a few details and giving Roy, Rosalind, Lola, and Luke a place to stand.

What led you to work with identical twins as characters? Is it true that paternity could not be determined between identical twins in 1976? How about now?

When I was growing up, many of the television shows loved to employ the device of the "evil twin." My favorite was *I Dream of Jeannie*. They changed her hair color and you suddenly had yourself a villain.

I hope that *Leaving Before It's Over* has little relationship to the sitcoms of my youth, but it's possible that my desire to explore a story that involved identical twins had its beginnings way back then.

All twins are fascinating, but especially identical twins. If you take a quick look at Wikipedia, you read that cultures throughout history have either demonized or revered identical twins. Through no effort (and quite often, I suspect, no desire) on their parts, they possess a mystical quality by their sheer existence.

The early seeds of this book came out of a book that I wrote years before. The unpublished manuscript had aspects that I decided I'd love to work with again. In that book, the character of Lola (then several years younger) took on the burden of the entire narrative. When I decided to pull some of her story out, make her older, and fashion a new story from bits and pieces of that one, I also employed additional points of view to tell the story. I gave Roy a twin, mostly because I thought it would be fascinating to dig into this kind of relationship. They were raised together, but separated for their adult years and this provided so much to explore.

In reading about twins, either in published research or in the tabloids, it seems that one is often more outgoing, more driven toward the spotlight. While eye color, body type, and even IQ correlate between the two, certain aspects of personality remain unique. It has always seemed to me that these differences had to represent the soul, or spirit, of the individual.

In this way, I began wanting to focus on the "separateness" of Mont and Roy rather than their similarities. Mont's ambition drove him in ways that a desire for love and stability drove Roy. Then, as the story progressed, I realized that it would be their sameness that helped to offer a final resolution to the conflict. Roy spent his adult life escaping from being identified with his brother, but in the end, he is able to use his "twin-ness" to save Luke from the family that mistreated him throughout his life.

The book is set in 1976, and as the battle for Luke heated up, I found I could use the identical DNA shared by the twins to give Roy and Rosalind leverage in their paternity claim. I felt reasonably sure this was a safe thing to do in that time period. Since identical twins share the same DNA, I assumed it would be impossible at that time to determine paternity if both twins claimed intimacy with the mother. As Rosalind points out in the later scenes of the book, according to science, Roy and Mont, "might as well be the same person."

While in the editing/revision stage of the book, I wanted to check this out to make sure my premise held solid ground underneath. What I found is that not only was it impossible in 1976, but for legal purposes, it is apparently still impossible today (or at least as of 2007).

I ran across a report on ABC News that ran in May 2007, where two identical twin brothers went to court to determine which one should pay child support for the child of a woman with whom they both had sex on the same day. According to the DNA testing ordered by the court, it could not be determined.

The law calls for a 98 percent or higher probability of a DNA match. With each of the identical brothers, there was a 99.9 percent match. The forensic expert brought in by the court said, "With identical twins, even if you sequenced their whole genome you wouldn't find a difference . . ." The doctor who served as the paternity testing expert for the story agreed. "There is simply no test that explains the difference between two identical twins."

So there you have it. If more definitive tests have been developed since the time of this court case, I'd be very interested to learn about it. I receive e-mail through my Web site.

In the meantime, I feel relieved that even today, as far as I know, the story holds up and Luke would remain safely with Roy's family.

Andy Ziskind

JEAN REYNOLDS PAGE is the author of *A Blessed Event, Accidental Happiness, The Space Between Before and After,* and *The Last Summer of Her Other Life*. She grew up in North Carolina and graduated with a degree in journalism from the University of North Carolina at Chapel Hill. She worked as an arts publicist in New York City, and for over a decade reviewed dance performances for numerous publications before turning full-time to fiction in 2001. In addition to North Carolina and New York, she has lived in Boston, Dallas, and Seattle. She and her family have recently moved to Madison, Wisconsin.

Jean Reynolds Page

BOOKS BY JEAN REYNOLDS PAGE

THE SPACE BETWEEN BEFORE AND AFTER
A Novel

ISBN 978-0-06-145218-5 (paperback)

"A beautifully told tale of family, secrets, long-festering misunderstandings, and the occasionally tangled bonds of love, that takes you on a journey you won't soon forget." —Eileen Goudge, *New York Times* bestselling author of *Woman in Red*

THE LAST SUMMER OF HER OTHER LIFE
A Novel

ISBN 978-0-06-145249-9 (paperback)

"Page's knack for characterization...helps nudge things toward an appropriately affirmative ending." —*Publishers Weekly*

LEAVING BEFORE IT'S OVER
A Novel

ISBN 978-0-06-187692-9 (paperback)

The true meaning of family is tested when a man, his wife, and two daughters must return to his childhood home in Virginia—where past conflicts, painful memories, and old family tensions are rekindled in full.